I WANT
SUPERPOWERS

STEVEN BEREZNAI

Jambor

First Printing: 2016

ISBN 978-0-97327928-8-6

Jambor Publishing

Cover design by Joey Wargachuk

Copy editing by Andrea Németh

Library and Archives Canada Cataloguing in Publication

Bereznai, Steven, author

    I want superpowers / by Steven Bereznai.

Issued in print and electronic formats.

ISBN 978-0-9732928-8-6 (paperback).--ISBN 978-0-9732928-9-3 (pdf)

    I. Title.

PS8553.E6358I12 2016   jC813'.6   C2016-906434-4

                                      C2016-906435-2

For my mom and dad.
Thank you for all your support.
I could not have done it without you.

Special thanks to: Joey Wargachuk for his ongoing enthusiasm, advice, and graphic design/marketing skills. You keep me inspired. Jamie Sherman, for his font wizardry. And to Andrea Németh, for her insightful edits.

CHAPTER 1

"I look ridiculous," I say, holding up the edges of my flouncy dress in an attempt to keep the hem from catching on the rough wood of our apartment's floorboards.

"Yes," my mother agrees. "You do."

Other moms would coo or reassure. Mine's too blunt for that. Think sledgehammer with hearts etched into the handle.

She kneels beside me in our dimly lit, one-room flat. Our drop-down bunks are latched against the wall to give us more space. The chipped and faded countertops in the kitchenette are scrubbed and our breakfast bowls are drying in the small sink with the rust stain running down its center. According to the label on our rations, we ate oats, though they were so pulverized it's hard to say for sure. Rumor is, they mix in sawdust.

"There will always be rumors," my mom often says.

We're both clothed in head-to-toe red. Me in the dress, she in her coveralls, ready for work. There's a round patch above her left breast with the image of a cog on it that marks her as a factory worker. Not the best of positions, but not the lowest either. Still, a far cry from when my father was alive.

She stands, turning me this way and that. At sixteen I'm taller than she is, which is weird. I'm used to looking up to her, not down. I'm bigger boned, too, meaty where she's porridge thin. I take after my dad that way.

"Stop fidgeting," she says, sliding a pin into place.

Her tone puts me on amber alert. I try something new—I keep my mouth shut, waiting to see if her impatience will balloon into something more.

Wait for it, part of me warns.

But today's a good day and the tirade doesn't come. Sometimes it's like that. She's...unpredictable. My mother keeps working and I let myself breathe. The only thing having a blow up at the moment is the booming thunder in the distance. We barely notice. It emanates from the roiling black clouds that hover just outside our borough, clouds that just sit there, day after day. I can see them outside the small window above the sink. The mass of condensed vapors never expands nor contracts. Never intensifies nor dissipates. They've been floating there, stuck, since before I was born.

"They're left over from the war," my dad told me once when I was little. "Boy, did they make you wail when you were a baby!"

Oh Papa, I think.

Today I feel the sadness that he's gone. Other times I'm flat out angry. But it's been so long now that the feelings are like the storm out there. Never gone, but after years and years of it, mostly relegated to the background.

Our borough was established exactly on the border where the clouds end. On a sunny day there's literally a dividing line. As kids we would dare each other to step over the shadow they cast, and when a kid did, we'd all run away squealing. The real danger lies on the other side of the electrified security fence that the shadow would creep over. I can see the chain links through the tiny window, separating us from the danger beyond. The glass is grimy from the billowing smokestacks of the factory where my mom works, but I can still make out the orange warning sign attached to the fence post. It's a triangle with the stylized black outline of a trio of animal heads; hound, lizard, and giant cat, their growling countenances budding like polyps within the triple crescents of a biohazard symbol, immediately recognizable as a mutant animal alert.

"And I think that should do it," my mom says, stepping back to admire her handiwork.

"Give us a twirl!" my brother says enthusiastically. His name's Nate. Nathorniel Jarod Feral when he's in trouble.

He's 12, with big brown eyes that give him a spooked owl look; they make him appear younger (and more innocent) than he is. His frame is such a perfect combination of our parents I sometimes think a mad scientist must've spliced his DNA together in a test tube rather than, you know, that *other* way. He gets all the luck. Currently, he's showing off his walking handstand, feet straight in the air, wearing just a pair of pink underwear. They were white until they accidentally got washed with Mom's coveralls. They've been his favorite ever since.

He maneuvers around the small wooden kitchen table on his hands as easily as he could on his feet, making good use of his ridiculously broad shoulders. Those he got from our dad. Combine that with our mom's narrow waist and his set of etched abs (honestly, what 12-year-old needs

2

that kind of muscle tone?) and the kid looks like he jumped off the cover of a comic book.

Some people were just born with the proportions to be awesome, I sigh inside my head. Petty jealousy aside, I love the brat, and give him what he wants, spinning about until the hem of my dress flutters around my ankles. He lands nimbly on his feet and starts to clap.

"Caitlin! Caitlin!" he chants.

"Please," I say, making shushing motions with my one hand while the other is egging him on. He presses his cheek against the fabric covering my belly and wraps his stupidly muscled arms around my back.

"It's so soft!" he gasps with wonder, as he still does at so many things, practically a teen, but still a big kid. "And slippery!"

My mother grabs his wrist and yanks him away from me so hard I trip into the side of the table.

"Ow!" I say.

The move is so sudden, so harsh, that it takes a moment to switch gears. For the hour it took to stitch me into the dress, she was a mom born of some dream. She fussed a bit too much, but she didn't call me "chunky" as she struggled to zip up the back. When we found a rip in the side she didn't break into hysterics, demanding to know "How the hell am I supposed to raise two children alone?" Instead she smiled and laughed and reassured me she'd get it fixed in plenty of time for Testing Day. She tricked me into lowering my guard.

"Are the headaches back?" I ask cautiously. Maybe it's a safe question. Maybe it's not.

"I'm fine," she says, her jaw tense. She's trying to convince herself as much as us. Her brow creases in pain and she forces herself to let Nate go. Her lips twitch. Invisible strings pull them into a marionette's smile.

"I'm fine," she repeats, patting his head with jerky, mechanical motions.

She's trying, a part of me sighs, giving myself a reminder. *It's hard for her.*

"Okay," Nate says, testily brushing her arm away.

She eyes me as if there's an internal pressure sensor inside of her, and the needle keeps veering from the far right danger zone to the far left safe zone and back. Finally, it settles somewhere in between. Her face relaxes. Unlike the lightning cloud on the other side of the fence, this storm seems to have passed—for now.

"You need to finish getting ready for school," my mother tells Nate quietly. I can tell she feels bad for flipping out. She's getting low on meds and she's been splitting the doses. End of the month is always the worst for rations.

"Yeah, yeah," he replies. It's his new favorite saying. I'm not sure where he picked it up and, though it's a bit sassy for my mom's taste, it's hard to tell him to stop when both of us have started imitating him.

"Yeah, yeah," my mom echoes, and it's as if the air comes back into the room. Unlike me, Nate has a way of breaking the tension. Mom smirks, pointing to the wardrobe we all share. It's built-in next to the worn kitchen cabinetry. "Put some clothes on already."

He decides to be obedient, in his own Nathorniel way. He performs a couple of dance steps, utterly unabashed. His feet are a blur as he twirls around me and does a majestic leap. He manages to be both a vision and a donk (what my mom calls a "dork") at the same time.

He moves aside his chess set and pulls clothes from his drawers, holding shirts against pants as he plans his outfit. Nate sings as he dresses, a tune our mom used to croon to us, but he's changed around the lyrics. It was a lullaby about jumping over the moon. He's transformed it into a love song. It's raw, and childish, but his pitch is perfect. There are rare moments where his voice breaks on a note he can't quite hit, yet somehow it makes the song even better. My mother's frown deepens. She's worried. The kid's got talent, but is it the regular kind, or the *special* kind? I can tell my mom's wondering the same thing.

I put a hand on hers, trying to be reassuring. The gesture feels borrowed from what I've seen other people doing. We're not the touchy-feely type and, true to form, she takes her hand away, resting it above her heart.

"His first testing isn't for another year," I say.

"I know," she says, "I just wish he wouldn't..."

"I know," I reply. "But if you try to stop him..."

"Yes, that *would* go badly wouldn't it?" She shakes it off, as if the consequences are too horrible to contemplate, and focuses on me. "At least I don't have to worry about you for much longer," she says, adjusting my dress around my shoulders. "Sweet sixteen. Just get through today. One last time, and then you're safe. Right?"

Safe. The word hangs in the air like a set of manacles.

"Sure," I say, because I know that's what she wants to hear.

4

She nods in relief and gives me an awkward hug. It's so rare that I just keep my arms at my side. The important thing is she believes me. If she knew what I was really thinking, it would just make her worry. Saying the right thing is a new skill I'm starting to develop because, growing up, we were told to always tell the truth. It's only recently that I've come to realize *that* is a lie. People don't want the truth. They want to hear what they want to hear. And sometimes the truth can be dangerous.

"I'm just glad we're past last year's nonsense, and the year before that," she says.

"And the year before that," I add.

"We *are* past that nonsense, aren't we?" she presses. "You've come to your senses. No more funny-business?"

"No more funny-business," I agree.

"Good. That stunt you pulled last year nearly did me in," she says. "Caitlin, it's okay to fail their test, no matter what they say about what an honor it is to pass."

"Of course," I lie again, and I feel my rib cage twisting as I do, because if I pass they'll take me from her, from Nate, forever. I try not to think about it, and yet as I do, I wonder, *Maybe she's right. Maybe I'm better off just as I am.*

"And, Caitlin," she says. "Please come back in one piece."

On that point, she and I do agree. The final testing is the most rigorous. Fatalities are rare, but broken bones, scars, and head trauma are common enough. Disfigurement is a possibility. Forcing a Manifestation is not a delicate process.

"Cross my heart," I say, tracing an X over my chest. I leave the rest of the expression unspoken.

My mom nods, but she's not paying attention to me anymore. Now that one child is almost safe, her fretful nature is honing in on a new target. My dad used to say she wasn't happy unless she was worrying about something. I follow her gaze and watch as my brother Nate decides between two equally garish tops. Is his thing for color and textures a sign that he's "special" or just another one of his quirks?

There have been so many alerts released about signs to watch for it's impossible to know what's bunk and what's not. One year it was "allergic reaction to shrimp causes girl to glow in the dark," another time "boy projects own shadow after winning bicycle race." For a year after that, anyone between 13 and 16 years old received packets of desiccated shrimp in their rations and were required to learn to ride a bike in extracurriculars.

"One more thing," Mom says. "This is for you."

She hands me a worn decorative box just slightly wider than the palm of my hand. The box has a ratty pink bow on it.

"Presents!" Nate says, coming over quickly. He's now got yellow pants on and a green shirt. No socks or shoes as of yet. "Open it! Open it!"

I do, lifting the lid off and my eyes sparkle at what's inside.

"I know it's a little on the girly side for you," Mom says. Her jaw is clenched. Only now do I realize she sometimes braces herself for my moods too.

"I love it," I say, and that is the truth.

It's a simple plastic coronet, but it looks like gold, if you ignore where the paint's peeled off. I place it atop of my blandly black hair, tied back with a strip of red ribbon.

"It was mine, when I was a girl," Mom says.

"Did you wear it at your Testing Day?" Nate asks as he puts on mismatched socks.

My mom has a faraway look on her face. "There was no Testing Day when I was young. This was from a costume party for a holiday called Halloween. I was younger than either of you are now. Of all the things for me to still have, I can't believe it's this. I was a fairy princess, if you can imagine it."

I can't, actually. My mom's hair is so short it's basically shaved. No need for a hair net, like some of the other factory workers.

"And now look at you," she says. "You're a princess too."

I gaze at my reflection in a cracked mirror between our bunks. I squint a little, to create a filter that distorts reality just enough so that I no longer see me. I don't see a fairy princess either. I see *her*. The me I wish to be, a girl with a cape and a hero's circlet around her brow. A girl who can fly, or lift a bus, or teleport away. Maybe all three.

Today is my final Testing Day.

Today I find out if that's the girl I get to be.

CHAPTER 2

At school, everyone in my age category will be tested for the final time. Our teacher Mrs. Cranberry eyes each of us as we enter.

Her figure reminds me of the stick people we draw on the chalkboard when playing hangman. She's so thin that her torso, arms and legs all seem to be made of broom sticks. Her face is gouged with wrinkles, and her hair is a mass of grey curls. I doubt she was ever pretty. The emblem on her suit jacket is of a book and ruler.

She purses her lips, eyeing my dress and coronet. I give her a twirl, mostly because I know it will annoy her.

"Acceptable," she snorts, waving for me to take my seat.

I reach my desk and pull out my stool, taking a moment to examine it to make sure it's safe. The girl one desk over notices and smirks. Her black hair is shiny and lustrous. Mine is a pit where light goes to curl up and die. My brown eyes bug out, hers are delicately lidded at a demure angle. And her dress—it's a vibrant yellow that brings out the flecks of gold in her hazel eyes. I bet her gown is brand new.

Her name's Lilianne. She's the worst.

In second grade she gave me the nickname "Puddle Pants" after I sat in a pool of water she'd left on my seat. All the kids chanted along with her.

Puddle Pants, Puddle Pants!

Today the seat is dry, so I plonk myself onto it. I focus on the pamphlet sitting on my desk staring up at me. All of us have the same one. One kid is turning his into a paper airplane. I read mine.

TESTING DAY: What it means for you!

There's an image of a smiling boy and girl on the front flap. The girl is shooting lasers from her eyes. The boy has angel wings.

Mrs. Cranberry does a head count and releases a rare grunt of satisfaction.

"Good. Everyone's here."

She sounds relieved. Just last year, one of my classmates, a pimply faced boy named Lore, failed to show up for testing. I heard his parents tried to run away with him and actually got past the security fence before the protectors caught them. The parents were executed. Lore was tested. Turns out he can communicate with butterflies, so they sent him across the river to be with his own kind. That's one version anyway. Others say his family got as far as the Red Zone only to be slaughtered by ravenous mutated animals. There was even a rumor that they got away, found land that had not been irradiated in the Genocide Wars, with potable water and soil to till, but nobody believes that. I choose to believe he's now safely in Jupitar City, where he can be happy with his own people—and his butterflies.

"And just look at the lot of you all dressed up," Mrs. Cranberry continues.

I'm not surprised that she's pleased. The kids who identify as boys are leashed with ties, sitting up straight in their hand-me-down jackets that have been patched and stitched over the years. The girls are in frayed dresses that force us to keep our legs closed. The students with parents who earn more credits wear the newer, fanciest clothes—like Lilianne.

I'm not jealous, I assure myself.

A pair of testing officials arrive at the open door. Their sleek helmets are strapped to the belts of their orange form-fitting hazmat suits, which bear the insignia of six lightning bolts in the shape of a star. Stools are shifted nervously. The kid making the paper airplane freezes as he's about to launch it at the redhead he's got a crush on. Even Lilianne's grip tightens on a purse studded with faux-crystals. I feel an excited ripple.

I recognize the older of the two testers. He's been at every one of my testings. The hunching of his back, the paunch at his belly, and the thickness of his round spectacles give him a Mole Man quality. The second tester is the new guy. He actually looks like he's just been taken out of a box. I half expect curly bits of foam packing to be sticking to him. He's not just handsome and younger than normal for his position, his hair is like shiny spun gold from a fairy tale.

Anyone who's into boys sits up straighter in their chairs. I realize I'm one of them. So is Mrs. Cranberry. He consults the electronic pad in his hand.

"Normand Bamford?" he calls out.

We all look at Normand at the back of the class. As he gets up from his stool, it scrapes on the floor. He's heavy-set, which is unusual since everyone's on rations. Both his parents are bureaucrats, which means more credits, more food stamps, more everything. His suit's brand new and freshly pressed, but looks awkward on his lumbering frame. He takes a moment to squeeze some antiseptic gel into his hands. He's always doing that. Makes me wonder how much of the stuff he must go through in a year.

What a waste of credits.

He limps forward, one foot turning out, his leg brace creaking with every step. He's been like that for all the years I've known him. I used to think his brace was so cool, like he was part robot. He doesn't look at anybody as he plods to the door. He's the one kid who's weirder and less popular than me.

We watch him go, each of us wondering: *Will he be back?*

As the minutes tick by, the air grows heavier, making me and my classmates sweat. The wooden window frames are warped and sealed shut from years of paint.

I doodle in my notebook, drawing an image of myself in a superhero costume: a glorified corset with a lightning bolt emblem on it, knee high boots, a cape (obviously) and the coronet about my brow. I confess, I may have misrepresented the length of my legs and inflated my breasts. I smile as I write underneath *NOT TO SCALE.*

I admire it, my reverie barely disturbed by the whirring of the small fan on Mrs. Cranberry's desk, decidedly pointed at her. She's leaning back in her chair. I'm pretty sure she's fallen asleep. It's then I realize Lilianne and her crew of girlfriends are whispering and looking toward me.

Lilianne leans over.

"Nice tiara," she says. Her friends giggle. Why is she like this? She's beautiful. Shouldn't that make her too happy to be mean?

"It's a coronet," I correct.

"It's garbage," she replies.

"Just like me," I say.

"Just like you." She stops, eyes narrowing. I beat her to the punch line. She doesn't care for that.

The way she scans me for weaknesses, I swear she must be Supergenic. Not that she needs x-ray vision to find my flaws. There are plenty right up front, such as my potato face and creepy-crawly eyebrows. But Lilianne's cruelty is growing more refined. She dismisses my obvious defects. They're too easy. Instead, she notices my sketch. I snap my workbook shut, but it's too late.

"Oh, Puddle Pants," she says. "You actually think *you're* going to Manifest?"

I blush. "I have as much chance as anyone else." The retort is, as my brother would say, "weak."

"Well then, let's hope wetting yourself is a superpower," she quips, burrowing through my thick skin like an irradiated tick. She looks to her friends who titter approvingly.

I stand and slam my palms on her desk.

"How about if I punch you in the face?" I ask. My mom's not the only one with a temper.

I see the fleeting fear in Lilianne's eyes. It's satisfying for less than a second.

"Does your mom want to start treating raw sewage?" she asks. "My dad could make that happen."

"Caitlin!" Mrs. Cranberry shouts, very much awake now. "Sit down!"

She's pointing her ruler at me. She wouldn't dare use it on me though, not on Testing Day. Would she?

"I will *not* have you making a fool of me again this year!"

I grudgingly take my seat.

"I own you," Lilianne says under her breath.

If I were a hero in a comic book, I'd turn the tables on her. I'd outsmart her, or win her over, or defeat her in a race at the end of the school year. But this is real life.

I don't have to do any of those things, I try to reassure myself. *All I have to do to beat her is Manifest. The lowliest Supergenic is still higher than the most powerful of dregs.*

Everyone's staring at me, and not in a good way. I nervously finger the pamphlet on my desk. I stare out the dirt-caked windows that won't open. Across the river, I see the tall gleaming towers of Jupitar City. There are people flying amongst the buildings, tiny specks in the distance.

I lose myself in their dizzying motion until I hear the classroom door creaking open. I glance over. Mole Man is looking at his electronic pad. Golden Boy has his arm wrapped around Normand and is helping to hold him up. There's dried blood just under his nose. Final Testing Day is especially rough.

"You okay to walk on your own?" Golden Boy asks.

"Stop fussing," Mole Man snorts. "The dreg's not our concern."

Golden Boy looks ready to argue.

"I shall be fine," Normand says in that formal way of his.

10

He takes a few faltering steps, wavers, and then he starts to go down. He grasps at a nearby desk, but his fingers are devoid of strength. I join the collective gasp as he collapses to the floor.

"Normand?" Mrs. Cranberry stands quickly, looking from the Supergenics, to Normand, then back to the Supergenics, waiting for them to tell her what to do.

Golden Boy moves toward him but Mole Man grabs him roughly by the arm and yanks him back. Golden Boy jerks his arm free and glares. He looks ready to argue but Mole Man holds up a silencing finger.

"He is *not* our concern," Mole Man reiterates.

"Of course he is," Golden Boy insists.

"A word," Mole Man says, using his free hand to close the classroom door. We hear Mole Man shouting, things like "fall in line," "we have a quota," and "there will be consequences."

I quickly get up from my desk and hurry over to Normand's side. I tap him on the shoulder. "Normand?"

His eyes flutter open.

"I passed out, didn't I?" he asks, gazing at the ceiling.

"You did," I reply.

"Caitlin!" Mrs. Cranberry snaps. "Help the boy up!"

I am *not* going to miss that woman.

I get my arm around him and nearly crumple under his weight. Finally I help him onto his feet. He winces as he slides into his chair, but I convince myself that he's otherwise all right, until his whole body shudders. Not just once but twice, then a third time, followed by a fourth and fifth.

"Normand, are you okay?" I ask.

He may have a concussion or worse.

He shudders again, and again, and again. His eyes roll back in their sockets, showing their whites.

"Mrs. Cranberry," I start to say, "I think he needs..."

His body jerks one more time and then his eyes pop back to normal. He grabs my forearms and yanks me in close.

"Caitlin," he begs. "Please don't make me go through that again!"

The other kids are staring. I ignore them.

"It's over. This is your final testing," I remind him. "You never have to do it again, not ever."

He pulls me closer, his mouth to my ear. This is the guy who wouldn't even take my hand without disinfecting it. He's *really* terrified. "I barely survived in there. They're not afraid to kill us. They're not afraid to kill *you*."

"Normand, that goes against the Treaty," I say.

I want to quote to him how the Supergenics can only test within reasonable parameters to find members of their own kind, but he shakes his head. "They don't care. They're desperate."

He looks ready to say more, but the door opens. Golden Boy stands there, handsome even in his hazmat suit. He's rubbing his arm as if it's in pain. The Mole Man is nowhere to be seen. Golden Boy looks at the e-pad in his free hand.

"Caitlin Feral?" he calls out.

"Caitlin," Normand hisses. I look at him. He's still holding onto my forearms. "Whatever it takes, live."

"Caitlin?" Golden Boy calls again. "Is Caitlin here?" Confused by the lack of response, he says to our teacher, "I was made to understand you had full attendance today."

"Caitlin!" Mrs. Cranberry shouts.

I'm trying to pull away from Normand but he still won't let me go.

"Promise me!" he hisses.

"Normand!" I snap.

"Now, Caitlin!" Mrs. Cranberry slams her ruler onto her desk. "Don't keep the young man waiting." She blushes apologetically and holds her hands up helplessly, giving him a cracked laugh. "She's utterly impossible!" To me, she levels a look that I know all too well, promising me I'm going to pay for this latest embarrassment. Everyone sees it. Lilianne and her friends smirk. The tester's golden brow lifts in what I assume is disdain.

"Fine," I say to Normand, if only to appease him. "I promise."

He lets me go, and I clumsily stagger back, jabbing my hip into a desk.

"Ow," I say.

Golden Boy winces. More titters from Lilianne and her squad. I smooth out my dress and stare at Mrs. Cranberry. If she had powers, she'd be shooting death rays at me. I tilt my head defiantly, the hero to her villain.

"Wish me luck," I say to her.

Her hand grips the ruler so hard it trembles.

Instead she says, "I'll see you soon, Caitlin."

CHAPTER 3

I do my best to forget about Mrs. Cranberry and Lilianne. Normand is tougher to put out of my mind. What did they do to him in there? What are they going to do to me?

It doesn't matter, I assure myself. Normand is weak. I am not. *So why is my heart beating so fast?*

I focus on Golden Boy as I follow him across the cracked asphalt of the outdoor recreational yard. It's a sea of black that surrounds the squat concrete school behind me. A rusty chain link fence pens us in. Just beyond, a bus rattles by. Thunder booms. Golden Boy flips his fingers across the surface of his e-pad, sometimes typing on it, not even giving me a second glance.

The things Normand said have rattled me more than I'd care to admit. What if he's right? What if the rules have changed? Am I willing to die on the off-chance of Manifesting? Is it really worth my life? The answer isn't "no," but is it "yes?"

We approach a squat building. For safety, it's set on the far end of the yard. It's been years since there's been an incident during Testing Day, but that story's still being told. Twelve students were killed. The kid Manifested, and immediately turned feral. Back then, the officials would just take over a classroom inside the school itself and fill it with their gadgets and probes. The kid broke out, wild with fangs, claws and quills.

He slaughtered three testing officials, two teachers, and half his class before the protectors managed to contain him in an electrified net. The Supergenics arrived to take him away, the families of the victims were compensated and, from then on, testing has taken place outside the school itself.

"There have been significant advances in testing protocols since then," Golden Boy says, sounding like he's reading from a manual. "I assure you, things like that don't happen anymore."

His words yank me from my thoughts. I look at him. He's still focused on his tablet.

"I didn't say anything," I yammer, which is when I realize what his power must be. He's a telepath.

I remember the mind reader from the previous three years. He was older, and smelled of alcohol. He didn't seem able to catch my thoughts unless he was touching me.

"Ah yes, Neville," Golden Boy says. "He's...retired."

I can tell from the way he's saying it that he's lying.

He shrugs at my unspoken accusation. "It's not easy being a telepath. One's own thoughts can be too much, let alone someone else's. Neville became... overwhelmed. I'm Joshua, by the way."

He pulls off the glove of his hazmat suit and holds out his hand for me to shake. I hesitate.

"I'm more powerful than Neville. I don't need physical contact to read minds, though it can still heighten the psychic connection."

I try to be comforted by his words, but it's more than unsettling having someone creeping around my thoughts, even if they assure us this isn't a Mind Audit.

His hand hangs there. I force myself to take it. As I do, I start singing a song in my head, a lullaby my mother taught me.

Two little puppies dancing in the rain...

"Please stop that," Joshua says. "It's very irritating, and hardly the way to fool a telepath."

It's possible to fool a telepath?

He blushes, his cheeks lighting up with a golden hue as he lets go of my hand. "Best that you forget I mentioned that or you'll get us both in trouble."

We reach the squat testing building. I want to ask him more.

"You always want to ask more, don't you?" he winks, pulling out what appears to be the Supergenic equivalent to an i-Dent card. It's shinier than ours.

"Mrs. Cranberry once said she wished that curiosity *would* kill the cat," I reply glumly. "I was the cat."

He laughs at that, and I can't help but smile.

"Well, I for one hope that the feline in question has many more lives," he replies. His words give me a warm glow inside.

He slides the i-Dent card through an electronic lock and punches in a code. I hear half-a-dozen thick bolts pull back.

"Just in case," he winks.

He really is ludicrously handsome.

14

"Thank you," he says.

I blush.

"That's really not fair," I say.

"Life's not fair," he agrees amiably. "Take you, for example."

He gestures up and down at me.

"What?" I ask, looking to see if I've spilled something on my dress.

"Do you have any idea how boring Testing Day is? I've been at this for months, school after school, and the closest I've come to getting a kid to Manifest was a 13-year-old with purplepox. You were supposed to liven things up for me."

"Me?" I demand.

"Yes, you. You're Caitlin Feral. Subject CF 1554 DASH 8. At least you're supposed to be. So where's the girl who showed up for her first Testing Day covered in wild berry juice that stained her skin blue? Or how about the following year when you plastered feathers all over your body with industrial glue?"

I remember both incidents all too well.

"My mom got the can of adhesive from the factory she works at. She brought it home to repair a mug," I reminisce. "It took two months to get all the feathers off, and another three for the skin to heal."

"Now *that's* what I'm talking about," he says. "*That's* the Caitlin Feral I was expecting. I mean, this is your last chance to Manifest. You know that, right? I figured you'd go all out. I've been looking forward to this for weeks and all I get is this," he waves at me. "Another average girl in a hand-me-down dress. You're supposed to be a legend."

"A legend? What? No. Really?" I ask.

"Caitlin," he says with this incredulous look on his face, as if he can't believe he has to tell me this. "You're *in* our training manual."

I can't help but be a little proud. At least I'm good at *something*.

"Exactly!" he says, his eyes literally shining bright as he catches the thought. "So *be* good at this."

I consider his challenge.

"You've got a plan, don't you?" he asks with excitement. "Don't tell me. Don't even think about it. I want to be surprised."

I want so bad to impress him. He's a handsome Supergenic who is not only paying attention to me, he thinks I'm a legend. It's like a dream come true. I want to drag this moment out for as long as I can. So, of course I muck it up. *That* is my superpower.

"This year is different," I say.

He contemplates me. Who knows what his psychic powers are picking up. Nothing good, as his golden brows furrow in disappointment.

"Yeah," he says. "I guess it is. Just my luck."

Joshua shrugs in acceptance. I'm not a legend anymore. I'm just a silly girl in a silly dress.

"Perhaps it's just as well. I'm not sure that my colleague would have the patience for your special brand of creativity," he rubs his arm as he says it. Makes me curious about the Mole Man's power. His ability is a matter of great debate in my class. In three years of testing, none of us has ever seen him use it. I'm starting to think that might be a good thing.

Joshua grips the door handle to the testing building and jerks his head toward it. "Your classmate Normand had reason to warn you about what to expect in there. We've had too few Manifestations. This year is worse than last. We need a win. Each classroom we've tested, my colleague has pushed the kids harder, made the tests more aggressive. We have the highest number of injuries on record. The dreg monitors are there to make sure we don't take it that far but they're too terrified of him to say anything. And me, well, I'm the new guy."

"You're not supposed to be telling me this, are you?" I ask.

"No," he admits. "But what he did to that kid before you, it was nasty business. And he was going easy on him. You won't be so lucky. My colleague knows your history. He's going to push you harder than anyone else."

Hard enough to kill me? I wonder.

Yes, I hear Joshua reply in my mind.

My heart is pounding. I could really die in there.

"Listen, I was just teasing you about putting on a show. If you have to, you beg us to stop. Maybe that will get the monitors to intervene. And *don't* antagonize him."

"So basically don't be myself."

"Yes!" he agrees with relief. "Exactly."

And with that he yanks the door open.

Inside, there's the Mole Man and three other officials in orange hazmat suits, all with the icon of the star made of lightning bolts. Their helmets

16

hang from their belts. One tester's seated at a desk inputting information on a data terminal, another is setting up a drip bag, the third is waving for us to enter. We step through and I feel all the hairs on my body lift lightly from the electrostatic decontamination sweeper.

The security door closes with a clang, stealing any natural light, leaving us with a dozen cones of luminescence from the LEDs in the ceiling. In here everything is shiny, polished stainless steel—a contrast to my usual world of grit and concrete. I hear and feel a slight hum as someone activates the containment field. It's apparently strong enough to smother the force of a D-bomb.

There's a treadmill, a lounge chair on a hydraulic lift, a silver sarcophagus leaning against a wall, and so on. Some I recognize from previous years. Others are new. Joshua hands me a vacuum sealed foil packet containing my testing suit. He turns away to talk with his fellow testing officials. Two of them are dregs like me, here to monitor. They're supposed to look out for me. The third would have powers, in case I Manifest and have to be restrained. And, there's Mole Man.

The tester at the desk motions me toward a door. What's left of his grey hair is slicked back, and a thin beard covers his cheeks.

"You can change in there," he says. "And fill this half-way."

He hands me a plastic pee bottle with a cap. I nod, and go into the other room. It's eight measures by eight measures, what my mom sometimes refers to as feet, which seems like a weird unit because everybody's foot is different. It's all gleaming white tile, with a porcelain toilet and sink, and a steel shelf with hooks in the wall. The smell of bleach burns my nose. I reach behind me and unzip my dress, stepping out of it in relief.

I can breathe.

I hang the dress on a hook then rip open the foil packet to pull out a thin pair of track pants, disposable socks, a t-shirt, and a pair of collapsible rubber shoes. I dress quickly. The last thing I do is take off the gold coronet and place it reverently on a hook on the wall.

Soon you won't need a crown to feel special, I assure myself, peeing into the bottle.

When I emerge, the testers all have their helmets on. One of them attaches a series of pads above each of my organs as well as an IV drip in my arm.

"We'll start you on the treadmill," one of the testers says, his voice coming through hidden speakers in his helmet. It's Joshua. His broad shoulders and lean waist are a dead give away. I wonder what it would be like to date a mind reader.

"Caitlin?" he asks.

"Yes," I say, stepping onto the machine. The track starts to whir and I jog lightly.

"Faster," Mole Man barks. Joshua turns a dial. It speeds up. Within moments I'm sprinting, sweat dripping down my face while the heart rate monitor starts beeping at a satisfactory rate.

Satisfactory is for losers.

"Faster!" I order.

What did I tell you? I hear Joshua ask in my mind.

"You heard the subject," Mole Man says.

I'm a legend, remember? I think at Joshua.

I hear his telepathic sigh as he dials it up.

The monitoring devices beep louder and quicker. A red light starts flashing.

I'm doing it! I think. *I'm Manifesting!*

The pads all over my body heat up as a variety of energy waves bombard my muscular, endocrine, and central nervous systems, prodding them to do something out of the ordinary. I feel a burst of energy building in me. I smile and grit my teeth against the burning in my legs, pushing even harder.

I'm doing it! I think. *It's happening!*

I'm on the verge of Manifesting. I know it. I can *feel* it. I give it everything I've got, wondering what sort of power is about to emerge, until a cramp in my leg makes my left side seize up. I cry out in pain. My thigh's gone so rigid it's like concrete.

Maybe it's turned to organic granite! I think in excitement.

Which is when my foot hits the spinning rubber pad at a funny angle, my ankle gives under my weight, and alarm bells erupt in my mind. I'm going down.

"Abort!" I hear Joshua order. He's already slamming his palm against a big red button, but it's too late. I fall flat onto the spinning tread, ripping the IV from my arm as the treadmill tosses me onto the floor. I land hard, knocking the breath from me.

I did it, is the only thought in my mind. *I Manifested.* I wait for the cheers and congratulations as I'm welcomed into the Supergenic Family. I'm met with cold silence instead. This is not as the brochures have led me to believe. I look down at my leg. The feeling is coming back into it. I touch it through the track pants. It feels normal, but it can't be, can it? I really thought it had turned into living rock.

"Augmented acceleration, fail," Mole Man says, making a note on his electronic pad. I realize my own stupidity. Of course that's what they were testing for—super speed, not geomorphication—but other Manifestations under the stress were not an impossibility. Joshua helps me to my feet.

"Are you all right?" he asks.

"Let's move on," Mole Man interrupts. Under his direction, I sit in the hydraulic chair, where Mole Man fastens restraints about my ankles and wrists. The heart rate monitor bleeps more quickly.

You've got this, I assure myself.

And yet what follows is an escalating series of torturous failures.

They use cold metal pincers to clamp my eyes open, making them burn with acidic drops. They're pushing me to exhibit some sort of ocular emission, be it lasers or x-rays or swirling hypnotic waves. The pads on my temples heat up. Pressure builds in my skull. I'm whimpering. My eyeballs bulge in their sockets, literally ready to explode from the strain, and not with an optic blast. My vision blurs.

I'm going to be blind, I realize in a panic. It's happened to others.

"It's too much," Joshua says as a warning light starts flashing. "Nerve damage is imminent!"

Mole Man throws a pencil. "Fine," he concedes. "Ocular emission is a fail."

Joshua presses a few buttons and the pressure decreases.

They hand me a variety of gemstones. I clutch them, one after the other.

"Mineralization, fail," Mole Man grunts angrily.

They put a respiration mask over my mouth and nose and I breathe in a chemical mist that's like a cheese grater against my throat and lungs.

"Sublimation, fail," Mole Man says.

Electrodes are attached to my adrenals. I writhe and gasp as I'm jolted with electricity.

"Shape shifting, fail," Mole Man says. The pace of testing accelerates, as do the pronouncements: "Telepathy, fail. Lycanthropy, fail. Weather control, elasticity, and flight…fail."

They bombard my brain with delta-waves in the hopes of triggering special cerebral abilities. Instead I go into synaptic shock, convulsing as bubbling froth overflows my lips.

I hear Normand in my head. *They're desperate.* I feel something warm dripping from my nose and running down into my mouth. It tastes of iron. *Blood*, I realize. The monitors remain silent. It's Joshua who finally yells, "Enough!"

Mole Man lifts a finger and sighs, "Agreed."

I'm not sure what's worse, the pain of the tests or being told how utterly ordinary I am. Not just subjectively. *Clinically.*

What I have to show for it is a sprained ankle, sunburnt skin (apparently my epidermis does *not* absorb UV and convert it into other forms of energy), and a migraine. But it's the test for super strength that nearly kills me.

They inject me with amphetamines and the pads all over my body supercharge my endocrine and central nervous systems as I attempt to deadlift a metal bar with plates that are being pulled downward by a magnet. I growl in defiance, and yank the bar upwards. My heart hammers, the room swims, and numbness spreads from my arm into my chest. I barely hear the weight clang to the ground as the room swims.

"She's going into cardio-pulmonary failure!" Joshua yells.

His voice is stolen from me as everything goes dark.

When I come to, Joshua's gesticulating at Mole Man. He has his helmet off. They all do.

"You're taking this too far!" Joshua yells.

"Need I remind you what's at stake?" Mole Man asks.

"You're not the one who can feel their pain," Joshua replies. "And you!" he points at the monitors. "Why are you even here?" They cringe, glancing from him to Mole Man uncertainly.

"You need to calm down," Mole Man says, reaching for Joshua. Joshua smacks his hand away and hastily steps back. "Don't you *ever* touch me again."

"Or what?" Mole Man snorts. "Your powers don't work on me." He lunges toward Joshua. I intentionally knock over a stainless steel pan. It clatters on the ground.

Everyone stops and turns. Mole Man contemplates me, then angles his body back toward Joshua. "She's awake. Let's get back to work."

Joshua kneels beside me, like he really is a prince from a fairytale.

"Your heart stopped briefly," he says. "You can ask us to stop."

He's got a lock of hair out of place, stuck to his sweaty forehead. I resist the urge to fix it.

"No," I say, standing up. "I can't."

I'm woozy, but I stay on my feet.

"Hold this around your body with your arms straight out to the sides," Mole Man instructs, making Joshua stand aside with a look while handing me what appears to be a glittering hula hoop. I hold it at waist height, as instructed. He presses a button and the hoop projects an energy sphere around me. I try to move my hands and feet but they're all glued to the edges of the pulsating ball.

"I haven't done this test before," I say. "What does it do exactly?"

"Just hold on," Mole Man says, as if I had a choice. He turns a dial and the sphere starts to spin me around, in every which way. He turns the dial more and I spin faster and faster and faster. I can't tell what's up, down or sideways. I see the testing officials from every angle, and then the floor, the ceiling, the walls. I'm pretty sure I'm going to throw up.

From there it gets worse. The hula hoop and the energy sphere start to expand, pulling on my arms and legs. At first it's just a light stretch in my limbs, but then it keeps going. The pressure starts to build in my joints. The pain is unlike anything I've ever felt. *They're going to pull me apart!*

"Stop!" I howl. "Please stop!"

They don't hear me or they simply don't care. The pulling intensifies. They're really going to kill me.

"Please!" I beg louder.

And just when I'm sure I'm about to be quartered, the pressure on my body eases off as the sphere contracts and the spinning slows down. The hoop grows still and with a spark the energy globe winks out. I immediately drop the torture device, and sway in place. My legs are jelly—not literally unfortunately—and I fall to one knee. The hoop does a little twirling dance around me until it settles to the floor.

Joshua steps forward with a stainless steel pan and holds my hair back as I barf into it. He's got his helmet off. They all do. I glare at the hoop.

"What is that even testing me for?" I ask.

"Nothing in particular," Joshua replies. "It's a last ditch effort to literally rip the power out of you."

"Last ditch? You mean..."

"You're finished, Caitlin Feral," he says. There's a note of relief in his voice.

"No," I insist, stepping toward the hoop. "I'll try it again."

"Remove the dreg," Mole Man says. He's not even looking at me. He's holding a hand mirror and checking his teeth for bits of food. "Prep the facility for the next subject."

"Caitlin," Joshua says, "You can go get changed." If only that were true. "You're done."

"No," I say to the whole room. "Put me back in the hoop. Give me one more chance. I know I can do it."

I expect Mole Man to order me out. Instead, he puts down the mirror and contemplates me. I can see the truth in his face. He *wants* to hook me up again. Joshua sees it too.

"Get this dreg out of here," Joshua barks, drawing himself up to his full height. There's a look of desperation on his face. "We have much more promising subjects to focus on."

Please, Caitlin, I hear his voice in my head. *Go, while you still can.*

"Wait a moment," Mole Man says, gesturing for Joshua to settle down. "I've always believed that if our subjects were to endure just a little more discomfort, we'd have a much higher success rate."

"The data speaks for itself," Joshua snorts. "She's a waste of our time."

I glare at him. He glares back.

Mole Man drums his chin with his fingertips, as if he's running our back and forth through an algorithm in his mind, calculating the cost benefit ratio of time and energy spent on each dreg versus Supergenic found, and what output of effort the subject in question is worth on the chance that she might yield the desired outcome. After all, every minute spent on a dreg who will never Manifest is time he could be investing on someone who actually does have enhanced abilities. But how can he ever know for sure? If I push now, I'm convinced he'll let me try again.

He'll kill you, I hear Joshua in my mind. *I won't be able to stop him.* It reminds me of what Normand said to me in class, begging me to live.

I'd rather die, I reply.

I'm about to say as much when I get a vision of my little brother prancing around in his pink underwear. I step toward the hoop, but that's as far as I get. Invisible hands hold me back. For a moment, I think Joshua is using his telepathy to short circuit my motor functions and freeze me in place. But no, this is me having second thoughts. I look at the hoop lying on the floor. For a split second I can feel it ripping me apart. There is blood and pain and then…nothing.

It will *kill me*, I realize. *Because I* don't *have any superpowers.*

The unexpected epiphany does something that all of their invasive tests could not. It breaks the protective casing deep inside of me that until now sheltered my beautiful lie, the one that gave me hope, so much so that I was almost willing to die for it. But exposed as it suddenly is, my delusion can't survive. It curdles in on itself, transforming into a dense stone of unpalatable truth.

"There's no point," I say. The words come unbidden, as if I've been through this already, and I know this on some deep, instinctual level. "There's nothing special about me. I'm just a dreg." My mom will be so pleased.

There's a long pause. I think I'm more shocked than anyone. Mole Man snorts and turns his back on me. A wave of panic strikes.

What have I just done?

I open my mouth to say I've changed my mind (again), and Joshua cuts me off. "Go," he says. "You're done here." He sees me deflating, and he adds, "For what it's worth, it was a pleasure meeting the Legend." He's trying to make me feel better. Like myself, it's a fail.

"Yeah, sure," I reply.

I keep my head up and shoulders straight as I walk to the washroom, though my attempt at dignity is pointless with a telepath who knows that all I want to do is to curl up in a ball. I don't even bother singing about puppies in the rain. After the humiliation of the past hour, I've got nothing to hide.

As soon as the washroom door closes behind me, I feel the tears.

No, I say. I'm burnt, inside and out, my eyes have broken blood vessels, and I'm covered in bruises, but I won't walk back into that classroom a cry baby. I'm not going to give Lilianne the satisfaction.

You can fall apart later, I assure myself.

I yank off the sweaty track suit, shoving it into a mesh bag with a draw string and I struggle to get back into my stupid gown. *Why the heck do we even have to dress up for this?* It's bull, is what it is. All of it.

It takes a lot of pulling but I get my dress over my hips and my arms through the sleeves. I twist to reach the zipper. I grasp the metal prong, triumphant in this at least, until I yank on it and hear the unmistakable sound of ripping cloth. I turn and, in the mirror, I can see the white of my underpants through a tear in the back side. Now the tears come. Just as I lack any other power, I'm devoid of the strength to hold them back.

It's not the dress that makes me crack. It's the black void inside me. Before there was always hope, the dream of a better tomorrow. Now I know this is who I'm stuck being for the rest of my life. Stupid, ordinary me.

I look at my mother's plastic coronet hanging from a hook on the wall, a final remnant of her previous life, before the Genocide Wars, when young people could dress up and pretend to be fairy princesses. I take it in my hands. It's so light and insignificant. An illusion of something more. I contemplate it for a moment, squeeze my hands on either side of it, and snap it in half. I shove the two broken pieces into the trash and I don't look back.

CHAPTER 4

I'm a mess when I emerge from the washroom. My eyes are bloodshot; my cheeks flushed and stained by my tears. All the officials have their helmets off now that they've confirmed that I'm powerless.

I emerge from the washroom and hand over my bag with the testing clothes in it. I briefly consider asking if I can hold onto the track pants since I've ripped the back of my dress, but I already know the answer to anything that contravenes testing protocol. I watch the female official shove the bag of clothes into a slot and hear it whooshed into a bin in the back of the building.

Adding to my humiliation, Joshua walks with me back to the school. Thunder booms from beyond the security fence. I would rather be alone, but part of his job is to make sure I return to class safely, and to fetch the next subject. At least Mole Man stayed behind.

"Do you ever get used to it?" he asks. "The thunder, I mean."

I want to ignore him, but then I might seem like I'm sulking.

"It doesn't wake me up anymore," I say. "So, I guess so."

"It's amazing," he says. "People can adapt to pretty much anything."

I suspect that's some sort of metaphor for my benefit. I wait for him to tell me that it's all right to fail the test, that I will be a valuable member of society as I'm given my work detail, and to generally just buck up and be grateful for what I have. I prepare myself to yell at him for such nonsense, but he says nothing of the sort.

Instead, he stops and stares at the broken city behind the fence, beyond the signs warning of mutated animals, out at the falling down buildings where the lightning strikes.

"We can see the storm from Jupitar City, off in the distance. I always wanted to see it up close. It's amazing. Scary in a way."

A flock of shadowrens wheel and dive amidst the lightning, never seeming to be hit, almost like they're taunting the great power above, reminding it that all things have their limits.

"It's powerful," I say. "Powerful enough to destroy a city."

He nods. "It wasn't just dreg bombs that broke our planet."

I stop breathing at his words. Nobody speaks like that, nor is that what I meant.

"The Supergenics were acting in self-defense," I say quickly.

He neither agrees nor disagrees.

"Do you ever wonder what it was like? Before the war I mean. Back when that city was full of people just going about their lives, off to work, buying groceries, planning birthday parties. And then something caused the very first Manifestations, right in the middle of all that. There was no Supergenic state. We all lived together."

I don't even have to consider my reply.

"When the first Supergenics Manifested, it should have been the dawn of a new golden age," I say automatically, reciting the words every dreg knows by heart. "But instead of seeing potential and promise, the dregs looked at their superpowered children in fear. When given the chance to nurture, the dregs tortured. When given the chance to evolve, they sought to cure. When given the chance to understand, they imprisoned instead. They did so in the name of Science. In the name of God. In the name of Family, Tradition, and Society. But really they did so out of Ignorance and Fear."

"And how is that different from what the Supergenics are doing to the dregs now?" he asks.

I step away from him and look about for black-clad agents to come swarming out with protectors at their side to take me away. He doesn't need to be a telepath to see my fear.

"I'm sorry," he apologizes. He sounds tired and sad. "It's not a test, a trick or a Mind Audit to gauge your loyalty. But it was unfair of me to ask, because you're right. It is a question with consequences, even for a Supergenic."

He starts walking again toward the school. Part of me wants to ask more but for once I keep my mouth shut. There's safety in silence. Say nothing and you can't say anything wrong.

We reach my classroom and he pauses, leaning on the door as if to keep it closed.

"I want you to know something, Caitlin Feral," he says. "I don't need any of those tests to see that you're different. You *are* special and we could use more people like you."

Before I can ask him what he means by that, he opens the door. My classmates stare at my bloodshot eyes, the suction marks all over my face, and my blistered skin. Even Mrs. Cranberry looks shocked, as if in all her years as a teacher she's never seen a testing go this far. Whatever pity she might feel, she quickly shakes it off.

"Well, Caitlin," she says with satisfaction. "I guess you'll be with us for a little while longer."

Her hand tightens on the ruler. I'd forgotten about the bottom beating saved up for me. Now that my testing is done, there's no need to hold back and apparently, no matter how rough I might look, she's still determined to get her licks in. The woman can hold a grudge. I expect her to make an example of me (again) here and now, but to my surprise, Mrs. Cranberry points the ruler at my desk and says, "Take your seat."

Finally, a bit of luck. I scurry past her, afraid she'll change her mind. Normand is staring through me, wide-eyed, his palms pressed to his cheeks as if he can't believe what he's seeing.

"You did it," he whispers in relief.

He's so weird! Lilianne eyes me up and down. Her face is a mix of amusement and disgust. My dress flops around my ankles as I set my bottom down, quick as I can in the hopes that she won't see the rip in my backside. I realize my mistake immediately as the cold wetness soaks through my underpants.

Lilianne strikes again. She laughs behind her hands, as do her friends, along with several others. Mrs. Cranberry gazes at me with a cold smile. Even she was in on it. Joshua contemplates them with an unimpressed arch to his golden eyebrow.

"Ow!" Mrs. Cranberry says suddenly putting her hand to her temple.

Joshua gives me a wink. Now it's my turn to smile. I briefly wonder what he looks like without his hazmat suit on.

I heard that, he says in my mind.

I refuse to blush. *Good*, is my reply.

I like you, Rebel, he says in my mind. *Let's have some fun at your classmate's expense.*

"Lilianne Whisper," he says.

Lilianne's head pops up in surprise.

"Yes, that's me," she says. Everyone else is confused too.

He gestures with one finger for her to join him. She gets up hesitantly. Usually we go alphabetically, and she would go last. She eyes my blistered skin, but it's no longer funny to her, because she's next. She grips her purse tightly, not leaving the side of her desk.

"Well, hurry up, Lilianne," Mrs. Cranberry says. "Don't keep the young man waiting."

Lilianne takes tiny steps to reach his side and as they leave, I hear Joshua say to her, "I hope you've got a strong stomach." A better person than I wouldn't be smiling.

As the clock ticks, I wait gleefully for Lilianne to return. Testing time varies from kid to kid, but usually not by much. Mine and Normand's were over in half an hour. Lilianne's been gone for 45 minutes. She should be back by now. An hour passes and finally Joshua is opening the door. He must've really tortured her. I almost feel bad. Almost. I'm ready to "console" her when I realize Lilianne isn't with him. His face is ashen. Even his golden hair has lost its luster. Mole Man is at his side, smiling and rubbing his hands together.

I expect Joshua to say something in my mind, but he does not.

"Eric Graymoor," he calls out.

A scrawny boy covered in freckles and wearing a pair of cracked glasses gets up. He walks forward, not taking his eyes off of Lilianne's empty seat. I stare at it too. She's not coming back.

But that means...

I choke the pamphlet on my desk. *It can't be! It just can't!* And yet it is. Lilianne's Manifested.

CHAPTER 5

On the walk home, I'm careful to keep my eyes down, averting them from the order-enforcing protectors in their form-fitting copper uniforms, all bearing the same chest patch of a fist clutching an all-seeing eye. There are more of them out than usual, at most street corners and driving around in their sleek patrol cars or skimming by on hover attack vehicles. There's even a truck that rumbles through the streets pulling a twenty-measure long metal wagon. Strapped to it is the corpse of a gigantic lizard with three tails that end in rows of deadly spikes. A mutant killed out in the Red Zone. Its skin has painful looking nodules, likely some type of cancer, and there are signs of ice burn. They've probably been keeping it in the freezer to pull out on an occasion such as this, a reminder to us of what's out there, of why we need to follow the rules, of what the protectors protect us against, and of why our alliance with the Supergenics is so important.

All of this is mostly for show. Mostly.

I stop at a street corner where some people are gathered, looking at one of the public info monitors up on a lamp pole.

There are shots of Lilianne waving goodbye as she boards a hovercraft, yellow dress fluttering around her as the vehicle powers up. This is a cause for celebration. There will be extra rations for the whole borough tonight, including cake. I'd rather chew on rusty barbed wire than have even a bite of Lilianne Whisper's Manifestation Day cake, even if it is chocolate, which it better be. What idiot serves vanilla? In a close up, her eyes are clearly bloodshot. Joshua and Mole Man flank her in their orange hazmat suits. No word on what her power is.

That should be me, I think.

"What a happy day indeed for the people of Borough 5," a stone-faced info clerk reports matter-of-factly on the screen. His hair is cut short, with just a touch of putty to hold it in place. His insignia is of a video monitor. "Appearances would indicate that someone's been crying tears of joy. How lucky she must feel. We go now to the male citizen who contributed half of Lilianne's DNA to hear his thoughts on this wonderful occasion."

Up comes an image of a broad-shouldered man with thinning salt and pepper hair. He wears a bureaucrat's navy blue suit and tie. The emblem on his breast pocket is a pointing finger pressing a circle—a button that guides the rest of the labor force. I've seen him before with Lilianne. She never tired of talking about how important her father was. Of course, now that's she's Supergenic, he's no longer legally her father. He's a sperm donor. Her mom not only gifted the egg, but had the added honor of incubating one of the chosen. She stands behind her husband. She's lean and trim like her daughter, with the same delicate features. She wears a rose dress with a necklace of fake white pearls. There's a perma-smile plastered to her face and a glossy drugged look to her eyes. She nods continuously as her husband speaks.

"This is an exciting day for our daugh..." he starts to say, then catches himself. He lowers his eyes, focusing on a piece of paper in front of him, and from then on reads from it verbatim, not daring to look up. "This is an exciting day for Lilianne. It has been an honor for my wife and me to be her caretakers for the past 16 years." He pauses, wiping at his eyes. If it were my mom up there, she'd be having a full-on meltdown.

But he's a bureaucrat, so he understands that Lilianne's better off with her own kind. How could he hope to raise her now? What does he know about superpowers? It's a hard truth in a world of hard truths.

On rare occasions though, the transfer doesn't go this smoothly. Not every parent is so willing to give up a child. There are the misguided Runners who never make it past the Yellow Zone and are executed on the spot. There have been riots, the protectors coming out with their shields and electrified batons; hence tonight's preemptive increase in security. I look up as a short-range cargo transport lands on the roof of a ration center to stock it up.

I take another look at the screen above. It's showing Lilianne again, waving goodbye. Several people wave back. I'm not one of them.

Instead, I stare at the ground and walk away, picking at my peeling sunburnt skin. I automatically step off the sidewalk to put some space between me and the protectors directly ahead.

To my right is the electrified security fence, with guard towers every two-hundred measures. I barely notice the warning signs for radioactivity and mutant animals. Beyond the fence is the Yellow Zone, where a once-great city sits in ruin.

Up above, the ever-present storm clouds rumble with thunder, shooting out blasts of electricity that are sucked into a network of energy syphons that poke up amidst the rubble. The Supergenic who created this phenomenon is long dead, but what the individual's power called forth remains. The lightning hits huge orbs of specially tempered glass set atop massive pylons, and the power is drawn into the electric grid that feeds the boroughs and beyond to Jupitar City.

I stare at the light show as I walk, wondering what it would be like to shoot lightning bolts from my hands, or to summon a hurricane with a thought. I sigh. Today is the day I have to start putting such thoughts aside, like when I was 12 and I packed up my small box of toys to give to the little girl three doors down.

I'm so caught up in myself I almost don't see the protector who steps in my way until his copper uniform fills my vision. The emblem of the fist holding the all-seeing eye glares at me.

"I-Dent card," he says, his voice coming through the mic in his helmet.

My heart is beating faster. I pull out my plastic i-Dent card from my worn-out purse. He swipes it through a card reader attached to his on-the-go device. I wait, feeling more and more guilty with every second that passes, even though I've done nothing wrong. They have a way of doing that —making a person feel as if they've committed an infraction simply by pulling them aside.

He hands the card back and waves me along. I scurry away. I think I hear his laughter as he catches sight of my ripped dress with the wet patch on my bottom. I pass two more groups of protectors on my way home, but none of them even glance at me. I'm trying not to think about what comes tomorrow.

Instead, I cling to the hope of a late Manifestation. I mean, it *could* happen, even if the odds are against it. At my age, it's something like a million to one. With every passing day, and month, and year, it gets exponentially less likely, and then even if I were to Manifest, the more time that passes, the greater the chance that my power would turn out to be either a pathetic nuisance, like incurable halitosis, or so powerful I'd die in the Manifestation and possibly take a chunk of my borough with me. A few years back there was an explosion two buildings over. A man in his fifties stumbled out of his burning apartment, belching fire. He died moments later of organ failure, his heart literally turned into a hunk of coal.

It's one of the reasons for Testing Day, to force Manifestations before they burn too low, or too hot.

As I enter the concrete hallway of my tenement building, I shove these thoughts aside. For now, I just want to get out of this dress.

I race up the stairs. The lift is broken. Again. Fortunately, I'm only three stories up. I unlock and swing open the door to our flat, just barely missing a rack with clothes drying on it. My mom stops stirring dough for dumplings and rushes over to wrap me tight in her arms. That's two hugs in one day.

"I can't even tell you how relieved I am," she says, disengaging and handing me a dented can with a homemade ointment in it. "For your skin," she explains. "When I heard about your classmate, I thought for a second that it was you."

"Lilianne," I say with distaste. She's all that anyone will talk about for the next month.

"That poor girl," my mother says, scooping spoonfuls of dough from the bowl and tossing them into a pot of boiling water.

I say nothing about my own disappointment because I know it will just upset her.

"Can you undo my zipper?" I ask. I'm afraid if I try to do it myself I'll just rip the dress even more.

"Of course, sweetheart."

It's such a relief to feel my full breath as I hear the *zzz-vitt* sound of the metal prong being drawn down those interlacing teeth. I slide the sleeves off, careful to keep the fabric clear of my damaged skin. She doesn't ask about the wet spot on my butt, either because she doesn't see it or because she knows better. Either way I'm relieved. I have my pride.

I hang the dress up on a hook. She'll mend it in the next few days then sell it or trade it. I pull on a pair of worn jeans and a plain white shirt. I stare at my mom's red coveralls thrown over the back of a chair. She notices.

"Soon you'll get a pair of your own," she winks.

I force a smile, fooling no one, but we pretend.

We don't wait for Nate to get home to eat. He's at that age where he's encouraged to pursue any hint of talent he's got in the hopes that it will lead to Manifestation. Tonight it's dance, followed by choir. There are competitions throughout the year. He's won loads of awards, which is how he's managed to accumulate so many colorful clothes. He's like a flower in a sea of grey, but even that's encouraged—for now. Poor kid has no idea what's in store if he doesn't develop powers.

Before I can start feeling too sorry for him, my mom pops a question out of nowhere. She's examining the tear in the dress, planning her attack to repair it.

"Honey, where's the coronet I gave you?"

Crap. I'd forgotten about it. She steps back to stir the dumplings.

"It broke," I reply. It's not exactly a lie.

"Damn it, Caitlin!" she shouts, picking up the pot of boiling water and slamming it down on the counter. The window gets sprayed. She glares at me, her hand on her hip.

"Well, let's see it," she snaps. "Maybe we can glue it back together."

"I...I threw it out," I say.

She shakes her head. "You did *what*? It wasn't yours to throw out. I *loaned* it to you. It *meant* something to me!"

"I...I'm sorry Mom. I should've brought it home," I stammer.

"*This* is why you have no friends," she says.

The verbal slap catches me off guard. She's right though. Breaking the coronet was childish, and it wasn't mine. It's probably all she had left of that different time, when all things seemed possible.

"Well, at least you still have me," I say, trying to lighten the mood, but it's hopeless. That's Nate's power. The anxiety she's been feeling all day drowns her relief that I'm still here. In an instant, whatever's been propping her up drops out from under her.

"Lucky me," is what she grumbles under her breath.

So begins the first day of the rest of my life.

CHAPTER 6

We eat in silence, and I think about my dad, about how much better things would be if he were here. Maybe if he hadn't died, Mom never would've developed her mood swings. After dinner, I wash the dishes and Mom starts mending the dress.

I put on my windbreaker jacket. My mom doesn't ask where I'm going and I don't say goodbye.

Outside I run through a series of back alleys, avoiding the protectors. I cut across a parkette with a towering stone statue of several legendary Supergenics. Their uniforms consist of tights and capes that accentuate their perfect bodies as they hold up the world, saving it from us.

A few minutes later I reach my destination: the library.

The library is beautiful. Unlike almost everything else in our borough, it's not made of cinderblocks coated in spray-on insulation and grey stucco. It looks like it was carved from a single piece of luminescent marble, with graceful columns, whimsical fairies, fiery demons, avenging angels, scaly dragons, along with armies of elves, and wizards, and dwarves.

"It's a pity project," Mom once said as we walked by, but despite her words I could tell from the way she looked at it that she was impressed.

Some famous Supergenic author, Marigold Mapleton, led the campaign to have it built, and she even came here, with her purple hair that stuck out like a pair of horns on either side of her head, praising the written word, extolling the virtues of reading books in print, not just off of a data screen.

"You simply *must* have that tactile experience!" she assured us.

I walk up the library's translucent steps. Everywhere my foot touches, the marble starts to glow. Strands of light swim within its hard surface, as if I'm walking on water and sending out ripples. Sometimes I'll prance up and down these stairs just for fun, until the librarian shoos me away. I reach the top and a pair of stainless steel doors etched with pixies slides open without a touch. Inside, I inhale that ever so slightly musty odor that swells my chest and widens my eyes. It's the smell of a building full of printed books.

The interior is just as fanciful as the exterior, lit by floating glowing globes, more marble columns, these ones crawling with stainless steel vines with metallic leaves, flowers and buds, pollinated by copper bees and butterflies that shimmer in the light. I wander amidst the stacks of books on shelves of wood so black they almost look like a rupture in space.

I come to a data terminal, a simple swipe screen atop a lectern, and I type in my material requests on the interface. They all come back with green check marks and the instruction to "PLEASE PROCEED TO THE WITHDRAWAL DESK."

I do so, and at the front counter is the librarian, Mrs. Sicklesop. She could pass for Mrs. Cranberry's crankier older sister. She takes my i-Dent card and swipes it. There's an unusual BEEP that makes her pause. She looks at the reserves I've placed, then at me.

"Aren't you a bit old for comic books, dear?"

"No," I reply.

"I'm terribly sorry." She's not. "But your access to comic books and other such literature has expired. That's what happens after you fail your final Testing Day." There's an "oh dear, what can I do about it?" hint to her tone. "Time to grow up. Those are the rules, and we musn't break the rules. Would you like to enter another request?"

She slides her keyboard toward me like it's a chess piece closing in on my king.

I tilt my head, look at her primly and tap her screen.

"My access doesn't expire until midnight," I reply. "It says so right here." I slide her keyboard back at her. Check mate. Her eyes narrow and she looks like she wants to shake her fist at me, a clichéd villain bested by some clever brat whose spunk and big heart make up for her rough edges.

I smile. "Those are the rules and we musn't break the rules."

She grunts and disappears into the back stacks, returning an unreasonably lengthy time later with five creased comic books. She takes her time scanning them. I keep looking at the clock. She notices, and goes even more slowly, fussing over one barcode that's crinkled, then entering it in manually. When she's finally done, I'm about to grab my reading material off the counter, until she slams her palm on top of the pile.

"We close in 35 minutes. Returns are over there," she points, as if I didn't know.

"Thanks," I say with sarcastic cheer as I take the comic books from her.

She scowls and pushes a cart of books into the back. I escape to my favorite reading place, a comfy blue seat that's practically a couch. I set all but one of the comic books onto a table, and stare at the one in my hand. It has a muscular woman on the cover. She holds a glowing spear, and wears battle armor reminiscent of a one-piece bathing suit that pushes her large breasts up and together. The outfit is stylized in yellow, black, and red, with a dazzling crescent moon in the middle of her chest.

She stands beneath the bold title *Lady Strength*. I've read it dozens of times, yet my eyes still linger, and it's with intentional slowness that I turn from page to page.

I'm just getting to the best part, where Lady Strength's been captured by the evil semi-sentient soldiers of the monstrously mutated Greyhounds, who've tied her in chains and are threatening a thermonuclear detonation in the boroughs, when who should come plodding through the stacks but my loser classmate Normand Bamford. I can call him that, because I'm a loser too.

I hear him before I see him, his bum leg slamming into the tile floor with every step. I roll my eyes in irritation. Yes, I jumped to help when he fell down this morning, and he did warn me about the new aggressive testing protocols, but we're not actual friends. To call him annoying is to be generous.

I hear the creaking of his leg brace drawing closer and I instinctively curl into myself, as if that can somehow protect me from the socially awkward scenario that's about to unfold.

"Greetings, Caitlin," he says in that nasal, overly formal way of his, pushing those awful oversized glasses up his slightly piggish nose. As always, he doesn't look at me when he talks, but rather at some ghost just over my right shoulder.

"Normand," I force myself to say.

He's got half-a-dozen comic books of his own, including one called *The Good Guy*, with a muscled man in a torn costume covered in gashes standing amidst a pile of monstrously deformed Greyhounds, dead at his feet. Normand sets his own pile of comics down and picks up mine, making me bristle as he flips through the titles.

Stop touching my stuff, I want to say, even though my sense of ownership is laughable. Comic books can't even be signed out.

"This one has merit," he says, pulling out an issue of *Polarmight*. On the cover, the title character is shooting blasts of ice from her hands.

He looks ready to settle back and start reading one of *my* comic books, even though he's got a pile of his own. He manages to hit nerves I didn't even know I had. I grab the comic book back.

"I'm going to read that one next," I lie.

He blinks in surprise.

"Am I to surmise from your tone that you are expressing displeasure?" he asks.

He sounds like a data terminal when he talks. I'm convinced he must've been dropped on his head as a kid. Only now do I notice how battered he is, with a black eye and swollen lip. This was by far the toughest Testing Day in history, and let's face it, Normand's something of a wimp, so I can only imagine how much rougher this must've been on him.

"Sorry," I say, handing the comic book back. "It's been a bad day."

"Indeed," he agrees. "Testing Day is...stressful. And disappointing for most."

He's the first person to acknowledge to me that it sucks.

"Yeah," I agree. "And then Lilianne Manifests? How unfair is that?"

"Statistically it is neither fair nor unfair," he replies. "It simply is. Someone must beat the odds. Why not her?"

Why not me? is my sullen unspoken reply, and I know that our brief bonding moment has passed.

"I wonder what kind of cake we'll get in our extra rations," he muses out loud.

I refuse to admit that I briefly wondered the same thing. It makes me feel like we might have too much in common. Besides, I have more important things to deal with. I need to enjoy my comic book time. After tonight, I won't be allowed to sign them out anymore. I could get Nate to do it for me, but that feels pathetic, like an eight year old who still sucks her thumb.

"Normand, it's almost closing time," I say. "I really just want to read."

"Tick tock goes the clock," he says, looking at the timepiece on his wrist. It's gold with moving hands instead of digital. Word is it came from Jupitar City. He's constantly looking at it, and I just want to shout at him, *yes, we get it! You have a watch!* Even Lilianne doesn't have a watch.

"Time is such a fickle mistress," he says. "And tomorrow is a big day."

"Job assignments," I agree. "Goodie."

"Just remember, when courage triumphs over fear, anyone can be anything. Even a hero," he says. "Someone told me that once."

He's looking at his leg in its brace. It makes me wonder how much harder that's made life for him. For the first time today I'm not feeling sorry for myself. I'm feeling super lucky.

"Normand, I..." I start to say, and surprising for me I reach out to pat his arm. He shifts away immediately. He's even more touch averse than I am.

"There's no need to spread germs." He stands, giving me an archaic bow. "Until the 'morrow."

I watch him limp away, into the stacks. When the creaking of his brace dissipates, I turn back to my comic books.

Way too soon, the floating globes start flashing, indicating that the library is closing. I flip shut a copy of *Amazingonians*. I check to make sure that I have all the comics I checked out. I do *not* have the credits to pay for a replacement.

I finish counting. This is wrong. I have six issues, but I only signed out five. Normand must have left one of his comic books behind. Testing Day must've really done a number on him, because this is utterly contrary to his compulsively fastidious nature. Obviously I will return it for him, but my goodness!

Get it together Normand! You're going to be starting work detail soon!

As I walk toward the front desk I slide free the comic book he left behind. Curiosity and all that. The crone at the front counter sees me and starts dinging the little bell on her desk, waving for me to hurry up. Instead, I freeze on the spot.

"What the heck?" I whisper to myself.

It's a comic book, clearly, but unlike any I've ever seen, and I've seen them all. Numerous times. Because we get so few new issues, I even read the titles I don't like (including that annoying goody goody RinRin and his cat Pokey). But *this*? What is this? The title of the comic book is *Tigara*, likely a play off the word tiger. Its chief character, as revealed on the cover, is a half-naked woman in a cone of light. She's pulling on an orange elbow-length glove with black stripes on it and claws at the end. The rest of her tigress inspired outfit lies on the floor.

I am instantly and utterly mesmerized.

I touch the cover with disbelief. It's almost too good to be true. There's barely a crease on it. This must be brand new! How could I have not known about this? Which is when the little red alert in my mind starts going off. Something isn't right here. I scan for the release date and my heart starts pounding faster.

1993.

That can't be. That was *before* the Genocide Wars. Decades before. This must be a gag from the comic book publisher, involving a time-traveling Supergenic, even though everyone knows time travel's impossible, even for them. The publisher has certainly gone all out to achieve a historical feel. All sorts of things are off. The colors are less saturated, the style of art is unlike any I've seen, gritty and harsh, an ode to a more primitive time perhaps, and even the paper feels different. Thinner. Frailer. These are the details I can explain away. There is one that I cannot. The sticker barcode—stuck on by Mrs. Sicklesop on every single comic book, no matter if it's covering up the villain's or hero's face in mid-battle (I swear she must do it on purpose)—it isn't there.

"Sweet Louise," I cuss under my breath.

This isn't part of the library's collection.

Mrs. Sicklesop starts banging harder on her bell. I should hand the comic book over to her. I should report Normand (where did he even get this? And why leave it for me? Brain damage or not, he's too much of a fusspot for this to be a mistake). I imagine giving the issue of *Tigara* to the librarian, and I instantly know I can't. There's no telling what she'll do with it. Certainly I'd never see it again. I turn my back on her, and I slip the *Tigara* comic book into my satchel.

Mrs. Sicklesop bangs harder on her little bell. I wonder how much force it would take to shove it up her you-know-where. *Then* let her ding her bell.

Breathe, Caitlin, I tell myself. *Don't think about the fact that you're about to commit treason. It's just a comic book.*

It's a lie and I know it's a lie. This is contraband.

Pony up, I tell myself, slowly releasing my breath.

I do a half-pirouette to face the librarian and walk as sweetly as I know how up to the counter. I return the comic books I checked out. She yanks them from my hand.

"I have better things to do than wait around for you all night," she snaps.

"Do you?" I challenge.

Her jaw juts and her eyes narrow. For a second, I think she's going to insist on searching my bag.

Crap, crap, crap!

"Get out of my library," she says, pointing at the door.

I don't argue. I want out of here as fast as I can. I back away a few steps, and give a little bow. That makes her glare. I get to the door. I'm almost safe.

"Caitlin Feral!" she shouts. I stop, heart pounding. I'm not a kid. Now that there's no hope of Manifesting, the protectors won't be lenient on me for breaking the rules. This comic book could land me into forced labor in an irradiated zone.

"I hope tomorrow you get assigned to garbage detail," she shouts.

I half-turn, answering over my shoulder.

"With my luck," I admit to her, "I probably will."

CHAPTER 7

The walk home is excruciating. I want to yank the impossible comic book from my bag and read it cover to cover. Instead I have to pretend everything is normal. I'm more aware than ever of the protectors on every street corner. The symbol of the all-seeing eye held in the fist on their copper uniforms glares at me from every direction.

I try to look down, but my eyes keep darting all over the place. *Are they staring at me?* My guilt feels like a flare. All viewing material goes through the Critic's Bureau, which oversees the dissemination of books, plays, and screenings. They boast: "We decide what you should see so you don't have to."

It's just one comic book, I assure myself. *What harm could it do?*

But as innocent as a comic book may seem, I'm sure it would be deemed against society's best interests. Almost anything from before the war is. A few things "of merit" are tagged and stored. The rest is simply destroyed "to prevent another Genocide War."

Normand would be in so much trouble if they found out I got this from him. *Where did he even get this? Why would he give it to me?* And…*does he have more?*

The possibility is like soda pop in my spine—bubbly, oh so sweet, and bad for me.

I pass a set of protectors just a block from the library. They loom over me, their visors turning my reflection into a distorted mask. I'm a few steps past them, ready to start breathing easier, when I hear the inhuman squawk of one of them talking through the mic inside her helmet.

"What's in the bag, girl?"

I freeze. *Why would she even ask me that?* And then I realize why. Because I'm clutching the satchel as if it has the most precious cargo in all the world —which it does.

"I'm talking to you!" she repeats.

I can't move, and yet I have to. As if I'm a wind up toy, I slowly pivot to face them.

"I said, what's in the bag?" she says.

I slide the strap off my shoulder and hold the satchel toward her. I might as well get this over with. It's an oddly perfect end for the worst day ever. Lilianne gets her powers and new life, while I'll be cuffed and made an example of. My thoughts trickle into my trembling hand.

Be stone Caitlin, I tell myself, *Be stone*. But I can't. In fact, I'm afraid I'm going to lose control of my bladder. I can practically hear Lilianne in the back of my head.

...puddle pants, puddle pants...

The protector jerks the bag out of my grasp, flips open the sash and starts rummaging through my belongings. There's not much. A half-eaten nutrition bar, my i-Dent card (which she gives to her fellow to swipe through his on-the-go), an empty beverage bottle, and a bronze ribbon I won in a race. I like to keep it on me for good luck.

Clearly, it doesn't work. The protector yanks out the comic book and stares at it.

"Where did you get this?" she demands, flopping the comic book in front of my face.

"Well?" she demands.

"The library," I say. It's sort of true, but she's not buying it.

"You're lying." The all-seeing eye in a fist atop her breast glares at me accusingly. She points her blaster at me. "On your knees. Hands behind your head."

My lips are trembling as I lower myself to the ground, one leg at a time. It's hard to keep my balance with my palms pressed into the back of my neck. Passers-by pick up the pace, heads lowered and shoulders hunched.

"I'm going to ask you one more time," the protector says. "Where did you get this?"

I stare at the barrel of her gun. "We have ways of making people talk," she says. She lifts my chin with the blaster, the point of it settling into the soft of my throat. I stare at my warped reflection in her visor. My cheeks are scraped and puffy from today's testing.

"We can do things to your mother," she says, looking at my i-Dent file, "Make you and your brother watch. Like when we took your father away."

My cheeks burn from the memory.

"That won't be necessary," I say.

I'm sorry Normand, I think.

"A classmate gave it to me," I say.

42

"I need a name," she says, jamming the gun deeper against my throat. "Normand," I yelp. "Normand Bamford."

Her partner types the name into his on-the-go then shows it to the protector who has me at gunpoint. She stares at it, then back at me. Thunder booms over the fence.

"On your feet," she says.

I start getting up and lose my balance. She grabs me and sets me right. She stuffs her gun into its holster and shoves my bag and the *Tigara* comic book into my chest.

"If I find out you stole it from him..." she draws a finger across her throat. "Do you understand?"

I nod vigorously, struggling to believe that she's giving it back to me. *Hasn't she noticed there's no seal of approval?*

"Good," she grunts. "Now get out of my sight."

I quickly hide around a corner and press my back against the wall. I'm panting and drenched in sweat. I stare at the cover of *Tigara*. I could blame Normand for all of this, but I'm the one who chose to keep it. I could've handed it over to the librarian, or just left it in the library, or thrown it into a trash bin. But no. I could not have done any of those things. I take in Tigara's fierce countenance. Her athletic physique. Her ferocious costume.

You better be worth this.

Somehow, I'm already convinced that she is.

When I get home, my Mom looks up from patching the dress.

"I was getting worried," she says. She's speaking to me again. She slides the dress onto a hanger. Nate's holding a wall handstand, counting under his breath and ignoring us both.

"That came for you," she says, nodding at a package on the table, wrapped in plain brown paper.

Nate lands on his feet, interested at last.

"Open it! Open it!" he says.

"Sure," I say, though I know he's going to be disappointed by what's inside.

I unwrap it, and there it is. A plain charcoal jacket and grey skirt, with a matching grey tie. My new school uniform. It's patched and worn in places, like everything else I own. It's being passed down through the Bureau of Education from last year's graduating class.

"Put it on! Put it on!" Nate says. The kid loves clothes in a way that I never have.

He sees my lack of enthusiasm. I knew this day was coming, I just told myself it would never come for me.

"Don't worry," he says, putting a hand on my arm. "We'll find a way to add some color."

The next day at school, Lilianne's desk is conspicuously empty. Oddly, so is Normand's. My eyes are heavy from not enough sleep. Last night, once Mom and Nate were breathing softly, I snuck behind the toilet screen and, using a flashlight that Nate won at a ballet competition, I lost myself in Tigara's world. At the end, Tigara is broken and bloody after being betrayed by her evil twin sister. Thugs surround the urban heroine, and it's a wonder I could sleep at all wondering what happens to her.

Now, I look over at Normand's empty seat. I'd been planning on grilling him about the comic book.

Is he okay? I wonder. *Did the protectors get him? Was that their plan all along? Let me go with the contraband comic book and follow me up the supply chain?*

I fidget and pull at my tie. We're all dressed in our uniforms. Those who identify as boys are in grey trousers held up by suspenders, white shirts with charcoal vests and matching ties. Those who identify as girls are similarly attired, but in skirts. The Ministry has access to all of our exact measurements from our Testing Day data, and yet most of our uniforms don't quite fit, either a little too tight or a little too loose. We all show the aftermath of testing—swollen and cut lips, bruises, and the occasional line of stitches across a cheek or forehead.

I play with a bright yellow bracelet of interlocking elastic bands around my left wrist. It's not part of the uniform. Nate gave it to me. He made it a few years ago during a "crafternoon." As promised, he found a way to sneak in some color.

"All right, class," Mrs. Cranberry claps. "We have a lot to do this morning."

My hand is in the air before I even realize it.

"Caitlin…" she sighs.

"It's about Normand," I say. Kids look to his empty desk. "Is he okay?"

"I would worry less about Normand and more about what I'll do to you if you don't stop interrupting," she replies.

It would've taken less time for her to just answer the question. She is so frustrating!

"Yes, Mrs. Cranberry," I force myself to say. I eye the door, wondering if I'll be the next to disappear.

She starts handing out sheets of paper, one to each of us.

"These are your individualized vocational proficiency scores based on your school results of the past several years," she says. "They will help determine which work stream you will ultimately be funneled into. You will see five potential occupational outcomes listed. They are in order of demonstrated aptitude. One is most likely the best fit for you. Five, the least."

My hand shoots into the air. She towers over me as she places my aptitude results face down in front of me.

"You may *not* request a vocation that is not on your sheet."

I slowly lower my hand. I stare at the blank back of the piece of paper before me. My future is on the other side. She pauses next to Normand's empty desk, and then keeps walking.

He's probably just sick, I lie to myself.

"You may turn your sheets over," Mrs. Cranberry barks.

I push Normand from my mind and flip the paper over, then stare at my list, starting at number 5 and working my way up.

5. Laborer (aptitude for heavy lifting)
4. Clerical (proficiency in reading)
3. Janitorial (minimal sense of smell, strong stomach)
2. Assembly Line Worker (able to perform repetitive tasks)
1. Protector (above average dexterity and physical stamina)

This can't be right. I check to make sure it's my name in the upper right hand corner. It is. With my birthdate. And address. But this *can't* be the sum total of what I'm capable of. With each number the list just gets worse and worse. How can protector be my number one occupational aptitude? They're the ones who took my dad away. They're the ones making life miserable for us all.

"You will each have one night to think about it," Mrs. Cranberry says. "Tomorrow you will choose three out of the five options listed. Keep in mind that while research demonstrates greater output when citizens have a level of choice in how they will contribute to our society, it is *strongly* recommended that you include your top two proficiencies in your selection."

I roll my eyes. So typical.

Why even pretend that this is up to us? Just tell us the top two are mandatory and be done with it.

"You will then receive preliminary practical training and evaluations in the three vocations of your choosing to determine your suitability for further development in *one* of those fields of work," Mrs. Cranberry concludes.

I stare at my proficiencies. Janitor is one of the worst. Laborer could be fine while I'm still young, but their bodies get so broken and battered that they wind up living in pain until they ultimately can't fulfill their work obligations and are left to live off the most meagre of pensions. Clerical would be amazing if I could get a job at the library, but fat chance of that ever happening. There's just the one in the whole borough, and there's a lineup to take Mrs. Sicklesop's position when she finally dies, which at the rate she's going will be never. Assembly line worker would mean I'd likely wind up working with my mom. I have a vision of her fussing over me amidst the conveyer belts, her voice loud with frustration, saying things like, "No, not like that. Like this. Oh, let me do it. Honestly, Caitlin! You're going to get us both reassigned."

Which just leaves protector. Dark memories twist my stomach.

I can't be a protector, I think to myself. *I* can't. Not after what they did to my dad. And yet I'm expected to at least try. As upsetting as the thought is to me, there's another that takes precedence.

Mom is going to kill me.

CHAPTER 8

"Well," my mom says the moment she gets home. "Let's see it."

I'm standing at the hotplate stirring a pot of stringy noodles. Nate hands me the foil flavor packet.

"It's on the table," I say.

She picks up the sheet, the one with my aptitude results and possible work streams on it.

Here we go.

My mom gazes at the list.

Nate senses the obvious. Something's up, and it's not good. He slides his fingers into mine. We both stare at our mom.

The word *protector* might as well be written in my father's dripping blood. Her grip tightens on the paper and her lips purse. I wait for her to yell at me. I wait to shout back that I didn't create the list, *they* did. I wait for her to break down in tears, sobbing, *have you forgotten what they did to your father?* I steel myself to comfort her when really I need her to comfort me.

Instead she sets the paper down and calmly takes a marker from her pocket. She marks a black X next to Clerical, Assembly Line Worker, and to my shock, Protector. She doesn't cry or rant. She hands the paper back to me. She sees my look of confusion.

"It's what they want," she says. "It's what's expected. You'll get basic training in all three disciplines. They'll score you and then assign you to your work detail based on your results and what vacancies most need to be filled."

"So..." I begin, knowing there's a connecting thought she's leaving out, something she thinks is obvious, but which I'm not getting.

"So," she says with exasperation: "When you do your basic training to be a protector, you do the absolute worst job possible. You make sure you flunk. Do you understand, Caitlin?"

This is so contrary to the way I expected this conversation to go that I hesitate in my reply. She shoos Nate away. He retreats to his bunk and pretends to work on a sketch, but keeps looking at us, ready to intervene. Man, I love that kid. My mom grabs me by the shoulders and gives me a hard shake. Nate tenses, ready to spring into action. I hold my palm up to him in the "let's see how this plays out" signal.

"I'm not fooling with you, Caitlin," my mother warns. "I *won't* have one of *them* in my home. I *will* disown you first. Do you understand?"

"Okay, yes, I understand," I say. She's staring me in the eyes, gauging if I really mean it, which is insulting. How could I ever want to be a protector? They say they protect us from what's beyond the fence, and from each other, but mostly they let us know that they are *always* watching. Practically begging us to screw up. That's how they got my dad and I never saw him again.

My mother lets me go, and I can start to breathe.

The next day at school, Normand still isn't there. My worry for him grows, and again I watch the door, expecting protectors in their copper uniforms to come for me. We hand in our vocational picks. Mrs. Cranberry collects them briskly. When she yanks mine from my hand her eyes fall on my selections. Her sour lips purse. "Protector," she mutters. Her bony fingers tighten, and I brace myself for a smacking, because apparently I have once again done something wrong, even though I've followed her instructions precisely.

"Sit up straight," she says half-heartedly.

I make a note of it. I *will* figure out the grown up world.

"Today," she says, "You will begin with your lowest scoring vocational option."

For me, that means clerical, which is actually my preferred choice. The pay is decent and the work conditions better than most other vocations. I just have to make sure I ace my placement, while sucking at the other two.

Mrs. Cranberry divides us up into six groups. I stand with the stockier boys and girls from my class, which seems odd. Our scholastic scores are publicly posted. We all know how we rank in everything because it encourages competition, and so I can definitively say that three of the kids in my group are not clerical material.

"And this lot," she says to my group. "Will be headed to the Growing Lands."

I gape. "But, I didn't pick farmhand," I protest. "It's not even on my top five list!"

She holds up a liver-spotted finger. "We have a deluge of *much* more qualified candidates for clerical positions, and a shortage of laborers. No, no, I think that you'd do well getting your hands dirty."

"But you said we couldn't pick anything that wasn't on the list!" I argue.

"Indeed you can't. But *I* can make recommendations. It's all arranged." There's a look of triumph on her face. "Make me proud."

I rage inside as we walk in a clump to the train station. Streams of other children our age merge with us. Groups of those who identify as boys push each other playfully as we walk, and groups of those who identify as girls whisper together in conspiratorial huddles. I'm conspicuously alone and I'm surprised to be missing my classroom. There, I always had something I could be reading, or an assignment I could be working on or daydreaming of better days ahead. I could forget nobody liked me. Here, every laugh is like a razor to my ear. My shoulders hunch, and if I could pick a power to have right now, it would be to pass through solid objects so I could sink deep into the ground.

Grey-clad overseers greet us at the grimy train station doors. The emblem on their chests are three arrows, each pointing from the center in a different direction. They shout out the various occupational groups while standing under signs representing them. There's a pick axe and light for the miners, a sheaf of wheat for farmhands, a set of cogs for the factory workers, a fist clasping an all-seeing eye for the protectors, and so on.

I hand an overseer my i-Dent card. She swipes it through her card reader, nods, and hands me a beige arm band with a sheaf of wheat on it.

"Track 8, car 52," she says, waving me toward the inside of the station.

I head in. The train station is one of the few grand buildings in our borough. It survived the war and is majestic with its sweeping staircases, antique giant clock, and steel girders that look more like works of art than structural support. It's covered in grime, and many of the window panes in the domed ceiling have been broken, replaced with wood or mismatched rusting steel. Black shadowrens with tufts of red on their chests flutter in dizzying patterns overhead.

They chirp all around and I imagine being part of their flock, a thing of speed and grace and precision, which is when I feel the wet and squishy plop of bird poop landing on my cheek. A few kids notice. They point and laugh.

I fish around in my pocket for something to wipe off the droppings. I've got nothing. I look down at the arm band with the wheat on it. It'll have to do.

"You may want to reconsider that course of action, Caitlin Feral," a familiar voice says.

I turn and stare into a round face, with doughy skin that's permanently flushed and framed by a bowl haircut. I feel a mix of relief and reflexive annoyance. It's Normand. He's wearing an armband with a data terminal and a screw driver on it.

"Normand, where have you been?" I ask. "I was worried. Why weren't you in class?"

He gazes to my right, avoiding eye contact, and blinks repeatedly, like a cursor on a screen.

"There was no need for concern, Caitlin," he replies. "Because of my greatly superior intellect I've already been given my permanent work stream, so I won't be taking part in the traditional selection process." He indicates the arm band around his charcoal jacket, with a screwdriver and data monitor on it.

"Okay," I say, wanting to point out that in addition to his "superior intellect" he's also got a crap leg, so it's not like he's a great option for most manual labor positions, and he's got two parents who are bureaucrats pulling strings beyond the reach of most dregs, so it makes perfect sense he'd be assigned to a cushy tech position. He may not have Manifested, but he's still got it made.

Caitlin, I say to myself. *For once keep your mouth shut and let him have this.*

"You still have bird feces on your face," he interjects, gazing at my cheek. "It would be advisable to remove it. Birds are known carriers for a host of diseases. For instance..."

I hold up my hand to stop him.

"Normand. This is not the time."

"Yes," he agrees, looking at his watch. "We are on a ticking clock as they say. But it would be rather *fowl* to use your armband as a sanitary napkin."

He makes a gasping sound that for a second sounds like he's having an asthma attack, and his shoulders move slightly up and down. I'm pretty sure he's laughing. All around us a mass of kids hurry to their platform, all of

50

them with armbands of their own. He stops laughing abruptly, as if a switch has been turned off.

"Here," he says, holding forth a plastic container with a moist tissue poking out. He stares over my left shoulder, avoiding eye contact. We can barely get gritty soap that practically dissolves our skin and he's got wet wipes?

"Thanks," I say, pulling one free and using it to clean the bird poop off my face.

"Did you know that birds defecate and urinate all in one?" he asks, as if this should be the most fascinating thing in the world. I confess, the nerd in me is intrigued. I refuse to let him know this.

"I should get to my train," I say.

The stream of kids around us is starting to lighten. The trains are all scheduled to start leaving soon. I'm screwed if I miss mine, yet still there's something I have to ask.

"The last time I saw you at the library, did you...leave anything there?"

My eyes dart around, noting where the protectors are, faceless with their visors. Can they hear us? Probably, with their spying tech, but there's a lot of noise in here. We should be safe. I hope.

"What an unorthodox query," he replies, looking once again at his watch.

My heart hammers. A protector is staring at us. He's walking our way. Is this what they've been waiting for? To catch us to together? Are they recording what I'm saying? What exactly did I say? I think back, trying to remember my precise choice of words. The protector is getting closer. Kids veer around him.

"Oh, well, never mind," I stammer. The protector is ten measures away. The back of my shirt is soaked in sweat. I step away from Normand. "I should go."

"Of course, I left you the *Tigara* comic book," he blurts out. He doesn't see the protector closing in. "I'd think that would be more than apparent. Did you find it to your liking?"

"Very much so," is what I want to say, but the protector is two measures away.

"Would reading issue 2 be of interest to you?" he asks.

He's talking loudly, perhaps to be heard over the din, or perhaps to sell me out. The protector doesn't need tech to hear us now. He's right next to me. Kids are giving us a wide berth.

I force myself to laugh. It's too shrill and hysterical to be real. My theater teacher would be disgusted.

"Oh, Normand," I snort. "You're so funny!"

He blinks rapidly, a sign that he's trying to process.

"What's happening now?" he asks.

"Vintage Normand," I say. "Such a clown."

I wipe the imaginary tears from my eyes. My little farce fails. The protector grabs me by the arm, ready to drag me away, just like others of his kind did to my dad. Is that why they've set me up? Because of the crimes of the father? It's exactly the kind of innately mean thing they would do.

"Why are you two loitering?" he demands.

I look to Normand, waiting for him to sell me out. He shudders twice like he sometimes does.

"What's wrong with him?" the protector asks.

My mind races, figuring I can use Normand's weird health issue to our advantage, but before I can say anything Normand stares at the protector's visor.

"Why did the chicken cross the road?" Normand asks.

My eyes widen in alarm. The protector's grip on my arm tightens. Normand's telling a joke? We're as good as dead.

"Why?" the protector's voice crackles from the hidden speakers in his helmet.

"To get laid," Normand replies.

There's a moment of silence. I close my eyes. I can't watch. I hear a muffled chortle from the protector's helmet speakers. My eyes pop open. Am I hearing this right? Is he *laughing*?

"That's terrible," the protector says. There's a hint of playfulness to his tone and his grip on my arm weakens. "Did you kids hear that story on the info update about the guy who got hit in the head with a can of soda pop?"

Normand's eyes widen in alarm. "No, I am unaware of…"

"It's okay," the protector cuts him off. "It was a soft drink."

Normand gets it before I do. His shoulders rise up and down and he wheezes out a laugh. The protector releases my arm and it's my turn to wonder, *what's happening now?* I'm too surprised to even play along. I just look from Normand to the protector and back.

Hold up. Is Normand *saving the day?*

"All right," the protector says through his mic. "You two move along now."

His tone is brusque, but there's no bite to his bark, and he waves us on like an indulgent uncle. I wait for him to change his mind as we rejoin the thinning crowd of kids, but when I glance over my shoulder he's walking the other way.

"Did that just happen?" I murmur.

"The evidence would indicate yes," Normand replies.

His leg brace creaks as we walk. I'm noticing it less and less. He stops at a set of stairs. "My track is in this direction."

I can't quite believe it but I'm a little sad to see him go.

"Well, have a good day." It seems like such a banal farewell after our mini adventure.

"A good day to you as well," he replies. "And before we were interrupted, I was asking if reading *Tigara* issue 2 would be of interest to you?"

My mouth is so dry I barely get the words out. "Yes, it would."

He gazes at his watch.

"Good. Then it's decided. Until then, fare you well."

And with that he grabs the hand rail and creaks his way up the steps.

"Wait. What?" I stare at his back. "What's been decided?"

I think of running after him. He reaches the top of the stairs and a grey-clad overseer is asking for his i-Dent card. Yellow lights start flashing all around the station and a crackling voice comes on over the intercom.

"Five minutes 'til departure. Five minutes."

"Damn it," I curse. *Why does Normand have to be so weird? And why am I allowing myself to be pulled in?* The hall is now empty except for a few overseers and several protectors. Before they can notice me I run for my track.

When I reach it, there's a few stragglers boarding their cars. I clamber aboard. There's grime on the windows. The bolts in the floor look like they are more rust than iron. The lights flicker.

I slide onto a seat. A spring pokes into my bottom. It's almost like someone went out of the way to make this ride as uncomfortable as possible. The wiry kid next to me seems oblivious. He's pressing his face to the window.

Like everyone else in our car, he's wearing the armband with a sheaf of wheat. He turns to me with wide eyes as I put mine on. The bridge of his nose is splattered with freckles and his black hair is a mess of beautiful curls.

"I've never been on a train before," he says, as if we've known each other for years. "I'm Bradie Lopez Nettle." He's cute in his own boyish way, getting squinty-eyed every time he smiles—which is often. Makes him look a touch simple.

He offers me his hand. It's oddly formal, but unlike Normand's quirks, it's also strangely charming. I'm instantly suspicious—charming people get away with far more than they should.

"Caitlin," I say, making sure to keep my guard up.

"My brother used to take me to watch the trains when I was little," he continues in that chummy way of his. "We'd make up their destinations. Impossible places. Like other planets, or into the center of the earth, or even cities beyond the Red Zone, carrying secret cargo, and there'd be a series of brutal murders on board, and it turns out the ticket taker did it."

For just a moment he wins me over, with his enthusiasm, with his talk of his brother, with the whimsical fantasies that remind me of the way I want to disappear into a world of capes and masks. But the part of me that sabotages any attempt at getting close to anyone whispers in my ear, *he's an idiot. And he's talking to you because you happen to be here. Don't think that he actually likes you.*

The thought makes me shrink away from him.

The other kids chirp excitedly around us. The PA system squawks something utterly incomprehensible, and a busybody type two seats behind me primly tells everyone to take their seats because the train's about to start moving. There's a mechanical grunt and a lurch, and we start chugging out of the station.

"So where are your friends?" Bradie asks.

The question makes me squirm.

"They were given different work assignments," I lie.

"Oh, that's too bad," he says.

"What about you?" I ask. "Where are *your* friends?"

If he's going to put me on the spot, I'm going to do the same to him.

"They're in Borough 10. I just moved here. I'm living with my aunt. It sucked when my brother became a protector and moved away for his work placement, so he pulled some strings so I could be closer to him."

His brother's a protector. I am instantly horrified.

"We can trade seats if you want the window," he offers.

"I'm good," I deflect.

"Check that out!" he says loud enough for the whole train to hear. To my surprise they listen, turning to see what's so interesting. He's only just arrived and he already has more clout than me. He suctions his face to the window as we pull out of the station.

The ever-present storm clouds are crackling on the other side of the security fence. Below the roiling black mass are the broken remains of a city decimated by the war with the Supergenics. We see that all the time. But today something is different.

We are heading directly toward the storm.

The train track leads to a gate of thick steel. Massive guard towers flank it, and to either side of them the security fence that separates us from the Yellow Zone winds its way to left and right. It's plastered with signs warning of radiation, toxic waste, and mutated animals.

The gate opens, and Bradie grabs my shoulder as if he needs an anchor.

"We're going outside the fence!" he says.

There's murmurs of "no way," "holy cow," and "badass." One kid is shaking and even starts to cry. I'm keenly aware of Bradie's fingers curling into me.

Should I touch him back?

I lift my hand, not quite sure where to put it. I hesitate and he lets me go, pressing both hands to the window. I run my fingers through my hair as if that's what I meant to do all along—not that anyone's noticing. Like a bunch of cattle, they're mesmerized as the gate opens.

I'm not sure why they're in such a tizzy. This isn't a surprise. We're on farm duty after all. That means we have to pass through the Yellow Zone. Yet despite my condescension, I feel it too. There's something momentous about this moment. None of us has ever been on the other side of that barrier. We speed through the open gate. We're now traveling directly under the black clouds.

We're on an elevated track, which puts the streets of the Yellow Zone directly below. I now wish I'd taken Bradie up on his offer to switch seats. I see the Yellow Zone in a way I've never seen before, gazing down at a pile up of cars, toppled buildings, and the ever-present wrens that have made the city their home. Lightning flares around us, but the many pulsating orbs dotting the city keep us safe. The orbs sit atop concrete towers, putting them almost level with us. I watch a burst of energy smashing into a globe merely twenty measures away, making it crackle with energy.

"Sweet chariot," Bradie swears.

I agree.

Inside one roofless homes I see a room with a toilet, tub, and sink that are surprisingly intact. Mushrooms poke up amidst the grimy tile floor. There's not much else that can grow under those clouds.

We pass a partially collapsed building with a large bell tower with a giant lowercase "t" on it, which seems to be a symbol of some sort.

Some areas are completely flattened. Others are filled with skyscrapers that look ready to crumble. One house is perfectly preserved, including shrubs and flowers, the whole property pulsating with an ethereal light. There's a public square filled with black statues of terrified people trying to run from something. My chest constricts. I'm not sure they're statues.

We leave them behind.

Our attention is soon diverted. We're quickly approaching a second gate, bigger than the first. There's another security fence, so formidable it makes the one around the boroughs look like a joke. That one is electrified chain link. This is a wall of steel and concrete, rising 20 measures high, armed with sonic mutant repellants that make our ears vibrate with a rising hum the closer we get. It too has warning signs, gigantic ones, with the heads of a mutated wolf, lizard, and lioness ensconced within the crescent moons of the biohazard symbol. It's dozens of measures across.

The gate opens and we speed through—into the Red Zone.

I'm met by a landscape unlike anything I've ever seen. Beyond the concrete confines of our borough and the smashed remains of the Yellow Zone, is a vista of golden wheat billowing in the breeze. We speed by it, and there are apple orchards, rows of grape vines, even pasture land with cows and sheep, just like in our farming books at school. It goes on and on.

"I don't understand," I say.

"What do you mean?" Bradie asks.

"There's so much of it."

"So?"

"So," I reply, "Why do we end up with so little?"

For the first time Bradie's smile withers.

Now what have I done? I wonder.

"Don't say that," he whispers. "Don't ever say that."

I'm about to ask why, but I don't. I know why. Dotting the farmlands are squat watchtowers, each bearing a flag with an emblem of a fist holding the all-seeing eye. There are protectors inside, ostensibly keeping a watchful eye for prowling mutant animals. In reality, we all know they are watching the farmhands just as much.

You're not a kid anymore, I hear my mother say. *You need to start keeping your mouth shut.*

"Our little secret," Bradie winks, and he's back to his smiling self, except the smile doesn't reach his eyes, and when he banters with the girls behind us he's a bit too loud, a bit too gregarious, a bit too forced.

He's scared.

As always, I want to know more. *Just how much of the food are the protectors taking?*

The train pulls to a stop and a grey-clad overseer opens the door to our car. He barks at us, "Come on, farmhands. Let's go."

We leave in orderly rank and file, just like at school. The train platform is open to the air. We crowd it and the overseers direct us down a wide flight of stairs. When the farmhand trainees like me and Bradie have disembarked, the train whistles and starts chugging away, deeper into the lands outside the boroughs, toward the mountains in the distance, toward the mines. The kids still on the train look at us enviously. A few wave. I wave back, sad for them. Those who are chosen to be miners will eventually die of black coughs, their lungs full of dust. For us, it's the chemicals used to treat fruits and vegetables that we need to worry about. They get us from the inside, or from the outside, but in the end they get us all.

CHAPTER 9

We're all given beige coveralls to wear over our uniforms, along with work boots, none of which fits us properly. We spend most of the morning standing in front of a conveyer belt, sorting the apples that rumble by into various categories.

The half-rotting ones are what I'm accustomed to in our rations pack so it's no surprise that these all go in bins marked DREGS. If any look mutated, we set them in a biohazard bin to be sent to a lab. It's the other apples that amaze me, with their glossy unmarked surfaces, firm bodies, and the promise of succulent interiors.

I hold one in my hand and stare at it. I've seen apples like this in pictures and assumed the images had been digitally altered. I had no idea an apple could actually be like this in real life. The cartoon apples with smiling worms poking out actually seemed more realistic.

"Don't get any ideas," a woman with grey hair and a stained apron says next to me. "They'll be happy to beat you."

She jerks her head at the protector by the door. He's staring at me. Of course he would. Apples like this are for people like him. I'm about to put it in a bin marked Protectorate when Apron Lady snorts.

"They wish," she says. "That one there, hon."

She points at a container labelled *Jupitar City*. It's already brimming with hundreds of similarly perfect specimens.

This can't be right, I think as I add it to the already-packed container.

"Okay, help me seal it up," Apron says to me.

I hold a circular lid in place above the barrel while Apron applies a device that seals the top into place. There are dozens of barrels marked for Jupitar City.

Everyone knows that the various boroughs and Jupitar City are trade partners; that some of the food and manufactured goods produced by dregs are shipped across the river, and in exchange the Supergenics keep the boroughs and the surrounding land radiation-free, as well as neutralizing any mutated animals that the protectors can't handle. Only now do I start to question how much the Supergenics are getting in return. The answer, it would seem, is a lot.

58

"You're catching on quick," Apron says to me.

"Yes," I agree. "I believe I am."

Later that day, we're taken into one of the orchards, and we spend hours pulling apples from trees. I keep thinking about all the perfect fruit headed for Jupitar City instead of to the people who grow and pick them. There must be some mistake. The Supergenics are heroes. Maybe they don't know how often we go hungry. I'm pulled from my thoughts by a group of giggling girls. Their laughter is high pitched and grating. I look over and there's Bradie at the center of the fawning cluster. It's making an already irritating task even worse. I try to refocus my attention. The kid who picks the most apples gets some sort of prize and part of me can't help but think, *maybe this time*.

I take a bit of satisfaction as an overseer snaps her fingers at their little group.

Good.

I should know better than to let my attention wander. I grope for an apple deep in the tree, the corner of my eye on Bradie. I overreach, my ladder teeters, and as I try to right myself, I know it's too late. The ladder is falling out from under me. I grab a branch just in time, my feet dangling in the air. Mrs. Cranberry is a train ride away, and yet I can still practically hear her yelling at me to "Get down from there."

I dangle, hesitant to drop to the uneven ground below for fear of spraining my ankle. I'm about to call for help when a loud siren fills the air. For a split second I think it's because I've screwed up, and the protectors are coming for me. Deeper down my pounding heart knows this is worse. We do drills several times a year. Whether it's here or in the boroughs, that siren means one thing. A perimeter breach.

I spin my head about in terror, searching for the safety shelter. All the other kids are doing the same. The overseers are nowhere to be seen. We were given cursory safety training when we arrived, and there are signs pointing toward evac zones. The workers wave at us, and shout, "This way, this way."

I look down at the ground and let go, landing like a cat, just like I learned in gymnastics. I'm so springy I don't even feel it in my joints. *Nailed it*.

My heart's pounding as I start to run. I don't get far, no more than five measures when my foot catches on a tree root and down I go. I hit hard, knocking the breath from me. I struggle to inhale as someone helps me up. I look into Bradie's dark eyes.

"There," he says, pointing toward a set of stairs leading to the train platform. People are running up them, the experienced workers doing so quickly but calmly, the trainees screaming and shoving their way in between.

"Ready?" he asks.

"Yeah," I nod.

We sprint toward safety. I'm fast. Bradie's faster. I struggle to keep up.

"Come on, Legs," he winks.

I push harder, wanting to show him up, but still remembering the roots all around. I weave and jump amongst them. So does he. I dart around a tree, and take the lead. I'm so exultant that I block out the sirens, and the panicked shouts of the other trainees. For an instant it's just him and me, racing for no other reason than to see who is the fastest. Which is when I smash right into a copper uniformed protector. He's not that much bigger than me and I bowl him over.

"Effing geez!" I hear him swearing through the mic in his closed helmet.

He grabs me by the arm and yanks me to my feet. I think he's going to demand to see my i-Dent card and have me formally charged. Instead he points to the crowd, "Go!" he shouts. "Get to safety, kid!"

I don't have time to obey before a muscled form covered in brown fur smashes into him, knocking him back to the ground. The thing growls, its sharp teeth ripping through the protector's body armor like it's tissue paper. He screams. I pant, backing away, and the monster on top of him rounds on me, staring at me with bloodshot eyes.

It's a hound, big as a cow, slavering at me with its bloody teeth. It has two heads, one in proportion to its massive body. The second head is smaller, wilder, snapping at nothing in the air. I've seen dead mutated animals on the backs of trucks, driven around to scare the populace. This is far more terrifying. The beast bunches up on its haunches and I know it's about to launch itself at me, ripping me apart the same as it did the protector.

I hear the sounds of gunfire, and shouting, more growls amongst the trees, muscled shapes covered in fur a blur as they sprint through the orchard.

Oh ,geez-us, I swear. *There's a pack.*

The monstrosity before me ignores them, all four of its bloodshot eyes on me. The little head yaps more wildly, egging the big head on. I'm dead. It's as simple as that.

"Leave her alone!" Bradie shouts. I stare at him. The idiot is clenching an apple in his hand. He winds it up, and throws it as hard as he can at the mutated creature. The apple hits the big head square in the brow. The apple bursts. The monstrosity yelps and the little head bites the big head on the ear. The big head shakes back and forth, and turns to face Bradie. It's so huge, he's a toy doll by comparison. He backs away slowly, holding another apple where big head can clearly see it. Little head keeps craning its neck to get a better view.

Around us are more gun shots, more shouting, more screams.

The mutated thing steps cautiously toward Bradie, ears back, showing its teeth as a low growl rumbles in its throat.

"Caitlin," Bradie says, "I need you to get the protector's gun."

The hound's tail swishes back and forth over the dead protector's feet. His gun is still in its holster.

"You can do it," Bradie says.

I nod. I *can* do it, but should I? An ordinary citizen brandishing a weapon? That's forbidden. And yet what choice do I have? Bradie's brother is a protector. Does that make this okay?

I swallow my fear, moving it from my throat to the pit of my stomach as I inch my way closer to the protector. The little hound head sees me, but before it can start barking at me, Bradie whips another apple at it, hitting the small one between the eyes. Bradie unleashes more apples, grabbing them from the ground and pitching them with surprising accuracy. He throws and the big head catches the apple in its jaws, chomping down hard. Juice, seeds, and saliva spray everywhere. I bend over the dead protector. The reinforced fabric of his uniform—allegedly as supple as silk yet stronger than steel—was useless against mutated fangs and claws. I can see his rib cage. I step in a pool of his blood, reaching over him to unclasp his holster and pull his firearm free. I lift it and point. My arms are shaking.

"You need to turn off the safety," Bradie says. "It's on the left side of the barrel."

I look and see a slide switch. I shove it with my thumb and it clicks, revealing a red rectangle that presumably means it's on.

"To load the chamber you pull back on the barrel."

He sees my confusion.

"The top of the gun! Pull it back!" he shouts, still lobbing apples.

I do and I hear something snap into place. The mutant hound finally loses it and charges at Bradie.

"Shoot it!" he shouts.

I point, aiming at the thing, and pull the trigger. The boom is loud in my ear. My arm jerks up and back from the force, and the gun flies from my grip, skittering across the ground. I slip on the blood around my feet, tripping over the dead protector. The force of hitting the ground reverberates right up into my jaw. I gaze at what I expect to be the animal's dead body, killed by my bullet, only to find the beast very much alive. My shot did hit it, if barely. One of the little head's ears is blown clean off. It's deathly quiet, staring back at me over its shoulder. So is the big one. Bradie throws more apples at it, but it ignores them. It lets loose a low growl and then charges me.

The gun is too far away. The protector's dead hand grasps a baton. I yank it from his fingers and shove it blindly toward the animal. It pays no mind, until it makes contact and a blue burst of electricity courses from the baton into the creature's chest. It yelps in agony, the two heads losing all control, smashing one into the other. It can't pull away, the electricity holding it trapped, and I push the baton harder into its chest.

I can smell burning flesh, and see the smoke rising from its singed fur. The baton grows hotter and hotter in my hands. My palms are burning but I don't let go. The baton sparks. The electricity grows brighter for just a moment, and then winks out as the battery runs dry. I drop the weapon and the monstrosity falls dead to the ground.

I'm panting, drenched in sweat, covered in blood. My senses are so wound up that I even hear the tiny crackle of a branch. I swivel and watch as another hound, this one with just one head, but twice as big as the other, comes out from the trees. It sprints toward me with impossible speed. There's no time to run or even scream. It launches off its haunches. I cover my face instinctively, but still I hear the boom and see the red burst of

62

blood as the side of its head blows out. It smashes into me with all its weight, pounding me into the ground. I struggle against its mass, my nostrils filled with the stink of wet fur and infected flesh crawling with maggots. I grit my teeth to keep its hair out of my mouth. I'm sure I'm going to die under here, slowly suffocating, when I hear Bradie shout, "Push, Caitlin!"

I do, and with him pulling I'm able to skitter out from under its mass. Bradie helps me up, and holds me tight, and before I know it he's kissing me, and I'm kissing him back. The shock wears off when I feel him grab my butt. I shove him so hard he lands on his ass. I'm panting, towering over him, fists clenched.

"What was that?" I demand.

"Me saving your life?"

"You kissing me!"

"I don't know," he shrugs. "You seemed into it."

"I wasn't," I say.

He's still holding the protector's gun. There's a bleeding red line across his cheek.

"You're hurt," I say.

"Yeah, well, it turns out that you're a really terrible shot," he replies.

"I did that?" I ask.

"And that," he jerks his head at the electrocuted mutant animal with the two heads.

He gets up and reaches out to me. I instinctively take a step back.

"Relax," he says. "You had your chance at this." He waves at himself up and down.

He takes one of my hands into his own and slowly uncurls my fist. My palms are red and starting to blister from overloading the baton. Matches my face from Testing Day.

"You'll be okay," he says. "I've seen worse."

He kisses me again, but this time on my forehead. It's so tender and unexpected and different than the lip kiss that all I want right now is to curl into him and listen to him tell me it will all be all right.

Those are just your daddy issues coming out, a part of me snips.

It doesn't matter. The moment passes and a group of protectors surround us.

They've got their weapons pointed at us. Bradie pulls away and drops the gun. He raises his arms in the air. My blistered hands go up. A protector's dead because of us *and* we took his weapons. We are in a *lot* of trouble.

The lead protector touches the side of his helmet and his visor slides back, revealing his face. He looks at the dead animals.

"Did you kids do this?"

There's no point in denying it. We nod.

He inclines his head to the side. "Not bad. Maybe you should become protectors."

Never, I swear to myself.

CHAPTER 10

The protector takes a look at my blistered hands and whistles.

"Gross," he says lightly. He takes out a tube from the med kit on his belt and squeezes a clear ointment into my palm.

"Rub it in," he says.

I wince as I do so.

He takes some bandages and wraps the gauzy material around my injured palms. They tingle from the cream, and already the pain is dulling to a light throb. I've never known a protector to be nice. An injured hound is dragging its hind legs behind it, growling as it pathetically comes toward us. The protector pauses in tending to me and shoots it in the head.

I wince at the sound, then look around, hoping to see the members of A.M.M.O. swooping in from Jupitar City to save the day.

"Is Captain Light here?" I ask.

The protector who's helping me chuckles. "Don't fool yourself, kid. The protectors are the first line of defense. We do the heavy lifting." He jerks his head in the direction of Jupitar City. "*They* only come around when the cameras are on them."

"Oh," I say with disappointment. I've always wanted to meet Captain Light, and this would've been the perfect chance to ask him about the apple distribution discrepancy. I know there must be some explanation.

The protectors escort us back toward the train platform. Through the trees I see more hound corpses. The smaller ones are being tossed onto the back of a flat bed truck. But some are as big as cars. Those ones are being stabbed with meat hooks from the slaughter house, and then attached to chains and lifted by hoists to be deposited next to the smaller members of their pack. One has three tails. Another has two heads, but different from the one that attacked us, as if their twin faces had been mashed together in the middle. All four of its dead eyes stare at us. Many are covered in boils, radiation burns or have other strange growths pushing out of their fur.

They're not going to feed that to us, I wonder. *Are they?*

There's always talk of what actually goes into the canned meat we receive as part of our rations. We've been told that any cattle that's born deformed is sent to a lab for analysis, just like the oddly shaped apples. Surely it's the same for these monstrosities. And that's when it hits me.

"I *killed* one of those things," I say out loud.

"Yeah," Bradie agrees. "That makes you a badass."

"You killed one of those things too," I reply. "I guess you're also a badass."

He smiles and winks. "*That* was never in question."

Such a brat. It's a step up from idiot.

As we are escorted up the concrete stairs to the train platform, a wave of cheers and applause rises with us. Many of the students and farmhands saw us from above. They know what we did. Bradie waves at them. I just stare like an oaf. The train is waiting, its doors open.

"*Please board the train now*," a crackling voice comes over the announcement system.

Nobody listens, staring as the protectors guide us away from the crowd, to a car at the very end of the train. We get on. It's an upgraded version of the car we rode in on. The vinyl upholstery is new and the chairs are stuffed with foam. This car must be for officials. When I sit I experience a foreign sensation: comfort.

The protectors leave us there, alone. I watch out the window as everyone else is herded onto the train, but none of them come into our car. Once the doors close, the train lurches to life, carrying us back toward our borough.

A grey-clad overseer comes in carrying a pair of dinner trays with foil on top. She sets them down on pull-out tables. Fancy.

"We thought you might be hungry," she says. "And for dessert..."

She hands us each a shiny, perfect apple. I hold it before me, gazing at it in awe. I almost want to eat it first, but I'm curious what's under the foil. I pull it back, and stare at what appears to be real meat loaf (not some mix of oats and animal fat), mashed potatoes, and some string beans. I've rarely experienced a meal like this and I devour it quickly, as if they might take it away. Bradie does the same with his. There's not even anything to lick by the time we're done.

I set my plastic utensils down and gaze at the apple in my hand, but I don't bite into it. Bradie shows no such restraint, taking a large chunk out of it with his slightly too large teeth. His face is pure ecstasy as he chews on it, and he's making weird grunting sounds of sheer delight.

"It's so good," he says.

He notices that I haven't tried mine yet.

"If you're thinking of saving it for your family, you can't. They won't let you take it with you," he says.

"What do you mean?" I ask. "Why not?"

He shrugs. "It's just another one of their rules."

I get the feeling that he was about to say, "One of their *stupid* rules," but caught himself just in time.

"How do you know?" I ask.

"Because my big brother's a protector, remember?" he replies. "He was never allowed to bring food home from the Cube when he came to visit, and that guy is sneaky."

My chest constricts involuntarily. I'd forgotten his brother was one of *them*. I was wondering where Bradie learned so much about guns, enough to shoot a mutant obscenity square between the eyes. That wasn't luck.

"He's the one who taught you to..."

He leans forward quickly and grabs my hand, his fingers pressing into my bandages.

"Ow!" I say, but he doesn't let go.

"Has anyone ever told you that you have the most beautiful eyes?"

I'm almost conned by Bradie's charm, but his dark eyes are framed by a terrified furrow in his brow. He's scared.

Before I can say another word, half-a-dozen dissemination screens around the cabin spring to life. There's an information clerk in navy blue on the monitor, seated behind a desk, reading off of a teleprompter.

"A breach today in the farming sector, where hundreds of lives were saved by the brave efforts of our protector forces."

We watch the footage of the protectors shooting at the rabid and deformed canines as they hunt amidst the trees. There are yelps of pain. A dramatic musical score has been laid underneath.

"Three officers were killed in the incursion, bravely defending the populace from these ravenous beasts."

Smiling head shots of the three fallen protectors appear on the screen, along with their names and ages. The youngest was just a few years older than us. I recognize him. He's the one I knocked over, the one who told me to run. He was barely more than a kid. He died trying to protect me. I've grown to hate them so much I'd stopped believing how dangerous their jobs outside the fence really are.

That's what they want you to focus on, I can hear my mom say.

The information clerk is back on screen.

"And some unexpected bravery from a pair of mentees during that incursion," he says.

Bradie sits up excitedly.

"He's talking about us!" he says.

New images begin to roll, taken from the cameras overlooking the fields from the security towers. There's a shot of the dual headed hound growling at me.

Bradie starts throwing apples at the mutant and it turns to attack him. Any images of me picking up or wielding the protector's gun are completely omitted. It cuts to the hound rushing me, right into the baton in my grip. The music swells triumphantly as the beast electrocutes itself.

The images cut out and up comes Chief Bureaucrat Sannvi Patel, dressed in a beige suit, extolling our bravery, saying how sure she is that we will "grow into our place within the system."

I'm barely listening. I'm thinking about what they haven't said; what they haven't shown. They've cut out the part where I fire a weapon, badly, as well as when Bradie picks up the gun and shoots the second dog, expertly.

Ordinary dregs shouldn't know how to fire a weapon. They shouldn't even think of picking one up. I'm sure to be penalized. But Bradie...he's clearly had practice—lots of it. That will earn him the death penalty—or worse. Bradie's turned pale. He's thinking the same thing. The protectors seemed so concerned about our well-being back in the orchard, I'd just assumed we were in the clear. That was before they had a chance to review the security footage.

I want to reassure Bradie, but my words are cut off as the door to our car slides open. In strides a man in a black uniform with red piping where the seams meet. The insignia on his chest is a red hangman's noose. A woman with that symbol oversaw the protectors taking my dad away. This man in black is an agent of the Cube, worse than a protector. He moves like an eel, and with the shaved strips on either side of his grey, slicked-back hair, he looks like one too. A pair of protectors in their copper uniforms walk behind him. I grip my apple tightly.

"I trust you've enjoyed your meal," the agent says.

"Y-y-yess," Bradie stutters.

"It was delicious," I add quickly.

68

"I'm sure," he says, wrinkling his nose as if we'd just been feeding from a trough. He reaches over and plucks the perfect apple from my hand. He appraises it, then polishes it on his black leather. "I need a word with the young man, in private."

"I..." I hesitate, and in an instant a massive protector is yanking me from my seat. My toes barely touch the ground as he drags me toward the door. I look back at Bradie. He's staring at the floor. I'm not sure, but I think he might be crying.

"Caitlin, my dear," the agent says, "Don't let that public broadcast give you any foolish fancies about being a hero. We do like to give the populace the occasional story of hope. We find it minimizes the suicide rate. But we both know that you simply got lucky, and by all rights you should have been torn to shreds. Understood?"

I gape, not saying a word.

"I said, do you *understand?*" he shouts.

"Yes, yes I do," I insist quickly. "And Bradie..."

"Goodbye, Caitlin," he says. He bites into the apple as the protector drags me from the car.

I stare over my shoulder. Bradie's body is heaving. I can't hear what the agent is saying to him. Apple juice drips run down the agent's chin and then the door is sliding shut.

CHAPTER 11

The protector shoves me into an empty cargo car. There are no seats and it reeks of fermenting fruit. I swat at buzzing flies. The shifting train jostles me and I fall to my hands and knees, sending jarring pain up my wrists. I sit on the bare metal floor for the rest of the ride, staring at the door, waiting for it to open, waiting for them to throw Bradie in with me, but they don't.

We pull into Central Station and I hear everybody else file out. Only once the platform is clear of people do the doors on my car pop open. I walk out cautiously, looking for Bradie.

A protector sees me loitering and points for me to be on my way. I obey. There's nothing else I can do.

At home, my mom gives me an awkward hug. She's seen the information update broadcasting the images of me electrocuting the mutant. I cry and she thinks that it's because I'm scared of what happened, and I am, but not because of the hounds. I don't know what they've done to Bradie, and I have no way of finding out.

That night, after my mom and brother have gone to bed, I lie in my own bunk, staring at nothing. I wonder if I'll ever be able to sleep again. I fish under my mattress and pull out Normand's comic book. I climb down from my bunk, careful not to step on my brother and go to the window where the light from a streetlamp streams in.

I flip through until I get to a page where Tigara is breaking a militia fighter's neck while slitting the throat of a mercenary with the claws on her feet.

I stare at her image and I wish that she was here to make the agent pay.

The next day at school kids come running up to me. They've all seen me on the information broadcast. All of a sudden everyone who has ignored, derided, or played tricks on me is now my best friend.

"Are those claw marks?" Julia asks of the scratches on my cheeks.

"Teeth," I reply dryly. Her eyes grow wide. It's nonsense, of course. They're scrapes from when I fell. If the hound had gotten that close to me with its gaping jaws I wouldn't have a face left.

"Here," she says, offering me a small plastic cup with a peel-back lid. It's got three spoonfuls of gelatinized vanilla pudding inside. I slide it into my pocket.

"Caitlin's sitting next to me in class!" she declares loudly to the crowd. Julia's the new Lilianne and has blossomed into a grade-A bossypants now that her domineering best friend is gone.

Even Mrs. Cranberry acts differently toward me.

"Still getting yourself into trouble I see," she says to me, but there are no threats of punishment or demerits or the dreaded "permanent file." Even her baleful glare is softened.

It's small consolation though. I still have no idea what happened to Bradie, and I can only think of one way to find out. I raise my hand.

With an exasperated sigh Mrs. Cranberry acknowledges me. "Yes, Caitlin?"

"I'd like to skip the rest of my farming apprenticeship," I say.

"Caitlin, I know you had an upsetting day," she snaps, "But that simply isn't done."

I'm undeterred.

"I'm ready to try being a protector," I say.

The entire class is silent. She stares at me. I wonder if she feels guilty. Farmhand wasn't even one of my options, but she sent me there anyway. She's the one who put me in danger in the first place. Maybe she can reason it away—that it wouldn't matter where I was, I'd find a way to get into trouble, but from the way her face constricts I'm not sure even she's buying that.

Finally, she says, "I'll look into it."

After that she breaks us up into groups based on which work stream we were in yesterday. We're required to discuss the things we learned at our trade, the things we have questions about, along with areas we'd like to improve upon. When it comes to my turn all the kids in my group want to know about the hounds.

"How big were they?" they ask.

"Like a truck," I reply.

"Did they have three heads?"

"Only two."

"Did you see anyone die?"

"Yes." And worse.

It's all a bit silly considering they were there, but I suppose the adult workers kept them from seeing much. After that we answer multiple choice questions about the work placement, and write essays about how this makes us contributing members of the larger society.

After school ends I'm at the center of a cluster of kids who identify as girls, followed by the boys who like them. Julia's got her arm looped through mine.

"We have got to talk about who your boyfriend is going to be!" she coos to me. "Or do you prefer girls? I have a cousin who's gender variant. She's an absolute riot. What about Cody? I think he likes you."

I glance back at Cody, one of the more athletic kids in our class, and I quickly look away. All I can think of is Bradie.

Black-winged wrens swoop through the air above us, gobbling up insects. We're passing the library and I see Normand's unmistakeable silhouette. He raises a hand in a wave. I try to do the same and Julia grabs my arm, forcing it down.

She's practically hissing. "Don't wave to that weirdo!"

We keep walking and I take a backward glance at Normand's form alone on the library's steps.

Little by little, our group shrinks as my classmates disappear into the various tenements near our school. It's down to just Julia and me. She gives me a huge hug.

"Caitlin Feral, I think you might be the bravest person I've ever met," she says. "I'm so glad you're my best friend."

"Sure," I say, waiting for the punchline.

She giggles and waves and skips to her front door, a townhouse in a world of apartments. It's been a longtime since my family lived in one of those. Her mother opens the door before she reaches it, as if she'd been waiting for her daughter's return. Behind her is Julia's father. And behind them, seated on the couch, is a man clad in a black uniform with red piping.

The door slams shut, and Julia is gone.

My heart is pumping loudly and my throat runs dry. I'm fairly certain it's the same agent who came for Bradie on the train. Eel Man. I hide behind a crumbling wall and a moment later I watch the agent emerge with Julia. They get into the back of a black car and drive away.

They're taking her too!

72

I want to go knock on her door, but a neighbor pops her head out.

"What are you doing?" she demands.

"Nothing," I say.

"Well, off with you," she orders. "Before I call the protectors."

I blanch at the thought and hurry home.

The next day I walk briskly to school, looking frequently over my shoulder. Every time a car, van, or hover vehicle drives by I tense, waiting for agents to pour out and nab me right off the street.

My nerves are wound tight by the time I get to school, and the screeches of the younger kids chasing after balls or jumping rope are like cymbals in my ears. I wander among them, searching for Julia, and to my shock I see her.

I smile in relief. She's surrounded by her pack, not a hint of torture or trauma to her pretty features. She does look different though—better actually. She wears a uniform just like the rest of us, but hers is now brand new, and fits her perfectly. She's also got hints of makeup, just enough to give her an air of glamor, with a jaunty beret that's probably all the rage in Jupitar City.

I rush up to her and give her a hug before I even realize I'm doing it.

"Julia!" I say. "I'm so relieved to see you!"

She pushes me away, a look of disdain on her face, like I'd just eaten a bushel of onions and was breathing all over her.

"Hands off!" she insists.

She gives me a puzzled look as if she has no idea why I would be talking to her. I pull back, confused. She's dusting herself off as if I've somehow contaminated her.

"Hey Feral," Cody asks, "Kill any more mutant hounds?"

There are nods of approval, but not from Julia.

"The *real* heroes are the protectors," she informs us. "Don't go taking on airs, Caitlin. Some people say *you* got those three protectors killed."

"What people?" I demand.

"People," she says pointedly.

Her clique goes quiet at that. They appraise me, as if I've just been caught in a lie and they're seeing me for who I really am. I have no idea what to say, and I mutely follow her and her posse into class. Once again we are divided into our groups. I'm placed with the farmhands. I put my arm up, but before I can ask my question Mrs. Cranberry says crisply, "I haven't heard back, Caitlin." I lower the limb.

After attendance, we are sent for another day of on the job training. I am conspicuously alone amidst the packs of teens marching to the train station. I tell myself I'm just imagining it but some of them seem to be giving me dirty looks, and then saying things to their friends. The dirty looks spread.

Focus, Caitlin, I tell myself.

I search for Bradie, and not just with my eyes. I listen for his tell-tale banter. I spot several look-a-likes (I never knew there were so many kids with freckles and unruly black hair in our borough). None of them are him. I'm about to head for my train when someone grabs my arm and spins me around. I face a huge kid who shoves me roughly to the ground.

"Hey!" I look for the protectors to intervene, but they all seem to have their backs turned.

"I heard how you put everyone in danger in the farmlands, attracting those mutant hounds into the orchards. My *mom* works in the orchards," he shouts, pointing his finger at me.

"I didn't," I insist. "Where did you hear that?"

"Come on," a friend of his says. "She ain't worth it."

He spits on me, and the two join the rest of the crowds heading for their trains. Nobody helps me up. Many avert their eyes. But there are a few who glance at me guiltily, as if they know what's going on, but don't dare get involved. It reminds me of how some of our neighbors treated us right after my dad was arrested. People I'd known my whole life wanted nothing to do with us. It was almost a relief to be relocated.

In the orchards, the blood of the mutant hounds has been hosed away. I pick apples in silence. At day's end nobody tries to walk home with me.

The next day I'm grouped with the other farmhands again.

"Mrs. Cranberry," I start to say, but she cuts me off.

"If this is about the protectors, Caitlin," she says with an edge to her voice.

"No, Mrs. Cranberry," I say. "Sorry, Mrs. Cranberry."

"Good," she snips. "If I have something to say about it, I'll say it."

She then shoos us off through the door.

All the way to the train station, as the next generation of workers come together into a horde, I search once more for Bradie. I reach the station in

74

disappointment. I hand an overseer my i-Dent card. She swipes it in her on-the-go. I wait for it to bleep cheerily. Instead it honks.

She looks at me more closely.

"You're the girl from the info update," she says. "The one who killed the mutant."

"Yes," I say.

"Come with me," she says.

"But...my train," I say.

"This way," she says.

There's a row of booths, all of them shuttered, advertising tickets for sale, from the days when people apparently travelled to far-flung parts of the continent, before most of it was turned into a radioactive wasteland. She opens a door and indicates for me to step inside a small windowless office.

It's been cleared out of any of its original contents, but some of the architectural detail remains, like the moulding and a lamp of rounded stained glass hanging from the ceiling by gilded chains. A single bulb flickers in it, casting shadows over the agent in black seated in a padded chair before a scratched up wooden table—the same agent who took Bradie away.

"Sit," he says, pointing at the stool.

I lick my lips and do as I'm told.

"Good girl," he says. It occurs to me that I don't know his name. He doesn't introduce himself. I continue to call him Eel Man in my mind. "Caitlin, you've had quite a few eventful days haven't you?" Eel Man asks.

I ignore the question.

"Where's Bradie?" I ask. "Is he okay?"

He shrugs. "Dead."

I struggle to keep breathing.

"Or alive," he adds. "I'm not handling his case personally so I really wouldn't know."

My fingers dig into my thighs. He's toying with me.

"It's obvious Bradie knew how to operate his weapon with proficiency," the agent continues. "That's why we took him so swiftly. You, on the other hand, clearly haven't a clue how to use a firearm."

"I really don't," I confess.

"Which is why we let you be a hero, for just a little while longer than him," he says. "You wouldn't want to get too full of yourself, now would you?"

"I would not," I force myself to say.

"Marvelous. You've had your little moment in the sun. Best you get comfortable with the shadows again. Are we clear?"

"Very much so," I reply.

"Off you go then," he says, making brushing motions, as if I'm a crumb to be flicked from the table.

I get up. The sound of the stool scraping on the floor is a razor to my ears. I wince. I walk to the door and open it, which is when he says, "One more thing."

I stop. Sweat drips down my neck.

"Yes?" I ask, staring out at the concourse.

"Turn around when I'm speaking to you."

I hate myself for obeying but I do it.

"You forgot to take this with you."

He slides something toward me across the table. To take it means walking back into the room. It could be my execution order for all I know. He might expect me to carry it to the protectors myself.

"Come, come," he waves impatiently.

I let the knob slide from my grasp and listen to the door whine shut as I step back toward the table. I reach it. He lifts his gloved hand and staring up at me is a trainee armband stenciled with a fist holding the all-seeing eye of a protector. I want to grab it and run, but I hear my dad's voice.

Nothing is ever free, Caitlin.

The agent's smirk hardens. "Those who hesitate miss out an all sorts of opportunities," he says. "And when you're offered what you've been asking for, you should take it."

I think of Bradie. I need to know what happened to him. My fingers close around the rough fabric and Eel Man strikes like a viper, grabbing my wrist. His grip squeezes hard enough to hurt. I suppress a whimper.

"Caitlin, the rules are in place for a reason," he says. "What are those reasons?"

I force myself to look at him.

"To maintain the peace," I say, reciting the lines I've learned since first year. "To honor the treaty with the Supergenics. To avoid another cataclysm. To fix what's been broken. To make this a better world."

"Yes," he says. "But to maintain the truce does require sacrifice. There are rewards though, for those who play by the rules. You requested an early transfer to the Protectorate Novice Program. Well, here it is. What do you say?"

"Thank you," I reply.

He lets a few seconds pass and all I can hear is my pounding heart. He lets go of me and sits back. I snatch my arm to safety, holding it and the armband to my chest.

"You're welcome," he replies.

"May I go?" I ask.

"Of course. You're not a prisoner here. Hurry, hurry. The train won't wait forever. Track 2, I believe. Who knows, we may yet put that rebellious nature of yours to good use after all."

He gestures me away, like he's waving off a foul smell.

As soon as the door snaps shut behind me, I start to run, and not just to catch my train. I crush the armband in my grip as I emerge onto my platform.

I clamber aboard the waiting train, and I'm met by row upon row of kids who stop chattering to stare at me as I walk past. I do my best to ignore them, my cheeks burning as I search for an empty seat. They're in their school uniforms, same as me, and they all wear the armband with the all-seeing eye clutched in a fist. What really strikes me is how they are all bigger than average, regardless of where they fall on the gender spectrum.

I see a couple of thugs from my own school, known for getting into scraps on the school yard. I also see the brute who shoved me to the ground yesterday. He gives me a dark look and sticks his foot out as I pass. He's not even subtle about it. I look at him, and simply say, "No."

The brute looks ready to say something when he's cut off by someone calling my name.

"Caitlin?" someone shouts. "Hey, Caitlin, over here! Come sit with us!"

I look at a pair of familiar faces. The kid who's calling my name is Liam. He's all muscles and square-jawed good looks. He should be in magazines. He waves for me to come over.

"So what are we doing here?" I ask the brute.

He grudgingly retracts his foot. "Whatever," he snorts.

I gratefully walk past and sit down opposite Liam and his girlfriend Sandie. She keeps touching her closely cropped, tightly curly black hair. The last time I saw her she had shoulder length dreads. In fact, everyone on board's been given a severe haircut. The days of self-expression are over.

Both Sandie and Liam are star athletes from another school. Everyone was sure one of them would Manifest. They always had a grace and sureness to their steps. Even sitting down, there's something elusively ethereal about them, as if they're actually at home in their own bodies. Their fingers lounge against each other on their arm rests.

It's a stretch for me to call them my friends, but they would always say, "Good job" to me after a discus throw, even when I'd beat Sandie—which was not often, or if I flubbed a pole vault they'd assure me, "Next time, tiger."

"Hey, hero," Sandie says.

I tense. "Please don't call me that."

Neither asks why not. They see it in my eyes and hear it in my tone. Now that we are officially dregs they too are figuring out that there's a fine line between standing out and fitting in that we must walk much more carefully.

"Here," Liam says, indicating the armband clutched in my hand. "Let me help you with that."

He snaps it into place overtop the sleeve of my dress jacket.

"There," he says. "Now you're one of us."

His words are paradoxically welcoming and alienating at the same time. What exactly am I going to have to give up to be a part of this?

Relax, I insist. *You're not really joining, remember? Just play along.*

Except I actually like these two. Even at their most competitive they've managed to be nice.

There's a soft hiss as the train gently starts to move. Unlike the train to the farmlands, there's no grinding of gears. It doesn't jerk back and forth. It glides along the tracks instead of clawing its way grudgingly toward its destination. There are other differences too. The seats are plumper. It's got carpeting. The windows are clean.

I remember the agent's words. *There are rewards for those who play by the rules.* And for those who enforce them.

The track takes us parallel to the security fence. Lightning flares and thunder rumbles.

"So, your first day," Liam says. "You think gym class was tough? You have no idea."

"Don't scare her," Sandie says, punching his arm. "But seriously Caitlin, I've never been so sore in my life. If you find yourself needing to cry, most of us sneak off into the equipment room. Just try to find a spot where someone else isn't already having a breakdown. It's a thing."

"Okay," I say, wondering if this was such a good idea.

Focus. You're just here to find Bradie's brother.

"Have you met any protectors with the last name Nettle?" I ask.

Liam and Sandie look to each other and shrug.

"Doesn't sound familiar," Liam says. "But we can ask around."

"That would be great," I say.

I tell myself not to be disappointed, that I'll find Bradie's brother soon enough, and I almost believe it, until the train rounds the bend and I stare at a gigantic white Cube in the distance. This is it. The Protectorate. I've seen if from afar, towering over our borough, reminding us of the ever-vigilant protectors and agents within.

"Impressive, huh?" Liam asks.

"It is," I agree.

It just keeps looming larger and larger the closer we get. It's so big that the train pulls right into the structure, stopping in the middle of a gigantic atrium. I follow after Liam and Sandie, and as I step into a concourse of white tiles that looks like plastic, I stare up and up. It makes me think of a bee hive as it teems with activity.

I see floor upon floor of training areas through clear glass. Sweaty male- and female-identified protectors train together, running on treadmills, or doing gymnastics exercises, or firing weapons at targets. Others are doing hand-to-hand combat, there's a sick bay with medics in lab coats, and what seems to be some sort of meditation room, with rows of protectors in tank tops and shorts sitting cross legged with helmets on that cover their eyes with a solid visor that keeps flashing strange colors.

A squadron of protectors march by us in their copper uniforms, and there's the occasional flash of black as an agent moves among the masses.

"Welcome to the Cube," Liam says. "It goes down underground almost as deep. That's where most of the weapons are, short and long range vehicles, hovercrafts, hover*boards*. They're amazing."

I nod, awed and overwhelmed. I try to spot an older version of Bradie, but it's impossible. There are thousands of people here. *I am so screwed.*

CHAPTER 12

"Come on," Liam says. "We need to sign in and get you your gear."

They take me to a counter where a puffy matron in an overseer uniform swipes my i-Dent card, then hands me two bundles of workout clothes, a towel, and a set of sneakers.

"You wash them yourself," she says. "At the end of your placement, you return them. *Clean.* You lose them, it's 100 credits. Here's your lock. Combo's on the back. Next!"

"One quick thing," I say.

She glares as if I couldn't possibly have any questions after such a thorough run down.

"What?" she demands.

"Everybody here must come to you at some point, right?"

She's tapping her fingers on the counter.

"And?"

"How would I find a guy with the last name Nettle?"

"I'm not a dating service," she snaps. "Next!"

She's waving at the person behind me. I turn to look, but there's no one there. I turn back and the matronly overseer is waddling away through a swinging door.

Sandie laughs, "I don't know who this mystery man of yours is, but I can't wait to meet him. Come on. Let's get changed."

They take me to a set of moving stairs that Liam calls an escalator and we're carried up along with a pack of other kids our age. There's an adjacent escalator carrying people down. There's a door that a bunch of kids head into. Sandie stops me in front of it.

"Have you ever been in a mixed locker room?" she asks.

"A what?" I reply.

She pushes open the door and drags me inside. I'm met with rows of benches and lockers, all made of the same white plastic that dominates the Cube. It smells of disinfectant and sweat. I barely notice, blinded by the mix of genders stripping down to their essentials.

"Oh," I say.

"If you got it," Liam shrugs.

He's already taken off his school jacket and tie. The first few buttons of his dress shirt are undone. He doesn't bother with the rest of the buttons. He just peels the shirt off over his head, revealing the firm mounds of his chest and the delineated lines of his mid-section.

A lot of the other kids are just as fit, Sandie among them. They may be dregs but as far as I can see they are still genetic winners, and the more gold medals they won over the years of athletic competitions, the better their food rations got. The rest of us are a mixed bag, though I'd say most of us are still above average in the fitness department. There are several hulks, including the brute who tripped me.

"His name's Gregor," Liam says, catching me staring at him. "Total douche."

Gregor glares worse than the matron who gave me my track suit. I turn away, wishing he'd stop staring at me while I get changed. I'm slow to take my clothes off, and then quick to get my shirt and track pants on.

I shove my uniform into an empty locker, memorize the combination, and click it shut. We're all dressed in beige shorts and tank tops, as if they are making us as indistinct as possible. We exit through a different door than the one we entered, passing a row of stainless steel toilets, all open to one another, and then a shower area that makes the toilets feel private.

We exit into a vast training area with a glass wall overlooking the atrium. Everything we do is on display. Hanging from the ceiling are numerous banners of the Protectorate's emblem, the all-seeing eye clenched in a fist. The protectors don't just watch everyone else, they watch each other.

The floor is covered in cushioned mats. Everyone else is already stretching, and I would do the same, but I see a man with flecks of grey in his hair wearing blue training pants and a matching t-shirt. He's chewing on a whistle while flipping through a data pad. I jog over to him.

"Hi," I say. "I'm Caitlin Feral."

He looks up at me.

"I was just wondering, do you know a protector with the last name Nettle?"

He gazes past me.

"Novice!" he shouts at the kid closest to us. It turns out to be Gregor.

He comes running over and stands at attention, puffing out his gorilla chest.

"Yes, sir!"

82

"Show your fellow novice here how to execute a take down. Do it as many times as it takes for her to get it right. The rest of you, in a circle!"

I open my mouth to protest, the same way that I would with Mrs. Cranberry—only here do I realize she was being patient with me.

"Come on, hero," Gregor says.

He grabs me by the arm and the next thing I know, he's tossing me to the ground. Everybody else is standing around us, watching. Most of them laugh. Liam and Sandie wince. I get to my feet, trying to remember what I learned in wrestling. I spent most of my time escaping drab reality by daydreaming about being able to fly. Today that dream comes true as Gregor grabs me by the shirt, lifts me up and slams me down.

I gasp as the breath gets knocked out of me.

"Get back up, novice!" the drill instructor yells.

Air comes flooding back in. It does not escape me that I came planning to suck. That plan is coming together a little too well. Gregor charges, and I know that there are dozens of counter defenses for a moving attacker, but I can't think of any of them. He closes his arms, about to engulf me in his grip, and I instinctively duck down, slide through his legs, and pop up right behind him. Again there are all sorts of maneuvers I could use from this vantage point. I can't recall any of them, so I grab his shorts and pull them down below his knees. He turns, his face an angry red, his hands instinctively reaching for me, and as he does his legs get tangled in his shorts. He windmills his arms as he tries, and fails, to catch his balance, falling flat on his front.

The drill instructor blows his whistle. There are cheers, led by Liam and Sandie. Gregor's friends glare. I don't have time to gloat.

"Clear a hole!" the instructor shouts.

My fellow novices open ranks and we all watch a muscled young man striding toward us. He's dressed in the yellow and blue tank top and short shorts that the protectors wear while training. His body owns the room with every step.

As he comes to the center of our semi-circle he contemplates us one by one, then holds his hand out. Our instructor passes him the tablet. The protector swipes through it a few times, grunting here and there, rolling his eyes on occasion, nodding to himself. He stops, lifting his eyes to stare right at me.

"Caitlin Feral," the protector says.

"Y-y-yes," I stammer. The instructor glares. "Yes, sir!" I shout.

The protector hands the tablet back to the drill master.

"The girl who took down a two-headed mutt," he says. I catch the dismissiveness in his voice. "Well, let's see how you do against me."

"She had a baton against the mutt," Liam says.

The drill instructor rounds on him.

"One hundred push ups!" he shouts.

Liam drops to the ground.

"Your baton," the protector in the tank top says, holding his hand out to the instructor.

I expect the instructor to protest. Instead he smirks, as if he's in on the joke. He hands it over, and the protector gives it to me. I hold it awkwardly.

"Well, come on then," the protector says. "Power it up."

I hesitate.

"Now!" shouts the drill instructor.

I flick it on and a crackle of blue energy sizzles along its length. As soon as it makes contact with something, it will automatically flare in power. The protector lunges at me and I swing clumsily. He evades, grabs my wrist, and twists. Pain runs up my arm. I drop the weapon, and before I know what's happening I'm landing hard on my stomach, his full weight crushing me against the mat.

He presses his lips to my ear and whispers, "Hi, my name's Trenton Lopez Nettle. Stop asking questions about me. Bradie's in enough trouble as it is. So am I."

My cheek is pressed into the mat. "Bradie, is he..."

Trenton hisses in my ear. "Stop talking. My brother's all right. You'll see him here soon. Now keep your mouth shut. And, get a haircut."

He gets off me, picks up the baton, turns it off, and hands it back to the instructor. Sandie helps me up. I rub my arm.

"There's a big difference between fighting an animal, and a person. Remember that," Bradie's brother says.

"Thank you, sir!" the circle of novices intones.

I wait for him to give me a special look, maybe a wink. Something to indicate our newly forged bond. He ignores me, turning without a word and I stare at his muscled back as he leaves. A giddy smile crosses my lips.

Bradie's alive. And I'll see him here soon.

CHAPTER 13

By mid-day, my body is covered in bruises, my palms are bloody where the skin's been ripped away, and the back of my neck itches from a hasty trip to the in-house barber shop. My newly shorn hair's barely long enough to tuck behind my ears.

We're ushered into the cafeteria, with its sleek white plastic chairs and rounded tulip base tables. There I'm expecting a mass of food, hoarded and kept from the general population, where the protectors gorge themselves and laugh at the less fortunate.

The reality is rather different. Each of us receive a foil covered platter, where the servings are larger than what we would get at school, and the food is better (in this case protein-based pasta with meatballs and a protein-enriched brownie for dessert), but it's not a free-for-all. It is enough to fill me up though, which is a foreign feeling. It doesn't last, as we're soon put through our paces once again, including survival training, obstacle courses, and a form of stretching known as yoga that leaves me feeling tighter than when we began.

By end of the day, we're all so exhausted the only sound on the train ride back to Central Station is the whistle of air outside, and the hum of the conveyance speeding along the track. It's joined by the *ploff* sound of rain hitting the windows as it starts to drizzle outside. Liam and Sandie lean against each other, eyes closed, her head on his shoulder, his head on her head.

I wish I could do the same, but as bruised and beaten as I am from today's training, I'm way too wired to rest. Out of everything that's happened today, one moment blares louder than the rest.

Bradie's okay!

When the train reaches the station, I walk with Liam and Sandie and a few other kids. It's strange not being alone. In ones, twos and threes, they all veer off down the streets leading to their homes, until I'm on my own in the rain. There's a weird battle in my stomach as part of me wonders, *am I actually fitting in?* followed by a warning: *Don't get attached. It won't end well.*

I pass a pair of protectors, and before I know what I'm doing I give them a salute. They see my arm band and they salute back. I feel a flush in my cheeks, as if I've somehow betrayed my mom, and more importantly my dad.

It's okay, I assure myself. *You're just playing along.*

As if to remind me of who I really am, I see a familiar figure waving to me from underneath an awning. It's Normand, in a plastic poncho with matching rain pants. I wave back and walk toward him. Only now do I realize that I haven't had time to think about Tigara or comic books or superpowers all day.

He gestures for to me to come, and starts walking away without waiting.

"You are the weirdest," I say, hurrying to catch up.

Normand takes us through side streets and narrow alleys. We turn, and right in front of us is the electrified, chain-link fence. The radiation and mutant warning signs make my wet skin prickle.

The black storm clouds over the broken city fire lightning bolts like crazy. My ear drums throb from the thunder. He pulls out an e-pad, leaning over it to protect it from the rain. I'd say he got it as part of his tech training, but it's definitely not standard issue. It looks old, beaten and scratched, with odd decals on the back that look like i-Dent insignias, but unlike any that I've seen. There's one with a black bat in it, another of a big X inside of a circle, and a third of a stylized golden eagle. In the middle of them all, and part of the e-pad itself, is a white apple with a bite taken out of it.

"Where did you get that?" I ask.

He lifts his fingers to his lips. Is he shushing me? An instant later I understand why. I hear the squawk of a pair of protectors talking to each other. I can't see them, but they're getting closer to the mouth of the alley. If they see us here, it's going to raise questions, but Normand doesn't flinch. There's a slew of odd looking icons on the e-pad. They're programs, GRAMS for short, but unlike any I've ever seen at school. One is of a cartoon clown, another a scowling red bird, another of a stylized hand with its middle finger up. He finds an icon that looks like a protector helmet and taps it. Up comes a map of our borough, with scores of red dots scattered about. Each of the red dots has a pair of horns and an angry face. He zooms in on what I'm pretty sure is our location. There are two red dots getting closer and closer to us.

"Normand!" I hiss. "Are all those red dots protectors?"

"Caitlin," he whispers urgently, "I must insist you be quiet or they might hear us."

"*Hear* us?" I demand. "They're going to *see* us!"

His finger nimbly presses onto another icon, of a happy face wearing a blindfold. He drags it over and drops it on top of the two red dots that are practically at the mouth of the alley. The red dots change into happy faces with blindfolds. I hear the squawk of their voices projected through their helmet speakers growing louder. On the screen they are almost here.

"The protectors can't see through their visors," Normand explains. "Their helmets are equipped with cameras, which project a 360 view of the world on internal screens. Since that visual stream is digital, it can be manipulated, like when the protector pulled out your Tigara comic book. I made her see a ministry-approved comic book instead."

I gape. So *that's* how I got away with it.

"What if she'd raised her visor?" I demand.

"You would have been in a significant level of trouble," he replies unapologetically.

That is an understatement and it's nothing compared to this. The blindfolded smiley faces are almost on top of us. This is treason! If I'm caught, they'll do to me what they did to my dad.

"I have to go," I say.

He steps in front of me. "That would be a mistake." He holds his strange-looking e-pad for me to see. On the screen is a picture of *Tigara*, issue number 2. She's in her full garb, jumping from a rooftop, claws at the ready. My instinct to run is suddenly anchored by my desire to stay. The conflict starts tearing me in two.

"And then I say to him," a protector's voice squawks through the speakers in his helmet, coming from around the corner. "I say, you call *that* a baton?"

Their electronic laughter rings in my ears.

"What are the chances that it won't work?" I demand through clenched teeth. Rain runs down my back, mixing with the sweat.

"The failure rate is down to 22 percent," he says.

"Are you kidding me?" I whisper.

"The audio reconfiguration sequences keep crashing. They shouldn't be able to see us, as long as we keep very still, but…"

He points to his ears and stops talking as he makes a slitting motion across this throat. The protectors reach the mouth of the alley and stop. They stare directly at us, just five measures away. They shine their lights into my face. One of them steps closer. His boot crunches on a discarded soda can as he approaches. He stops. If he were to open the visor's reflective sheath we'd be eye to eye.

My heart smashes at my sternum as I envision him doing so. I hear him ordering me to my knees, I feel him stabbing me in the gut with his electrified baton, then forcing my arms behind my back, cuffing them tightly together. I taste the mud in my mouth and I think of my poor mom. I envision her getting the news. It could literally kill her. And Nate. He's too young to remember what happened to dad, but I can tell it still affects him. Underneath his outgoing nature I sometimes see the insecurity, the need to belong, and his fragility when he doesn't.

I'm so sorry, I think.

"Status?" the second protector asks.

The one shining the light in my face lowers his arm. "Clear."

He steps back, the can crunching again underfoot. We watch them walk away, their squawking voices growing distant. I round on Normand.

"What is wrong with you? Do you have any idea what they would've done to us if we'd been caught?" I demand.

Normand nods, avoiding my gaze. "I know precisely what they would've done to us. We must step quickly before the next patrol arrives."

He reaches the end of the alley and doesn't even look to make sure the way is clear. He heads right for the fence. I'm about to call out, sure that he doesn't see the electrified barrier beyond the wall of rain, despite the brightly colored signs warning of mutants and radiation. He pulls out a round electronic gadget of shiny metal. Bands of blue energy rotate over its surface. He places it onto the key pad of the gate in the fence.

He refers to his worn swipe pad. Again his finger hovers over the slew of odd looking icons on it. He drags the image of a key with a skull and crossbones overtop an icon of a spider's web. The gadget on the lock hums to life, spinning first one way, then the other, then back. It stops and the gate clicks open.

"Effing eff," I swear under my breath.

The fence possesses a mythic quality. It stands between us and the deadly horrors beyond. And Normand—the timid loser at the back of the class—

just opened it. My head hurts as it does a mental reconfiguration. Who is this kid? Who is he *really*?

Normand tucks his e-pad under his arm and squirts disinfectant into his hand, rubbing it in. He looks at his watch and then at the pad. There are red dots moving toward us.

"We must go," he says.

He steps through the gate. I wait for alarms to sound and protectors to swarm him. They don't. Still I don't move.

"Caitlin, how do you think I procured a comic book from before the war?" He gestures toward the Yellow Zone, "A fallen city holds much more than bones."

"I..." It's so obvious now that he's said it. He's a pilferer, scavenging the Yellow Zone for anything of value that might have survived the war. That's where he got his electronic pad as well. He could have his hand cut off for that.

"The next patrol's running late, but it will be upon us shortly," he says, looking at his watch. "What say thee, Caitlin Feral? Dare ye venture outside the cage?"

No, a terrified part of me thinks and yet...Before I can talk myself out of it, I step beyond the chainlink fence.

There's an amused twitch to Normand's lips as the gate clicks shut behind us. My heart's pounding louder than before. *I'm in the Yellow Zone.* People get shot on sight for doing this. I gaze at a charred and half-melted car. This has to be the single stupidest thing I've ever done. I look at Normand, waiting for the joke to be over. Instead I see him doing something weird with his face. He still won't look me in the eye, but his twitchy mouth has turned into an actual smile. And that's when I realize what's weird. Normand's not scared. *How can he not be scared?*

"Here," he says, handing me a thin sticky pad with circuitry embedded in it. "Place this somewhere on your skin where it won't fall off."

"What is it?" I ask.

"There are motion and heat sensors all over the place, to detect mutants and to catch Runners. Once I patch it into the security system, this will tell it to ignore you."

How many times has he done this?

"Okay," I say, and slip it inside my soaked shirt, pressing it onto myself just under my collar bone. I feel microscopic hooks cling to me.

He turns to the swipe pad and drags the icon of a raccoon onto one of a girl with a superhero mask.

"It will take a moment for it to sync up with your bio readings," he says.

A moment later his pad *bings* and the superhero girl gives us a wink and a thumbs up.

"We may proceed," he says.

Walking the orderly streets of the borough, Normand is a snail, but here, in the jumbled ruins of the Yellow Zone, I struggle to keep up. The rain's making it impossible to see more than a measure in front of me, the terrain is completely unstable, and more than once Normand grabs me to steady me.

"Step where I step," he says.

"Sure," I nod.

At least the rain starts to let up.

"Almost there," he assures me.

We climb down what's left of a collapsed building and stop in front of a set of brick stairs that lead to more rubble. Normand bends over and grabs onto a twisted metal rod and yanks on it. I hear the distinctive clank of something mechanical falling into place. He steps back and, as if on hydraulics, a chunk of the debris lifts open, revealing a set of stairs that lead downward. A few pieces of broken concrete skitter off of it, but the rest holds together as if the mangled mesh of cement, steel rods, and refuse have all been glued together.

"This is it," he says, walking down.

I follow. How can I not?

I feel a rush of static electricity as my body crosses over the threshold.

"Notice anything different?" Normand asks.

I do. I'm not dry, but I've gone from soaked to damp. And although it's still raining out, I can't feel it anymore. I look back, and it's as if there's an invisible shield keeping the storm out.

"Humidity controllers," Normand says as he strips off his rain gear. "Prevents the water from getting in, otherwise all this would've flooded long ago."

"What is this place?" I ask.

His avoidant gaze is alight with excitement.

"Come," he says. "Showing you is always my favorite part."

He is *so* weird.

There's a handrail for support, but I still trip when I get to the last step. I hear another door open, and Normand guides me deeper. The door clicks shut behind us. We are in utter darkness, and only now do I realize that I could die here. That no one would ever know. Maybe there's something wrong with Normand, maybe he's funny in the head in a dangerous way, maybe…

Normand claps and twinkling multicolored lights on dangling strings come aglow all around and I stare in wonder at the impossible. I'm surrounded by walls and walls of comic books. Hundreds of issues all on display.

And that's not all.

There are life-sized statues of caped crusaders and costumed heroines, similar in many ways to the heroes I grew up with, though in costumes I've never seen before. There are glass display cases with busts of more characters in wild outfits wielding the primal elements with their dramatic poses. There's a counter with sets of multicolored dice in transparent containers in orderly rows, fanciful vinyl figurines with huge ears and adorable bellies plastered in an array of floral patterns, and posters, and books, and games.

I close my eyes, unable to believe them. When I open them I expect to be in my bunk at home, waking up from the most wonderful dream. But I'm still here. I pick up a box that touts itself as "a game for terrible people." Nowhere do I see the Ministry of Infotainment's seal of approval. I eye the comic books. I've never heard of a single one of them. I don't recognize even one hero or heroine or villain on all the covers. The titles are utterly foreign.

"All of this is from before the war," I realize out loud.

If the Protectorate ever found this place, they'd burn it to ash.

"Check this out," Normand says.

He pulls on a drawer and I gape in wonder. It's the perfect size for comic books, and its filled with row upon row of issues, all carefully preserved in plastic custom-sized bags with cardboard backings. There must be a hundred or more comics in that one retractable slot, and there are *dozens* of slots.

"What is this place?" I ask again, this time with a tone of utter awe.

Normand points to a battered sign on the wall, about six measures by two. The name of the store glows, made up of a strange type of tubular lighting.

"I Want Superpowers," I read. "Comic books 'n other kah-rap." There's a stylized image of a lightning bolt. The store sign tells me what I already know: this place gets me.

"I dragged it in from outside," he says. "Fixing the neon tubes was just shy of impossible."

I want to touch everything, but I'm afraid to touch anything, as if I'm at the museum and Mrs. Cranberry is ready to yell, "Put that down, Caitlin!"

"Is that how you found this place?" I ask.

"It was the moisture controllers that really gave it away. It warps the movement of water around here."

"What even brought you out into the Yellow Zone?" I ask.

"Ennui," he replies.

As if that's an explanation. *Weirdo.*

"Weren't you afraid the telepath at Testing Day would see this in your mind?" I ask.

"There are ways to fool everyone. Even mind readers," he replies. Joshua said as much himself. I want to ask how, but that's a question for another time.

I stare at a display shelf that rises as high as I can reach, with hundreds of comic books staring back at me. There are multiple copies of the *same* issue. I swear my brain is short circuiting. I don't pick any of them up. It almost seems impossible to choose the first one—though of course there is no actual choice to be made. I wander down the length of the shelf, following their alphabetical order to the T section.

And there she is. Tigara. I stare at issues 192 all the way up to a giant sized issue 200. My mind is about to snap. There are 200 issues in the series!!!

"You're probably wondering how this all even survived," he says.

"Yeah," I say distantly, picking up issue 192. Tigara is claw to claw with a leopard printed villainess who is just as fierce as her. If only the newest issues are on display, I wonder if all the other back copies are in one of those pull out drawers.

"This portion of the edifice was below grade. It's constructed of reinforced concrete," Normand explains. "In essence it is a bomb shelter."

"Uh-huh," I say, barely listening.

The comic book starts with Tigara in mid-battle. I flip the page, and it's a flash back with a yellow box that says, "Two Days Ago..." and I know this will lead up to the epic confrontation with Lady Leopard.

There's a sign that says, "You read it, you bought it! NO loitering." I sit cross-legged on the floor and slowly turn the pages. I forget the pain of my bruises and the dampness of my clothes as I'm swept into Tigara's gritty urban world, that is both like and utterly different from my own. I finish the issue, just as Lady Leopard is about to slice open Tigara's throat. Normand sits diagonal from me, quietly and contentedly reading a tale of a jacked guy with claws coming out of his forearms, fighting some other guy in weird metal armor.

I take a moment to soak in the feeling I'm having. I'm pretty sure it's happiness, and I think the words, *thank you.*

I read another issue of *Tigara*. Then another. I'm utterly mesmerized by Tigara's hot/cold love triangle with fellow nocturnal crime fighters Miss Thang, a crime lord trying to mend her ways, and Whamarang, a daytime "billionaire playboy" (whatever that is) by the name of Bryce Dayne, with a corporate legacy of corruption to atone for.

They clash with villains like the Ghouligan, Mesquite, and Hairantula— and sometimes the heroes battle each other as the path to justice grows more and more murky. When criminals run free, and their leaders are untouchable, how can Tigara not play judge, jury and executioner? Yet if she does, how is she any better than the villains she professes to fight? What is Tigara to do? Can she remain true to her own moral code or will the darkness in her soul prevail? And what will that mean for the citizens of Bright Lights Big City?

I'm so caught up in such questions that it's not until I'm turning the pages of the double-length anniversary special that something utterly revolutionary strikes me. When it does my stomach actually heaves as if from a physical blow, and I have to lower the issue in my hands.

First of all, the comic books that I usually read are all based on real people, like Captain Light. Did Tigara ever really exist? It seems improbable that a grown woman would go running around in a tiger-print leotard fighting crime.

It doesn't matter though. It's the *idea* of Tigara that burrows into my brain, because *she doesn't have any superpowers!* She's just a woman who's trained herself to be *almost* superhuman, but she's *not*. At the end of the day, she's a dreg.

Tigara and her world may be fiction, but they spark something very real.

She's like me, I realize. DNA regular. Does that mean that one day I could be like her? A superhero without superpowers?

Almost as revolutionary is my other realization. Superbeings—like the feline imbued Lady Leopard—can be evil, and it's sometimes up to DNA regulars like Tigara to stop them. And Tigara *does* defeat her!

In all the comic books that I've read, stamped with the Ministry of Infotainment's seal of approval, the heroes are *always* Supergenic, as if with great power comes immediate morality. The villains are always dregs, out to destroy the world out of spite and malice, or mutant animals grown grotesque from the irradiated aftermath of dreg bombs.

In the approved comic books, the Supergenics, being good and true, always prevail, and the dreg villains are made to pay for their crimes. Yet according to *this* comic book Tigara is not only a hero, but a *super*hero, even without enhanced abilities, and Supergenics, like anyone else, can be either good or bad.

I close the 200th issue, my world turned upside down. All this time I wanted to be a Supergenic because I thought it was the only way for me to be special, that it would fix everything that was wrong with my life, but what if I was wrong? What if there's another way? But if *that's* true, is it also true that the Supergenics are sometimes the *real* bad guys? I think of all the food destined for Jupitar City.

My mind is swirling with these thoughts when Normand announces in his abrupt way, "Our time here has come to an end." As he often does, he's looking at his watch.

I want to argue, but I know he's right. The stiffness from today's training is setting in. It's late. I have to get home. I reluctantly put the issues back. I can't believe all of this is real.

"Can we come back tomorrow?" I ask.

He nods. "And the day following that."

Getting back to the borough is slow going. Under the clouds it's perpetual twilight, lit only by the flashing globes high overhead that crackle as they absorb the lightning strikes. Finally, we reach the fence. It still feels weird being on this side of it. Normand uses his gadgets and swipe pad to open the gate, and we slip through. I expect a squad of protectors to be waiting for us, guns leveled, but it's just us and a rat scurrying by.

"Thank you," I say as I walk him to the bus stop. "For sharing your place with me."

"You know you can't tell anyone," he says. There's an intensity to his voice as he levels his indirect gaze at my shoulder.

"I know," I reply.

"Nobody," he repeats. "Not ever."

"Normand, trust me, I get it."

"Not even Bradie," he insists.

"Of course not!" I say.

"Good," Normand replies. The bus arrives and he clambers on. "You will find that Bradie is no longer as you remember him."

His words are like a brick to my chest.

"What does *that* mean?" I demand.

He swipes his i-Dent card in a reader and the doors close in my face. A second later he's being carried away, back to his fancy townhouse. As the bus carries him away, I ask another question.

"How do you know about Bradie?"

CHAPTER 14

A bit of sunlight fights its way through the dirty window in our tiny flat. My mom, Nate and I are eating protein-enriched cereal puffs with watery powdered milk. Nate's knocking one floating ball into another with his spoon, making *puh-RROOM* exploding noises.

"So, how did the protector training go yesterday?" Mom asks.

She's been quiet about it since I told her last night, after she spotted the bruises.

Nate catches the tone and looks up from playing with his food. He's quiet now. My armband with the all-seeing eye sits on the table, glaring at me accusingly.

"I got beat up a lot," I reply.

"It's just so odd that they would cut your farmhand training short," she says.

"Mom, I was almost killed," I reply.

"Dozens of farmhands are killed by animal attacks every year," she counters. Leave it to my mom to be so coldly logical. She's right to be worried, though. I haven't told her about Eel Man.

"Can we talk about this later?" I glance at Nate.

She catches my meaning and takes the bowl away from him, pouring half into mine, the other into hers.

"If you're not going to eat your food you might as well get going to school early," she says.

"Why?" he asks. "So you can talk about stuff behind my back?"

"Yes," she replies.

He looks ready to argue but I shake my head at him.

"Yeah, yeah," he says, grabbing his back sack and closing the door behind him.

"What happened?" Mom asks.

"An agent gave me this," I say, fingering the arm band.

Her grip on her spoon tightens.

"I'm such an idiot," she says. "Of course, they're going to pick on you. I loved your father, but that man has left us a heap of trouble."

"Mom..." I start to say.

96

"Okay," she interrupts. "We've been through worse. We just have to dance their little dance until they get bored of us and start picking on someone else." She takes the arm band with the protector emblem on it. Her hands are shaking as she snaps the band into place overtop of my school uniform.

"Listen to me very carefully," she says. "It's more important than ever that you fail the protector training."

Tears are coming to her eyes. I hate it when she cries. If this escalates it will turn into screaming and possibly throwing things. I never should have told her about the agent.

"It's okay Mom," I grasp her arm. "Trust me. I'm going to fail."

I get my chance to make good on my promise that very morning. It's another school day, where we sit in class under Mrs. Cranberry's glare and ruminate on the lessons learned at our work placement.

I'm the only one in the protectorate program so I'm in a corner alone, answering essay questions like "How does being a protector make me a contributing member of society?" and "What sacrifices am I prepared to make to keep the peace?"

I think of Tigara as I write answers like: "I'm learning to defend the defenseless against those who are stronger than them" and "I can ask lots of questions." They'll hate those responses. I also think relentlessly about the comic book store in the Yellow Zone, Normand, and what he said to me about Bradie.

I meet with Normand that night, in an alley near the security fence.

"How do you know about Bradie?" I demand. My tone is more accusatory than I intend.

Normand holds up his electronic pad, and plays security footage of Eel Man escorting Bradie off the train.

"How did you get that?" I whisper as the image freezes. Bradie looks terrified.

"I have many GRAMS," he explains.

"Do you know where he is?" I ask.

"Negative."

My shoulders slump and I wait for him to offer me reassurance. He does not; that's beyond him.

"Let us proceed," he says, putting his skeleton key on the gate's security pad.

"Normand, I can't stop thinking about Bradie and the danger he's in," I say.

"Why?" he asks matter of factly. "He'll be back."

The skeleton key starts spinning.

"You said he'd be different!" I say.

"He's been taken by agents. Of course that will alter him," he says.

"He'll be broken," I realize out loud.

"Broken things can often be fixed," Normand says.

His words catch me off guard. I'm pretty sure he has no idea that he's said exactly the right thing. The skeleton key stops spinning and the gate pops open.

I'm still thinking about Bradie as we travel through the Yellow Zone. We reach the pile of debris that's actually a door. Normand opens it and we descend the stairs. At the bottom he slaps his palms together, the lights come aglow, and I marvel at the effort someone's made to preserve this place.

"You say you just found it like this?" I ask as Normand pulls the door closed behind us.

"Correct," he says. "I postulate that the owner of this complex was some sort of billionaire genius. Those with lower intellects might describe him as eccentric."

I walk past a counter with a register. Next to it there are trading cards of various heroes and villains, none of whom I've ever seen, though we do have similar cards of the different members of A.M.M.O. There's also a pair of metal orbs, just the right size to hold in one hand, as well as a scarf with a big red S inside a diamond shape, and a black rectangular device labeled Taser, with two metal rods at its tip. It sits on top of what seems to be a charge pad. I'm about to pick up the scarf when Normand grabs my arm.

"Stop!" he shouts. His grip is surprisingly firm.

"Okay," I say, holding my hands up in peace. He lets go and quickly squirts disinfectant between his fingers.

He moves the scarf slightly one way, the metal balls the other, as if somehow that micro adjustment makes a big difference in the cosmic scheme of things.

98

"You may touch anything you wish in here, but nothing on this counter. These must stay exactly as they are," he says.

"Yeah, sure, okay," I say. Living with my mom, I've learned to keep the peace.

I quickly find two drawers of *Tigara* back issues and take out the first dozen. I stare at the cover of issue number 2. Normand is already leaning against a concrete column reading a comic called *Fighter Foes*.

At the end of the first issue, Tigara was surrounded by the shirtless muscled henchmen of the Conglomerate. The current issue picks up where that one left off. She's outnumbered and outgunned. She takes out two henchmen, dodges machine gun fire, and confronts The Man in Charge.

You think you are helping the oppressed, he says to her. *I help more people in a day than you will in a lifetime.*

At a cost, she says, stalking around him, cautious now.

Nothing is ever free, he replies. *There is always a price.*

Yours is too high.

She attacks. He points his gun, and fires. And that's where the issue ends. I reach for the next one, and my hand freezes above the pile. The next issue isn't there. There are fully six issues that are missing, jumping from issue 2 to 9.

"No," I whisper in horror.

Normand looks up. "What's the matter?"

"There are issues missing," I say.

"Indeed," he says. "I sometimes resort to creating my own."

I shake my head, like a data terminal that's frozen and needs to be turned off then on to get it working again.

"What do you mean you create your own?"

His brace creaks as he waddles over to the counter. He opens a drawer, pulls out a stack of papers, and shows them to me. They're filled with drawings in squares of various sizes. I like to doodle from time to time, but my sketches pale next to these. They're amazing, telling the lost tale of the Fighter Foes engaged in battle on an alien planet as they battle to save the Martian Princess *and* stop the evil Kahblang from detonating an intergalactic nuke.

"You did these?" I ask.

As I flip through the panels I quickly realize that while the art is amazing, the storytelling is terrible. His dialogue is all to the point, factual, bare bones. All the characters sound like robots programmed with formal speech. They sound like him.

"I once dreamed of penning tales like this for a living," he says. "My father informed me that all comic books come from Jupitar City. "I remember feeling as if something I treasured was being taken away from me, and there was nothing I could do about it."

I nod. "That's how I felt when I failed my final Testing Day."

I look at his drawings.

"I could do the same for your Tigara comics," he says.

"We can fill in the blanks," I realize out loud.

My words spark a powerful sensation; the opposite of helplessness. I can *do* something about this. Is *this* what Manifesting feels like?

In art classes, we were taught form, and color, and even storytelling. But we were only allowed to write and draw certain things, or draw in certain ways. It was so constrained, we might as well have been solving math formulas. But this, this is...

...*freedom*. The word is a mini-boom in my mind.

"Okay," I say. "But I want to do the writing."

"Excellent," he says. "That's the tedious part."

CHAPTER 15

My mother eyes me when I get home. She's stirring reheated beans in a pot on the hotplate on the counter. I enter slowly, gauging her mood.

"Where were you?" she asks.

"In the Yellow Zone," I reply.

She snorts. "Can you imagine?"

I smile weakly. "I was reading." So far I haven't had to lie.

She nods, assuming I was actually at the library. I feel a wave of guilt. What Normand and I are doing is dangerous. If we're caught, there will be consequences for more than just us. It's not worth the risk. And yet Tigara's all that I can think about. She even distracts me from worrying about Bradie.

"You must be hungry," she says.

"I am," I agree, my stomach gurgling.

She divides the beans into two bowls. As I shovel the beans into my mouth, I brace for what's to come.

"So, have they cut you from the Protectorate program yet?" she asks.

And there it is.

"Not yet," I say.

She's tapping her fingers on the chipped table top.

"Well, I'm sure this will all be sorted out soon. They haven't given you any pills or injections or anything, have they?"

"No," I say, confusion in my voice. "Why would they?"

"Just...don't take them," my mother says. "There's talk."

There's always talk.

She pats my hand. "You're a good girl."

Are you a good girl Caitlin? part of me asks. *Does a good girl sneak into the Yellow Zone and lie about it? Does a good girl put her family at risk for the sake of some silly comic books?*

Over the next two weeks, I spend less and less time at school, and more and more time at the Protectorate compound. On training days, I sit with Liam and Sandie staring out the train window, thinking about the comic book shop. Normand and I have started calling it the Lair.

I reminisce about the comics I read the night before, and the ones Normand and I have been creating. We argue over plot and character development. For someone uninterested in the nuances of writing, Normand is surprisingly opinionated on these matters.

One night at the Lair, he hands me a book from the before days, full of tips on how to write "good story." I learn about the crucible, stereotypes versus archetypes, and I have an *a-ha* moment when the book recommends creating some personal connection between the hero and the villain. Brother versus brother is more powerful than stranger versus stranger. Written in the margins is the question, *What about childhood enemies?*

"You could write about Lilianne," Normand suggests.

I start, snapping the book closed. "Normand! You scared me."

He gives off his wheezing laughter. I smile despite myself.

"Honestly," I shake my head, sounding like my mother. And then the smile lilts as I roll his words around in my head. "What did you just say?"

He repeats himself.

"We could create a character based on Lilianne, and then she and Tigara could fight."

Has Normand completely lost it? Lilianne is a Supergenic, and we are not to speak out against the Supergenics, not ever. And yet, inside this place of secrecy, maybe such thoughts *are* allowed.

I nod slowly, my smile returning. "Let's do it."

In reality, I'm sure Lilianne's developed some power that's enhanced her natural beauty, maybe gossamer fairy wings, her skin glittering with delicate crystals that are soft as satin. But here, I get to tell whatever story I want. Here, she does not get off so easy. Here, I can have justice.

After much discussion, Normand does some rough sketches, turning Lilianne into a monstrous creature covered in scales named Venomerella. The only thing that remains of the girl she once was are her beautiful eyes, and her all-too vicious human tongue. I almost feel a twinge of guilt. Almost.

In our tale, she and Tigara were once classmates, originally best (if competitive) friends, who become bitter enemies. In an egomaniacal rage, Venomeralla sets off an explosive device that levels five blocks of Bright Lights Big City. Amidst the rubble, she and Tigara fight it out. *Who shall be victorious?* I write. *Venomerella, with her cruel cunning, chameleon abilities, and poisonous fangs? Or Tigara, who has honed her abilities through hours of training, armed only with a whip and her wits, vowing to protect those weaker than herself?*

I read the words over and over, words that *I've* written, relishing them like the finest of meals, with no Mrs. Cranberry to tell me that it's terrible. A slew of possible outcomes dances in my head, each vying with each other. I honestly don't know what's going to happen next. I can't wait to find out.

The next morning I'm exhausted. I sit on the train with Liam and Sandie. I'm dying to tell them about Tigara, but that would raise too many questions. Once we arrive at the Cube, thoughts of my comic book heroine stop. There's no time here for distractions.

Day by day, the protector training intensifies, both physically and mentally. Some of it's individual, other times it's cooperative. I'm supposed to be trying to fail, but during the group challenges—whether it's flag football or an obstacle course—I can't let my teammates down, which is a foreign feeling. I'm a loner, not a joiner...aren't I?

And then weird things happen. Like I wind up *enjoying* the challenge. Or at lunch someone will call me over to sit with their group. Usually it's Liam and Sandie, but not always. Sometimes it's Denise or Reg or Claire or Bacon (I blush when Denise explains how he got the nickname). I expect them to be setting me up for some sort of social rejection, but instead they ask me questions and actually listen to the answers. I even crack some jokes. And then one day I realize that I have *friends*. Plural! At these times I have to remind myself that I only came to the Cube to make sure Bradie's okay.

In the cafeteria, as I eat my egg salad sandwich or munch on a morning muffin with protein-enriched hot chocolate, I keep an eye out for his mass of unruly hair. I casually search through novices and off-duty protectors, with no luck, but as I do I can't help but see the law enforcers differently than I used to.

Without all their gear—the guns, the batons, the on-the-go devices they use to report on people—they don't seem so different from the rest of us. Admittedly, many of them are bigger and certainly more fit than the general populous, with straighter backs, clearer skin, and better teeth, but that aside, they laugh and joke with each other. They have their romances. Their failures. I've seen friends become enemies. Enemies become friends. Just like everywhere else.

Stripped of their uniforms, I see the people behind those helmets. And they do serve our most important function: guarding the fence against the monstrosities beyond, and maintaining the rules that uphold our alliance with the Supergenics across the river. Maybe this place isn't so bad after all.

Could I be a part of this?

The irony isn't lost on me. During the day, I'm learning how to shut down any deviant behavior in the adult population that could lead to an upset of our societal order. By night I'm engaging in the very activities I'm training to suppress.

It creates a strange duality within me, as if my psyche is cleaving in half. Like so many of the heroes in the comic books I'm reading, I lead a double life. It raises questions, like which is the real me, and which is the mask? And what happens if one day I have to choose one over the other?

Such dilemmas are very much on my mind one morning in particular. Three months have passed, and it's the final day of my novice protector training. I'm sleepy-eyed at breakfast. I was up late again, huddled in the Lair with Normand.

We finally finished the battle between Tigara and Venomerella. Venomerella lay dying and bleeding on a shattered sidewalk. Her spine was broken. She grasped Tigara's arm, and with her last breath she hissed, "They did thissss to me. They made me a monsssssster. Ssssstop them!" Her words shook Tigara to the core, because once again good versus evil was no longer black and white, but shades of grey.

As for who "they" are, that is a mystery to be solved in another issue. Remembering it all makes me smile as I sit at the breakfast table, slurping down the remains of my cereal.

I'm actually humming as I reach Central Station, up until I get onto the train bound for the Cube. I look around at the other novices. The melody dies on my lips. Something's off.

A few people call out, "Hey, Caitlin" as I head for my seat. I greet people by name, and receive friendly nods of the head. I force myself to respond in kind, but I'm on edge.

What's different?

I walk toward Liam and Sandie. She won't look at me, staring forcibly out the window. Liam's lips keep twitching. My throat tightens. Practical jokes are part of our bonding, but I can't say that I'm a fan.

What are they going to do to me?

My heart beats faster. I try to relax, reassuring myself that this is different from when Lilianne would put water on my seat.

This means they like you.

Which is when I notice there's someone sitting in my usual seat. He smiles up at me, a spray of freckles across his nose.

"Hi Caitlin," he says.

I cover my mouth.

It's Bradie. His face is leaner, and he looks like he's put on some muscle, but it's him.

I sit down, not quite believing it. Liam and Sandie smile.

"You're here," I say.

"Yeah," he says, eyes twinkling, "I'm here. Can't get rid of me that easily."

I keep my voice low. "Where have you been?"

He replies at a normal volume, if a little off-key.

"I've been training, like all of you, just in a different compound," he says.

His cheeks twitch as he speaks. It's then I notice his hand. It's covered in angry scars that run up his fingers and wrist, disappearing into the cuff of his jacket. I'm staring, and before I can say a thing, he's rushing to explain.

"I hurt it when the mutant attacked," he says. His cheeks twitch again, as if a current's running from one to the other.

"No, you didn't," is my instant response.

He hides the scarred hand behind his back and squeezes my shoulder with his good one.

"I injured it when the mutant attacked. Do you understand?" he says it slowly and meaningfully.

I'm about to argue.

Caitlin, part of me blurts to myself in exasperation. *You need to go with this.*

All of a sudden I understand why Mrs. Cranberry was so angry with me all the time. She kept expecting me to play along, when I didn't know the rules and had no idea there was even a game that we were supposed to be playing. I think of the agent, I think of what Normand said, *You will find that Bradie is no longer as you remember him,* and it all falls into place. My throat constricts.

"Okay," I lie. "I remember that now."

Liam and Sandie nod in agreement, even though they weren't even there. *They* know how this game is played.

The train pulls out of the station. I'd imagined Bradie's and my reunion many times, many ways. Sometimes I would scold him. Sometimes we'd exchange teasing jokes. On occasion, I'd let him kiss me. I hadn't ever considered it would be like this. I feel that space growing between us, when two people have shared something intense, only to realize that they are strangers, and whatever illusion of closeness they'd felt is gone.

All that matters, I assure myself, *Is that Bradie's safe.*

"So how do you all know each other?" I ask, seeking safety in small talk.

"Bradie's brother introduced us at the station this morning," Liam replies. "Said we should all ride together. That you'd like the surprise."

I smile in relief. I was worried the agent had a hand in this.

Maybe he did, part of me still thinks.

We stick to safe subjects from then on. The lightning strikes beyond the fence. The food at the Protectorate and how much better it is than any of us are used to. How sad it is that pre-training is over and how exciting it is that cadet training will soon begin, for those of us who get in.

When the train arrives at the Cube, Liam and Sandie get up first. They squeeze each other's hand.

"They need to be careful," Bradie says, eyeing the pair as they walk ahead of us. "They'll use them against each other."

"What does that..." I start to ask, but Bradie cuts me off.

"Nothing," he insists.

The fear in his voice passes in an instant. Jovial Bradie is back, but not far under that veneer...It's then I pay attention to the band around Bradie's arm, the one that we all wear, of the all-seeing eye clenched in a fist. It makes me wonder if I've been getting too comfortable with that symbol.

"Okay," I say, and part of me wonders, *where were you really and what did they do to you?* And the scarier question, *Just how broken are you?*

CHAPTER 16

The rest of the morning turns out to be a snooze. We stand in line to hand in our gear, then another line to undergo a round of medical tests, just some blood work and a urine sample, and then it's lunch time.

The one remedy to the bureaucratic monotony is Bradie. Despite my worries, his charisma quickly asserts itself. While it's taken me the better part of three months to feel like I fit in, he somehow does it in half a day. I'm both relieved and faintly pissed.

"He's a good one," Sandie says in the cafeteria as we load up on double helpings of steaming pork and rice. And cookies. Oh the cookies! They're protein-based and sweetened with an inverted sugar that won't spike our insulin, but the bakers manage to get them gooey and chewy all the same. This could be our last meal here, and there's no grueling workout to follow, ready to make us puke, so we're going for it.

"Who?" I ask, though Sandie's clearly caught me staring as Bradie entertains a gaggle of female-identified cadets and a few moon-eyed guys. They all seem to be crushing on him as he does an impersonation of one of the instructors from the compound where he trained. There's a lot of dramatic finger waving followed by a flurry of martial arts chops and the occasional *hee-yah!* Sandie nudges my shoulder and winks.

"I think you'd make a lovely couple."

"What?" I say. "Bradie? With me? No. We're friends."

She rolls her eyes and makes an *mm-hmm* sound, clearly not buying what I'm selling.

After lunch, we stand at attention in one of the physical training rooms. There are hundreds of us. I note the missing faces from my cohort. The Protectorate was the one pre-work training program that one could opt out of at any point. *Culled* is the word the drill instructors use.

Those now absent either requested (or begged) for transfers after "tossing their salad," or breaking a bone, or worse, withering under the glare of their teammates after a failed challenge. Others were summarily cut, and sent to more suitable fields of training. I expected to be one of the latter, yet here I am.

A row of protectors stands along one wall. They're in uniform, but their helmets are buckled to their belts. Bradie's brother Trenton is among them. They salute briskly as a man slithers in, wearing a crisp black uniform with red piping and the insignia of a hangman's noose. I recognize him immediately. Eel Man.

My spine stiffens as I glance at Bradie. Sweat is beading on his forehead and he clenches his scarred hand. He recognizes Eel Man too.

Eel Man gazes along our tidy rows, quietly assessing us. When he speaks, it's like a serpent spitting.

"Bravo," he says curtly, "To some of you. Only the best will be invited to join the cadet program. The top three in this class will do so immediately. They are Liam Nelson, Sandie Marter, and Bradie Lopez Nettle."

I feel a twisting in my chest. The agents did that to Bradie's hand. I *know* they did. And yet he's being fast tracked into cadets? Is that his reward for playing his part? Or is this some kind of game, like when they put me on the airwaves as a hero, only to turn me into an example?

"Come forward," the agent waves.

For an instant, Bradie remains frozen. I almost think I will have to give him a shove, but he takes a jerky step, following after Liam and Sandie. The agent's face sags like heated plastic as he leads us in applause. Bradie's brother has a dark look on his face even as he claps. The agent gives us a brief jerk of the head, and walks out of the room. A grey-clad overseer steps forward

"Congratulations," the overseer says. "The rest of you will now move onto your next vocational stream. As you do, we will be carefully reviewing your results from your time here. Just be warned, what you have experienced so far has been *easy*. So *if* you are offered admission to the cadet program and you have any doubts about having what it takes, please *do* decline, because once you learn how to fire a weapon, there is *no* turning back."

I happen to be watching Bradie as she says that. I see the way his whole body tenses up and how he clenches his scarred hand. His brother is staring forward at nothing, his tan skin turning pale.

"I'd wish you luck," the overseer says, "But luck won't help you."

She salutes us, and we salute back. The sound of her boots smacking the floor echoes in the cavernous space, and a protector holds the door open as she leaves. The murmuring begins right away. I try to rejoin Liam, Sandie and Bradie, but they're surrounded by a horde of novices. I back away, weirdly hollow, once more on the outside looking in.

You knew this day was coming, a part of me chides. *This was the plan all along.*

I hear the words in my head, and I know they are right. Everything has worked out perfectly. I found Bradie. I made sure he's okay.

Is he though? I wonder. *Those scars on his hands, they run more than skin deep.* I hear my mom's response in my head. *There's nothing you can do about it, Caitlin. That's that. End of story.*

She's right, and for a second I hate her for it, because this isn't fair. As I watch people clap Liam, Sandie, and Bradie on the back, all I can think is, *I want to stay.*

On the train ride home, Liam and Sandie are being way too nice, almost apologetic for receiving immediate entry into cadets when I did not.

"You're getting in. You'll see!" Sandie says.

"Of course," I reply, not telling her about my abysmal written tests, nor that my mom would kill me if I went on to be a cadet.

I hug them good bye outside the station, along with a few others. There's a weird air of competitive camaraderie. Even Gregor gives me a head nod and grunts, "Good luck."

"Yeah," I say. "You too."

"Walk you home?" Bradie asks.

"Sure," I say.

Liam and Sandie look ready to join us but Sandie holds Liam back, giving us a thumbs up. Bradie slides his good hand into mine, his palm warm against my own.

"Let's go," he says.

We walk in silence for a bit. He looks at me and smiles. I smile back.

"What are you thinking?" he asks.

My gaze drifts down to his scarred hand.

He sighs. "All right, let's get this over with."

"What?" I ask.

He holds his hand up and pulls his sleeve past his elbow. The scarring ends right below the joint. I reach out to touch it and he angles his body so I can't.

I back off. "Does it hurt?"

"Not physically," he says, pulling down his sleeve and shoving his hand into a pocket. "The med techs did a good job. Cultured my own skin cells for the grafts and injected steroidals for muscular regen. The nerve rehabilitation was the worst."

"It doesn't make sense," I say. As usual, I'm trying to logic my way through the story. "They went to a lot of trouble to heal you, so why burn you in the first place?"

His cheek twitches.

"You know why. I broke a very important law. So did my brother. Trenton's got high standing in the Cube, and I've got 'potential,' so they're bending the rules for us; giving me a chance to become someone who *is* allowed to discharge a weapon. But nothing comes free. This..." he holds up his scarred hand. "This is the price I paid for our second chance."

CHAPTER 17

We're quiet after that. When Bradie and I reach my tenement building, our lack of words turns awkward.

"This is me," I say.

With his good hand, he brushes a lock of my hair behind my ear, his fingers grazing my cheek.

"I'll see you soon, Caitlin Feral," he says. Then he turns and walks away, disappearing around a corner. I can still feel his touch.

My smile widens as I walk up the concrete stairs. *Could we make a nice couple?* I feel an unexpected warmth in my belly. I reach my apartment, unlock the door and go inside. I'm humming.

"Welcome home," a foreign yet sinisterly familiar voice greets me.

It suffocates the warmth in my belly. Within the gloom of our tiny apartment, I make out the outline of a person. Eel Man.

"No pleasantries?" he asks. "Probably for the best. We haven't much time before your mother and brother get home. I don't imagine you're looking for me to stay for dinner."

The words are like barbed wire, but I force myself to say, "If you'd like."

He looks appalled, gazing around the flat. "I'll pass."

He snaps his fingers and points for me to stand in front of the kitchen table. I scurry forward like a trained mutt. He slides a data tablet across the table toward me and a series of holographic files pop up from its surface. I see my name and bits of my background floating in the air in front of me.

"You failed your cadet entry trial by one percent," he says.

My jaw clenches. I failed. I'm out. I should be happy. That was the goal after all, to come close, but not close enough to pass. *Yay for me*, I think. But surely he's not here just to tell me that.

"I gave you an opportunity," he says. "A gift wrapped up in a bow. And this is what you do with it?" He shakes his head and makes a *tsk-ing* sound.

"I'm sorry," I say.

He contemplates me.

"Can you keep a secret?" he asks.

His gaze bores through me. Does he know about the comic book shop? "Yes," I reply.

"We allow a modest margin of error in the trial results. A fudge factor."

My eyes widen.

"Does that mean...I'm in?"

"Dear me, no," he chuckles. "There was an exceptional crop of candidates this year. Anyone under 70 percent didn't stand a chance."

"Oh," I reply.

"But then what are we to do with you, Caitlin Feral? You killed a monstrosity. We know you discharged a weapon, though the angle of the videos can't prove it and the witness testimony is inconclusive. Your physical scores are well above average. And although your psyche profile categorizes you as a Solitary, during team training your bio readings, heart rate, voice analysis, and brain waves all tell a very different story."

He notes my look of shock.

"Yes, Caitlin, we've been monitoring all of the above. It's not enough to excel in combat. The skills that you've been learning, in the hands of someone opposed to the arrangement with the Supergenics, and the methods we use to enforce the treaty, well, that could be utterly revolutionary to the current world order. And we can't have that, now can we? It could destroy us all. These readings help us determine who we can count on."

"And what do your readings say about me?" I ask.

"That putting you in the general work force could be...troublesome," he says. "The Protectorate has been good for you. It's given you focus. Clarity. Community."

He slides an envelope toward me with a stamp bearing the all-seeing eye in a fist of the Protectorate.

"This is your last chance to be a part of that," he says.

I take the envelope. My heart beats wildly.

"I can see you're conflicted," he says. "Because of what we did to your father no doubt and to your friend's hand. Regrettable actions, but necessary. Your father was about to start a second gene war."

I can't hide the surprise in my eyes.

"He nearly killed us all," he says.

"No," I say.

"Yes," he replies. "I have no reason to lie."

I can't hear this.

"And Bradie?" I ask.

"Bradie, we could've executed. Instead we showed him mercy. The same as I'm now doing for you."

He taps the data tablet and the hologram gets sucked back into its smooth surface.

"I trust this will be our last conversation," he says.

It's strange watching him walk out the front door. He should slither, but in fact there's a dancer's grace to his stride, hiding the predator inside. The door closes, leaving me alone in the darkness. I think about what Eel Man said about my dad, and I can't help but wonder, *Is it true?*

When my mom gets home she flicks a switch and a bare bulb flickers to life. I'm sitting at the kitchen table. I don't look up.

"Caitlin?" she asks. "Why on earth are you sitting in the dark?"

She sees the envelope in my hand.

"Caitlin." There's a dangerous edge to her voice.

I tear the envelope open and pull out a thin sheet of paper.

"Attention, Caitlin Feral," I read out loud. "This notice is to advise you that you have been accepted for early admission into the Protectorate cadet program. If you choose to accept this position..."

There's more, but my mother grabs the sheet from my hand and tears it into little strips.

"You stupid girl!" she shouts. "You were supposed to fail!"

"I *did* fail," I shout back, slamming my fist on the table.

She stops, confused.

"The agent, he was *here*," I say. "He gave me the letter personally."

My mother leans on the counter for support.

"They're doing this to punish me," she says.

"This isn't about you!" I shout.

"Of course it is," she snaps back. "You're a teenage girl and you think an agent's going to take the time to oversee your choice of vocation? This is because of your father. As if giving me these blasted migraines weren't bad enough!"

I roll my eyes. She's insane. How many times have I heard her blame the protectors for something that's surely brought on by the fumes at the factory? Her mentioning my father sets me off even more.

"This *isn't* about you," I repeat. "This is about me, and Bradie, and those stupid mutant hounds. I fired a weapon. They're not going to just let that go." I think of Bradie's hand. With or without evidence, they could've done that to me. "I'm getting off lucky!"

She squeezes her eyes in pain, pressing her fist to her temple. Could the agents be responsible for her headaches? *Maybe. Or maybe she's conveniently having an episode to get you to do what she wants.* I hate myself for thinking it, and not for the first time, but right now my anger is stronger than my self-recriminations.

"You have to say no," my mom says. "That's all there is to it, consequences be damned."

"Mom," I reply as calmly as I can. "I'm going to say yes."

She grabs a chipped mug from the dish rack and she throws it at me as hard as she can. I duck, and it shatters against my closed bunk.

I'm shaking with anger. She *threw* it at me!

"No daughter of mine will ever be one of *them*," she insists.

"They're not all bad," I insist.

She shakes her head. "You did not just say that. You were there when they took your father. When they ruined our lives."

"You're the one ruining my life!" I snap.

Three months ago I would never have dared say such a thing. Think it, yes; say it, no. But that was before I failed my final Testing Day. Before I killed a two-headed ravenous hound. Before I snuck into the Yellow Zone. Before I had friends.

"I want to do this," I say calmly. "I'm happy there. And this is my decision to make."

"This isn't you," she says. "This is them brainwashing you, with their chemicals and their pills."

"There are no pills," I say. "Those are just stories. They're *all* just stories."

She's waving her hand in the air. "No, you're wrong. It's in the food then. Or the water."

"The food is just food," I reply. "And the water is just water."

"And what about the agent? What about him? He was *here*," she hisses. "You said so yourself. Coercing a sixteen-year-old girl. Turning her against her own mother. *That's* what you want to be a part of? That's the kind of person you want to be?"

"Of course not! He's an *agent*."

"Agent, protector, you think there's a difference?" my mom snorts.

"Yes!" I say. "There *is* a difference. I've seen it."

114

"No," she insists. "You go back to the Protectorate Caitlin, mark my words, you will do bad things, things you will regret."

"No," I insist. "I won't. Me and my friends..."

"Oh!" she throws up her hands. "She has friends now. Is that what this is about?"

I think of Liam, and Sandie, and Bradie. I think of that feeling I get at the Protectorate, of having a place where I fit.

"Yes," I say.

"They took your father!" she shouts at the top of her lungs.

"Well, maybe he had it coming!" I shout back.

My mom looks like I've just slapped her. I don't care. All these years, my mom's given me delusional half-truths that suit her version of reality, but what kind of person was my father really?

"Be very careful what you say, Caitlin," my mother warns. "There are some things you can't take back. Your father was a good man..."

"Then why did they arrest him?"

"*Because* he was trying to do something good," she says.

"He chose to break the law," I say. "And he left me and Nate without a dad."

"You don't know what you're saying. You have no idea what they were making him do to children just like you. Twisting their minds with his devices..."

"Enough!" I slam my palms onto the table. "I'm tired of your stories."

"They're not stories," she insists.

"Then why am I only hearing about this now?" I say.

"Their machines, they made me forget...but the memories, they come back with the headaches."

"Convenient," I say.

"Caitlin..."

"You're sick," I continue. "And you're not getting better and I just make you worse."

"Nate, he needs you. He's your little brother," she says. "You can't abandon him."

"Nate's going to leave us. He's going to Manifest. You know it. I know it. All the signs are there. It's just a matter of time."

She winces at the throbbing in her head, but I can see she's trying to find her cool. "Caitlin, I know you're scared, I'm scared too, but..."

"I'm not scared!" I shout. "I'm *choosing* this, not because of *them*, but because of *me*. I don't want to pick apples, or file requisition forms, or sweep garbage off the streets. I *want* to be a protector. I *want* to be one of *them*."

I can't believe I said it. I can't believe I mean it. Her arm swings in an attempt to slap me. The arc is wide, telegraphing her intent, and before I even know what I'm doing my newly honed reflexes kick in. I easily catch her arm in my grip.

"You do not lay a hand on me," I say. "Not ever."

She tries to jerk her arm free. I don't let her. For once in my life, I'm in control.

"I don't even know you anymore," she says. To be fair, I'm feeling like a stranger to myself. "Get out," she says. "Get out of my house!"

I snort, almost like a true protector, not just a cadet. Lines we've been forced to memorize at school come flowing out of my mouth before I even realize it. "You don't have a house. This is a residence where you are permitted to stay at the grace of the Housing Commission. Do *not* presume it can't be taken away."

"Caitlin," she whines. "You're hurting me."

I assume she means because of my words, until I realize my grip is tightening on her forearm. I release her, back away, and wonder if maybe there *is* something in the Protectorate food.

"I...I'm sorry. I didn't mean...You shouldn't make me angry like that."

I'm horrified by my own words. I sound like someone I recognize all too well. I sound like her.

My mother's quiet at that, so quiet it's scary, and when she speaks it's with a resolute coldness.

"Get out," my mother says quietly. "Get out of this government-owned residence. And don't ever come back."

CHAPTER 18

I stand outside of the apartment where up until a few seconds ago I used to live. I stare at the closed door separating me from my mom.

Now what?

I lift my open palm. Do I tap meekly or pound aggressively?

"That was quite the fight."

I whip around and face Bradie's brother. His form-fitting copper uniform shows off the curves of his muscled form. He's holding his helmet under one arm.

"Officer Trenton!" I snap my heels together and give a salute.

He's smirking. "At ease, cadet."

I lower my arm.

"You heard that?" I ask, standing protectively in front of the door.

"Whole block did, I imagine," he replies.

My mom could be in a lot of trouble.

"She didn't mean what she said," I assure him.

He shrugs. "At least you have a parent left who cares."

"You don't have parents?" I ask.

"Orphans," he says.

I remember now. Bradie lives with his aunt.

"Right. Sorry."

He shrugs. "It is what it is, cadet."

"You keep calling me that," I say.

"Cadet?" he asks.

"Yeah."

"You got your early admittance notification, right?"

I nod.

"So, are you in or are you out?"

I take a deep breath, and before I can change my mind I say in a quick exhale, "I'm in. Sir."

"Great. Let's get going, cadet."

I hesitate.

"Where?"

He winks, reminding me very much of Bradie. It's a side of him I haven't seen before.

"You'll see," he says.

I follow him down the concrete stairs and into the near empty streets. Evening lamps come to life around us.

We round a corner and waiting by the security fence are some familiar faces. Liam, Sandie, and Bradie. All three of them are still in their school ties and jackets, like me. Bradie winks. I try to wink back, but I know it just looks like I've developed a tic. I've tried practicing in the mirror. That's when I notice there's a fourth kid standing with them, wearing the yellow overalls of a technician, with the emblem of a computer monitor and screw driver on his chest.

"This is..." Trenton begins to introduce the odd man out.

"Normand," I say. My tone is heavy. My heart's hammering. *What's he doing here? Is this a trick? A trap? Do the protectors know about the Lair?*

Behind them black clouds roil and lightning blasts into the energy syphons.

"You two know each other?" Trenton asks. He seems genuinely surprised.

"We're in the same class," Normand explains, his avoidant gaze drifting.

"Huh," Trenton grunts. "I should've looked more closely at your files." He looks from one face to another. "Kind of weird that you all have a connection to Caitlin."

He's saying exactly what I'm thinking. Trenton shrugs.

"Just one of those things, I guess."

I almost believe he means it. Almost.

"Normand's been assigned as a techie for the Protectorate," Trenton explains. "Sometimes we'll take one along into the field. Tonight is one of those nights."

We all look at each other. *Into the field?*

Trenton starts punching a code into the gate's locking pad, and then swipes his i-Dent card through the reader. There's an electronic beep and a click. He shoves the gate open. We all look at each other confused. *Is this some kind of test?*

"Last person make sure to pull the gate shut behind you," Trenton says as he steps into the Yellow Zone. Lightning crackles into the energy absorbers set twenty measures back from the fence, lighting him up from behind.

"Is he serious?" Liam asks, staring at all the warning sign with the mutated animal heads on it. "He wants us to go in there, in our class uniforms, at night?"

"The evidence would indicate that to be the case," Normand says. He marches past us and through the gate.

"So...did Leg Brace just show us all up?" Bradie asks.

I smile, weirdly proud of Normand.

"Yeah," I say. "He did."

"Well, balls to that," Bradie snorts, marching after him.

"Are we doing this?" Liam asks Sandie.

She takes a deep breath.

"Looks like," she answers.

They snake their hands together, square their shoulders, and I'm suddenly the last one on the safe side of the fence.

"Hurry up!" Bradie yells at us as he forges ahead.

"Yeah, okay, we're coming!" Liam shouts in return.

I watch them go. Sandie turns to me. "Come on, Caitlin!"

She holds her hand out for me to take. I don't even know why I'm hesitating. I've been in the Yellow Zone before. It's not such a big deal. And yet as I embrace the path of the protector, the one that leads to the Cube and all that it represents, my mom's words haunt me.

You go back to the Protectorate, Caitlin, mark my words you will do bad things, things you will regret.

"Oh, screw it," I say. *What does she know?* I take Sandie's hand and she guides me through the gate. I pull it shut behind me and we set off after the others.

The pulsating globes of the energy syphons crackle above us, giving off an eerie light that's enough to see by. We're running, stumbling, sometimes crawling over debris and broken walls and through busted homes that for all we know could collapse on us at any moment. We chase Bradie, who chases Normand, who presumably is following Trenton. We're all grinning wildly.

Normand is surprisingly limber, as if he actually knows where he's going, just like getting to and from the Lair. I hope no one else notices. We catch up to Bradie. He offers me his good hand. I take it.

"Can you believe we're actually *in* the Yellow Zone?" he asks. His eyes are full moons, reminding me of Nate. Lightning flares from the perpetual black clouds above.

"Crazy, right?" I say. I've been in the Yellow Zone before, of course, but not with him, not like this.

We catch up to Normand. Trenton's nowhere to be seen. We've lost sight of our borough, and I realize that I'm not sure if I know how to get back.

"Guys, are we lost?" I ask.

Before anyone can answer the sizzling energy absorbers immediately around us go dead, casting us into pitch blackness. Fear is overtaking excitement.

"Do you hear that?" Sandie asks.

I do hear it. An animalistic growl. I turn toward it. A pair of glowing red eyes stare at us.

"Arm yourselves," Sandie says.

I reach down, feeling around. My hands close around a pipe. I lift it as the thing draws closer and closer. I draw the pipe back like a bat. The beast is almost on top of us when the red eyes wink out and a pair of headlights flare to life, blinding us. Trenton's laughter echoes around us.

"Effing eff," he swears. "You all look hilarious!"

He stands on the hood of a hover vehicle, laughing at us.

"Ha, ha," Bradie says, shaking his head. We all drop our makeshift weapons. Only Normand didn't arm himself. Figures he'd leave the fighting to us.

"Come on, losers," Trenton says, waving for us to join him as he nimbly swings over the windshield into the hovercraft.

We follow after him. There's a woman at the controls. She's got the air of a protector; strong jaw, slicked back hair, and an arrogant tilt to her head as she appraises us. She's not in uniform though. Instead she wears a tight tank top and a silver collar around her throat. A pair of goggles are up over her forehead.

"So *this* is the best this term has to offer?" she gazes at us, unimpressed.

"I didn't pick 'em," Trenton shrugs. "Besides, they can't all be as good as our year."

She nods as if that makes perfect sense.

"Get on," she orders.

There are handles and footholds to help us grapple our way aboard. We have to help Normand, who can't get his bum leg up. We half drag, half push him to get him on. The woman doesn't offer to help. Neither does

Trenton. Her disgust for Normand manifests in a clenched jaw that appears ready to spit on him.

"Techie?" she asks.

"He's apparently a genius," Trenton says.

"All right," she says, skeptical. "You're upfront genius."

Normand shuffles forward. For once he's not looking at his watch. He's staring at her breasts. She smirks.

"Everyone, this is Crystal Kapor," Trenton says.

She gives us all the finger, talking only to Normand.

"You know how to use a DRADIS?" she asks him.

He punches away on a control pad and a monitor flicks to life. It shows a rough cartography of our surroundings, with us as a blue blip on it. There are a multitude of red blips all around us. I grip the back of a chair tightly. I notice Liam, Sandie and Bradie doing the same. The red blips are other life-signs. Maybe there are mutants out there after all. If there's that many we're as good as dead.

"Eliminating non-threats," Normand says, typing away. The red dots blink out. "They were mostly rodents," he explains to us. "Possibly an alley cat."

"Not bad, rookie," Crystal says. "Keep an eye out. We did a sweep today but you never know when a mutie might slip through. All right, buckle up, grubs."

She doesn't wait, putting the craft into gear. I'm thrown backward, right into Bradie's lap. He's already belted into a chair and deftly catches me. Sandie does the same for Liam.

"My hero," he says to her.

Bradie puts his arms around my waist. It's not the worst. My gaze drifts down, to the scarred skin of his left hand. He sees me staring and he hides it under his thigh.

The hovercraft is open to the air, letting the wind beat our faces red as we speed through the broken city. The vehicle's front beams light the way, taking us among the electrodes that absorb the lightning all around us. I look up at the roiling clouds, the fight with my mother growing more and more distant the further from the borough we get.

We travel deep into what's left of the city, and we're not out here alone.

"Multiple contacts," Normand says. "Two dozen hovercraft closing in."

I see other high beams off in the distance. They seem to be coming from the direction of the other boroughs. Some are small craft like ours. I even spot a two-seater and the occasional single sling. Others are Juggernauts, capable of carrying up to a hundred people each.

What kind of mission is this? I wonder.

Bradie's grip tightens around my waist.

"Check that out!" he yells above the wind.

I stare at an enormous building in the shape of a gigantic bowl. Lightning arcs down into it, smashing into an energy absorbing globe rising from its center. We're speeding right toward it.

Crystal accelerates and we disappear into an opening in its side. The hovercraft's high beams light up our route. We skim along a huge hallway with reinforced concrete pillars all along the sides.

At the end of the hall is what appears to be an empty elevator shaft, framed by sliding steel doors that have been yanked from their housings.

"I hope you're all buckled in!" Crystal shouts.

We race toward the black maw of the elevator shaft and Crystal gives a sharp turn of the steering bracket. We do a 180 as we careen past the fallen steel doors and right into the portal of darkness, and then she shoves the gear into neutral. We slide into the elevator shaft and hover there.

She reaches for her gear shift. I grab a handle and grip it tight, my eyes locked on Bradie's.

"Don't you dare let go," I say.

"Never," he winks, squeezing me tight.

Crystal shoves the gear shift and the vibrations of the hovercraft shudders off. We drop straight down the shaft. I'm screaming. So are the others, including Trenton, but his is a wild whoop. Hearing it, I feel his thrill, and I echo it. I grip the handles so hard that my arms feel ready to be pulled from their sockets. Bradie pulls me in close with all his strength.

The walls are a blur. I lift off Bradie's lap and I swear I'm about to be wrenched into nothingness when Crystal rams the gear shift again. The hovercraft births a cloud of dirt beneath it as it vibrates to life. I feel a sudden upward pressure, pushing Bradie's thighs into me. We're all laughing, even Normand, in his weirdly wheezing way

He gives me a thumb up. I mirror it and feel oddly happy that Bradie, Liam, and Sandie are doing the same.

"Did we lose anybody?" Crystal asks hopefully.

122

"Negative," Normand replies.

"Well, there goes that bet," she says with disappointment, handing over a chocolate bar to Trenton.

Crystal propels the hovercraft forward through another hall. I see flashing multicolored lights ahead and I hear something growing louder. At first I think it's the omnipresent sound of thunder, but something's off about it. It sounds like...

"Music," Bradie says as we burst into the middle of the bowl-shaped building.

Bradie's right. It is music, but completely unlike the brass tubas and horns and flutes or the twang of violins or other string instruments that we all learn to play as children—and which a select few of us actually excel at. This is deep, then light, pounding, and then gentle waves, rhythmic and repetitive, as if the thumping of the heart, the inhale/exhale of the lungs, the sluicing of the blood, the crackle of synapses firing have all been turned into an infinitely repeating song that rises and falls with the ebb and flow of adrenaline, the cascade of hormones, the dilation of pupils. It's as if the music is somehow alive.

I gaze in wonder as Crystal drives us into the open air space. Trenton is unabashedly stripping out of his protector's gear, down to a pair of short shorts and sneakers, and nothing else.

Lightning flashes above, caught by the globe on its concrete pillar in the middle of the gigantic bowl. The electrode's clearly been modified, to not only absorb energy but to spit it back out in the form of lasers and light bursts, all in time to the music's throbbing beat. It's beautiful, and mesmerizing, and I can't believe this is actually happening. It takes me a moment to figure out what this place has to be. An arena of some sort, like the kind Tigara is thrown into to battle ferocious beasts in the middle of a savage jungle after she's marooned on a tropical island.

Seats rise up and up all around the periphery. Our various gymnasia have miniature versions of these stands at some of the schools, where the public can fill their short leisure hours by cheering on kids like my brother who may yet Manifest as they play team sports, or do gymnastics, or perform at a recital. On special occasions, the protectors will even do demonstration games against each other. But this is enormous. This could seat thousands. What kind of games did they play here?

Crystal powers down the hovercraft amidst dozens of other short range vehicles. More of them are arriving from various access points. Some of the drivers and passengers wave and holler at us as they pass.

Trenton and Crystal catcall in reply as they hop overboard. We help Normand clamber down, and we start walking toward the center of the stadium. The middle is full of people dancing and gyrating. Not just people. Protectors. Like Crystal, even out of uniform, they have a look to them, with their toned bodies and sure movements, and their metal i-Dent tags hanging about their necks.

Most wear the short shorts or loose track pants that we train in, and little else. Some of the female-identified wear sport bras or tank tops like Crystal. Others do not. Everyone has colorful accessories, bows and ribbons in their hair or tied around biceps or thighs. Collars, bracelets, and armbands made from shiny metals or shimmering beads. A lot of the men and women wear makeup, accentuating their eyes, lips and cheekbones.

I'm mesmerized and horrified at the same time. If regular dregs were to gather like this, they'd be arrested by these same people.

"What is this?" I ask.

"This," Trenton replies, "is something few cadets ever get to see or take part in, not until they are protectors themselves. Welcome to Revelry."

Crystal leans her arm on his shoulder in the way of old comrades, and she adds, "What he's saying is, *this* is where we party."

CHAPTER 19

Crystal takes out a round cylinder the size of a pinky finger and pops off its cap. She twists it and a red, waxy substance rolls out. She stands in front of Trenton and starts applying it to his lips. When she's done she tosses the cylinder at me.

"Here," Bradie says. "I'll help."

Bradie grazes my cheek gently as he applies the oddly sticky substance to my mouth. It's lipstick. Girls like Lilianne would sometimes wear it. I never thought I ever would.

He nods at his handiwork, handing over the tube. "Now you do me."

Crystal has us all add mascara to give our lashes "luster," and then she personally smears a black line with her thumb under each of our eyes. To my surprise the final effect is warrior-esque. I'd expected clownish. We leave our jackets in the hovercraft and are about to follow Crystal when she stops us with a commanding hand.

"Not you," she says to Normand. "You're over there."

She points to a group of young techies in coveralls at a multitiered array of consoles.

"That's not fair," I say.

"It's all right, Caitlin," Normand says. "*Someone* has to keep the lights on."

"But..." I start to argue and he cuts me off.

"I would never partake in that drug-addled hoopla," Normand gestures at the throng of bodies. "It's a petri dish of sweat and germs."

Bradie is hiding a smirk behind his good hand. Normand points a finger at Bradie.

"Staphylococcus infections are no joke!"

"Fair enough, my man," Bradie says, holding his good hand up in peace.

"From what alternate universe do you hail in which I am in any way your man?"

"Easy, tough guy," Bradie replies.

"We shall see who is the 'tough guy,'" Normand bristles.

He does a stiff bow and limps over to the double-decked control center. I want to say something, but I don't know what. I've never seen him actually angry.

"He's a bit odd, isn't he?" Crystal asks.

"You should read his personnel file," Trenton says.

Up until now Normand was a part of this evening. They even made him up like the rest of us. Now they shut him out? It reminds me of how I was treated at school. I feel a tug to go over to him, but the selfish side of me wants to stay. Besides, I really can't imagine him having fun with a bunch of dancing protectors. That would just be weird.

"The techie's right about one thing," Crystal says. "We do need some pharmacological enhancement."

She pulls a pill box from her pocket and opens it. Inside are six capsules with a glowing orange gel in them.

"What's that?" I ask.

"The chemical composition is dioxymantangulate. We call it Mango Tango."

She sees the concern on my face. "Relax," she says. "It's brain food. It enhances your ability to absorb new information and learn faster under guided conditions. We take it before our Calibration sessions."

"What are those?" Liam asks.

"They're like guided meditations," Trenton says. "Only way more kick-ass."

Crystal holds the pill box to us and one by one we each take a capsule. I hold the glowing orange gel tab up to the cascading light show, and through it's translucent shell I look at the throng of dancing protectors.

"This doesn't look like a guided situation," I say.

"That's what makes it so much fun," Trenton says. He holds up a canteen and knocks his capsule back with a chug.

"And when you throw a bit of booze into the mix, the effects are, admittedly, moderately hallucinogenic," Crystal winks.

Trenton passes the canister to Bradie, who follows his older brother's lead. Crystal's next, then Sandie and Liam. It's down to just me. I put the pill in my mouth, take the canteen from Liam, and suck it back. The liquid is definitely not water. It tingles and burns and sends a rush of peppermint up through my nasal cavity and out my nose.

It's only as the Mango Tango capsule slides down my throat that I remember my mom's words.

This is them brainwashing you, with their chemicals and their pills.

Shut up, I tell her. But part of me isn't angry. It's afraid. *What have I taken? What will it do to me?*

Fear is a funny emotion though; it can easily be replaced by a bigger, more immediate one. We move into the crowd.

I was always a disaster in dance class. I had no rhythm, and could never keep time with my classmates, and I'd constantly lose track of the choreography. My instructor was relieved when she was finally allowed to flunk me. Those feelings of humiliation start churning up in me now as we move amidst the sweating, gyrating bodies, and I look longingly over to the central command, where the techies are overseeing the music and power flow.

Normand got it lucky.

The protectors stare at us. It's clear we don't belong. Only Trenton and Crystal are dressed to their party code, not only stripped down to the barest of outfits, but unabashedly dancing in a sea of gyrating physiques.

"Come on!" Trenton waves at us, disengaging from a boy-girl couple who had him sandwiched and now start to make out.

He leads us deeper into the throng. Protectors press him for high fives and fist bumps, which he happily dishes out. Our school uniforms are earning dirty looks.

"Screw this," Bradie says, and he yanks off his shirt, bunching it up into a ball and throwing it into the crowd. There are loud cheers all around. Trenton beams proudly, grabs his brother and lifts him onto his shoulder. Bradie still has his tie around his neck, hanging between the surprisingly muscular mounds of his chest.

"This is my baby brother everyone!" Trenton shouts to a chorus of approval all around him.

Liam and Sandie look to each other and shrug, then they too are tossing their shirts away. More cheers ensue. Now everyone's looking at me. All I want to do is run. Every bit of insecurity that Lilianne and her friends have bashed into me over the years comes flooding back.

But then I think of Tigara, and I ask myself what that urban huntress would do. My fingers feel like claws that yank my shirt open, buttons popping everywhere. There are screams of approval as I pull my shirt off and twirl it over my head. A gust of air pulls at the cloth and I let it go. The updraft whisks it away, higher and higher until a burst of stato-electric energy grabs it and slams the cloth into the sizzling energy sphere up above. It makes a *whu-zip* sound and a tiny burst of flame.

The cheers are deafening as drinks are shoved into all of our hands. I hold a plastic cup, filled with a frothy red liquid that's giving off a thick vapor and the stench of strawberries.

Crystal sees me hesitate. "They're phytochemicals!" she shouts over the music. "They're good for you!"

Trenton holds his cup up for a toast, and we all clink together, sticky foaming liquid sloshing all over the place. The fear is gone. I feel a thrill of belonging, and this time, as the bubbly sweet concoction washes down my throat my mother's voice is wonderfully silent, the music holds sway, and when I catch what must be an imagined glimpse of a man in black watching from the shadows, I don't even give him a second look.

CHAPTER 20

I feel a foreign rush of euphoria and giddiness, as if a power washer has swept through me and cleared out all the junk from my mind. I dance—not the choreographed steps from the classes I failed, but random and wild movements, arms swinging and hips swaying to the paradoxically predictable yet ever-shifting beat.

Bradie reaches his good hand out to me, his scarred one safely behind his back. Our fingers entwine and I pull him toward me. He's grinning like a goof. I had no idea it was possible to feel this way. So light. So free.

So what happens when tonight ends? the naysayer in me wonders.

I don't care, is my honest answer.

"Look!" Bradie points.

A floating stage is slowly descending toward us. On it is a band and singers and dancers. The band starts to play wildly, on a slew of electronic instruments, and the dancers are among the best I've ever seen. The singer is tall and willowy, her voice like melting nougats and honey.

She sings a song we all know, of sacrifice and strength and solidarity, but with an added verse about the protectors standing tallest and shining brightest against the things that growl and shred in the night. Dozens of smaller floating podiums come down, each with a pole in the center, and athletic physiques costumed in copper undergarments and a protector's helmet and nothing else are upon each dais, whirling and twirling around the poles in dizzying displays.

Loud cheers rise from all around. The dancers on the main stage are a frenzy of hips and dips, and I realize all the performers are protectors. All of them were once candidates for Manifestation. All of them went through years and years of study to learn these crafts—singing, ballet, gymnastics. None of them have special powers, and yet they are all amazing.

Does that mean I can be amazing too?

I squeeze Bradie's hand and look to him for a kiss, but he doesn't squeeze back. His gaze meets his brother's, and Bradie points to himself, then at the main stage, hovering right before us, about 10 measures off the ground. Trenton laughs, and shakes his head. Bradie's eyes widen into full moons and he nods vigorously. Trenton sighs and shrugs and hands his drink to Crystal. She rolls her eyes and steps back.

"Clear a hole!" she shouts, loud enough that the protectors nearby step back, their smirks full of curiosity. Bradie takes his hand from mine.

"Wish me luck!" he says as he pulls away.

"For what?" I ask.

"For this!"

He sprints toward his brother, who crouches down, hands cupped together. Bradie jumps his right foot into Trenton's grip. Trenton's legs and arms explode upwards and Bradie goes sailing up into the air. He's like a missile, his body perfectly aligned, and, as if it's the easiest thing in the world, he flips and lands right on the stage. He holds his arms out to the side and the crowd goes wild. I feel a surge of pride, and unbidden I think, *he's my boyfriend!*

Is he?

My heart trembles uncertainly and into the euphoria creep black pits of neediness.

I don't know.

But you want him to be, don't you?

I think I do.

I'm rescued by a gentle numbness as I drink my strawberry elixir. The crowd is screaming its approval as Bradie does a series of flips, turns, and somersaults. He dives into splits and bounds right back out of them. It's part dance, part acrobatics and pure wondrousness. The band plays off of him, and he plays off of them.

He builds to a climax of a dozen flips in a row all around the stage, bounding into a twirl where he rips his pants right off to everyone's amazement and then he slides forward toward the crowd on his knees in just his underpants.

He throws his arms wide open. He's panting and covered in sweat. There's a moment of silence. Even the music has stopped, as if it too needs a moment to process what it's just witnessed. I can feel the crowd's awe gathering itself together, about to erupt in thunderous applause that will deafen even the roiling storm clouds above.

I'm about to lead the charge, but before any of our palms can clap together screeching feedback bursts from the sound system. It's a jagged razor against our ear drums. We gasp and wince and cover the sides of our heads, Bradie included. As we hunch down in pain, something else is happening too. Lightning is still striking the globe atop the electric rod in the center of us, but it's no longer spraying out a technicolor light show. It's absorbing the energy and holding it within the sphere, where it crackles hungrily for release. It starts to whine, like a dam ready to burst. People start backing away from it.

"Please turn off all cell phones and any other mobile communications devices," an antiquated computerized voice counsels us from the loudspeakers. "So that everyone can enjoy the show."

The whine in the electrified power absorbing sphere peaks and a giant bolt of lightning shoots out of it toward the rear of the stadium. As one, our eyes turn to follow it, and we see a single figure on a round floating dais right in the lightning bolt's path. I recognize the dropped shoulders, the girth of the waist, the gimpy out-turned leg in a brace.

"Normand," I whisper. And then in a shriek, "Normand!"

I want to look away, but the lightning is too fast, and I'm too slow. He's going to be electrocuted. Burnt to a husk. It's an image that will wake me with nightmares for years to come.

Except the lightning, impossibly, *doesn't* kill him. He holds up a palm with a metallic disc strapped to it. The lightning breaks into smaller bolts, cresting around the disc like a wave smashing against a rock. The streams of electricity dance about him in a swirling globe. He's got more of the weird metal discs attached all over his torso, arms and legs. He holds his hand forward, palm up. The energy forms a crackling sphere right above it. Another bolt of lightning fires right at him from the energy sucking globe. He harnesses it with the disc stuck to his other palm, and a second globe of crackling energy hovers over that hand.

The floating podium moves toward us, and he starts to sing into the microphone strapped about his head. It's an opera, in one of the old tongues. I can't understand a word of it, but it's beautiful. His voice! Who knew he had such a voice? It vibrates in a way that sends shudders up and down my spine. It's beauty, and ugliness, and triumph, and failure in its rawest of forms.

He moves his arms in sinewy arcs, and the lightning becomes two dancing energy dragons, twirling about each other. He looks down at me, and I up at him. I give him a double thumbs up. He draws his arms back and the dragons land like trained hawks, one coming to crouch on each of his forearms. The crackling electric dragons sizzle hungrily as they bite at the air, eyes on their target: me.

"Norman! What are you doing?" I demand. He doesn't flinch.

I look to Bradie. He sees the danger too. Normand's lost it.

"Caitlin!" Bradie screams. He somersaults off the podium and runs toward me.

"Stay back!" I shout at him, "Everybody, get away from me!"

The protectors closest to me edge away in a panic. Normand winds up his right arm, and throws a lightning dragon directly at me. It travels at the speed of light, but for me it's as if everything slows down. I see with relief that Trenton is grabbing his near-naked brother, jerking him off his feet and holding him tight with one arm around his neck, the other about his lean waist as he struggles futilely, calling my name. Sandie buries her head into Liam's chest, and he too turns away, neither of them able to watch. Crystal's eyes widen in shock, her head shaking in disbelief, her scream of "No!" lost to my ears.

And then the lightning hits.

CHAPTER 21

I wait for the pain. I expect it to be unendurable, an instant of ultimate suffering as my central nervous system completely overloads and my blood boils within my veins. I hear Sandie scream. I see Bradie elbow his brother in the face and slip free, running toward me. But I don't feel pain. In fact, I'd say it kind of tickles.

I look at my arms and the hairs on them are gently rising. The screaming has stopped. People stare in wonder. Bradie approaches slowly, a goofy grin on his face.

"Your hair," he says. "It's sticking right up."

Normand is still extending his arm toward me, channeling energy into my form, but it's not lightning. Whatever it is, it's much lighter. His song continues, but subdued now, fallen to the background, but I can sense it building. Bradie is close enough to touch.

"Are you okay?" Bradie asks me.

"I...I am," I reply. I'm surrounded by a glow. I feel like a superhero.

He's so mesmerized, he forgets to hide his scarred hand. He lifts it toward me until he catches sight of the mottled tissue winding up his forearm to just below the elbow. He looks ready to pull it back.

"Stay," I say.

He hesitates, and then his shoulders soften.

"Okay," he says.

I hold my fingers a breath away from his scarred hand. He gently presses the pitted flesh of his fingertips against mine, and Normand's song hits a crescendo. The glow around me spreads to Bradie, dancing up his arm. Steam rises off of him as the sweat covering his muscled form evaporates. He laughs, entwining his fingers in mine.

He kisses me in the most wonderful way: touching his free hand to my cheek, a gentle spark exchanging between his skin and mine, our lips approaching, and before they even make contact, the tingly electric current flows back and forth between our open mouths, and when our lips do meet, that sensation travels up and down my spine, spending just a few extra moments in the center of my hips. Our bodies press into each other, and seem to melt together.

I don't know for how long that goes on. The whole world fades away, and all I want to do is swallow him and be swallowed by him as the energy swirls not only around us, but within as well. There's an instant where it's all too much and I just need to hold him and be held by him, and he gives me that, my head tucked into his shoulder, him stroking my hair as we grudgingly come up for air.

He whispers into my ear, "Should we share this with the rest of them?"

The selfish part of me wants to say *no*, but instead I nod, and still holding his scarred hand I withdraw, feeling a million minute connections coming undone. Bradie holds his hand out to his brother, who takes it, curiosity clear on his face. The glow spreads from us into him, and Trenton's smile widens. He offers his hand to Crystal, who joins our effervescent ranks. I hold my free hand out to Sandie, who takes it, still holding Liam, and his hair slowly rises as the energy enters his form.

The current Normand is firing into me spreads as more people join our circuit, some taking hands, others pressing palms to neighbor's shoulder or back or chest or hip. Normand's song rises and descends, and soon we are all linked, all aglow, mist rising from us, and we look up to him as if he were Supergenic himself.

He lifts his free hand, which still holds a second energy dragon. It wiggles its bottom excitedly, ready to launch. He fires it upwards. It takes on the shape of an electrified bird, soaring in a circle that leaves behind a blazing trail of light. There are gasps of awe and murmurs rippling through the crowd, "It's a hawk!" some say. "No, it's a phoenix!"

I shake my head. It's a shadowren, winged rodent of the Yellow Zone. An odd choice.

Normand squeezes his fingers tight, extinguishing the light that fills us. We all gasp collectively as the energy pulsing through our forms is cut off. The stadium goes immediately and completely dark. For the first time in my entire life there's not a single bolt of lightning in the clouds above, and the electrode in our midst doesn't even hum. Our shocked silence matches the darkness, and if not for Bradie's hand in my own I would think this is what death feels like.

It lasts for a full 10 seconds. I know because I count them, and then as if someone's flicked a switch the lightning rears to life in the clouds once more, firing into the electrode, and the stadium flares with the lasers it emits and the synthesized music blasts once more from the speakers.

Everyone cheers and dances more frenetically than before, jumping up and down and pounding the air with their fists. Normand is gone from above us, his floating podium hidden away.

"Did you like it?" a familiar voice asks.

We turn and Normand is standing there, covered in the discs that enabled him to convert and manipulate the energy.

"Wow," Bradie says. "That was *awesome!*"

Normand stares off over my right shoulder, but I can tell by the smile twitching at his lips that he's pleased.

"What are your thoughts on the matter, Caitlin?" he asks.

"I don't think anyone will get to experience anything as magnificent as that ever again," I reply.

He looks ready to say something but before he can, Trenton is clapping him on the back.

"That was epic!" he says.

Crystal pushes Trenton aside, takes Normand's cheeks in her hands and kisses him on the lips. I expect him to freak out and deliver a diatribe about how the mouth is the most bacteria-filled part of the body, but instead he blushes deeply and, if I'm not mistaken, he would not have been opposed to the moment lasting a bit longer.

"You are definitely coming back next year," Crystal says. A shadow crosses Normand's face.

"Well," he says. "That is 365 days away. For the moment, I should rejoin the other technicians."

"No way," Trenton interjects. "You're going to party."

He shoves a frothy strawberry drink into Normand's hand. He sips it tentatively, and keeps eyeing Crystal's figure. She thrusts her breasts out ever so casually.

Bradie laughs. "Caitlin, I think you're jealous."

"What? No," I insist. "Crystal who?"

He laughs more. "It's okay. It's pretty obvious the guy's at least a little in love with you. And I gotta give him props. He definitely showed me up. I can't compete with that."

It takes me a moment to process. Normand's not in love with me, is he? And what does Bradie mean he can't compete? Is there a competition? Am I the prize? I should be horrified. I'm not some object. Yet I smile, just a little.

"Oh geez, there goes the girl's ego," Bradie rolls his eyes.

"Hush," I say, in a way that actually means, "go on." "Normand's not like that. He's different."

"Caitlin, he's a guy. Trust me. He's like that."

I watch Normand shuffle awkwardly as Crystal dances suggestively around him.

"I should go rescue him," I say, taking a step in his direction.

Bradie grabs me by the arm and holds me back.

"Dude does not need to be rescued," he says.

"But..." I try to argue.

"Let him have this night," Bradie says. "And we can have ours."

He kisses me, and when he does, I feel the electricity all over again.

CHAPTER 22

Morning comes far too soon. Although the dark clouds roil above, we can tell it's day because all around us time pieces start beeping. The protectors look at their alarms. The music and lasers cut out and the electrode above returns to absorbing energy instead of spitting it back out. There are moans of disappointment, but the protectors dutifully head back to their hovercrafts.

Normand gives Crystal a big hug. She kisses him on the lips. I wave and watch him leave with the other techies.

"He's a character, that one," Bradie says.

"He is," I agree, glad that Bradie didn't call him a weirdo or a donk. Only I'm allowed to do that.

It takes us a while to find our hovercraft amidst all the others. Once onboard, Crystal drives us back toward our borough. Liam and Sandie doze in each other's arms. Liam has his tie tied around his forehead. Bradie and I cuddle. He's only dressed in his underwear and waves of heat are coming off of him. Trenton is up front, monitoring the DRADIS and chattering with Crystal. We see the sun rising beyond the towers of Jupitar City, where there is no perpetual storm cloud full of thunder and lightning.

So this is what happiness feels like, I muse. I know it can't last, and it scares me as I wonder to what lengths I'll go to get it back.

The closer we get to the security fence, the more relevant that question becomes. I'm remembering the fight with my mom. I have no idea how I'm going to fix things with her. The euphoria of the evening is wearing off, and all I want is to sleep.

We skim along parallel to the fence, taking us away from the center of our borough. It doesn't take me long to realize where we're headed. I see the giant shiny white Cube that is the Protectorate, gleaming in the rising sun. There are cleaners dangling from ropes attached to the roof, wiping it down with squeegees.

The protectors at the guard tower nod as a set of gates slides open, and a dozen hovercraft whizz through. Crystal guides us into an underground parking garage. It smells of fuel fumes, the lights above crackle sporadically, and in a corner are several rusting jeeps and hovercrafts waiting to be junked.

It hits me all of a sudden. *I'm home.*

"Come on, grubs," Crystal says. "We need to get you washed and into uniform."

We stumble out of the vehicle and along the concrete floor, bumping into each other, giggling childishly. There's a slight throbbing in my temples, and a pleasant tingling everywhere else. Crystal directs the four of us to stand in front of a concrete wall in single file.

"Face me," Crystal says. "Yup, that'll work." She picks up a fire hose. It's the only warning I get before a freezing blast of water hits me.

I screech. I'm not the only one. Bradie, Liam and Sandie are all cursing around me as Trenton unleashes a second stream of brutally frigid water. They increase the flow, hitting us so hard we're knocked off our feet. My hip slams into the concrete floor. I try to crawl away, but wherever I go the water follows. I get brief relief as Crystal turns her hose on Sandie, but it doesn't last long. I'm coughing up water, my throat is raw and my skin burns. Who knew water could hurt so much?

There are hoots and hollers as more hovercraft return.

"Grubs! Grubs! Grubs!" the out-of-uniform protectors chant.

Trenton and Crystal thankfully cut the flow of water. We cough and sputter, wiping the water from our eyes. Our hands and knees are muddy with dirt.

"On your feet, grubs!" Trenton yells.

We force ourselves to obey. Our skin is red and painfully numb as we shiver uncontrollably.

"Clean yourself up, grubs," Crystal yells, and I'm hit with something hard and round. At first I think it's a stone, but I see the oval object that's landed in front of me. Soap. They make us all strip naked, peeling off our underclothes, and we pass the single bar of soap around. I dip my hands into the puddles of murky water at our feet, rinsing away the lipstick and eyeshadow and mascara. My fingers are so cold and numb, the soap keeps slipping through them.

"Good enough," Trenton shouts, and we're hit with another spray that must be taking off layers of skin along with the soapy film.

The water cuts out. We drip, teeth chattering. Crystal gathers up our old school clothes and dumps them in a pile. She pours fuel on them, then drops a burning match. They go up in flames.

"Say goodbye to your old lives, grubs, and hello to the new," she smiles.

Trenton tosses towels at us and I barely grab mine before it falls into a puddle. The water's turned my skin redder than hot coals and the sandpapery texture of the towel scratches me all over.

The protectors from the party are disappearing into several elevators, being whisked up and away.

"Get dressed," Trenton says, and he drops four foil clothing packs in front of us. They splatter on the wet concrete. "Come find us. You've got 10 minutes."

They enter the last elevator.

"Find you where?" Bradie asks.

Trenton and Crystal give us the finger as the doors close. As soon as they do, signs light up above each elevator with the words, "Out of Service."

"Effing eff," Bradie swears.

Sandie is yanking and pulling on her foil pack.

"How the deuce do you get these things open?"

She tries with her teeth, but no go. Bradie races over to one of the junked vehicles and slices his open on a piece of sharp metal.

I'm expecting the package to contain disposable track uniforms similar to what we use on Testing Day. Instead he pulls out a fun fur animal hat in tiger print, with matching trunks.

"Seriously?" Liam asks as he yanks out a similar leopard-inspired outfit. Sandy's is zebra striped, and comes with a matching bra. Mine is snake skin.

"Sssssexy," Bradie winks.

The get-ups are worn and patchy. A couple have an ear missing. They smell funky, even amidst the diesel fumes. As we dress, I try not to think where they came from or how many cadets have been forced to wear them.

"Hustle!" Liam orders and we hurry over to the stairs as quickly as we can, careful not to slip on the slick floor in our bare feet.

We open the stairwell door and gaze up and up and up.

"We don't even know where we're supposed to go," Sandie points out.

I look at how we're dressed. "Yes, we do."

We're gasping and drenched in sweat when we reach the desk where our novice gear was dispensed months ago. The overseer lowers her glasses to look at us reprovingly. She slams four uniforms onto the counter.

"Have you seen a pair of protectors by the name of…" I start to ask.

"No," she snaps, and resumes reading a book.

"Guys, there they are!" Sandie points.

We see them dozens of floor below, waving up at us.

"Really?" Bradie demands.

We grab the uniforms and run.

Crystal and Trenton are sitting on a white polymer bench and sipping tea as we stumble into the glass hallway where they're waiting. They're laughing at some sort of video on an e-pad. From the audio I'm guessing it's us being hosed down.

"You're out of uniform," Trenton snaps at us.

We strip and change quickly. Our novice uniforms are baby blue and made of some sort of webbed material that fits perfectly. Our furry costumes make a sad carcass on the floor.

"Line up," Crystal orders.

We comply, backs to the wall, wondering what fresh torture awaits us.

"So," Trenton asks. "Who's first?"

We look to each other, none of us having a clue what he's setting us up for. Liam steps forward.

"I'll go first," he says.

"Enjoy," Trenton says as a door disengages from the wall and hisses open on its hydraulic hinges.

A medic in purple waits there and gestures for Liam to come in.

"I'm Sewzanne," she says. "Welcome, welcome. Your first Calibration. How exciting!"

There's a syringe on the emblem on her chest. Beyond her is a lie-back chair that reminds me of Testing Day.

"Ah yes," she says, noting our inquisitive looks. "The Chair."

It's surrounded by data monitors, an IV attached to a canister encased in coolant, and there's a circuitry enmeshed helmet on a retractable chord dangling above it. Bradie's eyes grow wide and he immediately presses his back against the glass wall.

"Is everything all right?" the medic asks him.

"Everything's fine," Trenton replies, then shouting at his brother, "Isn't that right, grub?"

Bradie turns his attention to Trenton. Trenton is nodding at his brother, eyes and voice full of meaning. Bradie steadies himself with an effort.

"Yes," he forces himself to say.

"Yes, *sir*!" Trenton corrects.

"YES, SIR!" Bradie echoes forcefully. Beads of sweat are forming on his forehead.

"All righty," the medic smiles comfortingly. "Officers, it's time for you to join your squadron for group Calibration preps. Please take the props with you."

Crystal dutifully gathers up the furry outfits.

"You go ahead," Trenton says to Crystal. "I'll catch up."

She raises an inquisitive eyebrow, then glances briefly at Bradie, who is staring hard at the floor.

I expect Trenton to say something to his brother. Instead he talks to me.

"Cadet Feral, walk with me."

Bradie's eyes beg me not to go.

"I'll be right back," I say.

"Okay," Bradie says meekly.

I follow Trenton around the corner. He looks over his shoulder, as if to make sure no one is listening.

"I need you to keep an eye on Bradie," he says.

"Sure," I say. "Why? What's up with him?"

"Nothing," he says defensively.

A pair of protectors walk by. He nods at them. They smirk, assuming he's got some new special initiation in mind for the grub.

"Nothing," he repeats. "Just…help him keep calm."

Things had been going so well, I'd almost forgotten. Bradie's broken.

"It would help if you told me what was going on," I say.

"I'm sure he'll be fine," Trenton says. "But I've been looking out for that kid for a long time; old habits and all that."

"What exactly am I looking for him to do?" I ask.

"I don't know," Trenton says with growing exasperation, as if I'm asking him to describe the color blue. "Weird stuff. Just use your judgment."

I'm neither convinced nor comforted and it must show on my face because he gets more brusque.

"Well, grub, what are you standing around for? Back in line!"

He's worried. I can tell by the lack of rigor in his dismissal.

I salute, not entirely feeling it myself.

"Yes, sir," I say half-heartedly. He doesn't call me on it. He just waves me away, and I join the others around the corner, sitting next to Bradie.

"What was that about?" Sandie asks.

Bradie's foot is tapping up and down next to mine, making his whole leg shake. I put my hand on his knee and he stops.

"Nothing," I say. "Just Trenton being a dick. Bradie, you okay?"

He looks at me, forcing a smile. "Yeah, fine. You?"

His whole face has gone pale.

"Is anyone else hot?" he asks.

Sandie shakes her head.

"So that was some party last night," I say, trying to change the topic. "I still can't believe what an amazing acrobat you are. You were *epic*."

I figure it can't hurt to stroke his ego a bit.

"Did anybody else notice how none of the older protectors were there last night?" he asks. "Don't you think that's weird?" His other leg is shaking now.

He starts scratching at the scars on his hand. He's leaving behind long red marks. His breathing speeds up. Sandie's watching him closely now.

"I guess they're too old for it now," Sandie suggests. "Or maybe they have their own party. You know, with fancy stemware and the women wear slinky dresses and the men talk in funny deep voices, like in the screenings."

Bradie's wringing his hands.

"Could be," he says doubtfully.

"Maybe we should go for a quick walk," I suggest.

Bradie shakes his head, standing up and starting to pace.

"It just doesn't make sense. Why even let us have a party like that?"

"To let off some steam?" I suggest.

He waves his finger at me. "This is the Protectorate, and we just go out into the middle of the Yellow Zone to play music, and sing, and dance, and turn an energy syphon into a light show for acrobats on poles, as if we were still kids who might one day be special enough to Manifest? Am I the only one who thinks that's off?"

He keeps looking at the door the medic disappeared behind.

"I guess they want us to get it out of our systems," I suggest.

"Does that get it out of our systems? Or does it just make us want it even more?" he presses. "What's their end game?"

I've been too tired to really think about it, but he's right. That party last night, the brightest best moment of my entire life, so alien to anything else I've experienced, what was it really all about?

The door to the chamber hisses compressed air and slides open. Bradie flinches and his cheek starts twitching uncontrollably. Liam comes out looking oddly relaxed and refreshed. I think that Liam's lethargic state will help put Bradie's mind at ease, reassuring him that nothing horrible is going on in there. But he's not paying any attention to Liam. He's staring at the Chair beyond, with its helmet and sensor pads and needles hooked up to tubes.

"I can't go in there," Bradie whispers, just loud enough for me and Sandie to hear. His chest starts heaving. His freakout is different than my mom's, but I know what I'm seeing, and it isn't good.

The medic in purple looks at us.

"Who's next?" she asks.

"I'll go," Sandie replies quickly, rushing forward, using her body to block the medic's view of Brady.

"Is this going to hurt?" Sandie asks.

"Quite the opposite," Sewzanne assures her.

Sandie nods, giving us a worried look over her shoulder as the door slides closed behind her. Liam cocks his head, smiling a goofy smile, contemplating Brady.

"What's up with him?" Liam asks.

"I'm not sure," I say.

"Hey, it's okay buddy," Liam says, coming over and rubbing Bradie's back. "Just relax. It's totally chill in there."

"That Chair," Bradie says, "It's..."

Just like at Testing Day, I think.

"It's just a chair," I assure him.

Bradie's throat starts to constrict.

"I can't breathe," he gasps. His scarred hand clenches into the shape of a claw.

Liam remains utterly calm. "Maybe we should get the medic out here. She was cool."

He gets up, headed for the door that Sandie just disappeared behind.

"No!" Bradie rasps. "You can't. They can't know about this or they'll kick me out."

"Okay, man," Liam says, still super cool, holding his hands up in surrender.

Bradie's face is turning red. His knuckles are white.

"I don't know if I can do this," Bradie says.

I do the only thing I can think of. I sing to him.

"...blue moon..." It's an oldie. My mom and dad used to sing it to each other. I can't quite remember all the words, but I do my best. Bradie wraps his arms around me, holding onto me like a lifeline.

"Sing with me," I say.

When I repeat the refrain, he struggles to join in. After a few lines, he starts to get it. His grip on me slackens. I hold his cheek.

"You got this," I say.

Brady nods, wiping tears from his eyes.

"Yeah," he says. "I'm good."

When the door hisses open, Bradie and I are sitting next to each other.

"Everything all right?" the medic asks, as she guides Sandie out. Sandie has the same dreamy look on her face as Liam.

"Fine," I say, giving Bradie a slight push on his back, prompting him to get up.

"Yeah," he agrees, staring at the Chair beyond the open door.

"Nothing to be afraid of," the medic says.

"Sure," he says.

I hear him quietly singing "...blue moon..." as the door steals him from view.

CHAPTER 23

As I wait with Liam and Sandie, my stomach clenches in a way that I've only ever felt for Nate before, when he's late coming home from extracurriculars, or just before he's about to go on stage for a recital. To have this feeling for Bradie is foreign and new.

Twenty minutes later the door slides open and Bradie comes out. His shoulders and eyelids sag. His cheek keeps twitching. He looks nothing like Liam and Sandie when they emerged. They're still serene. Bradie's so pale it's like he's been smeared with white chalk.

"Are you okay?" I ask.

"Tired," he answers.

The medic pats him on the shoulder. "You did well. It will get easier. You just need to relax and let the Chair do all the work." She looks at him in a way that reminds me of the butcher in the Protectorate kitchen trying to figure out if he can salvage a crummy cut of meat. "Okay," she looks at me, motioning with her hand. "Last one."

I follow her in, looking over my shoulder one last time, expecting Bradie to give me a thumbs up like I did for him. Instead, he's staring blindly at something only he can see on the plain white wall. The door slides shut.

"Is he okay?" I ask the medic.

"Perfectly normal," Sewzanne replies. "About 20 percent of subjects have that kind of reaction. It's completely temporary. Come, come. Your turn."

She directs me to the Chair. I slide onto its smooth surface. Above my head dangles the helmet with wires plugged into it.

"So is this some sort of physical?" I ask.

"Not quite," she replies, attaching various pads to my body. She rolls up one of my sleeves. "Make a fist."

She taps my forearm and then slides a needle into me. It's attached to a clear tube that runs into a canister. She tapes the needle into place, then flicks a switch. The vat vibrates, pumping a glowing orange liquid into my arm.

She taps on her tablet and a holographic image pops up, with a slew of body readings, labelled heart rate, cerebral output, and pulmonary function.

"Electrolytes are low, but that's to be expected. I'd say someone had a good night," she winks.

"I haven't gotten any sleep actually," I say as I watch the bright orange liquid being fed into me. "Maybe we should do this after I'm better rested."

"On the contrary, cadet. You are both physiologically and neurologically primed."

"For what?" I ask.

"For Calibration. Watch your head," she says, and the helmet starts lowering toward me.

She helps me get it on, strapping it in place under my chin. I can't see a thing.

I hear Sewzanne's polished lacquered nails pecking away at her pad and images start flashing across the inside of the visor. Some are flat and colorful. Others are 3-D, black and white geometric designs, that bulge in and out. I try to speak but a strange lightness is filling me up. Dreamy, pulsating music fills my ears.

And then...and then the images and sounds are gone and the helmet is lifting off of my head.

"Well done, cadet," the medic says.

"But, I didn't do anything," I say.

"Exactly!" she says.

"Nothing happened," I insist, thinking that I've somehow failed. "That was like two minutes."

"Would you believe that it was an hour?" she asks.

I gape. "For real?"

"It's one of the longest first sessions I've ever done. Even longer than Trenton's! But don't tell him I said so," she winks. "You're lucky. Not everyone takes to the process this quickly or deeply."

I struggle to process this.

"I'm good at this?" I say more to myself than her.

"You're a natural," she smiles. "You must have a good imagination."

The part of me that drove Mrs. Cranberry crazy with questions immediately blurts out, "A natural at what?"

She's draining the excess Mango Tango from the rubber tube into a disposal canister.

"We're Calibrating your brain for learning," she says. "The better you do in here, the better you're going to do out there. And you did *very* well in here."

"But...I don't remember any of it," I say.

"Not consciously," she agrees. "But it's there. Trust me. You're going to find that certain physical and mental skills are going to start coming *very* naturally to you, much more so than many of your fellow cadets. And as the sessions progress, so will you. The trick is to stay receptive. We can only put in what you are open to. In fact, if you keep going like this, you'll soon be on the fast track for group Calibration."

I open my mouth to ask more, an endless stream of questions ready to pour out, but she presses a finger to my lips.

"You feel very good right now, don't you?" she asks.

I nod.

"Good. Then go with that, and let's just see what happens."

"Okay," I mumble from behind her finger.

"Good luck, cadet," she says. "I'm going to be keeping my eye on you."

Over the next week, we do more and more Calibration sessions and the medic was right: I do notice a marked acceleration in my protector training.

I'm in the combat center with the others. The floor is covered in padded mats. We're running through physical drills. When we spar, my body moves as if I were born to this, and I easily turn Bradie's weight against him, tossing him to the floor and wrenching his arm behind his back.

"Auntie! Auntie!" he cries.

The next day in the weapons range, Trenton shows us how to load a sidearm, and as I slide the clip into place it instantly feels like second nature. I aim it at a paper outline of a man hanging 20 measures away. I vividly recall my inability to shoot a giant mutated hound only five paces away. Liam, Sandie, and Bradie are all watching. I should be nervous. And yet as soon as I lift the gun, all that falls away. It's like it's a part of me. I squeeze the trigger, and the bullet hits the target right through the heart.

"Beginner's luck," Trenton snorts.

I fire again. The bullet pierces the target's forehead.

"Huh," he grunts, not entirely pleased by my success.

A surge of confidence washes through me. I give Trenton a wink, aim, pull the trigger three times, and a trio of slugs rips through the outline's baby maker. Trenton's eyebrows go up. His jaw goes down.

"Wowzer," Liam says, clapping me on the back.

Trenton gives him a dirty look.

"Okay then," he says. "Moving on."

It's not just these physical changes either. All the questions in my mind that used to buzz around like a hive of agitated bees are quieting down. I feel strangely at peace. Why was I always throwing up resistance when it's so much easier to go with the flow?

At the end of the week, Bradie, Liam, and Sandie all go home for Recuperation Day. I could go visit Nate and try to smooth things over with my mom. The thought skitters along the surface of my mind, and then sinks.

Next week, I assure myself.

Instead, Normand and I sneak into the Yellow Zone to hang out in the Lair. It's our first opportunity to do so since I moved into the Cube. As we descend the concrete steps and clap on the twinkling strands of lights that illuminate the displays of comic books, I wait for the usual rush of excitement at being here.

Huh, I think to myself. *That's odd.*

Instead of experiencing a thrill, I'm numb inside. Coming here used to feel like magic, but now it's as if there's a haze over the whole store. It's a disconnect that starts to extend to my friendship with Normand.

Over the next several months little things start to grate on me; the creak of Normand's brace, the constant disinfecting of his hands, the way he constantly checks his watch. And then there's his nonsensical "codes of conduct." Some stuff in the Lair I can touch, some stuff I can't. I intentionally move the scarf with the red S in a diamond just to watch him freak out.

I start cutting our visits to the Lair shorter and shorter, spacing them out longer and longer, and more and more I cancel at the last minute. I passive-aggressively wait for Normand to realize that I'm phasing him out. He doesn't get it.

Finally, the day comes when we finish creating the last issue of *Tigara*. In it she hangs up her costume. Her days of fighting the forces of evil in Bright Lights Big City are over. I stare at it.

"Normand," I say. "We can't come back here anymore."

"Yes," he says, a sad resignation in his voice, "I am aware."

I expected him to argue. He does not. I guess he did see this coming.

"You're going to have to destroy your e-pad and erase the GRAMS that you've created," I say. "Otherwise, I have to turn us both in."

I brace myself, expecting him to argue. To beg. To rationalize. He does not.

"We will require it one last time," he says. "To get back to the fence undetected."

"Agreed," I say.

His brace creaks as he shifts his weight and puts his satchel over his shoulder.

I take one last look, my gaze scanning over the shelves of comic books, at the varied costumes on the wall, the posters, games, screening discs, and busts of imaginary superheroes with impossible ideals. There's a faint wave of nostalgia tinged with sadness, and then it's done.

By unspoken agreement, Normand and I ignore each other after that, and our time together in the Lair starts to feel like it never happened. Meanwhile, my Calibration sessions grow longer and longer.

"Any vivid dreams at night?" Sewznanne asks.

"Yes," I admit.

"Good," she says. "Your subconscious is working things out. There's a lot to process. You're setting records with the length of your Calibrations."

"Longer than Trenton's?" I ask.

"I'm not saying yes," she chides, and then with a wink, "but I'm not saying no."

I swell with pride as the Mango Tango fills the rubber tube running into my arm. Everything is coming together—almost. While my sessions are getting longer, Bradie's have barely changed at all. Later that day, I'm eating with him, Liam, and Sandie in the cafeteria. Bradie's griping about a migraine after his Calibration today.

"You just have to relax," I tell him. "It's easy."

He's pushing around a protein-based chocolate pudding with his spoon. Liam and Sandie tense at my words, though I'm not sure why.

"You don't know what it's like," he says. "It's as if they're trying to hammer a square peg into a circular hole *in my head*."

He looks terrible, like he's trying to curl in on himself.

"You must be doing something wrong," I say. He gives me cut eye. I ignore it. He's annoying me more and more of late and I barely catch myself from asking him to please stop being such a whiner.

"Hey," I say. "The new recruits."

We watch as more than a hundred kids our age file in, all in the same uniforms as us. They've completed their final placements and are the last group in our age level to make the cut for cadets. I recognize a bunch of them from novice training, but most of them come from other cohorts. I wonder which ones will make it to protector and which will wash out.

"We should go say hi," I say.

Bradie eyes me in a way that he's been doing of late. Part suspicion. Part glare.

"That's rather sociable of you," he says.

"It is, isn't it?" I agree.

"That machine is changing you," he says.

"Yes," I say. "For the better."

"Says you," he counters.

"Says my test scores. You're just jealous because you can't keep up."

Liam and Sandie freeze, their pudding-filled spoons hovering in the air. My temples are throbbing and my cheeks are burning. I've gone too far and I know it.

"I'm sorry," I say. "I didn't mean..."

"Yeah," he says. "You did."

I wait for him to remind me that he saved my life once, but he doesn't.

"Excuse me," he says. "I should probably go hang with someone my own speed."

I watch him stalk out, wondering if I should go after him. Liam and Sandie are *very* focused on their pudding now. The new cadets eye Bradie and I expect him to crack some jokes as he cozies up to them. But that Bradie seems to have checked out some time ago. Instead he exits through a set of sliding glass doors, not looking back.

The Chair is changing him too, and definitely not for the better.

"He's struggling," Sandie says. With his difficulties in Calibration, he's barely keeping up with training. He's getting by on his natural athleticism—for now.

Pull it together, Bradie, I think. But despite my impatience, I feel a flicker of guilt. First Normand, now him. *You can't let them hold you back,* a part of me insists. It's a foreign and uncomfortable thought, so I focus on the new recruits.

"We should introduce ourselves," I say. I don't wait for Liam or Sandie to agree, I just pick up my tray and walk over to the newbies. As I sit down and shake hands, I notice Bradie on the other side of the glass wall enclosing the cafeteria. He's talking with Normand.

Bradie says something and they both laugh, Bradie in his gregarious way, like the Bradie I first met on the train, while Normand's shoulders bob up and down, no doubt wheezing the way he does when he finds something amusing.

When did they become so tight? I wonder.

I force myself to ignore them as the cadets bombard me with questions.

"What's training like?"

"Who's the toughest instructor?"

"Are we allowed to date other cadets?"

I answer their questions in order.

"Training is awesome. You're going to be challenged like you won't believe. Trenton is the worst. And can you date another cadet? I am, but no PDAs," I wink. They lean closer. Their eyes are like shining spotlights.

So *this* is what it feels like to be Lilianne.

Within the first few weeks, a third of the new recruits is culled. A lot of our training is all together, but sometimes they will still take Sandie, Liam, Bradie and me apart from the rest. We're held up as examples. That gets some of the other kids sucking up to us. Others can't hide their jealousy, showing it with petty remarks or going out of their way to get in our space. I make a point of sparring with each of them to reinforce that I'm better than them—and I am.

Not that any of this is easy. Each day is more grueling than the one before. They are also the most rewarding of my life. I climb through, over and under obstacle courses with electrified wires, icy waters, thick mud, and brick walls. I engage in hand-to-hand combat. I learn survival skills, electronics repair, and how to read body language. Considering my mother's shifting moods, I could likely teach the latter. My body's a web of bruises, aches and pains.

I grow stronger, faster, and deadlier. I no longer think about Tigara. I don't need childish fantasies. I've got me. During Calibration, my brainwaves are going deeper and deeper, with impressive real world results. I'm fast tracking like crazy.

The next hurdle to pass is my cadet field trial.

When the time for it comes, I'm grabbed without warning from a sound sleep in my bunk. A bag is pulled tightly around my head and my wrists tied behind my back. I'm dragged in my skivvies down flight after flight of stairs, my ankles smacking each downward step. My heart is a train flying off its track.

You're ready for this, Cadet Feral, I assure myself.

I better be. This is the hardest challenge ever assigned to a cadet before he/she/ze can graduate. My abductors say nothing as they toss me into some sort of metal container that clangs as I land. They put noise dampening headphones over my ears, filling my world with the grating sound of rusty nails scraping on stone. The floor starts to vibrate and lift, which is when I realize I'm in the back of a hovercraft.

We bob along, for an hour? Two? Time loses meaning. When we finally stop I'm shoved out of the still-moving vehicle and left there. I feel a sharp stone and use it to cut my bonds. I yank the headphones and blindfold off, and almost wish I hadn't. I cough on exhaust as I watch the hovercraft speed away. Lightning bursts overhead, followed by the rumble of thunder. Rubble surrounds me. I'm alone in the middle of the Yellow Zone with no food, water or compass. There's a basic survival kit on the broken sidewalk next to me, a cadet uniform, and a note in Trenton's handwriting.

Get the flag. Bring it back. Good luck beating my record. 73:41:15.

Seventy-three hours, forty-one minutes, fifteen seconds.

He's goading me, hoping to make me reckless in an attempt to beat him.

Forget about him, I tell myself, and I do. Ish. I quickly set the countdown on the timepiece around my wrist with the number of Trenton's score. I look around, and my stomach contracts. I see the red flag at the tip of a towering building that looks ready to topple over if I so much as breathe on it. I will have to scale it, capture the flapping crimson fabric, and then find my way back to the Cube. I dress, grab the survival kit, and start running toward the hollowed-out tower.

Four hours later, I'm scraped, bruised, and bloody, but I've got the flag in hand and I'm back on the ground.

For the next three days, I navigate the streets like a stealthy urban cat. Tigara has been buried deep in my mind but she starts creeping upwards. I feed off birds I capture, and seeds that blow in from the farmlands. I test for radiological dangers. Twice, I take shelter from deadly windstorms that last an hour or two. By day three, the borough is in sight. My nose is burnt and peeling. My lips are cracked and the inside of my mouth is like a desiccated prune. Dirt has carved out a home in every exposed pore.

I ignore the discomfort. I stride along a crumbling street with scraggly white weeds and mushrooms poking through. I look at the timekeeper on my wrist. Just under two hours left. Reaching the Cube is the only thing on my mind when something catches my eye. I stop, not sure what it is at first, but I've learned to pay attention. If something seems out of place, it probably is. It's not just my sight and hearing that have become sharper; it's as if my whole body vibrates like a sensor pad. I stare at a mound of rubble that is like any other mound of rubble in this wasteland, and yet it's not. It's familiar. I feel a warmth in my belly. I smile childishly. It's the Lair.

Only now do I realize just how successfully I'd forgotten about it. Between severing my friendship with Normand and focusing on my training, there was no reason to think about it anymore. It briefly makes me wonder what exactly the Mango Tango is doing to my brain. The whole point is to rewire it, to make it better, but what does that actually mean? The thought is like a tiny pebble skittering into a deep dark lake, instantly lost, with barely a ripple.

I stare at the mound of concrete hiding the Lair. It's been months since I've been inside.

Well, now's certainly not the time, a part of me snorts, egging me to pick up the pace. Yet I don't. I check the counter on my wrist, the numbers ticking down second by second. My eyes move back to the entrance to the Lair.

You could go in, another part of me says. She sounds like the old me, lonely and needy, yet whimsical and full of dreams. I feel like I haven't talked to her in a very long time.

No! the cadet in me snaps, but I ignore her. I'm not sure why, but being out here all alone has rubbed me raw in more ways than one. I clutch the red flag in my fingers.

The sensible thing would be to get going, to truly forget about this place forever, and yet I feel a tug, as if there's unfinished business. The cadet considers this and seems to have a change of heart. *All right*, she says. *Go take a look.*

I've barely had the thought and I'm already yanking on a rusted steel bar. It releases a hiss of air and the door to the Lair swings open. I pull it shut behind me. I'm down the stairs and inside the store within seconds. I clap and strands of lights flutter to life, twinkling like floating stars. There's a smell of paper and dust, and the images of larger than life heroes and heroines gaze at me from the posters on the wall. I wait to feel a sense of wonder like when I'd come here with Normand. Instead I feel like something's been scooped out of my chest and concrete's been poured in its place.

I take in the ceiling-high displays of comic books, the costumes on the wall, the stack of antiquated screening discs.

Burn it, the cadet in me whispers.

I feel a packet of matches in my hand. *When did I take them out of my survival kit?*

Do it, the cadet urges. *Burn the past. Burn it all.*

I strike one of my few remaining matches and let the flaming stick fall onto the stained carpet. The moisture controllers have kept the place so dry that the fibers catch alight immediately. Yellow licks of flame rise up. It's beautiful, and I feel a sense of ease at the thought of that rising flame burning away all the ridiculousness of my former life.

Freedom, the cadet sighs. I used to think freedom meant an escape from rules. My definition has changed.

The counter on my wrist beeps unexpectedly and I snap out of my reverie. I look at the ticking clock. I only have 20 minutes to make it back to the Protectorate to beat Trenton's record.

I see the tiny fire at my feet and curse in horror.

"Geez-us!"

I stamp it out with my boots as quickly as I can. The smell of smoke fills my nostrils. *Normand is going to kill me!*

For just a second, that matters to me, as if I'm the old Caitlin, the one who used to come here, getting lost in this place of fantasy. I'd sworn to never come back to the Lair so why should I care if it burns? Why should I care what Normand thinks?

Because you believe that as long as it's here, you can always change your mind, you can come back, and that comforts you, I hear Sewzanne's preprogrammed voice explain, speaking in that hypnotic way of hers. *To move forward, you must burn the attachments of the past. You must burn it all.*

I gaze about at the comic books, horrified at the thought of it all going up in flames. I turn and run, staggering up the stairs. I stumble outside and yank the door shut behind me. My heart is hammering, louder somehow than the thunder above. I turn the rusted metal rod to seal the door shut, and then I sprint toward the Cube without looking back.

With five minutes to spare, I drop a tattered red flag in front of Trenton's face as he grunts his way through a set of shirtless push-ups in one of the training areas in the Cube. It's just the two of us. The alarm on my counter starts chirping loudly, echoing in the cavernous space. I made it, with seconds to spare.

I smirk. I win.

"Congratulations," he says. "If you'd been an hour sooner, you'd have beaten my record."

My eyes widen but I keep my mouth from dropping. He lied on the note he left me, leading me to think I had an hour more than I did. If I hadn't stopped at the Lair…

He moves into side plank. I wait for him to revel in his victory. He doesn't. The silence stretches on.

"You're dismissed, cadet," he adds.

"That's it?" I ask suspiciously.

He switches to the other side, showing me his sweaty back as he reaches his free hand to the ceiling.

"That's it," he replies. "You know the drill. Mission complete. Report for Calibration."

I shrug and obey.

"A word of advice," he says. I pause. I knew it wouldn't be that easy. He picks up a jump rope and takes himself through a series of skipping patterns. I force myself to smile.

And here it is.

"Be careful how good you get," he says.

"I'll keep that in mind," I reply, biting my tongue from saying what's really on my mind. He's still an officer, and I'm still just a cadet.

He chuckles, but there's no humor in his eyes. "You've still got a lot to learn, little bird, about this place, about what it takes to survive here."

"I seem to be doing fine," I reply.

"No," he corrects. "Fine would be perfect. But you're not doing fine. You're excelling. Fast. Winning. Lots."

He drops the rope and switches to air squats.

"Scared I might be better than you?" I ask.

"One day we may just get to answer that question, if I can keep you alive long enough."

"What's that supposed to mean?"

He advances to one-legged air squats.

"Caitlin, you need to start paying closer attention to the *real* rules of this game. After you shot the mutant, they put you all over the information updates. Made you sound like a regular hero. Then what happened?"

I think of the agent visiting me, warning me to watch myself, but I don't share this with Trenton. From the way he nods, I don't need to.

"Yeah," he says, "That's what I thought. First they propped you up. Then they knocked you down. Want to know why?"

He begins moving through a series of stretches.

"Yes, sir," I say sarcastically.

"Do you know what happens to an object when you heat it, then freeze it, then repeat that over and over?"

I don't answer.

"It expands and contracts, again and again. It develops fault lines. And that's how they want us. Brittle. Makes us easier to smash. Then they sweep us aside and start with the next generation. They want us to be good enough to keep the population in check, but not so strong that we would ever overthrow the bureaus—or worse."

I don't ask him what could be worse than a coup. There are some things one doesn't talk about. Like challenging the Supergenics.

"Sounds like you're afraid," I say.

"I am," he agrees. "Killing you isn't the worst thing that they can do. I learned that the hard way."

"Is that why you're clinging to your records?" I challenge.

He snorts. "Trust me. I'm holding back. You need to as well. Be good, Caitlin, not great, and maybe you'll survive."

"Thank you for the teachable moment," I say.

He hops up and starts air punching a breath from my face. I stare him down, refusing to flinch.

"One last thing," he says, making sharp exhales as he contracts his core. "I'm looking out for you because you saved my brother's life, and he seems to have a thing for girls with flat chests and no hips and whatever it is that's going on with your face. I'd do anything for that kid. But if he ever gets hurt because of you, if they ever punish him for something that you did, we'll find out just how good you really are."

His punch is about to connect with my nose. I move aside just in time, and as he overextends his reach my instinct is to grab his arm and toss him to the ground. He waits, biceps grazing my cheek, daring me to do it. I barely restrain myself.

"Noted," I say.

I brush his arm aside, turn my back on him and walk away.

He's full of crap, I scoff. At least that's what I tell myself.

CHAPTER 24

I shower, change and head for Calibration. Sewzanne hugs me warmly, like the mother I never knew I could have. I hug back. There's a comfort to sliding into the Chair and the drill that follows. I'm so used to it that I actually help her attach the pads to my body and even correct her when one gets misplaced. We gab about who's dating who in the Protectorate, along with various other bits of dish. It's a mindless relief.

After Calibration is over we remove the pads. Sewzanne's looking at me funny.

"What?" I ask.

"Nothing," she insists, her eyes misting over. "I'm just so proud of you."

I'm taken aback.

"Well, I'm glad someone is," I say.

"Trenton?" she asks.

"Trenton," I agree.

She gets a mischievous look on her face and types away on her e-pad.

"Caitlin dear, how would you like to become the youngest cadet to go on a field mission?"

My eyes widen with hope and disbelief.

"When?" I ask.

"Before Trenton can do anything to interfere," she replies.

She's gazing at me meaningfully.

"Wait," I say. "Do you mean right now? But I just got back from my field test."

"If you don't think you can handle it…"

I hop up out of the Chair.

I can't believe I'm getting this opportunity.

Wait 'til Trenton finds out.

I'm jonesing as I ride the elevator down to the subfloor where the hover vehicles are kept. The suddenness of it is hard to believe.

The elevator doors glide open and Crystal's squad is there, doing last minute vehicle and weapons checks. There are six of them, all in protector copper. I'm still in the blue of a cadet. Crystal hands me a baton and a sidearm. I try to conceal my look of surprise. I check the barrel of the gun. It's loaded.

"Don't get too excited," she says. "They're stunners. Rubber laced with a paralytic. Still pack a wallop though, so be careful where you point that thing."

"Understood," I say, holstering it to my thigh. I eye the multi-variant rifle poking up from Crystal's back.

"Don't even think about it, grub, you're still just a cadet," she says. "You'll also need this."

She hands me a helmet similar to the kind the protectors wear. I slide it over my head. I can't see through the visor. Instead of a direct view, it hums to life with a 360-degree visual of what's around and above me, in a series of six floating holographic images. We've been practicing with these. It can be dizzying and takes some getting used to. Liam threw up the first time he put one on.

I clamber aboard the hovercraft. I watch Crystal moving icons around on her tablet to sync up all our communicators. A moment later, I hear the protectors in my ear as each does a mic check. It gets to my turn and I dutifully say, "Cadet Feral, check." Half-a-dozen voices reply back one by one, "Check," "Check," "Check."

Crystal's seated next to me. I hear the whir of the engines and feel the pressure of the seat pressing into me as the hovercraft rises. Air rushes over us as we zoom up a ramp and out into the open air.

"Guard tower delta, patrol niner on approach, anything to report?" Crystal asks as we whisk toward the gate. I can't believe this is actually happening. The chain link barrier draws aside for us, and we skim out into the broken city, lightning flaring and crashing into the spherical energy syphons on their rearing pylons spread amidst the wreckage of toppled buildings.

The wireless crackles in response. "We've got some anomalous readings in sector 18-dash-G."

"Acknowledged guard tower delta. Sector 18-dash-G. Will check it out. Over," Crystal says. She switches her COMM to address me alone, "Probably just some sensor glitches, but we'll make sure the area's clear. If it's something simple we'll fix it ourselves, otherwise central will send out a tech crew to deal with it."

"Understood," I reply.

We follow a grid pattern as we skim along the streets of the broken city.

"Nothing on DRADIS," the navigating officer reports.

"Approaching sector 18-dash-G," the helmsman replies.

"Eyes sharp," the navigator says, his voice coming through the ear jacks in my helmet. "I think I've got something."

On one of my internal screens is a smaller version of the DRADIS readout. I see a trio of blue dots huddled together until a sharp buzz of feedback rages through our helmets. We all grunt in surprise and momentary pain. The DRADIS crackles in and out. The navigator gives it a couple of smacks and it pops back on. Its circling cone of light now shows zero contacts. The protectors all pull out their weapons. My heart's hammering. Something's out there, and it knows how to hide.

"Patrol niner to guard tower delta, we have potential mutagenic animal presence in sector 18-dash-G," Crystal says into the wireless. "Suspected chameleon creature."

"Confirmed patrol niner," the guard tower replies. "Mobilizing back up. Over."

The Helmsman stops in an open square next to a row of blown over carts, which once sold flowers, or pretzels or sausages and patties. The hovercraft lowers onto the ground. There's a slowing of the *whoop-ah whoop-ah* sound the vehicle makes, and it shudders as the engine cuts out. We're all standing, visors scanning the vicinity, ready to dismount.

"You stay here," Crystal says to me.

"But..." I start.

"Don't make me repeat it," she says. Any thought that I'm a full-fledged protector is swept away. "Eyes and sensors peeled, cadet. You see anything, you think you see anything, you let us know. The rest of you, beta formation and fan out. This is recon only until back up gets here."

I watch them go. Working in pairs, they disappear into the surrounding rubble. I scan the landscape through my visor. The screens before me show crumbling walls, a car with its roof caved in, and a wire push cart. I switch to infraspectro vision, casting the dead city in dull tones of green. The small infrared outlines of rodents and felines light up on the view screens, along with a flock of shadowrens that suddenly take flight. I ignore them, turning my body to scan in a circle—which only serves to make me dizzy. I've already got a 360-degree view.

160

You have to learn to trust the screens, Trenton told us. *Remember which one is front, which one is back, which one is left, which one is right, and which ones are in between.*

There's a jut of concrete and the image of it fizzles out for just a moment, then snaps back to as if nothing had happened, just like the DRADIS. Suspicious.

"Lead Officer," I say into my mic. "This is Cadet Feral. I think I may have found something. Repeat, I think I may have found something. Over."

"Understood," Crystal replies.

I switch back to high def view and take out my sidearm. I take two steps toward the pile of concrete.

"Stay put," Crystal says, her voice coming clearly through the ear jacks.

I stop, raising my gun, and a man literally bursts out from within the concrete as if he'd somehow been a part of it. He's dressed in worn grey clothes, helping him to blend with the urban blight all around us.

"Freeze!" I shout, but he doesn't listen, running as fast as he can right in front of me.

My finger tightens on the trigger and I'm hit by some invisible force that knocks me up and over. I land on my side three measures from where I was standing. I shake my head. My gun is on the ground, a measure away from me. I grab it and fire three shots. Two go wide, but one hits the man square in the back. He staggers from the impact, tripping, but he catches himself. He runs a few more steps, then slows as the paralytic takes effect. I'm about to shoot again when something smacks the gun from my hand.

I twist around quickly, making the screens swirl and my gut wrenches up, but only for a moment. I'm ready to fight hand-to-hand, if only there were something to fight. No one's there. This time I remember to look at the screens instead of turning my head this way and that. I can see that behind me the man who ran is flat on a busted up sidewalk. My gun is only a few measures away on the ground. I crouch down and reach for the weapon and I feel a sharp electrostatic shock run through me. I jerk back.

There's something blocking me from touching the gun, like it's surrounded by an invisible force field. The field seems to contract, smaller and smaller until it slowly crushes the gun into a twisted ball of metal.

"Lead Officer," I say into my mic, "This is *not* a mutated animal. I've tagged one Runner. Adult male. There's also a Supergenic. I have not made visual. Suspected abilities include invisibility and force field manipulation. Repeat, we are dealing with a Supergenic. Over."

I wait for her reply, but nothing comes through. "Lead Officer, do you copy?" I ask. "Does anybody copy?"

No response. Something's interfering with the signal.

"Crap," I swear to myself. I turn toward the hovercraft, starting to run for its superior transmission capabilities, and I smack right into an invisible wall. I stagger back and hit another invisible wall behind me. The screens in my visor show nothing there. I reach up and down—it's above and below me as well. I'm completely encased and to my horror, it starts pushing me back. It's closing in. I stare at what's left of my gun, a crumpled metal ball, and I start banging on the barrier, shouting into my mic, "Crystal!"

A pair of protectors emerge from the rubble. They've got their rifles pointed at the man that I shot. One of them grabs him by the hair, pulling him up and onto his knees. He's still conscious. He stares right at me. I pound harder on the invisible enclosure, but no one can hear me.

Is he the Supergenic? I wonder. *No.* He'd be using his powers on his captors instead of me if that were the case.

I look back at the concrete mound where the guy was hiding, from where he seemed to burst out of nowhere. I think about the visor sensor glitch when it passed over that one area. That's where the Supergenic is hiding. It's probably his kid. The dad ran to draw us away. The kid must be terrified. I look at the protectors. They must think the dad is alone, a desperate fool who believes the stories of habitable lands and a better life beyond the fence. The punishment for his crime is immediate and summary execution. The protector holding the guy's hair puts a gun to the back of his head.

I slam the bottom of my fist into the shrinking shield. It's forcing me to crouch down. The kid but must be too far away to use his/her/zir power on the protectors. I kick futilely at the field that's closing around me. I shout. The protector pulls the trigger. I barely hear it, just a tiny pop, and a red bullet hole blooms in the guy's head. He falls dead onto the cracked concrete. The shield around me evaporates and I fall sideways in surprise.

"Papa!" I hear a wail rise from behind me.

A kid a few years younger than Nate comes running out from the slabs of concrete where his power was keeping him hidden. A woman dressed in grey is chasing after him, limping with every stride, unable to catch up. His mother, I presume, hidden by the kid's power until he freaked out.

"Mattaius!" she screams.

The other protectors emerge in a wide circle around us.

"He's Supergenic!" I yell into my mic. "I repeat, the boy is Supergenic!"

He passes the hovercraft and it explodes as an expanding force rips it apart from the inside. Shrapnel flies everywhere. I hear screams of pain from two of the protectors. An invisible force slams into the protector who stood by while the kid's father was executed, sending the man flying off his feet.

Crystal opens her visor.

"It's okay!" she shouts at him. "We're not here to hurt you!"

An unseen power rams into her gut and she's thrown back. She lands a few measures from me, unconscious. The mother is still chasing the kid.

"Mattaius, please!" she cries futilely.

The kid corners the protector who acted as executioner. The mother finally reaches the boy's side and hugs him tight. The protector slowly puts down his gun. The other protectors who are still on their feet are doing the same, holding their hands up in peace. The kid lifts his hand and an unseen force lifts the protector who killed his dad. The protector clutches at his throat as if grasping a rope that is slowly choking him. His visor cracks, and he screams from the pressure on his skull as an invisible sphere compresses about his head, just like it did around my gun.

"Please stop, Mattaius," his mom begs. "Please!"

Instead, Mattaius jerks his arm to the right and the invisible force slams the protector's body against a pile of asphalt. The kid jerks his arm to the left and the protector is thrown into the side of a collapsed building.

"Stop this at once!" a commanding voice booms. It cuts through everything.

I open my visor and stare at the floating radiance of a muscled man who is impossible not to recognize, dressed in form-fitting silver, with a lightning bolt on his chest. Captain Light. He floats ten measures off the ground in a globe of radiance. Of course. Protocol when any child Manifests is to contact Jupitar City.

Mattaius glares up at him. "He killed my dad."

"No," Captain Light shakes his head. "The man you call 'Dad' may have provided the seed that helped give you life, but he is *not* your father. He selfishly tried to keep you from your *real* Supergenic family. He tried to Run. The punishment for that is death. The protector was doing his duty."

As the Captain speaks, a slowly moving mist is drifting along the ground. There's a light breeze but the mist seems unbothered by it. It swirls around the boy's ankles. It ignores the mother at his side.

"That's a load of crap!" the kid shouts.

"Please," the mom begs. "Please don't take him away."

"We're not taking him away," the Captain replies. "That's what you were trying to do. We thank you for providing the egg and the womb that led to this boy's birth. But he is not your son. He has loving parents waiting for him back in Jupitar City. You would've been richly rewarded for your service. But kidnapping cannot be permitted. Runners *will* be punished."

He holds his palm toward her and fires a beam of light. I expect it to slice her in half or disintegrate her or burn her to dust. Instead it's surprisingly gentle, forming a wall between her and her son, slowly pushing her away. She beats at it with her fists, and helplessly tries to force it back. Gravel skitters from under her heels as she digs them into the ground. From the wail that rises from her lungs, I think she'd rather die than let him go.

"Mom!" the kid cries, trying to go after her.

Captain Light fires a second beam from his other palm. The energy wraps around the kid like a tether, holding him back.

"Your *real* parents can't wait to meet you, Mattaius," Captain Light says.

"No!" he shouts. "I'm not going anywhere!"

He lifts his palm up toward Captain Light and I can only guess that a shield forms around the muscled figure, cutting off the beams of light. The kid's mother trips to her knees as the photonic wall disappears. She scrambles to her feet and is about to run to him when a small part of the body of mist forms a swirling hand that rises up from the greater cloud, and it hovers in front of her in the well-recognized symbol for STOP.

She does, out of surprise I think. Tentatively she passes her own hand through the cloudy one, and the movement makes the shape disperse.

"Mattaius," she breathes, stepping forward.

But it's too late. The mist swirls up the boy's body and into his mouth and nostrils. He inhales the twirling air and his arms drop listless to his side while his head falls back. The whites of his eyes are showing. The mist lifts him a few measures off of the ground, his whole body slack.

164

"Thank you, Cloud," Captain Light says, clearly freed from the kid's power. He floats closer to the ground.

"Mattaius?" the kid's mom calls. "Mattaius!"

She tries to rush toward him, her legs flailing through the swirling mist, and Captain Light fires a beam of light that sends her flying back. He's not so gentle now. She hits the side of a crumbling building with a grunt. She tries to get up but a pair of protectors grab her and hold her. She struggles against them, sobbing in a way that reminds me of my own mother.

"Noooooo!" she cries.

The mist lifts the boy up and up, into Captain Light's reach. He grabs the boy gruffly and slings him over one shoulder as if he were a sack of potatoes.

"As per our treaty, we will leave you to govern your own people as we take our leave with ours," Captain Light says to us. The cloud swirls into the air, undulating around him. I watch them hover away, rising higher into the sky, floating across the river to Jupitar City, leaving a misty trail that sparkles with Captain Light's exhaust.

The woman sobs, the sound of a spirit completely and utterly broken. I want to say *it's going to be all right*, but it won't be. She's broken our most sacred law. She's failed in her duty. I turn away. I don't want to see what happens next.

"Mango is the new tango," I hear a voice in my ear bud. It's Sewzanne. The words are like a switch in my brain. Without even thinking about it, I press the button on my helmet and my visor lowers back down. The screens pop back to life one by one. The mom is on the screen that shows what's behind me. To do what I must do, I have to face her. I turn in her direction and the screens change. What was front is now back, and what was back is now front. I'm getting used to this.

I stare at the mother being held by the protectors.

I step forward like a puppet in a dream and pick up Crystal's rifle. Part of me can tell that the Runner woman is begging, but I can't hear her. As if this were target practice and nothing more, I aim and fire. Her head whips back, and the protectors drop her dead at their feet.

You just killed a woman, a part of me says in horror as I lower the rifle. *A woman who was just trying to hold onto her son.*

The rest of me should be equally horrified, but it's not, and I know on some level that's not how a normal person reacts after taking a life. *This isn't real,* I assure myself. I press the button on the side of my helmet and my visor slides open. I stare at the face of the executed woman. I drop the rifle from listless fingers. This is real.

What have they turned me into? I wonder.

I tried to warn you, I hear my mother reply. *Now it's too late.*

CHAPTER 25

Back at the Cube, I'm taken to a debrief room. It takes all of ten minutes for a pair of overseers to take my statement. They dismiss me and as I step into the hall, Sewzanne comes bustling over. She's beaming, as if I were her kid and I'd just aced a Spelling Bee. She hugs me tight. I don't hug back.

"I knew you were ready," she says. "Caitlin, I'm so proud."

This morning, those words from her would've made me swell with pleasure. Now, I struggle to feel anything.

"The boy, is he all right?" I ask.

"The Supergenic child?" Sewzanne replies, arching a plucked brow as she releases her hold on me. "He's with his own kind, where he belongs."

Her tone is dismissive, almost relieved that we are rid of him. She touches my arm in that conspiratorial way of hers that I used to love, because it felt like she was going to share some juicy tidbit that was just between us. "The boy was unusually young to Manifest," she whispers, as if that were some great secret. "Some people are saying we should start testing even sooner than we do."

I nod, trying to feign interest, but all I can think is, *I killed his mom.*

"I should go eat," I say.

"Yes, yes, you must be starving," she shoos me away amiably. I nod, turning toward the elevator. In truth, I have no appetite.

I go to my locker, strip, shower and change into a fresh cadet's uniform. I close my locker door and immediately punch it as hard as I can. I hear something crack. It's either my fingers or the door. There's so little feeling in me I can't tell which.

"Tough day?" Bradie asks.

I wheel about. He's seated on the bench in a corner. I lower my fists.

"I killed a woman," I say matter-of-factly.

"I heard," he replies. "Figured you'd need to talk. How do you feel?"

"How do you think?" I reply, as if it were the most redundant question in the world.

He shrugs. "Honestly, with the way you've been changing, I have no idea."

His words are like a needle, pricking at my heart.

How can he say that? a part of me asks.

Because it's true, another part answers.

"Numb," is what I finally say. "Like I have to keep reminding myself i happened. Like it would be easy to do it again."

He comes over and takes me in his arms. My every instinct is to shove him away. Instead, I try to remember how good this used to feel.

"Caitlin," he says, brushing my cheek with his scarred hand, "Are you still in there?"

I shake my head.

"I don't know," I say. My voice trembles, but I can't say why. It's as i someone else is speaking.

I take his wrist and gently remove his hand from my face.

"Don't pull away, Caitlin," he says. "Please."

"I can't go back to being the girl that I was," I say. "But I don't want to be who I've become."

"Who says those are your only choices?" he asks.

I struggle to find an answer.

You don't deserve him, a part of me realizes.

"I'm going to get some air," I say. I just need to be away from this place Maybe if I give myself enough room, that part of me that's gone dorman can come crawling back out.

And then what?

The truth is I don't know. Everything's such a mess, people are dead, anc the words "they broke the law, they put us all in danger, they could've ruined the peace" are not enough.

He nods. "I'll come with you."

"No," I say. And now I do push him away, gently but firmly. "I don' think I can be around people right now."

"Which is exactly when you should be around people," he answers.

He's probably right, but it's me, so I don't listen.

"I'm not going to do anything stupid," I assure him. "I just need to clea my head."

He takes my hand and stands on tip-toe, kissing me on the forehead. It' tender and familiar, reminding me of the Bradie I first met, and of the Caitlin he first met. I wipe at my eyes reflexively, expecting there to be tears.

There aren't.

168

I take a bus to the center of the borough. It passes a huge billboard of a beaming muscled teen boy in short shorts and nothing else, sticking to a sheer wall with his bare hands and feet. He's looking over his shoulder and seems to be staring right at me. In bold words it says, HE CAN CLIMB WALLS...WHAT CAN YOU DO? MANIFEST AND BE SPECIAL!

The bus rumbles to a halt, and something about the sign bids me to get off. The door whines as it opens, slapping me with cool, crisp air. A balding man with hunched shoulders disembarks ahead of me. His coat is worn and he coughs every two seconds. He eyes me, looking at my cadet's uniform. He wears orange coveralls.

"Don't expect them to take care of you once you're no longer of use to them," he says.

He doesn't wait for a response, limping away down the street. I can only assume that he was once a protector, injured in the line of duty. Now he wears coveralls with the insignia of a toxic waste worker.

I wander, seemingly aimlessly, until I'm standing in front of the security fence separating the borough from the Yellow Zone. I stare at a mutant hazard sign.

My eyes are burning. I touch them and my fingers come away wet with tears.

Weakness water, Trenton calls it.

I laugh, and cry a bit more. There's a swell of relief. If I can still cry, that means I can still feel, and if I can still feel, maybe I can find more of me amidst whatever else they've shoved into my head.

"Hi, Caitlin."

I whip around at the familiar voice. It's Normand.

"What are you doing here?" I ask.

"Saving you," he says.

I don't ask him what he means, I just watch as he pulls out his skeleton key, puts it on the key pad of a gate and with a swipe of his new tablet the lock clicks with a merry chirp. Of course he kept copies of his GRAMS. He hands me a motion detector suppressor—just like old times. Normand jerks the gate open and steps through.

"You coming?" he asks.

I hesitate. It's my job to report activity like this. We're creating all sorts of risks. And for what? So I can read children's comics books? This is a self-indulgence. *Duty before all.*

What about the woman you killed? a part of me asks.

That settles it. I follow after Normand.

The first time he brought me into the Yellow Zone was less than a year ago and yet a lifetime seems to have passed. Back then I was halting and tripping as I followed him. Now I lead, sure of foot, moving with an agility he'll never match. I scout ahead, watchful. I feel a flicker of excitement as we get closer to the Lair—only a flicker mind you, but it's there.

Pay attention, the cadet in me orders, extinguishing the delicate glimmer with a cold iciness.

This time she's right. I'm in the Yellow Zone. This isn't a playground. My eyes rove everywhere for threats; traps leftover from the Genocide Wars, sinkholes, and for mutants that have gotten past the outer wall. Thankfully, all I see are shadowrens.

We reach the Lair and as we enter the comic book shop I brace myself, not sure what to expect. Part of me worries that I came back in a fugue state and burnt it down after all. Normand claps and the twinkling strings of light come on. It's still here, the comic books, the costumes on the wall, the posters, the busts, and the board games.

As usual he shuffles in and adjusts the position of the scarf with the red S on it on the counter. The comforting familiarity of it makes me want to hug him, if only for a second.

I wait for Normand to freak out over the scorch mark on the carpet. He doesn't, and not because he hasn't noticed. This is Normand, after all.

He forgives me, I realize. I'm just not sure if I can forgive myself.

I wander around the store, too amped to read, and I find myself drawn to the costumes covering the store's rear wall. There's a giant rubber hammer, a green lantern, more masks than I care to count, along with capes, wigs, fangs, and crazy contact lenses that I definitely would've worn on Testing Day given the chance.

I'm drawn to one costume in particular. I lift it off of its hook and hold it before me. The cadet in me sees it for the ridiculousness that it is: a clingy blue top with a strange insignia emblazoned in gold on the chest and a red mini skirt with matching knee high boots. But the other part of me is thawing out, little by little. That part of me loves it.

I remove my uniform. I don't feel like being a cadet right now. Nor can I handle being Caitlin. I want to be this superpowered heroine, with abilities and a backstory beyond imagining, who always does the right thing, and never fails to save the day.

I slide the satiny top over my skin and slip into the skirt, feeling the way the fabric clings to me. There's a cape, which I drape over my shoulders, a belt, and the boots. I gaze at myself in a cracked stand up mirror and I'm surprised at how well it all fits, showing off the muscles I've developed over the last year. I pull on a blond wig with curls that tickle my shoulders and neck.

Normand is staring at me.

"How do I look?" I ask.

"Like a hooker," he says.

My jaw juts. His mouth widens into a smile.

"Did you just make a joke?" I ask.

"Bradie's been teaching me how," he replies. "Did you know there are rules to humor?"

"I did not," I confess.

"You can even plan jokes in advance."

"Is that so?"

"Bradie says anytime someone asks how they look, they want a compliment, so first you give them a little insult, smile so they know you're joking, and *then* say something nice. I fail to understand why, but it works."

Hearing him talk like this, it makes me feel lighter, more innocent, like we're back in the world we inhabited before we entered the Cube.

"I'm waiting," I say.

"For what?" he asks.

"You said that first you insult me, then you say something nice."

"Indeed. That is the formula. Well, you do have the appearance of a woman who barters for sex..."

I roll my eyes, but keep quiet. I get the feeling that saying the words "hooker" and "sex" are making Normand feel like a bad boy. I indulge him. I owe him that much.

"...but only because that's the way superheroes dress." He waves his hand at the shelves displaying comics with muscled men and large-breasted women on the covers, villains and heroes both, all in skin-tight clothes that reveal more than they conceal. "Which means you look like a superhero, which means you look awesome."

His words bring sudden and unexpected tears to my eyes.

"Bradie says when people cry it's sometimes because they're happy, sometimes because they're sad. What is your current emotional status?" he asks.

"Both," I smile, wiping the tears away.

I like him, I realize. *I like Normand. And I've missed him.*

"You should put on a costume too," I say.

He shakes his head, wringing his hands and squirting sanitizer into them.

"That option is closed to me," he says.

"Nonsense," I say, using Normand-speak.

"None of the costumes can accommodate my proportions," he explains.

"That sounds like something a quitter would say. And we," I wave at us, "are not quitters."

I start going through the packaged costumes in the cubbies beneath the display wall.

"Caitlin. I'm simply stating the facts," he insists. "I'm too big."

I wave my index finger at him, having none of it.

"Small, small, medium, large..." I mutter to myself, reading off the labels.

"Caitlin! This is a waste of time," he insists, and I'm starting to think he's right. I find an extra large of some furry blue creature who is into cookies, but even that won't accommodate Normand's girth. I look around the shop in defeat.

"As you can see, I'm right," Normand says.

"No," I say. I'm on a mission, to do something nice for my friend, my *best* friend, and I *have* to complete my mission.

I stare at the cash register. Something about it has caught my eye, and I've learned to pay attention to my instincts. I walk toward it.

"Remember the rules Caitlin," he says. "That is a no-touch zone."

There's a warning edge to his voice.

"Yeah, yeah," I say, sounding like Nate.

I stare past the forbidden objects. He watches as I circle around the counter and stare at the register. Right under it is a giant bin on wheels with a large label that says, RETURNS.

I pull it out. There's all sorts of toys, games, and books in it. I dig through and find a miracle within. I pull out a triple-extra-large set of beige coveralls, with lots of pockets on it. As if it were an official job in the borough, it even has a round insignia on it: a red circle and slash overtop of a white cartoon ghost.

"Hey, weirdo," I say to him. "Check this out."

He sees the voluminous costume hanging in my hands and his brace creaks as he takes quick shuffling steps toward me.

"Do you really think it will fit?" His eyes are a mix of hope and fear.

"Only one way to find out."

It's a bit of a struggle getting the coveralls overtop of his leg brace, but after much tugging and swearing he finally zips it up. It fits. It actually fits!

"This is part of it," I say, helping him don a square padded backpack with a cord attached to a fake rifle. He looks both ridiculous and awesome. I cheerfully punch my fist into the air and shout, "Ghost Fighters!"

He pretends to fire the plastic rifle with *pew pew* sounds, annihilating a slew of unseen foes. When did he get so playful? And that's when I realize what's really different about him.

"Normand, are you making eye contact?" I ask.

He blushes but doesn't look away. In fact, he's staring at me so intensely it's starting to make me feel uncomfortable.

"Bradie taught me how," he replies. "He says avoiding eye contact makes people think they can't trust me. It's body language for 'I'm hiding or lying about something.' People give away a lot with their body language."

"They do," I agree.

"Want to know a secret?" he asks.

"Sure," I say.

"I'm not really looking you in the eyes."

"Really?" I ask, and as I do I intentionally move my eyes one way and then the other. His gaze doesn't follow. It remains perfectly fixed. "Then what are you looking at?"

"Your forehead," he says proudly. "It was Bradie's idea."

Part of me is actually jealous that they've become such pals. Makes me feel like the outsider again.

What did you expect? I chastise myself. *You neglected them both. They found each other.*

"Normand, I'm sorry for being such a bad friend."

"We've both had very busy itineraries," he replies, as if it were simply a question of scheduling.

I think that's his way of saying he forgives me. It prompts another confession.

"Normand, I don't think I can be a protector," I say.

He nods. It looks mechanical and rehearsed, like a robot that's initiated a program in response to preset circumstances. "Do you want to talk about it?"

I laugh a bit. Who is this person?

"Did Bradie teach you to say that?" I ask.

"Yes," he replies, factual and straight-faced.

"There's the Normand I know," I say.

"Where else would I be?" he replies. He blinks again rapidly. It's like he's flipping through the pages of a book with his eyelids. He stops. "Is this where we discuss what happened while you were on patrol?"

I feel a vacuum inside of me. "Normand, how do I live with this? I turned a kid into an orphan. I don't deserve this, any of it."

"Clarify," he says. "What is it you do not deserve?"

"This!" I yell, gesturing around the comic book store. "The escape from what I've done. You," I point to him. "You being nice to me. You should be telling me I'm garbage."

Only then do I realize how right Lilianne was about me all along.

Normand blinks repeatedly as he processes this. Most people would say I had no choice. That I did what I had to do. Normand is not most people.

"I have a proposition for you," he says. "I move that we commence working on a new comic book project."

It's a preposterous suggestion. A comic book can't fix this. And yet guilt fights with intrigue.

"Yeah? Like what?" I ask.

He makes a few quick pencil strokes on a pad of yellowed paper.

"This," he says, holding it up.

It's rough, but the images are clearly of him and me. He's drawn me in the lycra outfit I'm now wearing, and himself as a muscled doppelganger of himself in a form-fitting version of his anti-ghost jump suit. My heart

174

hammers. Our own comic book. Of us. Not as we are or were or how the Cube wants us to be. But as we choose to imagine ourselves. Mind blown.

"Yes," I say.

He checks his watch, and we get started. We spend the next hour lying on the floor, him drawing, me filling in the thought and word bubbles of the premiere issue of our very own series. I've missed our collaborations. I hold up a full-page panel. My superheroine alter ego has an evil henchman in a headlock while kicking another across the face. Normand's ghost brawler is holding off a battalion of henchpeople with his blaster gun. I stop. The way he's drawn the henchpeople, they look very much like protectors.

"Normand," I say. "Have I become a villain?"

He stares at my forehead, and says, "Yes."

With anyone else I'd go into a rage, but with Normand I've trained myself to hear his truth because there is no filter, and as far as I can tell, no agenda. It's like getting mad at a data pod. Satisfying for a moment, but ultimately futile.

Instead, sourcing a word that he would use, I say, "Elaborate."

He puts a finger to his temple and replies, "Accessing files," he says, then he makes *beep, boop, bop* sounds.

"I may punch Bradie for teaching you that one," I say.

He holds up the finger of his other hand. The middle finger. My jaw juts again. His smile is definitely that of a guy who is feeling like a badass.

"Data retrieved," he says. "Based on my readings of thousands of comic books from hundreds of titles, I have determined the different classifications for heroes. There are those who have powers, and those who have honed their normal human abilities to near superhuman levels. Many are guided by high-minded moral principles. Others are best described as 'anti-heroes,' meting out violent justice to those who escape the punitive arm of the judicial system. Some are born to greatness, others have it thrust upon them by a quirk of fate. But they all have something in common. They stick up for the weak. The broken. The powerless."

"And those who don't..." I begin.

"...those who don't," he continues. "Even if they have good intentions, those are the villains."

I'm quiet after that. He goes back to the drawing he's working on, of me evading a henchperson's laser fire as Normand blasts him with some sort of goo.

"Stop," I say.

He keeps sketching and I put my hand top of his.

"Stop," I say again.

"But I'm almost done," he replies.

"I need you to do a different drawing for me."

He doesn't ask why. He doesn't ask what. He shakes with repressed excitement and says, "Finally."

CHAPTER 26

I ransack the wall of costumes, my hands a blur as I grab anything made of black or red lycra. I'm even more ruthless in the weapons section, taking knives, a mini-crossbow, fighting sticks, and a projectile grappling hook. They're all props, light weight plastic that will crack if I squeeze too hard.

I pull off the blond wig, I strip out of the red and blue lycra, and don my selected gear. It's mostly black, intermixed with swathes of red. I attach the weaponry all over my body, except for the fighting sticks. Those I hold onto.

"Here," Normand says, handing me a dark red wig.

I put it on. He adjusts it for me, moving locks here and there.

"How do I look?" I ask.

I wait for him to say like a hooker, but he doesn't. I think he gets that we're not playing anymore.

"Inspiring to the good. Terrifying to the bad," he answers.

He gets it.

I strike a pose with the fighting sticks. Normand starts to draw, with quick sure strokes.

"What are you going to call yourself?" he asks. "The red hair, with the black costume, it's just like…"

"A shadowren," I finish for him.

He nods approvingly. "Many consider it a rodent with wings, because it not only survives on the ashes of the broken city, it actually thrives where little else can," he says. "They are fierce, and loyal. I've seen a flock massacre half-a-dozen rats to defend a single nest."

I nod. He *really* gets it.

When he's done, he shows me the drawing and I can scarcely breathe as I look at it. I knew that Normand was a talented artist, but this is something else. It's as if Normand's captured my essence in a way that a mirror or photograph never could; they are mere reflections of the physical, and this goes so much deeper.

This is the version of me I need to see, a larger-than-life character, perfectly formed and battle ready, instead of a conflicted, brainwashed teenage girl. He's even done the lettering behind me in bold. *Shadowren*, Issue 1. There's a heap of defeated agents and protectors at her feet.

At my *feet*.

I pin it up on the wall. I'm not sure how long I stare at it. I never want to look away. But eventually I must, as Normand reminds me.

"We have to go," he says in his matter of fact way.

I reluctantly undress. As I slide back into my cadet's uniform, I burn the idealized image of Shadowren into my brain, memorizing the feeling of being her, willing that to override anything that Sewzanne and her Calibration procedure have uploaded into my brain.

"The obvious course of action would be for you to tender your resignation," he says. "As the saying goes, you're not a protector until you're a protector."

I think of the man from the bus, in his toxic waste coveralls.

"I know how to shoot," I say. "If I quit now I'll be assigned a job with a 100 percent mortality rate."

"Would you prefer to be put in a position where you are required to destroy another family?" he asks.

There is something tempting about walking away. I'd have a few years of misery, and then die. The punishment I deserve, followed by the ultimate freedom.

I look at the Shadowren drawing. "And then what?" I ask. "Just pretend I don't know what they do to the cadets during Calibration? Do I let those brainwashed cadets become protectors? My father knew what was happening. I think he was involved. My mom all but told me, but I wouldn't listen. He died trying to stop it. Maybe now it's my turn."

Normand nods. "Spoken like a true hero."

"Yeah," I snort. "I execute a woman trying to keep her son. I join the organization that killed my father. I turn on my mom, my brother, on Bradie, and you. And then I come here and play dress up. I'm a real hero."

"With that being the case, what course of action do you anticipate taking?"

It's like he's *trying* to sound like a robot.

"I don't know," I reply. "How do I unbrainwash the brainwashed? And then what? Fight the Supergenics the next time they come to take a kid away? It all seems so impossible."

"That sounds like a quitter talking," he says, using my own words against me.

"I know, it's just..." my thought trails off. I don't finish the sentence. My eyes have landed on an issue of *Tigara*, in which she's fighting the mesmerizing hypnotic powers of GazeFatale. The villainess wears a skin-tight outfit of swirling circles. It gets me thinking dangerous thoughts.

"Normand, hypothetically, would it be possible for us to insert our own program into the Calibration Chair's data bank?" I ask.

"Affirmative," he says, following my stare to GazeFatale. "And I have something that I believe you will find useful."

He takes me behind the counter. I give a wide berth to the forbidden objects. He pulls out a book and hands it to me. On the cover is a dove transforming into an eagle. I read the title. *The Power of Suggestion: A Guide to Hypnosis, the Subconscious, and Trance-Formation*, by some guy named Eugene Towers. In his creepy bio pic, he's wearing an ill-fitting suit, has shaggy hair to his shoulders, and a drooping mustache.

"Am I to understand the fate of the world rests in this guy's hands?" I say.

"No," Normand says. "It rests in ours."

We're quiet as we leave the Lair, feeling the magnitude of what we are about to attempt. As we walk up the concrete stairs, I touch *The Power of Suggestion* book, tucked inside my uniform.

"Normand, do you really think my plan could work?" I ask.

His response is drowned out as he opens the outer doors and we're deafened by rumbling thunder. I wonder if I'll ever be back here again.

The thought stays with me as we sneak our way back to the fence. We wait for a patrol to pass, Normand swipes a few GRAMS on his tablet to put the security camera on a loop, and we slip through the gate.

"Finally," a familiar voice says.

I stare at Bradie leaning against the wall, eating a nutrition bar.

"Bradie!" I stammer, searching for a workable lie. "We were on a special patrol."

He snorts. "A cadet, sneaking out from behind the fence, with a techie, and *that's* your cover story?"

"It's not like that," I insist.

"Yeah, it is," he says. He jerks his head in a brotherly way toward Normand and holds his hand up. "Hey, buddy."

"Salutations," Normand replies.

They high five. Normand sanitizes his hand. I look around nervously. Another patrol could come at any moment.

"Bradie, you shouldn't be here," I say.

"Neither should you," he replies.

His eyes twinkle, not as brightly as when we first met, but just like me, he's still in there. It's not too late. For him. For me. For us.

"Bradie, you're not going to tell on us, are you?"

"Depends," Bradie replies.

"On what?" I ask.

He shrugs. "On whether you're ready."

I look to Normand. "I am as bemused as you." There's an edge to his robot voice. I get the feeling he's lying.

"Ready for what?" I ask Bradie.

He gazes out at the Cube in the distance.

"A revolution."

CHAPTER 27

At training the next morning, it's as if the old Bradie is back. I watch him as I fill up my water bottle at a dispensing station. He's regaling the other cadets as we wait for the drill master.

I catch the tail end of his anecdote as I join them.

"...and then she says, well, maybe if you could levitate. Womp womp."

They all laugh. I force myself to smile. It's a good story, one that changes a bit every time. There's an edge to his voice as he tells it. The punch line is rushed. His laugh louder. His grin wider. He's nervous, just like me. If anyone notices...

Steady, Caitlin, I tell myself. *Steady.*

He winks at me. I try to wink back, but it still feels like I've developed a tic. Hopefully Normand's doing better.

I'm thankful to hear the drill master's whistle pierce the air. As I sweat through a series of swings, push-ups, tumbles, jumps, and flips I'm able to lose myself in the physicality of it. I'm no mere pawn of the Protectorate. I'm Shadowren. I channel her, and as I do I push harder when I need to, feel supple when I require finesse, and strategically retreat when necessary.

I'm not sure what Bradie is channeling, but as we spar he kicks my feet out from under me. Even though his Calibration sessions have gone terribly, he's a natural at this, which is why he hasn't been culled from cadets. I land on my back and he pins me. I don't fully mind, but Shadowren does. She's got him in a headlock moments later. He flips me. I roll. He counters. And on we dance.

In the showers, I notice his muscles and in my mind I dress him in a mask and tights, with a crow sigil in the middle of his chest—a fitting match for his Shadowren girlfriend. He catches me looking and blows me a kiss. I give him the finger. He responds with a moon-eyed "awe shucks" look and presses his hands over his heart.

I see the scars covering the fingers and knuckles of one hand, running up his forearm; mottled flesh that still looks raw, and always will. Again, he sees that I'm staring. He curls his scarred hand into a fist, and punches it into his other palm.

I nod. It's payback time.

I report for my first group Calibration session that afternoon. The set-up is a very different experience than the Chair. Instead of being in a small room on my own with Sewzanne, we're in a large glassed-in chamber overlooking the atrium. Hundreds of protectors are sitting cross-legged on the white rubber floor. The male-identified wear short shorts and little else, while the female-identified also have their sports tops on. Above each of them hangs a helmet with a visor.

There's a slew of technicians and medics bustling around them, attaching sensory pads to various parts of their bodies. Sewzanne sees me and waves me over.

"Caitlin," she says, giving me a hug. "Big day! How are you?"

"Ready to do my duty," I reply.

"That a girl," she says approvingly. "Let's get you hooked up. CeeCee?" she asks, looking around. "Honestly, where is that...CeeCee!" she shouts, gesturing impatiently at a rotund woman with her hair pinned in a bun on the top of her head. She's chatting animatedly with a muscled shirtless protector covered in sensory pads. Her hand lingers on his biceps.

"CeeCee!" Sewzanne shouts again.

CeeCee holds up a "just a minute" finger to Sewzanne, says something that makes the handsome protector laugh, and then comes bustling over.

"CeeCee, this is Cailtin, the girl I was telling you about. CeeCee's one of my best," Sewzanne prattles on. "She'll take very good care of you."

"Come on, Cay," CeeCee says.

She loops her arm into mine, winking at her handsome protector as we pass, and whispers in my ear, "Massive," showing me a space between her palms one measure long as she leads me to a dangling helmet. I'm flustered and blushing, but part of me wonders, *Is making me uncomfortable part of it? Does it make the Calibration more effective?*

It's hard to say what's an act and what's genuine anymore.

Game on, CeeCee, I think. *Game on.*

I strip down to my short shorts and tank top.

"So, you had quite the day yesterday," CeeCee says as she applies the sensory pads to various points on my body. "Runners, nasty business that."

She's silent then, letting the uncomfortable lull in conversation drag on. We've been taught to use this technique ourselves. Most people will automatically rush to fill the quiet, and will often let slip something they

182

didn't intend to. CeeCee is good, with her disarming, and slightly flirty manner. One of the best, just as Sewzanne promised.

I take a moment to calm my heart, to let any tension drain away, and then I answer, "It is what it is."

CeeCee looks at her data pad. There are no bleeps betraying what I'm really thinking. She nods imperceptibly. The system can be fooled.

"All set," she says, handing me a gel cap with a bright orange liquid in it. Mango Tango. I swallow it with a swig from my water canteen.

"Good luck," she winks.

I sit cross-legged, just like everyone else. All around the room, the helmets lower and we all ease them over our heads. They quiver to life, and I already know something is different from individual Calibration. I have this sense of the others all around me. It's subtle, as if we're all humming the same mantra with our minds. Occasionally it will feel as though someone's out of sync or off tune. Sometimes that person is me, sometimes a neighbor, but each of us is guided back by the vibrations of the others, and within only a few minutes we are all in harmony.

Once we maintain that unified state for a few minutes, the images begin, along with gentle instructions to aid the body and mind even deeper into a relaxed state. I've started reading Eugene's book, so I have some understanding of what's happening. The images and vocal induction are quieting down my conscious mind, prepping my subconscious for new input. In theory, they can't put anything in there that I don't already believe and they can't make me do anything I don't want to do. But, according to Eugene, we all have different parts.

The Calibration process is focusing in on the parts of me that want to be a protector, the parts that believe that the treaty with the Supergenics must be upheld at all cost, and it makes those aspects of myself louder, brighter, stronger, programming them to kick in without me even thinking about it, while bit by bit quieting down my other parts, the parts that question, that hold autonomy as a virtue, and ultimately turning them off. The Mango Tango intensifies the trance-formation. But even drugged, we still have some agency.

Just remember, Eugene wrote, *who you are, and who you will be, is ultimately up to you.*

I'm done wondering who that is.

I am Shadowren, I intone in my mind. *Shadowren is me. Shadowren defends the weak. Shadowren is a hero.* I say it over and over to myself. I feel a weird vibration around me as I fall out of sync with the others. It's as if I'm in the middle of a giant choreographed dance that relies on all the dancers doing the same moves all at the same time. Now that I'm stepping my own steps, I'm bumping into the dancers immediately around me, which throws them off, and they bump into the dancers around them. Like a pebble thrown into clear waters, the ripples spread outwards.

I picture myself in the Shadowren costume, decked out in her armor. I see myself standing between Captain Light and the boy he took away. I feel a few of the vibrations around me spike, as I find a kindred spirit or two. Instead of bumping into me as I dance, they start dancing my steps, creating a new harmony which challenges the one being imposed on us. Others start to join us, and as our invisible circle expands, I can sense the rest of our group growing agitated, doing the old steps one moment, then tripping as they accidentally incorporate a few of ours. There's a hum of discord.

This could actually work, I think, and just as I do, the hum dies out. The images on the inside of my visor go dark and the voice and relaxing melody coming from my earbuds fall silent. There's a tug as my helmet is pulled upwards by the retractable hose attached to it. I ease it off my head.

Is that it? I wonder.

The protectors seem as confused as I am.

"My apologies," Sewzanne says from the front of the room. "We seem to be having some technical issues. We'll have to run a diagnostic and reschedule for later in the week."

As we file out, I hear CeeCee saying to Sewzanne in a hushed tone, "I don't know where the anomaly came from." Her eyes flick at me. "But there was only one new person in the room."

It's both a victory and a defeat. My thoughts alone were able to affect the thoughts of the protectors around me. Some of them anyway. But it won't be enough to reach the entire Protectorate, and we have to keep Sewzanne from realizing the protectors' brainwaves are changing.

Over the next several weeks, we plan and scheme. One day I meet with Normand and Bradie inside a custodial closet. There are brooms, mops, scrub pads, and vats of industrial cleaner. Normand holds his hand before us and we stare at a round processor pod sitting in his palm.

"How did you get it?" Bradie asks, a hint of awe in his voice.

"I found it lodged in a pipeline during my first week at the Cube. Maintenance tech probably dropped it by mistake when he was switching it out. I held onto it, just in case."

"Wonder what happened to the guy when he couldn't account for it," Bradie says.

"Nothing good," Normand replies.

"But it works?" I ask.

"It does now," Normand answers. "We just need to populate it."

I hand him a pilfered data cylinder the size and shape of a pill. Hopefully no one will realize it's missing, and if they do, can't track it back to us. Even if they do, it should be too late by then. Should be. Normand slides it into a round port on the pod. A red light blinks at us three times and then the rewrite is complete.

"You guys sure this will actually work?" Bradie asks.

"Yes," Normand says so emphatically I can't help but believe him.

"Well, I guess we're going to find out," Bradie adds.

"Tomorrow, when you hear the perimeter breach alarm, that's the signal," Normand says.

"You're going to activate the perimeter siren?" I ask. "I thought we didn't want to attract attention."

"I can assure you, no one will be paying attention to us," Normand says. "There's a very powerful mutant headed for the Yellow Zone. It will be *very* distracting."

We don't ask how he knows that. In Normand we trust, him and his hacking GRAMS. Bradie flexes and stretches his scarred fingers.

"All right," he says, "Let's do this." He puts his hand at waist height in front of us, palm down in the center of our triangle.

I put my hand on top of his. I feel the heat coming off the scars. Normand makes a delighted squeal.

"This is precisely like issue 52 of the *Aerobots*!" he explains, putting his hand on top of mine.

"We're really going to do this," Bradie says. There's a glassy look to his eyes, and a shallowness to the rise and fall of his chest.

I don't need to be a telepath or an empath or a syphon to know what he's feeling. I'm feeling it too. Scared…and powerful.

The next day, even though I know it's coming, I'm still unprepared when I hear the piercing wail of the perimeter sirens rising through the air. We're in the outdoor training yard running laps. There's a light drizzle. Bradie and I make eye contact. It's time. A voice comes booming over the loudspeaker.

"Mutant alert! Repeat, mutant alert! Seismic sensors indicate subterranean approach!"

A squad of protectors is running toward us, visors down, rifles in hand.

"Cadets, into the hall! Now!" our instructor shouts.

We run toward the Cube, two rows of cadets parting to either side of the squad of protectors sprinting the other way. The ground shakes and we're all thrown from our feet, cadets and protectors alike, tossed together like so many bits of grizzled meat being churned into a stew. I slam into a protector in full uniform and we both fall to the ground.

My arm flails, hitting the side of his helmet, which causes his visor to slide open. It's Trenton. He gives me a dark look, as if he blames me for this and far more. He presses the button that slides his visor shut again. I'd forgotten about the little heart to heart we had. He has not.

"Move cadets!" he shouts at us through the speakers in his helmet. "Protectors, with me!"

We are like trained dogs at this point, scrambling to our feet, turning to obey so that we can get out of the way of the real protectors, but even the most beaten canine would stop and look back at what happens next. The unseen underground creature races closer and closer to the surface, its burrowing throwing chunks of broken concrete and beat-up vehicles in the Yellow Zone into the air, leaving a clear trail of upraised streets and sidewalks behind it.

The rising ridge snaking toward us gets within twenty measures of the fence, and then stops. Everything is silent except for the wail of the proximity siren—but only for a moment. A terrifying growl rises up, the ground shakes worse than before, chunks as big as a tank are launched upwards, along with a rusted car. It flies all the way over the security fence and crashes a few measures away from us.

A sink hole forms in the Yellow Zone, collapsing downward and creating a cloud of rising dirt. From within it, an enormous paw ending in jagged claws reaches up and out, stabbing into the ground like it's soft butter. It's followed by a second paw with deadly talons that grip the base of a concrete pylon with an energy sphere on top. The creature flexes and pulls itself up. Bright spotlights along the fence spin toward it, casting huge shadows as it emerges.

It's gigantic, about 20 measures tall, lumbering on two legs thicker than tree stumps, its long muscled arms dragging across the ground. Its skin is rough, thick, and looks like slabs of rock. Its face is bestial, with beady eyes and a huge snout that rises up into a gigantic horn at its tip. It reminds me of pictures I've seen of an extinct species called a rhino. I've seen mutated animals, but nothing like this.

Lightning arcs down from the billowing black clouds above, striking the beast. There are cheers as it writhes, defeated by a stroke of luck before it could do any real damage, but as the cheers die down we realize something's wrong. The same strike of lightning is still hitting it.

That's not right.

Giant pustules are rising up all over its body. They pulse with an inner glow. The thing huffs and snorts, like a dog slavering over the most delicious of T-bones. It's feeding off the energy from the clouds. When the lighting finally flares out, the mutant animal's entire form is aglow.

"All units, mutant threat can absorb energy," I hear Trenton say. He's forgotten to turn off his external speakers. "Repeat, the mutant threat can absorb energy. Ballistic weapons only. No plasma rifles or photonics. I repeat, ballistic weapons only!"

The thing roars and the energy it absorbed surges out of its mouth. It fires a blast of pink electricity at the closest guard tower. The pink power cascades through the structure. Spotlights burst and the protectors on the platform writhe in agony.

The sirens grow louder and, beyond the Cube, those who work in the borough scramble for the mutant raid shelters. The schools and factories have their own underground bunkers. I think of Nate and Mom hunkering down with classmates and coworkers. Someone grabs me. I assume it's Bradie but instead I stare into the drill master's angry face.

"Move!" he shouts, pushing me in the direction of the protective walls of the Cube.

I run toward it, searching for Bradie. He finds me first, the mottled flesh of his injured hand snaking into mine, giving my fingers a squeeze.

Normand was right. No one is going to be paying attention to us. In fact, I almost forgot about our plan entirely. Ahead of us the rest of the cadets are fleeing into the Cube when a burst of pink lightning flies over our heads and slams into the compound's sleek white surface. The energy sprays outwards, like dozens of serpents slithering along the wall, and one of the white panels covering the Cube's exterior shatters, spraying glass onto the cadet below.

He screams, protecting his face with his arms, the bare skin sliced in half-a-dozen places. Underneath where the panel used to be is a series of wires and circuitry. They spark and smoke.

The beast behind us roars again, and fires another bolt, this time of green electricity. It hits the Cube a dozen floors up, and once again the lightning cascades outward along the building's surface. It seems to fizzle out, until I see the exposed circuits just a few measures away from us start to spark with emerald energy.

It's traveled!

I shove Bradie to the ground as power the color of radioactive limes shoots out of the exposed cables, and right into our fellow cadet. His body goes rigid, making him shake uncontrollably as he's fried by the green electricity. The surge stops and he topples to the ground, scorched from head to toe.

I look back at the rhino monstrosity. It's glowing all colors of the rainbow. It takes another lumbering step toward the fence and a hover attack vehicle zooms by, firing a missile. It strikes the rhinonstrosity and explodes. The creature staggers back, banging into one of the concrete pylons with a power nodule up top.

Lightning flares from the clouds into the nodule. The beast looks up and reaches its thick fingers toward the crackling globe, and energy bursts out of the sphere, arcing down into its outstretched hand. The mutant grasps the bolt of power and swings it like a whip, cutting the hover vehicle in half. The front half skids along the ground, the back half goes into a wild tailspin, smashing and exploding against a half-collapsed building. There's a crash of bricks as it brings the edifice the rest of the way down.

The protectors at the fence crouch behind plastic shields and open fire with their ballistic weapons. The bullets sound like pellets as they bounce off the creature's thick hide.

The mutant roars—and the door shuts behind us.

188

We're the last of the cadets to make it in. Red lights flash all around. Down the hall are the rest of the cadets.

"To your bunks!" the drill master shouts at them.

"Hurry," Bradie says, pushing me in the opposite direction and toward the stairwell.

We skitter down the steps as quickly and as quietly as we can, making sharp turns at each landing, until we get three floors below. I smell something burning.

There's a smoldering medic lying facedown before us. One of her hands is fused to the handle of the door we need to get through. Her other hand is melded with her smoking i-Dent card, which is partially melted into the security swiper.

"That's a problem," Bradie says.

The door opens from the other side, breaking the medic's arm at the wrist as it pushes her body aside. Normand stands there. He's looking at his watch.

"You need to accelerate your pace," he says. "We're off schedule."

"That means crank it," I translate.

"I speak Normand," Bradie says.

He grabs my hand, both of us jumping over the dead medic as we follow after Normand. He's all business, taking the lead, limping as fast as he can, his brace creaking like crazy. He navigates us through the underground maze, taking lefts and rights through white corridors that all look the same to me, except for the occasional number with a letter to identify where we are. He doesn't even use his e-pad—"too much interference from the EM waves."

I convince myself that we're the only ones down there, that everyone else is fighting the rhinonstrosity or in their bunks, until we round a corner and come face to face with a pair of protectors with their helmets strapped to their belts.

"Balderdash," Normand swears. "They were supposed to be in the next corridor. That's the problem with..."

"What are you doing here?" the bigger one demands.

"We..." Bradie starts.

I take two running steps and propel myself off the ground. My legs are wrapped around the protector's neck before Bradie can say another word. The protector topples to the floor, I grab his baton and shove it into his stomach. He writhes in a spastic dance. I pull the baton away and feel the barrel of his partner's gun against the back of my head.

"There's two of them," Bradie points out.

"I sort of assumed you'd deal with the second one," I reply.

"I was going for smooth-talking our way out of it," he says.

"Noted," I say.

I spin with greased precision as all the skills they rammed into me during Calibration snap into auto. I smack the gun from his hand. It fires. Bradie kicks the protector's legs out from under him. We've got the jump on him and it's two against one, but the guy's bigger and has more training than we do. He drops, rolls and is back on his feet, kicking me in the gut so hard I slam into a wall. Bradie unleashes a flurry of blows into the guy's kidney and he punches Bradie across the jaw. His head snaps back.

"Not cool," Bradie says.

"I'm going to enjoy kicking your..." the protector starts to say when his body suddenly starts quivering like he's a bowl of shaking jelly. He drops to the ground. Normand is standing behind him, baton in hand. He shudders once, like he's shaking off the heebie jeebies. His body settles.

"I'd really rather not do that again," he says. He looks at his watch. "Let's press on."

"What do we do when they wake up?" Bradie asks.

"They won't be saying anything to anybody," Normand replies. "Come on."

Bradie and I look at each other. The protectors aren't dead, so what's Normand talking about? I know I won't get an answer now. He's already limping down the hall and stops in front of a door that blends almost seamlessly with the wall. We flank him, standing guard. He presses his card to the door's surface and a square keypad lights up. The door hisses open. We go in and stare at banks of processor drives stacked one atop the other. The whir of fans hums in our ears.

Normand looks at his watch. "Here it comes," he whispers.

A loud beeping fills the room.

"Get down," Normand says.

We obey, and just in time. All over the room, the towers begin to spark as a power overload surges through them, dancing with pink electricity. I can only imagine what's going on up at the surface. The rhinonstrosity must be putting up quite the fight. The processor towers spark for a few more moments, and then they return to their normal hum. I look to Normand.

"All clear," he says.

He leads us unerringly through the maze of smoking towers and stops in front of one computer drive in particular. We hear the whine of fans louder than before, many of them misshapen from the pulse of energy yet still trying to do their duty. He unholsters a mechanized drill from his belt. It whirs as he undoes six screws. He pulls off a panel. Inside we see row upon row of round processor pods. Several of them are smoking from the power surge. He gently touches one blackened processor pod that's completely fried.

"Don't worry," he says to the burnt out node, "I'm going to make you better than new."

He reaches in and grips the damaged spherical device, which fits nicely between his thumb and index finger. He gives it a hearty twist until there's a soft pop and then pulls it free. He gingerly places our processor pod in its stead, snapping it into place with a decisive turn. We stare at it as it whirs to life, spinning first one way, then the other.

"So that's the thing that's going to spark a revolution," Bradie says.

"The revolution has already been sparked," Normand replies. "This is the fan to the flame."

CHAPTER 28

Two minutes later Normand finishes screwing the panel back into place.

"It seems so easy," Bradie says. "*Too* easy."

He winks at me, like he's some clichéd hero in a comic book.

"We should go," Normand replies. There's something weary in his voice. And he won't look at either of us in our foreheads. If it were anyone else I'd assume he was up to something, but as much progress as Normand's made with basic social interaction, he's falling back to old patterns under the stress.

We leave the room of processor towers behind us. I'm actually thinking the worst is over. I'm daring to believe we got away with it. I'm foolishly anticipating a world where we get to think for ourselves, where they won't take Nate away if he Manifests, and it all starts here. Instead, as we stand in the hall of white panels outside the processor room, I find myself in not only a metaphorical cage, but a literal one.

I look left and right. Shiny white polymer security barriers have dropped down, blocking both ends of the hall.

"Guys, are we trapped?" Bradie asks.

Normand nods, weirdly calm.

"When the power surge ripped through the data banks the area was automatically sealed off," he explains, as if he knew this would happen and assumed we would as well. Must mean he knows how to get us out. Would've been nice if he'd mentioned it during our planning session.

I look down at the two protectors we knocked out, locked in here with us. They're starting to stir.

I pick up one of their fallen batons, ready to zap them again.

"No!" Normand shouts at me. "Throw it away!"

"We need to baton them again," I say, which still won't solve our long-term problem that they can identify us. I take a step toward them but Normand grabs my arm.

"It might as well be a lightning rod!" He grabs it from my hand and tosses it, sending it skittering across the smooth floor.

I look at him, confused. He's quickly undoing his tool belt and throwing that away too. He even takes off his watch and sets it on the floor, quickly

192

stepping back. His gaze locks onto the timepiece. It's counting down. 10...9...8...

"Against the security gate," he says to me. "Both of you. Tight as you can."

"Normand," I start to argue, but he's not paying any attention.

...7...6...

He drags me toward one of the security doors that's dropped into place. It's made of the same plastic as the walls.

"Five," he says as we press our backs against the barrier. The guards are shakily getting up.

"Normand," I say.

"...four..."

Bradie takes my hand.

"...three..."

The bigger of the protectors pulls out his blaster.

"...two..."

The other protector picks his gun off the floor him. The bigger one's finger is tensing, ready to fire.

"What are you counting down to?" he demands.

"...one," Normand says and a panel between us and the protectors explodes off the wall. Black lightning shoots out of it, snaking into their metal guns and ripping into their arms. They spasm. The seams of their uniforms start to burst with tiny pops. Smoke rises out from the breaches. The smell of cooking flesh fills the room. The black lightning winks out and the protectors collapse to the floor.

There are black scorch marks on the floor, walls and ceiling where the lightning hit. Normand's watch and tool belt are fried. We were standing in the one safe place in the penned up hallway. Bradie and I are panting. It all happened within seconds. If I'd kept the baton, I'd be dead. I look at Bradie. He's thinking the same thing.

"You're okay," he assures me. "Normand, can you get the security gates open?"

"No," he replies.

"What do you mean 'no'?" I demand.

"We will require assistance," he says, "From someone on the other side. Bradie, there's a communication console in the wall."

"Normand, who do you think he's going to call?" I ask.

"My brother," Bradie replies. "He's going to kill me."

And me, I realize.

Brady goes over to the console and dutifully punches in Trenton's COMM code. The connection comes to life. We hear the sounds of firing and animalistic growls from Trenton's end as the protectors fight to take down the mutated animal outside the fence.

"Trenton, it's Bradie," he says.

"Bradie? What the eff! Get off my COMM line!" Trenton shouts.

"Trenton," Bradie says, forcing the words out. "I'm in trouble."

Trenton is momentarily silent. We hear more shots, explosions, a monstrous howl. And protectors screaming in pain.

"Where are you?" Trenton asks.

"Sending you my location," Bradie replies. "We're sealed in by drop doors."

Trenton doesn't curse. He doesn't yell. His anger seeps through the preternatural steadiness of his voice. "What are you doing on sub-level 3?"

Bradie doesn't answer.

Trenton releases a defeated sigh and we hear him squawk, "I can't. You're on your own."

"Please," Bradie says. And then as if he's been saving this for the most desperate of situations, he adds, "You owe me."

It's so broken and beseeching I try to go to him, to hold his hand, to squeeze it in my own. But Normand holds me back. In fact, he yanks and drags me away from Bradie with two big steps. I look at him in confusion, jerk my arm free, and turn toward Bradie just as pink lightning bursts out of the COMM console. It slams into Bradie so hard it sends him flying into the opposite wall, pinning him there as his body gyrates like pulsating jelly.

His head is thrown back, jaws locked in a silent howl, unable to control a single muscle in his body. He starts to smoke and I can smell the hairs on his arms as they smolder. The pink lightning winks out and he collapses. Only a few heartbeats have passed.

"No," I breathe. "No, no, no, no, no!"

I collapse to my knees next to him. An animalistic howl shreds its way out of my lungs, worse even than the woman in the Yellow Zone crying over her son. I cradle Bradie's head. I'm sobbing. Blisters rise up all over his skin, red, raw and angry. He's gasping for air, like a fish deprived of water.

"Bradie? Bradie!" I shout. "Hang on." I turn to Normand. "We have to get him to sick bay."

Normand's shaking. If I didn't know better, I'd say there were tears in his eyes. It must be from the smoke. Except he's staring at Bradie, and he says, "I'm sorry, Bradie. I'm so sorry."

"Bradie? Bradie!" It's Trenton's voice. The COMM is somehow still working. "Bradie, are you all right? Caitlin, what's happened?"

"He's been hit!" I sob. "An energy surge. He's covered in burns."

I hear broken blips of swearing as the COMM fitfully flutters on and off, and then it goes dead. Is he coming for us? I don't know.

"Caitlin?" Bradie sobs. "It hurts." He's passing in and out of consciousness. When he comes to, I lie and say, "It's going to be okay, baby."

After what seems like forever, there's a hiss of compressed air and the security barrier is sliding up. Trenton stands there. His visor is open. He takes the scene in at a glance and if Bradie weren't still alive I have no doubt that Normand and I would soon be dead.

"You blasted morons!" he swears, kneeling down beside his brother.

He checks Bradie's pulse and scans his brother's injuries.

"We have to get him to sick bay," I say.

Trenton glares at me. He's thinking what I'm thinking, what neither of us will say out loud. That Bradie is going to die.

Trenton scoops his brother in his strong arms, and we run for the elevator.

Come on, I think as we wait for the doors to open. They finally do. We ride it up to the health unit and as soon as we arrive we step into chaos. Burned protectors are everywhere, crying and screaming. Doctors and medics rush amongst them. Trenton places his brother on a gurney. A doctor is at Trenton's side in an instant.

"Where are you hurt?" the doctor asks. His light purple uniform is splattered with blood.

"I...I rescued these cadets," Trenton replies.

"Well, get back to the battle field before that thing gets through," the doctor shouts.

Trenton looks ready to punch him in the face. I put a restraining hand on his arm. He rounds on me as if he's about to beat me to death. Part of me wants him to. This is my fault.

"Go," I say. "You can deal with me later."

"Don't think I won't," he promises.

The doctor is filling a syringe with a glowing blue liquid, which he injects into Bradie.

"We need a drip!" he yells.

A medic hurries over and hooks Bradie up to an IV and places sensor pads on his heart and other organs.

The doctor injects Bradie with a clear liquid, "for the pain," and then half-a-dozen protectors are being brought in, covered in electric burns and scorch marks. One of them has been mauled, his arm completely ripped off. His screams fill my ears, and the doctor abandons us, rushing to him. A medic starts cutting Bradie's clothes and peeling them off. They come away dark with blood and skin. I can't even recognize him.

"He'll need grafts," the medic says as she starts wrapping him in gauze soaked with some sort of steroidal cocktail. "Lots of them."

She covers him head to toe in the bandages, and then she's turning to another patient, a screaming protector with blood squirting from his neck. Two stocky orderlies are pinning him down and another medic is trying to stem the flow of blood. I gaze at Bradie.

"I want to hold his hand," I say to Normand, "But I can't because that will just hurt him more."

"Would you like me to hold yours?" he asks. "Is that the appropriate course of action under the circumstances?"

"Yes," I say, nodding fervently. "Yes, it is."

He takes my wrist, holding it as if his fingers were pincers, and squirts a clear disinfectant onto my palm He rubs it in with his finger tips, and only then takes my hand in his. I laugh and cry at the same time.

"You're a good friend," I say, giving his hand a squeeze.

This is where he should squeeze back, but he doesn't, because such nuances are beyond him.

"Thank you," he says. "I appreciate the positive reinforcement."

And then I can't take it anymore. I think I'm going to laugh but instead my throat catches and breaks into sobs. The tears pour from my eyes and I fold into Normand's soft body. He puts his arms around me, just like he's been taught. They rest there like heavy dough.

"There, there," he says, as if reading from a script Bradie had given him for when someone cries. "There, there."

CHAPTER 29

All night, I refuse to leave Bradie's side. I sit in a padded chair, wracked with guilt as I stare at his mummified form. Whatever numbness the Chair granted me, it's gone. I have no idea what Trenton will do to me when he gets back, but I'll be here for his punishment when he's ready to dish it out.

At some point, exhaustion overtakes me, and I manage to doze off. When I wake, there's sun streaming in from the translucent window. The first thing I see is Bradie, lying peacefully in his medically induced coma. The second is Trenton with two protectors, their copper uniforms laced with black piping. The all-seeing eye in a fist on their vocation patch is similarly black.

I knock over my chair as I get to my feet. A medic shushes me and gives me the evil eye, then she sees the protectors with black piping and scurries away with a mouse-like squeak. These are not ordinary protectors. They work directly with the agents.

"Trenton," I say. "What have you done?"

"It's *Officer* Trenton, *cadet*," he replies. "And *I* did my duty."

"Come with us, cadet," one of the protectors says.

I glare at Trenton as I walk past him and he grabs me by the arm.

"I warned you," he says. "I would do *anything* for my brother."

"You're going to get him killed," I whisper.

"Good," he replies. "Because my brother's better off dead."

He shoves me into the protectors. My heart hammers as they push me toward the elevators. *What did Trenton tell them? What does Trenton even know?* His words echo in my ears. *My brother's better off dead.* There's a part of me that wonders, *Is he right?*

The protectors take me several floors up. When the elevator doors open, I'm not greeted by the familiar white walls, floor and ceiling that are ubiquitous in the Cube. This hallway is all shiny black. They shove me forward. I trip, but catch myself. Our boots make tapping sounds as we stride forward, the protectors just behind me. There's instrumental music playing from speakers hidden in the walls.

They stop in front of a door that blends with the rest of the hall. It hisses open and they push me inside. I stare at a familiar face seated behind a shiny black desk. It's the agent who took Bradie away on the train, and coerced me into joining the Protectorate cadet program. Eel Man.

He doesn't look at me. He's watching a holo projection of the infocast that's been running nonstop since the mutant was stopped. A soft glow from the emitter reflects off the red logo of a noose on his chest. Fixated on the infocast, he snaps his fingers in my direction and points at a shiny, curvy black chair.

I sit. Still staring at the image of the rhinonstrosity slaughtering protectors, Eel Man snaps once at the protector on my left, then snaps once at the protector on my right, and then waves for them to leave. They salute stiffly and the door clicks shut behind them.

Down in the corner of the holo update is Informant Aarav Chandar providing the details of what took place. He's handsome, with a square jaw and slicked back hair, dressed in a muted yellow jacket buttoned all the way up to its short collar. The emblem on his chest is of a microphone.

"And as you can see here a valiant, though futile, effort on the part of protectors to defend themselves against this beast, that was ironically birthed in the aftermath of the very war we dregs started so long ago."

I gaze at the images of the mutant slaughtering dozens of protectors, smashing through hover tanks, blasting energy into heli-fighters, ripping a protector to pieces in its jaws.

"It's almost too much to watch," the agent says without blinking.

"Yes," I agree, "It's..."

Eel Man snaps his fingers at me. "No talking. Ah, here it comes."

In the holo image, I see Jupitar City in the background. From its gleaming towers comes a ball of light. It flies like a comet across the river leaving a glowing trail in its wake.

"But ever the humanitarians, the good denizens of Jupitar City won't leave their far weaker neighbors across the river to fend for themselves," Informant Aarav Chandar beams on the info cast. "You can see here Captain Light is reporting for duty."

As the comet gets closer I can see the outline of a muscular man with a form fitting cowl hiding his face. I immediately remember him taking the boy from his family. He barely gets within 50 measures of the gigantic mutant when a ball of light the size of a fist breaks off from the larger globe he's emitting. It drops, falling fast. Twenty measures from the ground, it jerks to life and fires like a missile toward the rhinonstrosity.

The howling creature is sucking up lightning from the energy syphons positioned all around him. It sees the ball coming and pauses amidst a battalion of corpses lying at its feet. The protectors quickly fall back. The mutant squints at the energy ball racing through the air toward it. It roars and the ball of light shoots right into its mouth and down its throat. The look on the creature's face is almost comical, like a person who has swallowed a bug.

The creature burps and staggers, its face screwed up in pain. The ball is bouncing around inside of it. I can see its stomach bulge every time the ball strikes its innards. In a corner of the screen appears a box with a bald man with thick spectacles, wearing a bright blue suit. He's an expert from Jupitar City.

"Now some of you dregs might be wondering why this mutant creature doesn't just absorb the energy of Captain Light's projectile. I believe that it's the creature's *epidermis* that has the necessary cellular configuration for that ability. It's internal digestive system is limited to absorption of a more conventional kind." The image of the expert fades away.

Captain Light floats in a luminescent bubble above the suffering mutant. Finally, the photon ball burst out of the rhinonstrosity's chest, and the creature falls dead to the ground. The deadly globe sizzles as it burns off the creature's blood, then arcs back up into the air, and coalesces with the larger aura surrounding Captain Light's densely muscled physique.

There are loud cheers from the protectors below. He salutes them, and without a word flies back across the river.

"Now that is just classic Captain Light," the informant says. "Not a word. He says it all with a simple salute. What a hero!"

I stare at the dead protectors surrounding the mutant's corpse. Eel Man hits rewind, pausing it as the rhinonstrosity belches up a stream of pink lightning.

"More than a hundred protectors were killed in the end. Unfortunately for you, Officer Trenton was not one of them," Eel Man says.

I stiffen.

What did Trenton tell him?

"Did you know there was a second mutant attack last night?" the agent asks.

"No," I say with surprise.

"Yes, it failed to make the info broadcasts, but let's see," he says, tapping at the smooth surface of his desk. The holo image of the rhinonstrosity fizzles and is replaced by another. I watch as dozens of protectors fire plasma weapons at a cat-like-mutant. It evades them with dizzying movements, disappearing amidst the debris of the Yellow Zone.

"Not what we pay them for," he says. "They will face disciplinary action, but at least they chased it back out into the Red Zone. We've also been tracking a third mutant that broke through the outer perimeter using the breach the first monstrosity created, but it's somehow dropped off the grid. Our best intel is it's somewhere in the Yellow Zone. It'll turn up. But listen to me go on. Why would I even tell you such a thing?"

"Because I'll be a protector one day?" I offer.

He laughs gaily. "My dear! Here you are sitting in the office of an agent after some rather questionable behavior, and you think it's because you're going to be a protector one day? Caitlin, I'm telling you this because you've clearly figured out that it's no coincidence that three mutated animals breached the perimeter within days of Runners trying to make off with a Supergenic. We're being punished."

"I...What? By who?" I ask.

He eyes me, as if trying to figure out if I'm serious. "How utterly clueless you are," he says with shock. "The Supergenics, of course. We almost let one of theirs get away. They're not going to let that stand."

"But, it's not our fault!" I insist.

"Isn't it? If our security measures were tighter, our propaganda more effective, our citizens more cooperative, there would be no Runners."

I stare at all the bodies. I know those people. And they're dead, to teach us a lesson.

"I had no idea," I admit. *But Normand did*, I realize. He figured it out, and not with his GRAMS. He saw the pattern. *That's how he knew when we had to be ready.*

Eel Man swivels in his chair one way then the other. He stops and wags his finger at me.

"Well, you and your friends were certainly prepared for the distraction the mutant provided, allowing you to do this."

He taps away on his computer and up pops a security feed of me, Bradie, and Normand.

"I had to do quite a lot of digging to recover this footage. Someone is very good at covering their tracks."

Not good enough apparently. I watch the images of us taking down the two protectors who caught us outside the processor room. I sting one with his own electrified baton and he falls to the ground. The footage cuts out for a moment, then resumes with us emerging from the processor room.

"The cameras inside the processor chamber short circuited from the electrical overload," the agent says, "But according to the time code, the three of you were in there for just over ten minutes."

"I can explain," I begin, but of course I can't.

"Can you?" Eel Man replies. "While you're at it…"

He presses more buttons on his desk, and the image of us gets sucked away, replaced by another. I stare in shock. It can't be, but it is.

No. Please no.

It's an image of the most recent comic book Normand and I created. *Shadowren*, Issue 1.

"I confess, my son is a sucker for comic books, but I'm not familiar with this title."

I watch the emission flip through the pages projected in front of me.

There's a black and white drawing of a girl. She's beaming triumphantly, dressed in a skirt with a cleavage-revealing top and a cape.

"A young girl dreams of Manifesting superpowers," the agent says reading the text boxes. The image shifts to page two. It's a twisted mirror of the first image. "But alas," the agent gasps melodramatically, still reading, "She fails her final Testing Day. She must face reality. She is nothing more than a mere dreg! This is the future she has to look forward to."

The panel shows the girl staring at her shoes, shoulders hunched in defeat. She's wearing baggie coveralls as she sweeps up contaminated waste.

"Aww," the agent says. "You mean she's going to have to *work*? How awful."

The page flips, and a series of fresh panels emerge.

"Such would have been her fate, but walking home one day, she sees protectors beating her neighbor, Mr. Fantome. The protectors are taking away his grandson because the boy has Manifested."

In the next square, the girl lifts her broom and smashes it over the protector's head. The protectors corner her against a wall.

"You're going to wish you hadn't done that," a protector says. They are looming shadows towering over her quaking frame, until...

"I'm through playing with you," Mr. Fantome says. He holds two pieces of the broken broom handle. He attacks, twirling them like cyclones. In a series of *BAMs! WHACKs!* and *POWs!* the old man lays the four protectors low.

"What happens when the protectors wake up?" the girl in the comic book asks.

"Grandson," Mr. Fantome says. "Can you make them forget?"

"I can try," the little Supergenic boy replies, holding up his hands as he uses his powers to strip the protectors of their memories.

From there, old man Fantome offers to train the girl in the ways of the warrior. She accepts. There's a montage of the withered man teaching her how to fight hand-to-hand, scale walls, do flips, and use an array of blades.

"When they look at me, they want to see a broken old man, so that is what I show them," Mr. Fantome says in a dialogue bubble. "You will wear a mask of a different kind."

I get so engrossed I actually forget I'm sitting in Eel Man's office, and that he's reading it aloud. I'm mouthing the words along with him. It's then the story takes a turn. In a bid to infiltrate the protectors, the comic book girl joins their ranks—except little by little she's brainwashed. She turns on her own ideals, and betrays old man Fantome. She turns him in, and to prove her loyalty to the protectors she once vowed to defeat, she beats him —to death.

"Only then," Eel Man reads aloud, "As he dies in her arms does she realize what a monster she's become. Protectors should protect the weak— not make them live in fear."

The issue ends with the girl vowing to make right her wrongs. She dons her Shadowren costume, and her thoughts appear in bold letters:

We can be more than they will let us be. You can *be more. They use us as indentured servants. They turn us against each other. They take our children, our brothers, our sisters, then expect us to thank them for it. They try to break us, but we are stronger than they know. You* are *stronger than you know. This is our land. This is our home. These are our people. It's time to fight back.*

The image of Shadowren hangs there. I will face the death penalty for this. So will Bradie and Normand. And yet I can't help myself. I'm dying for issue number 2.

CHAPTER 30

We both stare at Shadowren, floating there. Several heartbeats pass. I cough. Eel Man taps his chin.

"So, I don't get it," he says. "If the little boy can make them forget, why doesn't he just do that to the protectors in the first place? And old man Fantome, if he's so rough and tumble, why did he even need this girl's help?"

I say nothing.

"Well?" he demands. "You went to all this trouble to sneak this comic book into the mind Calibration system. Defend your plot holes."

I lick my dry lips. I was ready for the agent to put a gun to my head. Somehow, his critique still hurts. Normand and I worked really hard on this.

"Come on," he says. "I'm a fan. Do tell."

"Well," I say hesitantly, "the little boy doesn't fully control his mental powers. And, in fact, the protectors *will* start to remember what happened, causing some to hunt Shadowren, others to turn to her cause."

Eel Man arches his brow. "It's plausible, I suppose. And the old man?"

I shrug. "He's an old man. They caught him off guard. It happens."

"Yes," he agrees soberly. "Even to me. So what am I to do with this?"

With those words it suddenly occurs to me that I'm sitting in his office. Not an Audit Room. *Why is that?*

He's trying to trick you, I realize, by putting me at ease.

"I've had the cadets and protectors run through their Calibrations with your little story embedded within the sessions, just out of curiosity," he says.

"And?" I ask, emoting just a bit too much excitement.

"And...nothing," he replies. "All the readings come back normal."

The slightest of smirks gives me away. I might as well be doing an evil laugh. His eyes narrow.

"Your leg-brace friend added a subroutine to alter the output results," he realizes out loud. "Clever. Even that little light show at the Revelry, it was all part of it."

He's referring to my first night as a cadet, when Crystal drove us out to the arena in the middle of the Yellow Zone. He was there. *I knew it!* But it takes me a few seconds to realize what light show he's talking about.

"Normand linked us with an energy field," I say. Even now there's a shiver of pleasure as I remember the electricity between me and Bradie. But if I'm understanding Eel Man correctly, it went deeper than that. "We felt as one." He's right, I realize. It felt like group Calibration.

He gets up and walks to a side table by the window. There's a steaming pot of tea with several dainty cups and a three-tier dessert plate with various scones and cream-filled pastries. He pours himself a cup of tea, drops in a few sugar cubes along with some cream and puts a pastry on a plate. He takes a loud sip, not offering me any.

"The caffeine is hell on my nerves but I just can't switch to decaf," he explains. He flips through the pages of the comic book until it stops on the cover. He stares at it. "The question is, do I let this run its course, or do I shut it down?"

My heart is hammering in my ears. Did I hear him right?

"The latter would be easier," he continues. "Safer. I'd have to execute you and your friends, of course. I've certainly made greater moral compromises."

I grip the arms of my chair.

"Do your worst, monster," I say.

He does his little side-to-side finger wave. "Careful. You have no idea what my worst can look like." The insignia on his chest reminds me that this is not a casual threat.

I chew the insides of my cheeks to keep from saying any more.

"My quandary is this," he muses, almost to himself. "I recruited you, and a few others like you, over the years, children with specific brain wave patterns that could upset the group Calibration process."

I cock a brow and snort. "Specific brain wave patterns?" I ask. "You almost make it sound like I'm Supergenic."

He considers this. "Tell me, what is the difference between a mediocre Supergenic and an exceptional dreg?"

I have no answer to a question I'd never thought to ask.

"That's the thing about genetic variation," he says. "It's varied. Even in dregs. Not that it matters. Although your uniqueness allowed you to create a bit of a stir during your first group Calibration, it had no lasting effect. But this! You've inserted suggestions into the Calibration process to create

204

dissent. If I expose you, the new security protocols will be even more difficult to break through. We won't get another chance at this."

Only now does the truth hit me. Eel Man's a rebel!

"So, you're *not* going to execute me?"

He sips his tea, and with a hint of disappointment admits, "No. I'm not. Your little comic book is admittedly crude, but…effective."

I struggle to process all of this.

"You're going to let this play out, aren't you?" I ask. He sets down his tea cup, and stares out at the huge hole that the mutant created. Bulldozers slowly fill it in.

"Yes," he agrees. "I suppose I am."

CHAPTER 31

I feel like I'm on sedatives when I exit Eel Man's office. The protectors assigned to the agent glare at me, clearly disappointed to see me still alive. I want to sprint as fast as I can to the elevator, but I feel like they are like any other predator. If I run, they'll have no choice but to hunt me down. That's their nature. I control my steps by pretending there's glue all over the floor. I do, in fact, see a sticky strip with a cockroach stuck to it. I can empathize.

What have you gotten yourself into?

Eel Man is a subversive. He wanted me in here all along to stir up trouble. Now that I've exceeded expectation, what does that actually mean? Are we allies? We're certainly not partners. Am I his lackey? The latter seems most likely. I finally reach the elevator. I can feel the protectors staring at my back.

"Come on, come on," I mutter at the elevator, willing it to come faster.

The door opens, I get on, push the button for the medical floor, then wave to the protectors down the hall. Even now, I can't help myself. I'm starting to get why Mrs. Cranberry couldn't stand me.

The sliding doors steal them from view and I lean against the slick wall, cupping my face in my hands. I allow myself this momentary weakness for the count of three floors as the elevator descends. I feel the tears building, for all my mistakes, and their consequences, but if I fall apart now there will be more mistakes, and more consequences. I sniffle, wipe my eyes dry, and force my head up.

There's an overly cheery ding as the elevator comes to a stop.

"Medical bay," a computerized voice announces.

I face my mess. Moans rise up from the dozens of protectors injured in yesterday's battle. They lie in their cots, separated one from the other by flimsy white curtains. Machines blip and bleep next to them.

I go to Bradie. Trenton is there, holding his little brother's hand. A machine bleats next to him, monitoring the faint pulse of Bradie's heart. Trenton's eyes are bloodshot from tears.

"Caitlin," he says.

He's not surprised to see me. The agent's already been in touch with him. Trenton looks ready to kill me himself.

"I guess you've already heard," I reply. "That the data stream you sent him was corrupt and unwatchable."

I wait to see if he buys my lie. For his own sake, I hope he does. Trenton is a complication. He could still try to expose me and Normand. Eel Man's solution was to kill him.

"I got the message," Trenton says. "I guess your little techie friend had something to do with that. I guess everyone's buying your story that you got lost during the attack. Doesn't matter," he says. "One way or another, you're going to pay for what you did to my brother."

"Yes," I agree. "I know."

I look down at Bradie. Whatever Trenton plans to dish out, I deserve it. I just hope he doesn't get himself killed in the process. I want to take Bradie's other hand, the one that the agents burned to punish him what seems a lifetime ago, but I can't. His hand is gone. The whole bottom half of his arm has been amputated up to the elbow. Even if he survives, he won't be a protector after this.

Once you learn to fire a gun, there's no turning back. I'm surprised they haven't simply put him out of his misery. I suspect Trenton has something to do with that.

We were such stupid idiots, I say to myself.

I play it over and over in my mind. Bradie at the panel, calling his brother for help, me reaching for him, Normand yanking me back.

I compulsively gorge myself on the memory, in part to figure out what we could've done differently, in part to torture myself. But this time there's something about the memory that makes me pause. Maybe it's Trenton mentioning Normand. Maybe it's Eel Man talking about the light show at the Revelry, the one that Calibrated everyone to me, the one that was created by one person alone, without my consent.

"Normand," I whisper.

When Bradie was being electrocuted, the same thing could've happened to me. It didn't because Normand pulled me to safety. If not for him I'd be lying here too, my skin covered in ointment soaked bandages, my central nervous system fried, and my extremities turning necrotic. It's what I deserve. If that were me lying there, Trenton wouldn't hesitate to pull the breathing tube from my throat and press a pillow over my face.

Instead I'm here, healthy and haunted, and as that brutal moment wrenches my gut, a horrible thought occurs to me.

Normand was so sure of himself when he jerked me away from the panel, it was almost as if he knew there was going to be a power surge. I rewind further, to when the two protectors were drawing their guns on us. Normand was *so* insistent that I throw away my baton, that I not engage them, that I press myself against the wall. And then seconds later the hallway was filled with bolts of lightning.

Effing eff.

I can't be thinking what I'm thinking, and what I'm thinking can't be right. And yet, Normand knew exactly which node had burnt out. He knew not only that the mutant was coming, but that it was going to cause electrical havoc within the Cube, taking out the security measures that would've ruined our plan.

And then the final piece of evidence. Eel Man said that at Revelry Normand created a bond between everyone there. As I relive that moment, I see Normand on a floating platform above a crowd of protectors in the arena in the Yellow Zone. Lightning pulsed around him as if he were a god, and he transformed it into a different kind of energy. I thought he did it with tech, but what if he didn't? What if he didn't need gadgets and gizmos to manipulate electricity?

What if Normand's Supergenic?

Trenton is glaring at me. I barely notice.

Normand can control energy.

I'm reeling at the possibility. Trenton stands up. Do I share my suspicions with him?

"You need to leave," Trenton says. His fists are clenched.

That would be a "no."

"Sure," I say. My mind's working fast, searching for flaws in my "Normand has powers" theory. Normand failed his final testing, but false negatives do happen. But if he knows he has powers, why keep them a secret? Why not move to Jupitar City?

Because he's Normand, I think. *He is such a weirdo.* And a rebel. He's here because he wants to be here, where he can take down the Protectorate. There are still holes in my theory, questions that need answers. Like, how could he do this to Bradie?

Trenton takes a threatening step toward me.

I hold my hands up in peace. "I'm going."

I retreat to the elevator, the impossible racing through my mind. More pieces are falling into place. When we were trapped outside the data node chamber by the drop down walls, the lightning hit Bradie only *after* Trenton refused to help us. Normand knew there was no way Trenton would leave his brother suffering if he was critically injured. To get the king you must sacrifice the pawn.

Trenton was right about one thing. Someone *is* going to pay for what happened to Bradie. That someone is Normand.

CHAPTER 32

I immediately start searching for Normand all over the compound. So many systems are either fried or rebooting that I can't track him down using internal sensors. I ask around but the Cube is huge, and the techies are working triple shifts to get it all fixed. Most are on amphetamines to get them through and want nothing to do with me.

"If you have a work request, put it in through the proper channels," a sallow-faced tech girl tells me. "We'll get to it when we get to it."

By midday, my hunger flares. I can't remember the last time I ate. In the cafeteria, Liam slides in next to me.

"I ran into your tech friend," he says.

"Normand?" I ask, dropping my spoon into my split-pea soup. "Where? When?"

"Twenty minutes ago," he says. "He had a weird message. Says that if you want your questions answered, meet him in your special place."

My hand tightens on a knife. Liam notices.

"Caitlin, if something's up, if you need back up..."

"I don't. You want to stay out of this."

He nods. "I'm pretty sure I do."

He'll have questions later. I'll make up some lie. I'm good at that. I hurry out of the cafeteria, into the hall, past all the tech squads with their soldering equipment and lengths of cable. I get outside just in time to see Normand's distinct figure hobbling onto a bus. He says something to the driver, and it waits for me to catch up.

I'm panting as I get on. Normand stares at my forehead.

"Come," he says to me curtly, limping past the half-dozen people in their seats, to the rear of the bus.

I stare at his back, barely restraining myself. He sits. I force myself to sit next to him.

"I know what you did," I say between clenched teeth.

"Not here," he replies. "Too many eyes. Too many ears."

It galls me, but he's right. The bus ride lasts ten minutes, and it feels like the longest of my life. Normand pulls the notice cord, making a bell ding and the "Next Stop" sign lights up. The bus jerks to a halt and we get off in

210

front of the billboard of a muscled spider kid encouraging teens to Manifest.

The sun is setting and the street lamps are coming alight. We walk side by side to the security fence, where he uses his swipe pad and skeleton key to open the gate. As I follow him into the Yellow Zone, I see him differently forevermore. I should've known better than to trust him. Heroes and villains are both outsiders in their own way; the difference is heroes we look up to. Villains are outcasts, just like Normand.

We move undetected amidst the motion sensors. The real trick is avoiding the sight lines of the crews repairing the fence damaged by the monstrosity, and the heightened patrols searching for the mutated animal that may still be in the Yellow Zone.

"Down low," he says, gesturing for me to duck. I do, the pair of us cramming into a moist alcove.

Moments later I hear the *whumf* of displaced air as a hovercraft whizzes by. I'm tempted to shove him out in front of it. The protector patrol passes. He didn't even look at his swipe pad or the illicit GRAM that allows him to track protector movements. Maybe he doesn't need to. Maybe he never did. If he can control electricity, maybe he can sense it too, tuning into the cells that help power the hovercraft or even the helmets and body packs the protectors wear on patrol. Soon the hovercraft is beyond hearing, leaving only the echo of my labored breathing in the confined space.

"Let us continue," he says.

We're both dressed in our uniforms, him in his coveralls, me in cadet's blue. We reach the Lair and my baton bounces at my side as we pull back the door. He's unusually quiet as we walk down the stairs and enter the old comic book shop. The suspicious part of me suddenly wonders if this is a trap.

Normand turns to face me and I go into a fighting stance, whipping my baton into the air. He doesn't move. Doesn't lift his hands to fire lightning into me. Instead, framed by rows of comic books, and a wall of plastic shields, blasters, and capes he gazes at me, and he sighs sadly.

"So," he says to me. "Today's the day."

He sounds tired. Not the kind of tired I'd expect from someone who's worked three shifts in a row. There's worn out and then there's this, as if his very soul had grown weary—not that there's any such thing as a soul.

He looks around the comic book store. He picks up an issue with a muscled man in a loin cloth swinging on a vine on the cover. He puts it down.

"You blame me for what happened to Bradie," he says, staring at my forehead.

I had a whole ranting speech planned. Instead I ask for the simple truth.

"Is it your fault?"

"Yes."

I wait for him to elaborate. He doesn't. He is *so* frustrating!

"Explain," I demand.

He looks at his new watch, then back at me. "Caitlin, as you have already guessed, I am Supergenic."

My grip tightens on my baton. *I knew it!*

"I'm going to kill you for what you did to Bradie," I say.

He cocks his head, surprised by my words. "That's not what you say. You're supposed to ask me why. Why would I hurt Bradie? You're supposed to remind me he's your boyfriend." That is, in fact, what I was thinking. It's like he can read my mind. Can he read my mind?

I raise my baton and I lunge at him. He cowers and raises his arms over his head.

"I did it because of you!" he shouts in a panic.

I freeze, baton overhead. I'm shaking. "Don't you put this on me!"

And yet, despite my rage, I know the truth. It *is* on me. I suspected that Normand might have a crush on me. Everybody said so. But it was harmless. And then he and Bradie became friends. And he had a bigger crush on Crystal. And it was never weird with us, meaning it was always weird with us, because Normand's weird. He did this *because* Bradie's my boyfriend.

"I know what you're thinking," he says. "That I was jealous and that's why I hurt him." He's still holding his hands up defensively.

If he can *read my mind then...*

"Caitlin," he interrupts my thoughts. "I can see the future. That's how I knew when and where the lightning would strike, how to evade the patrols, and which node would burn out. It's how I knew when the mutant would attack. It's also how I know some of what you're thinking, because in the future, you tell me."

I shake my head. "There's no such thing as precognition. Even the Supergenics say so."

"It's rare," he says. "And most precogs go insane from what they see, or from trying to change what's to come."

"But not you?" I say skeptically.

"My brain works differently. I'm a weirdo, remember? But yes, it will kill me too in the end."

"You failed your Testing Day," I object.

"The tests are flawed," he replies. "And telepaths can't seem to access the temporal distortion in my mind."

I punch a cardboard cut-out of a robot.

"No!" I shout. "I came here to punish you, not to listen to this crap."

"My punishment is coming," he assures me. "There's so much I wish to tell you. About how I Manifested. The things I've seen. The lives I've led. And to confess the horrible things I've done in those futures that will never be."

I shake my head. "What are you even saying? The lives you've led? What does that mean?"

"That's how my power works. I only see *my* future. Perhaps 'see' is the wrong word. I experience it. I *live* it. That future is then fed back to me in the past, at which point I can let it play out, re-live it the same as before, or sometimes I can change it, then that new future is also sent back into the past. And then I can change it again, and again, and again. Out of all those lives, can you believe this is the first time Bradie and I have become friends?"

At the mention of Bradie, I suddenly decide to believe everything Normand's telling me. Normand can see the future. And he can change it through the past. That means he can fix everything.

"Save him," I say. "You tell your younger self to save Bradie. You do it, and you do it right now. This future, it never gets to happen. Do you understand me?" I wait for him to obey. I wait to disappear as this present gets erased like the mistake that it is. But nothing changes. I remember everything. The robot still has my fist mark in it.

"Why are we still here?" I demand.

I grab Normand and shove him against the wall. "You can save Bradie, so you do it."

"No," he shakes his head.

I've got him pinned in between a rubber mask of some old guy with grey hair and a big chin and another white-faced grinning villain. Normand's gazing at his watch. Only now do I accept that it's not some OCD tick. He's counting down to something. He knows what will take place. He knows *when* it will take place. His watch isn't a watch. It's a timer.

"What is it?" I demand. "What's about to happen?"

He shakes his head. "If I tell you, it could change things."

"No," I say. "You don't get to play the all-seeing and all-knowing. You don't get to pronounce who lives and who dies."

"You're referring to Bradie," he says.

Obviously.

"That wasn't my decision," he insists. "It was yours."

My heart throbs. My face burns. My fists are ready to lash out.

"It doesn't matter what we attempt," he says. "In every timeline where we rebel against the Protectorate, Bradie ends up mortally wounded. Time is... tricky."

"Time is *tricky*?" I demand. "What does that even mean?"

"It means..." he starts to explain.

"Shut up!" I yell. I'm thinking fast. He said something important. *Very* important.

In every timeline where we rebel against the Protectorate, Bradie ends up mortally wounded.

"What happens to Bradie if we don't rebel?" I ask.

He's silent.

"Tell me!" I demand, but he doesn't have to. I see it in his avoidant gaze, unable to even look me in the forehead. He *has* saved Bradie, in one of his futures, in one of his pasts. I'm not sure what to call them.

"Then stop us," I say. "Stop us from defying the Protectorate."

"No," he replies.

"Why not?" I slam the palm of my hand onto the wall next to his face.

"Because you told me not to," he replies.

That makes me pause.

"In the timelines where we don't fight back, you and Bradie get married," Normand says. "You have a daughter. She Manifests. You know what that means, so you Run, the three of you, into the Yellow Zone. You don't get far. No one ever does. Not even you. They kill Bradie immediately. You, they want to suffer. They make you watch as they change your daughter."

214

I don't believe a word of this, and yet the comic book girl in me needs to know…

"What do you mean they *change* her?"

"Her power is intermittent and if left alone likely to go dormant. The gene therapy required to make it 'take' is brutal. There's no anesthetic. It drives her clinically insane, so when they're done, the Supergenics dump her in the Yellow Zone to attack the boroughs."

Now I know he's lying. "They wouldn't. Not to one of their own."

"Yes, they will, and they do. Where do you think so many of the monstrosities come from? Some Supergenics are more animal than human. Not fit for civilized society. But they still have their uses. To attack us. To remind us we need heroes to come to our rescue. To keep us so afraid of what the fence is keeping out we accept that it's also keeping us in."

"You're lying," I say without conviction. And then I beg. "Please tell me it's all a lie. Please tell me you'll save him."

"In the futures where I do, your daughter pays the price. In those futures where I manage to reach you in your cell, and you know about my power, you beg me, *beg* me to not let that future happen, no matter what. I owe you that. You *and* Bradie."

"This isn't happening," I insist.

"You have to go," he says.

"I'm not going anywhere until you change all this!" I shout.

"I've tried. Hundreds of time. It's either him, or your daughter. I can't save them both."

I shake my head.

"I can't have known what this would mean for him. How could I? You can't hold yourself to a promise I've yet to ask of you."

"I can and I will. I told you everything that I could in the time that we had about the consequences of your request. That Bradie would never regain proper function of the right side of his body. That he'd lose bladder control. That the headaches would slowly drive him to chemical dependency. That he'd come to blame you for his broken body, mind and life before taking his own."

"I hate you," I say.

"I know," he says sadly. "But I love you. And this is one of the hard things I have to do because of it."

"You know nothing about love, and you never will."

I wait for him to crumble, this man with his soft and weak body, his gimpy leg, his eyes that need glasses as thick as a deck of cards. Instead he stares me right in the eyes—not at my forehead, but in the eyes—and says unflinchingly, "A lot of people think love is that wild feeling they get in their belly when they see or think about or touch that other person. At least that's how they've described it. I wouldn't know. But I do know that isn't love. That's infatuation. *This* is love. When things get hard and ugly and the one you love stumbles under the weight, and you take it on yourself so that other person can keep going. My love for you has deepened over many different lifetimes. You have no idea the adventures we have shared. The revolutions we have fought. The dark times you have seen me through. My love for you is not the romantic kind. It runs so much deeper than that. You saved me from myself. Now I will do the same for you."

His refusal makes me snap. I want to hurt him the way Lilianne would. With my words.

"You will always be alone," I say.

He nods. "There is but one future where I experience romantic love." He looks around at the comic book store, at the images of muscled men and busty women in their tights. "How I wish you could meet her! She loved me, she really did. And I loved her. But some lives can only be lived once. I can't go back there, not without losing myself and others suffering for it. Nothing is free. This is the price we must pay."

I look at "the no-touch zone," the countertop where everything has to stay in its exact place. I sweep my arms across it, shoving everything off. The metal balls clang against the floor. I stomp on the red S on the scarf, and I kick the Taser away. My actions are stupidly childish, and for a heartbeat, utterly satisfying.

I turn on Normand and shove my finger in his face. He's not looking me in the eyes anymore. He's staring at the floor.

"This isn't done," I say.

I turn my back on him. My eyes drift to a poster of Tigara watching me leave. I ignore her, stepping over the burn mark in the carpet and yanking open the door to the stairs.

As it whines shut behind me, I catch Normand looking at his watch. He never did tell me what he was counting down to. He mutters to himself, "She better not be late."

CHAPTER 33

As I emerge into the open air, I know that this is my last time in the Lair. I can't ever come back. It's tainted and ruined, just like the rest of the Yellow Zone.

I told you to burn it, a part of me chastises.

I duck down to avoid the sight lines of the crews repairing the security fence. That's when I hear it, a piece of rubble skittering softly off a wall, hitting the ground roughly 10 measures behind me. In this city that's ready to collapse in on itself a bit of falling debris is common place. Except there's not a shadowren to be heard. That's weird. Added to that is an odd sense of familiarity to this scene, as if it's played out before, and I know the truth.

I'm not alone out here.

I take the baton from my hip. I turn and scan the wreckage of the Yellow Zone—glancing over a fire hydrant leaning at a weird angle, a utility pole that somehow has managed to remain standing straight up after all these years, and a busted up sign for "oca-Cola." There's no one there; except there is.

This isn't the first time I've faced invisible foes out here. I flash back to the Runners; of the dad being executed, of the kid flipping out and throwing force fields left and right, of the mom chasing after him, of me picking up a rifle and...

I shake the memory off. I won't hurt anybody, not this time. I set the baton down, and step back. Someone must've taken advantage of the damage to the fence to try to get out. I'm going to help them.

"It's okay," I say. "I'm not going to hurt you."

There's a boom of thunder, and in the space between lightning strikes, I hear a low animalistic growl. That's not a Runner. It sounds big, whatever it is. Too big to be one of the feral tomcats that live in the Yellow Zone.

"Easy there," I say, as if it were a trained dog. I eye my baton a measure in front of me.

Only now do I remember what Eel Man said. *We've been tracking a third mutant that broke through the outer perimeter.*

At first, it's hard to see the thing. It's got grey scales with flecks of brown that help it blend with the surrounding concrete and rusty metal rods sticking up from the collapsed buildings all around. Like many of the mutated animals that make it through the outer fence, it's disturbingly human in its proportions, with long lean arms and legs, rounded buttocks and well-proportioned breasts.

It's a she, I realize. Not that it matters.

The mutated animal sniffs at the air through a shrunken nose that is only slightly more than a pair of nostrils on a bump in the middle of her face. I'm downwind, but I don't think it's me she's smelling. In the distance, I can see a series of hovercrafts whisking toward us.

She hisses. I'm expecting a forked tongue, but it's round and pink, and her eyes, they aren't yellow with vertical pupils. They're hazel and round at the center, with flecks of gold. They're beautiful.

Doesn't matter. My fear turns to something else: the need to hit something; the need to *kill* something. I want it to be Normand, but this monstrosity will have to do.

She crouches low and her skin shifts with every move. She's clearly got chameleon abilities, sophisticated enough to fool the motion sensors, up to a point anyway. I lunge and grab my baton. It's firm in my grip and I strike it against the concrete where she stood a moment ago. I'm too slow. She's already gone and I feel the reverberation of the stick running up my arm.

Where is she?

I spin and she lands a solid blow, slashing me across the back. If not for the reinforced lining of my training uniform, I'd be shredded from my shoulder blade down to my opposite hip. As is, I stumble and roll.

I catch a glimpse of rippling air and I sweep my foot across the ground, knocking her legs out from under her—for all the good it does me. She lands on all fours and launches herself at me.

She's on top of me, her smooth reptilian palms wrapped around my throat. As she chokes me a part of me realizes I have to stop thinking of it as a her. She's a thing. An it. And yet, her hazel eyes are hauntingly familiar and all too human—not reptilian at all. And the way she fights, something's not right about it. She's got claws and jagged teeth, yet she's choking me. It's like she doesn't know what to do with her own arsenal.

She lifts me up by the throat, drawing one hand back, claws growing longer. She looks at them. She's starting to figure it out. I get a solid hold of the thumb around my jugular and crush it in on itself. She hisses in pain as I break her hold. I land a solid kick in her abdomen and she slams into a

218

jagged piece of concrete, leaving behind the telltale sign of blood. Caught in freeze-frame it looks oddly like a panel taken from one of our comic books.

I hear cheers behind me and realize there's a semi-circle of hovercrafts bobbing 15 measures away. Outside the fence, a crowd of local workers and retirees is forming. The mutant hisses at them angrily. The protectors point their rifles at the mutated creature, but they don't fire. All of this is against protocol. They should be killing her, *it*, and arresting me for being in the Yellow Zone without permission. But they're not. Many of the protectors have their visors up. I can see their faces, and there's something in their eyes, like they need me to do this, hand-to-hand, to prove that we too have power, to make the stories about human heroes true.

Maybe the Calibration program we inserted is working. And maybe I need to stop worrying about that and start focusing on staying alive.

The mutant comes at me and I smash the baton hard against her face. I'm about to do it again when she shakes her head and it's as if the blow clears something inside of her. She looks at the crowd differently. She's not hissing at them anymore. She appears...confused. I get another weird sense of déjà vu. She gazes at me, and in a voice that is oddly familiar, she says, "Puddle Pants?"

I stare into those beautiful eyes flecked with gold, the eyes that I long ago realized camouflaged a monster, and now the monster is before me, revealed.

"Lilianne?" I whisper.

It can't be. Lilianne's not a mutated animal. She's a Supergenic. And I've been beating the crap out of her! That's an offense punishable by death. Then again, so are most of my offenses. But this time I'm *really* caught, with dozens of witnesses. She sees the fear in my eyes. She looks back at the crowd. Is she searching for her parents? Her friends?

What is she doing here? Why does she look like this? The things Normand said, about my unborn daughter, of her being dumped in the Yellow Zone, could they be true? Could the Supergenics really be doing this to their own? Out off all the fantasies I've had of kicking her ass, I never imagined this.

Yes, you did, a part of me says.

And that's when I realize why all of this feels so familiar.

"Venomerella," I whisper. Normand drew this—a version of it anyway.

Lilianne looks at me and I wait for her treacherous *I got you now* smile. Instead she says quietly, so only I can hear, "Hit me."

"What?"

"Hit me, as hard as you can. Then you rescue me. Do you understand? Do *not* let them cut me open. Not again."

People are watching. The protectors see that something's changed. The hovercrafts start closing in.

"Make it look good," she says. She lunges at me, hissing loudly. "Come on Puddle Pants."

I swing my baton, smashing her as hard as I can, first one way, then again with a backhand. Twin cracks fill my ears, joined by the ever-present rumbling of thunder in the background.

Venomerella falls unconscious to the ground and loud cheers fill the air.

CHAPTER 34

The crowd and the protectors are chanting my name. It's what I've always wanted. This moment to shine, where the world gets to see all the specialness within me. I drop the bloody baton. It clatters against asphalt. The anger and adrenaline are dissolving away, leaving me hollow.

None of this will help Bradie. None of this will fix my broken friendship with Normand. Mending things with my mom seems easy by comparison. And none of this explains what the hell Lilianne is doing here. I still can't bring myself to believe Normand's story. I look down at her unconscious form, her lizard scales, more animalistic than ever now that I can't see her human eyes.

What did they do to you? I wonder. *All that jealousy over the years, and for what? To see her end up like this?*

A black-clad female agent leads a swarm of protectors in their copper uniforms through the gate. The shouts of my name die down.

"Get that filth back!" she yells to the protectors, pointing at the people gathered by the gate. Protectors with plastic shields grudgingly start forcing them away. The red noose on her chest seems to glare at us.

The protectors assigned to the agent surround me, shoving me roughly away from Lilianne. I expect them to shoot her, like the mutant animal they believe her to be, but instead they manacle her arms and legs, and toss her into a holding van.

Do not let them cut me open, she said. *Not again.*

I take a step toward the vehicle and the agent grabs my arm.

"You've got questions to answer."

Half a dozen of the agent's protectors surround me. I stare at the distorted reflection of my face in their visors. No one's cheering now, but the rest of the protectors clench their weapons tightly.

Are they thinking of coming to my rescue?

A couple step forward. I shake my head at them and they stop. I'm shoved into the back of a vehicle. The agent slides in next to me.

"I can explain," I say.

"You tell me *nothing*," she insists.

"I don't understand," I reply. "I thought..."

"That I was going to interrogate you?" she snorts. "Do I look like I have a death wish? You've pissed off some *very* important people. The Supergenics are sending a telepath to Mind Audit you, and anyone who's been in contact with you, so whatever it is they think you know, you keep it to yourself. You're not taking me down with you."

I stare out the window of the truck, at the river separating us from Jupitar City. A hovercraft with the lightning bolt insignia on it is skimming across the water toward the Cube. I keep my eyes on it as best I can as we drive through the borough.

This is about Lilianne, I realize. She's a secret. An important secret. When I hit her head, she changed. She was no longer a wild animal. *I'm not supposed to know that she's not a mutant. I'm not supposed to know that they sent her back to the borough to die, and for what? To keep us scared of what's outside the fence?*

I see the Cube ahead of us, massive and white. We disappear down a ramp that takes us under its surface into the parking garage below. The protectors shackle my hands and throw a hood over my head. I'm led into a room, shoved into a seat and only then is the hood yanked off. The restraints they leave on. The door hisses closed behind me. I'm alone, in a room of all black, lit by a purple glow that comes from the seams in the ceiling. The air is intentionally warm and damp. This is an interrogation chamber.

"You might as well make yourself comfortable," the female agent says over an intercom. "The telepath will be here shortly."

Normand says it's possible to trick telepaths. Joshua said the same. Neither explained how.

I'm guessing an hour goes by before the door hisses open. The moment the man with the grey flecks in his hair steps in, I know I'm as good as dead. He wears a crisp uniform of blue with bands of yellow. It's the same man from my Testing Day. The one that filled Joshua with pain and fear, and nearly killed me. His insignia is not that of a tester though. It's of a lightning bolt atop of a brain. He's a mind auditor.

"You," I say in surprise.

He arches a brow. "We have never met," he says. "Though I understand your confusion. According to my records, my twin brother was in charge of the team that tested you. Fair warning, he's the weak one. All he can do with his abilities is cause pain. I can do that, and so much more."

"I'm not afraid of telepaths," I lie.

"You will be."

He's trying to scare me. He needn't bother. I'm actually terrified. I've heard the stories of mind auditors. Part weasel. Part snake. And I'm the hen in the house. A one-way mirror along one wall gives me a good view of just how screwed I am.

"That was quite the display you put on out there," he says. "Hand-to-hand combat with a rabid mutant."

She's not a... I catch myself and start singing in my head.

...blue moon...

He moves with the swiftness of a viper. Grabbing my throat, he lifts my whole body out of the chair. He's impossibly strong, and with all my training, all I can do is flail my limbs as he slams me to the floor. I try to hit him, but my mind is mush. All the moves ingrained in me for fighting from the ground are gone. He rips at my clothes, pawing at my breasts. His hand moves lower.

"Stop it!" I yelp, sounding like a pathetic mutt.

All of a sudden, I'm back in the chair. Despite the vision of a second ago, I never left it. I'm panting, drenched in sweat. My uniform is exactly as it was when I walked into the room. Dirty, bloody, ragged where Lilianne shredded it with her claws, but he hasn't added to the rips.

He is touching me though, if barely, the tips of two fingers against my left temple.

"I can make you see and believe anything," he says. "I can fill your mind with all sorts of horrors. Your brother being tortured. Or I can make you believe Bradie is healed. You'll be overjoyed by the miracle. And then I'll take it away, and you'll hear him scream from the pain of his burns, from the endless skin grafts, from the humiliation of soiling himself. Do you understand?"

I nod.

"Say it," he insists.

"I understand."

"Good. Then no more melodies or attempts to hide your thoughts," he says. "Say it again."

I force the words from my mouth. "I understand."

"Why did you break protocol and attack the mutant?"

I don't dare hesitate.

"I was angry."

"Yes, I can see that. You had a fight. With your friend, Normand. You'r in a store, surrounded by contraband. My, my, and you've been going ther for some time now."

My fingers tighten into fists and instantly a coil of blinding agony sear down my spine. A moment later, it's gone.

"Say you'll play nice," the mind auditor commands.

"I'll play nice," I say, panting and wincing at an echo of pain.

"Good girl. Now let's see...For some unfathomable reason, this Norman has developed quite the attachment to you, not that he's a prize himsel And...you've infiltrated the Calibration system, implanting it wit subversive programming. You've been a *very* naughty girl. But that's no what I'm looking for." He's practically nonchalant about it.

"I've watched the security footage of you fighting the mutant," h continues. "At the very end, it looks like you're speaking with the creature."

"I..."

"Shhtt," he hushes me, holding up a finger for silence. He moves hi head to one side as if listening to a sound only he can hear. "There it is."

Against my will, I replay Lilianne staring at me with those gold flecke brown eyes of hers. *Do not let them cut me open*, she says. *Not again.*

His face darkens. "So you know," he says quietly. "Not everything, bu far too much. What is it with the girls from this borough? Such troublemakers."

"Why?" I ask. "Why send Lilianne back to die? She's a Supergenic."

"We all have to follow the rules," he replies. "Lilianne could have had new life, a new family, but she threw that opportunity away. So yes, we sen her back here with a mind chip to kill a few protectors, and then to b killed in return."

I know that I'm not leaving this room alive, but I won't go down withou a fight. I try to launch myself from my chair, but nothing happens.

"I've cut off your access to the motor control centers of your mind," h explains. "Now it's time for you to serve your sentence. Mere execution i too simple."

He opens his black case and removes a needle filled with a glowing gree liquid. "Most of the mutants who attack your borough *are*, in fact, animal that have been altered by the radiation unleashed by the Genocide Wars growing in size and ferocity. Some form packs. A few are crafty or hav powers. Very occasionally they evolve into a new species. But it's simply not enough to convince you dregs that you need us. Sometimes we have to give a helping hand. Peace is pricey."

He flicks the needle a few times to get the air bubbles to rise to the top, and then he squeezes the syringe until a drop of glowing green liquid dribbles out. "This won't give you powers, but it will turn you into a monstrosity. We'll set you loose on the outer fence, and the protectors will gun you down. It gives them a sense of purpose."

"You're evil," I seethe, futilely trying to fight the paralysis.

He snorts as he slides the needle into my vein.

"I forgot that you fancy yourself a hero. You are a terrorist."

He squeezes the needle, sending green liquid toward my veins.

The door hisses open and he looks up in surprise. So do I. My head seems to be the only thing that can still move. Normand stands there, dressed in his coveralls with the emblem of a computer and a screw driver.

"The accomplice," the mind auditor says.

"Accomplice?" Normand says. "I'm the mastermind."

I head butt the telepath and he staggers back, taking the needle with him. It slides out of me and blood squirts from my arm. Normand hurries over and grabs a cotton ball from the black bag on the table and puts pressure on the pinprick in my skin.

"Forget that," I say. "Get him."

"I will," Normand replies calmly. He tapes the cotton ball in place, then places his electronic skeleton key on my shackles. He pulls out his swipe pad and drags the icon of a key onto a lock and my restraints pop open.

The telepath winces as he touches his nose and his fingers come away bloody.

"I am going to eviscerate your minds," he says.

"You may begin with mine," Normand challenges.

There's a coldness to his voice, a finality that I've never heard in him before.

"Normand, you don't want him in your head," I warn.

"I'm fairly certain that I do."

He stands between me and the mind auditor, but not the way a protector would. There's no fighter stance, no arrogant cock to his chin, no weapon at the ready to cow his opponent. Instead Normand looks down at himself, patting his coveralls, as if he's lost something. The mind auditor hesitates, unsure of what to make of this odd behavior, so different than the fear he's used to inspiring.

"What are you up to?" the mind auditor asks. He's confused. Normand's mind is not so easy to read. "You can't keep me out of your brain forever," the auditor says.

"I very much look forward to letting you in," Normand replies.

He pulls out a round metallic disc from a pocket. The disc looks familiar.

"Catch," he says, tossing it at me. My fingers close around its smooth surface. I recognize it now. It's from Normand's outfit, the one he wore at Revelry, the one that filled me with energy and temporarily linked me with all the other protectors who were there. I could use that connection now, but it was based on physical contact. So why would Normand give me this?

Because he's already been through this, I realize. Which means he's figured out some other way of reaching them using what's in this room. I look at the mind auditor differently now. He reads my thoughts.

"You think *you're* going to use *me* as a conduit to connect with the protectors in this base?" he snorts. "You're going to be a catatonic drooling imbecile by the time I'm done with..."

I don't let him finish. I grab his wrist.

"Bring it," I say.

CHAPTER 35

I wait for light to emerge from the disc in my other hand, to fill me up, and reach out through the mind auditor using his telepathic abilities to reach the protectors. Nothing happens. He smiles wickedly and before I can pull away he twists his hand and clamps his fingers around my forearm.

Pain sears through me and I drop to my knees. The metal disc clatters from my grip as my fingers go into spasms. I scream in agony. Normand is fiddling with his e-pad.

"And...activate," he says.

Tears fill my eyes, clouding my view, so it takes me a moment to realize the metal disc has started glowing. I snatch it off the floor and the energy flows into me, pushing the pain away. My skin is aglow, but it goes deeper than that. It's in my every vein, my every cell, my every synapse. I pull forward the image of Shadowren from its storage place in my mind. In the mirror on the wall, I can see the glow around me change, growing wings and a beak.

I imagine that image clawing its way into the auditor, and through him reaching the protectors in the Cube. It's like slamming into a brick wall.

"Did you really think this would work," he mocks. "That you, a mere dreg, were going to somehow turn my own power against me? Allow me to show you what I can really do."

He grins, and pain even greater than what he's already unleashed on me sears through me. I howl in agony, but also in defiance. I lock even more firmly onto my Shadowren persona, and I push back. The pain recedes, and I'm filled with a sense of strength. As if we are a pair of arm wrestlers, we go back and forth like this, him forcing the pain back in, me using Shadowren to focus the energy of the metal disc to excise the mind auditor from my central nervous system. I grit my teeth, dig my heels in, and with a will I didn't know I possessed, I force the light into him.

The wall keeping me out crumbles, dissolving to dust, and for a moment the mind auditor's form comes aglow. Through him, I can sense the protectors in the Cube. At least I think I can. It's subtle, not unlike group Calibration, but it's enough. I imagine Shadowren in all her fierceness, and as I'm about to send her out into their minds that sense of unity suddenly and unexpectedly fizzles away. The metal disc in my hand glows extra bright for a moment, and then its light dies out. The outline of Shadowren disappears from my form.

The mind auditor grins. "You've failed." He grabs me by the throat, nails digging into the side of my jaw. He just holds me like that as I squirm, letting the seconds tick by.

"Please," I beg.

"Oh, the fun I'm going to have with…"

His words are drowned out by a deafening boom. The room rocks. Bits of dust filter down from the ceiling. He staggers back, losing his grip on me as he falls to one knee. I hear gunfire and shouting. The auditor stares up at the ceiling, as if he's seeing through it.

"It can't be," he says in shock. "The protectors are rebelling."

"Some of them," Normand agrees.

"That's not possible," the mind auditor says. "I stopped her transmission. She never got through."

"I did," Normand replies. "You were smart to disengage the cameras and mics from this room. But I turned them back on and while Caitlin distracted you, I broadcast your interrogation to the entire compound. They now know what you've been doing to children like Lilianne. The ones you were supposed to be taking to a better life. The ones you changed and sent back for the protectors to kill. The protectors are not pleased about that. Contrary to what some may believe, most of them take great pride in their job. Protecting us from the dangers outside the fence. Turns out that's you."

A third explosion goes off above us. The mind auditor's disbelief transforms into rage.

"You have no idea what you've done!" he shouts, grabbing Normand's face in both his hands. "I will destroy you for this!"

And yet it's the mind auditor's eyes that start to twitch. "What…what are you?"

"I'm a precog," Normand explains calmly.

"That…that's not possible," the auditor says.

He tries to pull his hands away but Normand grabs him by the wrists and holds him fast. I can suddenly move and I jump up from the chair.

"Normand, what are you doing?"

"I'm showing him everything," he replies.

"But you can't," I say. "You said telepaths have a blind spot for your premonitions."

His laugh comes out as a wheeze. His nose starts to bleed. So does the mind auditor's.

"I'm way beyond premonitions. The divides in my mind, the segregation of future memories from past from present, from all the timelines that once were but will never be, it's all collapsing together. The cell membranes are breaking down. My synapses are misfiring. Things are leaking all over the places as the temporal anomaly in my brain implodes. I told you, precogs don't live long. This is how I pay for what happened to Bradie."

"Normand, you have to stop. All those things I said, I didn't mean them," I say. "Please!"

He shakes his head.

"I told you my powers would kill me one day. *Really* kill me. Today is that day. No more do-overs."

The mind auditor and Normand cough blood in unison, spraying each other with red droplets.

"Please," the auditor begs. "Please stop."

"My brain's pulling you in," Normand responds. "Like a black hole. Hurts, doesn't it?"

Normand chokes on his own blood. It bubbles out of his mouth. The same happens to the auditor.

"Tastes like iron," Normand says.

"Don't joke," I say, grabbing his arm. "Don't go. I take back everything I said. You know how to love more than anyone, and you'll never be alone, because you'll always have me."

"Sounds like you love me too."

I nod vigorously. "I do. I love you. Now stop. Stop downloading from the future, just be here with me now."

"I'm not downloading from the future. I have no more future. The flow's reversed. I'm uploading from the past. My past and my futures, they're the same. All those memories, of timelines redone, of moments never to be, they're all coming back."

"It's too much," the auditor sobs.

"He's right," Normand agrees. "The human mind, even a Supergenic one, even an oddity like me, can only handle so much."

"You can't die here," I insist. "You told me all about things yet to come. You told me about my daughter. That's years away. I *know* you didn't make that up. That means you live through this."

He and the auditor cough more blood in unison, and when Normand talks, the auditor says exactly the same thing, on just the slightest of delays. It gives him an otherworldly echo to his voice.

"I lived longer that time," Normand says, his voice more mechanical than ever. "Different decisions, different outcomes, different life expectancies."

"But then how do you know this decision leads to the right outcome if you don't see how it turns out?!"

They shrug.

"Because this is the only one where Bradie and I become friends. This is the one where I don't die alone. This time I'm a hero, not a villain. Believe me, there are worse endings."

I don't want to ask, but I do, "Does it hurt?"

"The temporal distortion in my brain is collapsing," he and the auditor reply as one. "It…pinches. But there is an odd beauty to it. My lives are literally flashing before me, and I must confess, I find myself thinking how nice it would feel to be in love just one more time. Oh, and to party again. That was *awesome*."

The Bradie speak makes me smile even as I wipe the tears from my eyes. Blood starts dribbling from Normand and the auditor's ears.

"And here I thought I'd be the only girl you ever liked."

"I like lots of girls," they say. "I'm a dude, remember?"

More Bradie speak. I laugh a bit. Such a pair of tools, even now. I think that is Normand's dying breath, but even now he finds a way to be verbose. I wish he'd go on talking forever.

"I've made arrangements for Bradie," they say together. "I hope it works out."

"What do you mean arrangements?" I ask.

"No time to explain. Take my skeleton key and slide pad. And Caitlin?"

"Yes?"

"Thanks for my best life yet."

They burp once, blood bubbling from their mouths, and then he and the mind auditor collapse head first into each other, and fall dead to the ground.

230

CHAPTER 36

"Normand? Normand!" I kneel next to him, I shake him, I press repeatedly on his chest and breathe into his mouth, just like I've been taught.

"Come on!" I yell, pounding harder on his sternum.

The door behind me hisses open. I don't look. I don't turn. I keep trying to save Normand. I know it's too late, for us both. I wait for the pop of a protector's gun and the sharp smack of a bullet blasting open the back of my skull as I'm executed for being a traitor.

Instead, I feel a hand on my shoulder and my instincts kick in. I throw the person over me, grab the needle with the glowing green liquid, and press it to an agent's throat. It's the same agent who cajoled me into joining the protectorate. Eel Man. He holds his hands up in peace.

"I'm ever so glad we're on the same side," he says.

My hand's shaking as I throw the needle into the corner and I get off him. He jumps nimbly to his feet.

"What's happening out there?" I ask.

"Half the base is fighting the other half of the base. The loyalists have cut off rebel communications, so we're the only borough that heard the truth, and we can't reach the other compounds to tell them."

My brain's working fast.

"The other bases are sending attack squads against us, aren't they?"

He nods.

"We'll be slaughtered." My voice is neutral. Matter of fact. I sound like Normand. I look at his remains. At the blood on his face. I don't want to leave him here. I also don't want his sacrifice, his *many* sacrifices, over countless lifetimes, to be in vain.

"The base is the most secure stronghold we've got. If we manage to take it, how long do you think we can hold out?" I ask.

"Against other protectors? A few days. Against Supergenics? An hour, if we're lucky."

I nod. They'll burn us in fire and light and ice and acid. We'll choke on toxic gases. We'll be ripped by claws and pulverized by brute strength. Our bullets will bounce off flesh made of organic steel. Our cries for mercy will be lost in sonic screams that turn our brains to pulp. And when we die our carcasses will be strung up and used as an example to any dregs who would defy those more powerful than themselves.

We could run, but never fast enough to outrace their speedsters and flyers and teleporters. We could hide, but they'd find us with sniffers and readers and trackers. And it won't just be those of us who picked up arms who will suffer, it will be our families as well. The entire borough.

I say the unthinkable.

"We have to surrender."

The agent looks at me in shock.

"We won't get another chance like this," he says.

"Exactly," I reply. "And the only way we're going to win is if we give up."

"You're not making any sense."

"I've got a plan."

I talk fast, too fast probably, but he keeps nodding, mumbling "very well" and "indeed" in a way that lets me know he's getting it.

"It's rather daring," he says when my torrent of words finally ebbs.

"It might work," I say.

"Perhaps," he agrees.

I close Normand's eyes. *I'll come back for you*, I silently promise him. *If survive.*

"Your friend did an utterly brave thing," Eel Man says.

"Brave doesn't cover it," I reply, wiping the weakness water from my eyes. I force myself to turn my back on Normand. "All right. Where are the holding cells?"

"You're quite certain about this?" he asks. "She's one of *them*, you know."

"No," I disagree. "*This* is her home. She's one of us. Besides, we need her."

The agent looks like there are tectonic plates shifting in his head as part of his brain struggles to accept the truth, and the other clings to his own prejudices, anger and hate.

"Very well," he finally concedes. "Go save the lizard girl. Now if you'll excuse me, I've got a rebellion to destroy."

CHAPTER 37

The agent and I sprint in opposite directions down the hallway. I round a corner, then another. I look at Normand's swipe pad, following the blinking dot through the maze of underground corridors. Unlike him, I don't have the place memorized. I think of him dead on the ground. His blood is on my lips from the mouth-to-mouth. I sprint harder, as if I can run from the memory. Instead, the world mimics my emotions and a wall explodes in front of me, throwing me off of my feet.

A group of rebel protectors emerges from the busted up wall. They are backing out of it, firing their rifles, and being fired upon. A pair of them kneels down and provides cover for the rest. As soon as they're all clear, they break and run toward me. The one in the lead sees me and points a rifle at my face. He's not wearing a helmet. He's young. Barely older than me. His hair's been shaved down to little more than stubble. Handsome. I hold my hands up, clearly unarmed.

"You're the girl from the broadcast," he says, lowering his weapon.

"Assemble!" someone shouts. He turns and kneels along with the rest of his cadre. The *wuppa-wuppa* of automatic weapons discharge thuds in my ears as they fire at a squad of protectors brandishing plasma rifles. I duck down, back against the wall. A plasma beam bursts through the air, followed by a second energy blast. It barely misses my face. I smell scorched hair and skin and muscle. The rebel protector who recognized me stares up at the ceiling. There's a charred hole the size of a fist burnt clear through his chest. Three others have met a similar fate.

"Retreat!" someone orders, and the surviving rebels fall back. I lie next to the dead, pretending to be one of them.

I hear the thud of the protectors' boots beating the ground as they give chase and I see flashes of their black soles. There's more gunfire, shouts and screams, the twanging sound of the plasma rifles being discharged, and someone yelling, "To me!"

I struggle to my feet, and step carefully over the bodies, expecting there to be pools of blood. There are not. The plasma beams cauterized the wounds even as they tore through the protectors' vital organs. I stagger forward, sweating, panting, constantly looking over my shoulder for fear of what might be coming up behind me. The corridor bends to the left. I turn, ready to sprint, and a pair of women stumble right into me. One is a protector. She grasps her bleeding shoulder and can barely hold her injured arm to point her gun at me. Her visor is cracked. There's a cut across one leg. She's been in a knife fight.

Sewzanne is holding her up.

"You," the medic sneers. "You've destroyed us."

Apparently I'm not her favorite anymore. The injured protector's finger tenses on the trigger. I become a thing of violence. My leg is a whip, kicking the gun from the protector's hand. She growls, coming at me. A punch to her injured shoulder distracts her. I smack the side of her helmet and her cracked bullet proof visor recedes, exposing her face. I grab her other gun from its holster, stare into her surprised eyes swelling with bruises, her nose broken, possibly pretty on a better day, and I shoot her in the forehead.

I point the gun at Sewzanne.

"Mango is the new tango," she says.

I feel the switch go off in my brain.

She smiles. "Now kill yourself."

I feel far away as the gun in my hand starts pointing at my temple.

"Ironic, isn't it?" she says. "There are protectors out there who have managed to cast off years of programming after your little worm got inside my calibrator. But not you. You're my prize pupil after all. And you don't even fully believe your own story."

The barrel of the weapon I'm holding is cold against my temple.

"You can't make me do anything I don't want to do," I say. "You said so yourself."

She makes a mock guilty face. "I may have fibbed, just a bit." She holds her thumb and index finger a space apart. "With the addition of the pharmachemicals to the Calibration process, and a bit of psychoanalysis to identify your trigger points, we can make you want to do pretty much anything. I just need to know what buttons to push. For instance, I know you want to kill yourself. You want to die, because of all the horrible things you've done."

I think of Normand. I think of Bradie. I think of abandoning my mom and Nate. Sewzanne sees it in my eyes.

"That's it," she says. "Punish yourself."

Sewzanne is right. I deserve to die. I squeeze the trigger, more relieved than afraid. Finally, I'm going to pay for my failures. Finally, this can all stop. My finger tenses, I hear the pop of the gun firing, and Sewzanne falls dead at my feet. Standing behind her is her subordinate CeeCee, a smoking sidearm in her hand. I've still got the gun to my temple.

"Lower your weapon, soldier," she says.

"I can't," I say. My arm feels frozen in place.

"You're stronger than the Chair's programming," she says.

I press the gun more firmly against my head.

CeeCee takes a deep breath. "We saw the mind auditor's interrogation. Everyone did. You're not Caitlin Feral, you're the Shadowren. And this is not how or when the Shadowren dies."

Her words flick another switch in my brain. I see Normand's drawing of that urban huntress come to life in my mind, strong, focused, and relentless. The gun trembles against my temple. It would be so easy to end it all.

You're not done fighting, Shadowren says to me.

That may be true, and yet my finger pulls on the trigger.

I call to mind that moment in the Audit Room, when I grew wings of light and a sharp Shadowren beak, when I truly was that hero. I don't have access to that energy source now, but I call on the feeling it gave me, willing it to well inside of me. My trigger finger relaxes. The barrel of the weapon pulls away from my skull and my arm drops to my side. The limb hangs limply and the gun shakes against my thigh.

Did Normand know about this moment in one of his futures? Did he give me that disc not half an hour ago to prepare me for it? I suppose I'll never know.

"Go," CeeCee says. "Finish what you've started."

I run. I use Normand's e-pad and GRAMS to follow a layout of the Cube with blinking dots that tell me where protectors are located. It's not perfect. Not everyone's in uniform; many were just in their sweats when the fighting broke out, but it helps me steer clear of the worst of the conflict. I see clusters of dots wink out as other clusters of dots annihilate them.

The Supergenics won't have to kill us, I realize. *We're killing ourselves.*

Finally, I reach the corridor I've been looking for. The holding cells. Dozens of doors are open all along the hallway. My heart spasms. I'm too late. I walk slowly, looking in each room, gun at the ready. They're all the

same. Each holds a pile of rags on the floor which served as beds for th
political prisoners held here. In every tiny room is a refuse bucket that reek
of human waste. The occupants are all dead, each dressed in a coarse, sack
like garment. Most are skeletal. They make the most food-deprivec
members of our borough look meaty. The first few look like they were mad
to kneel before being shot in the back of the head, but the further I go, th
more rushed the executions became. Two tried crawling to the door befor
bleeding out.

My heart is hammering as I search for one body in particular, covered i
scales. I don't see her. Lilianne is not among the dead, or so I pray. I used to
mock my mom for clinging to superstitions, but not now. If there is a God
please, *please* let Lilianne still be alive. If she's not, we're all going to end u
just like this.

The hall seems to dead end, but I spot the nearly undetectable door
given away by the slight seam where it connects with the wall. I us
Normand's skeleton key, sticking it atop a hidden push pad. The door hisse
compressed air. Inside, the lights flicker as the power surges. There's a ful
surgical suite set up, with an operating table, and a slew of vicious looking
tools for poking, prodding, and cutting. A tray of scalpels and needles ha
been knocked over and litter the floor.

Beyond is the holding room, separated by a clear barrier of impregnabl
glass. The pen is stark, with barely enough room to walk six paces. There's a
bench, and a rubberized bucket for relieving oneself. Otherwise the cell i
empty.

"Mother f…"

There's a patch of fuzziness in the grey plastic wall of the prison. A blurr
outline steps forward and solidifies into Lilianne's green-scaled form. Sh
presses her webbed hand to the glass. Her claws don't make a scratch. She'
saying something, but I can't hear her. I pull out the skeleton key and th
barrier slides back.

"It's about bloody time," she snorts. Even as a lizard, she has a way o
making me feel inadequate. And yet despite her words and tone, she wrap
her sinewy arms around me, and with a ragged breath hugs me tight. He
scales are surprisingly smooth.

"Let's get out of here," I say as we disengage.

She picks a scalpel off the floor and I step back, gun raised. She pays n
mind, feeling around on the side of her skull.

"There it is," she says.

She cuts into herself.

"They were controlling me..." she pauses, concentrating. "...with this." She pulls out a small metal chip. I must have disrupted it when I hit her with my baton. She crushes it and drops the remains of the bloody circuit into a metal bowl.

"There," she says. "That feels better."

"Good," I say. "Now we just have to get you out of here."

CHAPTER 38

"So what's the plan?" Lilianne asks.

"Stand by," I reply.

I look at Normand's swipe pad and flick to the home screen. There's a slew of icons on it—all of them are his personalized GRAMS. One is of a ninja wearing a headset. Underneath, it says COMMS.

"I really hope this works," I say.

Lilianne blinks at me with her eyes that still incite jealousy. What can I say? They're more gorgeous than ever against the green of her skin, which ripples with flecks of gold.

"What do you mean, you *hope* it works?" she asks.

"It'll work," I reply, trying to sound more confident than I am. I press on the ninja's face and up comes a slew of audio feeds from all over the base.

"...we're pinned down! I repeat, we are pinned down..."

"...we need back up!"

"...the rebels are targeting the munitions depot..."

And screams, lots of them, in utter agony.

I quickly double tap to shut the program down, silencing the voices. But they're still in my head.

"What's happening?" Lilianne asks.

"Chaos," I reply.

"So, we use that to get out."

"It's not that simple," I reply.

"It is for me," she says, walking toward the door.

"You won't make it," I warn. There's an icon on the pad, of a guy with antique binoculars for eyes. Underneath it says CAMS. I press it and it taps into the security feeds. Hundreds of windows pop up on the screen, one after the other in quick succession, showing me every camera view in the building.

"Damn it, Normand," I curse. "I don't need to see this much."

"Now that I've got that chip out of my head, they won't find me or hurt me ever again," Lilianne insists.

I've used some of these GRAMS before, but I'm nowhere near as adept as Normand. I start closing one security feed at a time, feeling far too slow as I search for something I can use. I miss Normand looking at his watch right about now, counting down. They're coming, I just don't know when, and I have to be ready by the time they get here.

"I wouldn't be so sure of that," I say.

I show her the pad, and we gaze at the video of an armored short-range jet landing on the roof. On its side is a lightning bolt and the words A.M.M.O. It touches down and a side door pops open, unfurling a set of stairs. Five Supergenics emerge, clearly identifiable by their silver suits with a lightning bolt emblazoned on their chests. Captain Light is among them.

"No," Lilianne says. "No, no, no. I won't let them get me. I won't!"

She's trembling, tears falling from her eyes.

"They won't," I say, hoping to heck I can keep my promise. *Please let this work.*

I swipe faster through the camera feeds.

"Come on, come on," I say, and finally I find what I'm looking for. A group of agents and protector loyalists firing at a small cadre of rebel protectors and cadets defending the communications bay. I minimize the rest of the windows and look for another GRAM. I see one with a stylized version of my Shadowren mask. It's labeled, CAITLIN, USE THIS ONE.

"We have to get out of here," Liliane says.

"No," I reply. "We have to wear a mask."

She looks at me like I'm mentally delayed.

Normand would've gotten my comic book speak, I think defensively.

Lilianne and I may be allies, but I doubt we will ever be friends.

"Here," I say. "I'll show you."

I drag the Shadowren icon atop of the window with the rebels and loyalists fighting against each other. Another window pops up. A computerized voice says aloud, "Establishing COMM link. COMM link established."

"Flank the rebels!" I hear their leader order. I've patched into the loyalist's communications bandwidth.

"Normand, you brilliant beautiful bastard," I whisper.

"Pin them down!"

"Belay that order," I say in a tone that I hope is commanding.

"Who the hell is this?" the squad leader yells back at me.

"Check my i-Dent specialist," I snap back. I cringe in the intervening silence. Lilianne has an "I didn't know you had it in you" look on her face.

I'm betting (and hoping) that Normand's program has created a false authentication signature for my audiograph.

In a corner of the screen, I watch the feed of Captain Light pointing a something on the roof.

We're running out of time, I imagine Normand saying.

"What are your orders?" the agent asks.

"Reroute to the roof. We've got rebels up there about to take the whole Cube down," I reply. "They're armed with blasters and explosives. You need to go in hot. I repeat. You need to go in hot. You open fire immediately Understood?"

"Understood," I hear back, and we watch as the loyalists pull back, and disappear into a stairwell.

"Do you actually think they're going to shoot at Supergenics?" Lilianne asks.

"They will if they don't realize they're Supergenic," I reply.

I look at the swipe pad and there's an icon of a ghost inside a red circle with a line through it. I think of Normand in his Ghost Fighters costume The GRAM is labelled VISUAL RECONFIGURATOR.

What seems a lifetime ago, before I was put in an accelerated learning Chair, when I was mousy Caitlin Feral walking home from the library with a contraband issue of *Tigara*, Normand used this GRAM to fool a protector into seeing a ministry-approved comic book instead. Now it's my turn.

"Here goes everything," I say.

I drag the icon on top of the image of the loyalist squadron headed to the roof. Up pop a dozen windows, and I see what they see inside their visors, a 360-degree digital view of their surroundings. And since it's digital I can manipulate it, just like the Protectorate manipulated me into executing the woman trying to flee with her Supergenic son.

"You screw with me," I say. "Now I screw with you."

A few taps of my fingers and it's done. The loyalists reach the roof and quickly blow open the door. Normand's swipe pad feeds a false image to their visors. Instead of Supergenics, they see a group of rebel protectors.

"Open fire!" I shout.

They do. Bullets and plasma beams fly.

One of the silver-clad superpowered members of A.M.M.O. is hit and falls immediately. The other Supergenics cringe and duck down in fear and surprise. Captain Light's photonic force field pops up around them. The spray of bullets and the undulating power streams bounce off, right back at the loyalist protectors. They're wearing protective suits but the backlash still packs a punch. A few visors crack. There are grunts of pain. Several copper-clad protectors stagger back, clutching themselves where they've been hit. The smarter of the loyalists realize something's wrong. I've disabled their microphones, so they can barely hear each other through their helmets, but I watch as several of them slide their visors back, blinking as their vision adjusts, and they stare in horror at the Supergenics.

"Hold fire! Hold fire!" someone's shouting. More visors pop open. More looks of utter terror. Guns are placed on the roof. Hands are held up in surrender. Captain Light's energy shield drops and a man with red blistered skin steps forward. He holds his palms toward them and blasts fire into the surrendered troops. They scream, their smoldering body armor falling around skeletons of brittle ash.

Their CAM windows go dark one by one as their helmets burst from the heat. I take a shuddering breath.

"What am I doing?" I ask out loud.

Lilianne puts a webbed hand on top of mine. "What you have to." We're both shaking. I'm not sure if she's trying to convince me or herself. I think of Normand. I think of Bradie. I think of Nate.

"We can't change the world in a day," I rationalize. "But I *will* make sure this rebellion has a tomorrow."

I find a second band of loyalist troops on the swipe pad, then a third, and a fourth. I take another ragged breath. *This isn't their fault*, a part of me reasons. I ignore the guilty side of me and send hundreds of people to the roof to die.

CHAPTER 39

I hear their screams through the COMM link. I know they will haunt me, like so much else that I have done. Maybe I can blame this on the Calibration they put all of us through. Maybe. I turn to Lilianne.

"Now we go," I say.

We escape through a combination of service tunnels and air shafts, using cunning, cruelty, and luck. I know which way to go but without Lilianne I would never have made it. She blends with the walls and on several occasions strikes at bands of loyalists without mercy. With her chameleon abilities, she's practically invisible. A dozen protectors are blocking a hatch we need to access. She slithers from a vent and knocks them off their feet. Her tail chokes one while her claws slice another across the throat.

She ducks and dodges bullet fire, turning one guy into a human shield. His body shudders under a spray of slugs. She careens off the walls then clings and drops from the ceiling. She reaches her arm over her head and grabs a chin as she lands, jerking it so hard the sound of a neck snapping fills the air. The dead protector falls. His baton flies from her hand, hitting one woman while Lilianne drop kicks another. It takes less than a minute.

And she wasn't lying about not being trackable. She can hide her thermogenic signature. She's silent as death. For all I know, even telepaths can't detect her. No wonder they put a chip in her and sent her to die: they don't want people they can't control.

We reach the Cube's outer wall. I push open an emergency exit and the sound of thunder cracks the air as lightning flares on the other side of the security fence.

"I never thought I'd miss that sound," Lilianne says.

The chaos inside the compound is matched outside as we step into the open air. Loyalists and rebels are shooting wildly at each other. Lilianne pulls me back inside the door, and points upwards. I watch as Captain Light blazes off the roof and into the sky. Small balls of luminescence drop from his body, falling several measures before coming alive, and blasting for their targets. They shoot into the mouths of fighters on both sides. Their bodies glow and they start to spasm as the photonic pellets beat them to death from the inside. He can't tell friend from foe, so he kills them all.

I huddle down and on the swipe pad I open a file drawer labelled INTEL. There's a slew of personnel folders, including me, Bradie, and even one for Normand himself. Another is labelled AGENTS. I open that. A whack of head shots pop up, of people dressed in black. I find the agent who got me into this in the first place. Eel Man. AGENT SAMSON, it says. It's the first time I've seen his name. I want to read everything about him, but that will clearly have to wait. I use his i-Dent info to patch through to him on the COMM link.

"Agent Samson," I say.

"Caitlin," he replies. "You're alive." I'm not sure if he's surprised, irritated or relieved.

"You need to surrender to the Supergenics," I say. "Convince them of your loyalty before they slaughter everyone."

I hear a garbled reply. I have no idea if my message went through, or if he's even still in command of the communication center. I want to go back, Bradie's in there, helpless, but I'm just one person, and I have my mission. If it fails, we're all of us done.

"Come on," I say to Lilianne, and we scurry for the fence.

We escape into the Yellow Zone through a section in the chain link that's been damaged by the fighting. Lilianne basically disappears once she's in the broken city, blending with the busted up concrete. I'm far more conspicuous. Fortunately, no one is paying attention to what's beyond the fence.

The sound of fighting—gunfire, explosions, screams—grows distant, but doesn't disappear. As we get further away from the compound, I jump over a crumbling wall and freeze. We're not alone out here.

I point my gun. A family stares at me. Two Moms and twin boys, all with hastily packed bags. Their faces are filled with fear. I lower my gun.

"What are you doing here?" I demand.

Mom One efforts an answer, her mouth working soundlessly as she tries to come up with a plausible lie. The answer of course is obvious. They're Runners, taking advantage of the chaos to escape from the boroughs. They're headed for certain death, or so we've been told. I think of the woman I executed. There's no Sewzanne in my ear. Today I make my own choice, and I leave them to theirs.

"Good luck," I say. I hope they make it out there, beyond the Protectorate's squeezing grip and the Supergenics' choking leash.

They scramble away, unable to believe I'm just letting them go. I want to look back, but I don't.

Finally, we reach the Lair. I will always call it that, and it belongs to Normand and me, never mine alone.

Lilianne grabs my arm. "Your scent, it's all over the place. I think this is what drew me here when I attacked you earlier."

"There are no coincidences," I reply.

"But I'm smelling a male as well," she says. "Stronger than the rest."

"Yes," I say sadly. *Normand should be here.* "I know."

I open up the doors. Lilianne goes ahead, slithering down the stairs. I follow, closing the door behind me. Down in the store, I clap, but the lights don't turn on. Have they been damaged? If so I have no idea how to fix them, or anything. How long will this place survive without Normand to keep it running? A worry for another time, if I should live so long. I bump into Lilianne. She's tense, her body a wall of muscle.

"Someone's here," she says. I turn on my flashlight. Her large nostrils on her tiny nose flutter rapidly.

A faint *whuzzphm whuzzphm* sound breaks the silence as someone fires a dart gun. Lilianne grunts and bumps into me drunkenly. I try to grab her but my grip slides off her smooth scales and she thumps to the floor.

The tiny lights on strings come to life. Trenton comes out from behind the counter with the register. Lilianne said she smelled a male. She wasn't talking about Normand.

"It wasn't easy finding your hiding place, he says. "But I kept wondering, how did Caitlin get to that lizard mutant so fast? And what was Caitlin doing on the wrong side of the fence? Then I checked the sensor logs, and there's no record of you passing through a gate, and the motion detectors didn't pick you up until all of a sudden you were just there. Led me right to the front door."

I knew we'd outsmart ourselves, with our little technology tricks, foolishly believing that we were beating the system. It just never occurred to me that it would be Trenton who figured it out.

He points the dart gun at me and fires.

Whuzzphm whuzzphm whuzzphm.

I drop and roll. Three darts hit the wall. He tosses the gun with its empty cartridge aside.

"Trenton, don't do this," I say. "Bradie…"

"You don't get to say his name," he growls. "He's why I'm here. I would do anything for that kid. *Anything.* Now because of you he'll never walk again, he'll have a bag for a gut, he'll be lucky if he ever forms a complete sentence. You took my brother from me."

"I love him, too," I say.

There's weakness water in Trenton's eyes.

"You love him? Really? You think as much as me? Did Bradie ever tell you how he got the scars on his hand?" he asks.

I swallow hard, thinking of how long it took for Bradie to let me hold his injured hand, how pained he was by the wound long after it was physically healed. There were the scars I could see. And then there were the other ones.

"He told me that was his punishment," I say. "For firing a weapon."

"That much is true. Do you want to hear the whole story?" Trenton asks. His jaw juts at a dangerous angle.

My heart hammers. *Yes,* I want to reply.

"No," I say to my own surprise. "That's for Bradie to tell, or not tell."

"That's where you're wrong," Trenton replies. "*I* did that to him. Literally and figuratively. He had to be punished for firing a weapon, but I'm the one who taught him how to shoot. So to teach *me* a lesson, the agents gave me a choice. I could watch as they shattered Bradie's knees and ankles with sledgehammers and then dumped him to die in the Red Zone, picked apart by mutated scavengers, or I could shove his hand into boiling water, and hold it there for 30 seconds."

I'm so horrified by what he's saying, I struggle to respond.

"Trenton, I..."

"Shut up!" he shouts. He wipes tears away and half-chokes on his own words. "They strapped him down in this chair that was bolted to the floor. It looked a lot like the one in the Calibration chamber. I had this thick rubber glove on so *I* wouldn't get burned. They made sure of that. The pain they wanted me to suffer was not my own. Bradie gave me the go ahead. Just a quiet nod and look as I held his hand over a boiling vat. But he didn't know what he was in for. How could he? He screamed. Oh man, did he scream. He begged me to stop. *Please,* he said. But I kept going. I had to. I could smell it *cooking* him. It killed, me Caitlin, but to save my brother, I'd do it again. So what do you think I'm willing to do to you?"

His story enrages me, and I've plenty of blame to throw back at him.

"I'm not the idiot who taught him how to shoot," I say.

His jaw clenches. I try a different tact.

"Help me," I say. "Help me stop the people who did that to him, and to you."

He shakes his head. "It is going to feel so good when I snap your neck."

He was always fast, but now he's like a bolt of supercharged lightning. try to run, back toward the stairs, hoping to draw him away from Lilianne In two bounds, he closes the distance between us. Pain like fire shoot through my ankle as he sweeps my legs out from under me with a wicked kick.

I drop, roll and kick back. He catches my foot in his hands. He's smiling He's enjoying this. He lifts my whole body off the ground, wrenching m hip as he gives my leg a harsh twist, twirling me like a toy. I crash into shelf, and a slew of plastic figurines topples on top of me.

"Don't do this," I say. "Don't be their puppet. We have a chance to b free."

He flicks open a knife. "Tell that to my brother."

I search for a weapon of my own. Everything in here is useless props.

He charges. My hand closes on the scarf with the red S on it—the on Normand insisted I never move. Even after my fit where I threw everythin on the counter to the ground, he made sure to put it all back—because h knew I would need it. That's why everything near the register had to stay i its place.

Thank you, thank you, thank you.

I yank the scarf off the countertop. It's so old, I'm sure it will rip apart i my hands, but it holds, and as I dodge left, I press it against Trenton's wrist deflecting his assault. I'm behind him a heartbeat later, the cloth wrappe around his neck. He half turns and smashes me in the face with his ope palm.

I try to roll with the punch, but he's too fast, and so strong that even glancing blow sends me off my feet. I try to sweep his legs out from unde him. He told me once that his strategy for avoiding the wrong kind o attention was to no longer show how good he really was. Now he's showin me everything. It's like kicking a concrete wall. I yelp in surprise and pain.

He grabs me by the throat, lifts me up and starts to squeeze. He's cuttin the flow from the carotid artery to my brain. I try to crush his thumb like did with Lilianne. He smirks. I have seconds before I pass out. He lifts th

246

knife and aims it at my eye. I grab blindly, my fingers wrapping around a plastic object, and I shove it into his temple.

Blue electricity flares from the Taser in my hand. The refurbished battery doesn't pack much of a punch, and quickly fizzles out. Still, he staggers back, breathless and bent over. I fall, gasping to the ground.

"You are dead!" he spits.

"I don't think so," I reply, and I smash him across the face with the metal balls Normand left for me on the counter.

He reels dizzily. I hit him again. The balls come away bloody. His body wavers, arms flailing comically as they grab at nothing in an attempt to keep his balance. It's a lost cause. He uses what control he has left to drop to his knees.

"You can't win," he says. "The system...It's too big. Those on top...They're too powerful. They can read minds. Turn invisible. Smell our lies. We can't keep secrets from them. We can't run. We can't hide. We can't fight."

"I know," I say. "That's why I need as many of them as possible to join us."

His eyes flutter, and I have no idea if he heard me. I wrap my arms around his neck in a sleeper hold. When his form goes limp, I gently lower him to the ground. I tie his arms with the scarf, just in case, and go over to Lilianne. I pull the darts from her torso and toss them aside. She's already coming to, far quicker than I expected. It must be something in her Supergenic DNA. She blinks at me groggily, smiling like a little girl. I can't help but smile back. She knows how to work an audience. No wonder she got away with so much growing up. Then as if remembering where she is and how she got here, she suddenly sits up.

"Where is he?" she demands, sniffing the air.

"Taken care of," I reply.

She sees Trenton unconscious on the ground.

"Can I eat him?" she asks.

"Maybe," I reply.

Neither of us seems sure if the other is joking.

"Lilianne, I don't know how much time we have."

She nods. "I think you're crazy. I've always thought you were crazy. But I'm ready. Let's do this."

I insert a data key into Normand's tablet and then set it up to do a video record.

"Ready?" I ask Lilianne.

"Caitlin," she smiles her lizard smile. "I was born ready."

When we're done, I press stop, pull the data key from the tablet, and hand the recording to her.

"Do you think this will actually work?" she asks.

"I guess we'll find out," I reply. She stares at the key like it will open a door, or lock it shut.

I pick up the pile of papers that comprise *Shadowren*, Issue 1, drawn by Normand, written by me, and I stare at them reverently. They are all in black and white, on yellowed paper. The pencil marks still show through underneath the ink. There's the occasional spelling mistake. Some of the transitions are questionable at best. Compared to the glossy and slick computer-rendered comic books all around us, they are rough and raw. To me, they are the most exquisite things I've ever seen.

"Here," I say. My hands are shaking as I hand it over.

I can't believe I'm going to part with it, even though that was always the plan: to show the world our story. I just never dared believe we'd ever actually live in a world that would allow anyone to see it.

"So this is how we spread a revolution," she says skeptically, flipping through the pages.

"This is your story," I point to the data key that contains the video recording we just made of her. "The rights the Supergenics violated. The laws they broke. And what they were willing to do to one of their own."

"That I get," she replies. "But the comic books?"

"That's my story, mine and Normand's," I explain. "The video of what they did to you will give the Supergenics a reason to rebel. The comic books —I hope—will show them how."

CHAPTER 40

Lilianne helps me get Trenton's unconscious and ridiculously heavy body back inside the perimeter fence. There are no more sounds of explosions coming from the compound, and a loud speaker flares to life.

"Citizens, the terrorist attack against the Protectorate has been terminated. For your own safety, return to your homes for further instructions. Anyone remaining in the streets will be deemed a terrorist, and will be met with maximum force. I repeat..."

It's Agent Samson's voice. There's an edge to it. He's scared. So am I. We haven't gotten away with this yet. The metaphorical Supergenic missile that's always been casually pointed at us from across the river has flown over and is now aggressively pressed against our gates.

"This can't actually work, can it?" Lilianne asks.

I shrug. Her guess is as good as mine.

"Do your part," I say. "I'll do mine. Let's see where that gets us."

"Yeah," she agrees emphatically, her brain clearly twisting my words into something way more rah-rah than they actually are. "We'll show them."

She hugs me and, before I know it, I'm hugging her back. It's hard to remember that this is Lilianne, my childhood nemesis. I lose sight of her camouflaged form as she slithers and coils her way toward the river.

The next morning, I stand at Trenton's side. He's strapped into the Chair in a Calibration chamber. There's a tube feeding a bright amber liquid into his blood stream. The helmet over his head covers half his face, but not his lips. His jaw twitches, and from time to time his whole body tenses.

CeeCee watches his vitals carefully.

"We can't actually erase memories," she says. "At best, we can overwrite them. It's been done to dissidents, but the results are inconsistent."

I think of my mom, of how I didn't believe her.

"I understand," I say.

When Trenton wakes, he's in sick bay. He blinks at me, confused. I'm wearing a full-fledged protector's uniform. My mom's worst nightmare has come true.

"What happened?" he asks.

"There was an uprising," I reply. "You were hurt in the battle."

I watch him and wait for his response. All his vitals are being monitored. If he fakes believing me, we should know.

"Did we crush them?" he asks.

"Of course," I reply. "But you suffered a head injury. We found you in the Yellow Zone. What do you remember?"

"There was...a mutant. A lizard. I...I think I killed it," he says.

I nod. "That's exactly what happened."

"What about Bradie? Was he hurt in the attack?" he asks.

"Yes," I say. "Very badly."

Trenton starts to cry. "I have to see him."

"Of course," I say, snapping my fingers at a medic. "She'll take you to him."

"What about you?" he says, surprised.

My ear piece beeps.

"They're here," Agent Samson tells me.

"I'm on my way," I reply. To Trenton I add, "I have to go."

I walk through a hallway of melted plastic. The malformed resin runs the length of the entire corridor, its scorched and distorted surface looking like petrified magma. There are dozens of half-melted protector helmets and pieces of body armor melded into the twisted walls, all that remains of the people who died here. Their bodies were burned down to the bone. What's left has to be hacked out of the walls. There's no blood. It boiled inside their veins as the elemental Supergenic scorched his way through here.

I get to the elevator. Repair crews work behind yellow hazard tape, using blow torches to weld broken mechanisms back together. I take the stairs and pass by a wall where I can see the imprint of a giant fist smashed into the concrete. A steel railing's been bent outwards by the passing of a huge body. There's debris everywhere. A door has been ripped off its hinges, finger prints five times the average human size indented in the solid metal. keep going down and emerge into the sub-basement. The Audit Rooms are here.

I choke momentarily on the fumes from chemical disinfectants. I could put on my helmet, use the built-in respirator, but I refuse. People died down here. My people. Even the ones we were fighting. They were ours, they just didn't know it. The bodies have all been removed. There were so many, it was hosed down to prevent the spread of any disease. I run my hand along the slash marks in the plastic walls, from claws that cut deeper than any animal's. The Supergenics sent a pack of animalistics down here, with their heightened senses and primal urges, most likely to take down Lilianne.

Except she doesn't leave a scent, I think with relief. *You do*, another part of me warns. *They could follow your trail to Normand's secret place.* I snort. *That's the least of my worries.*

I'm about to have my brain raped, and there's nothing I can do about it.

I stand in the Audit Room, waiting. I stare at myself in the one-way mirror. For all I know the mind auditor is on the other side, already doing his/her/zir's dirty work. Then again, maybe not. I know a lot more about telepaths than I used to, that they're much rarer than the propaganda would have us believe. The weaker ones need physical contact to pick up a single thought, and the most powerful telepaths, the ones who can rip a mind to pieces, rarely survive long after Manifesting, suffering from aneurysms, strokes and all sorts of neurological disorders as their brains literally explode from being inundated by other people's thoughts.

I think of Normand, and his ability to fool telepaths, a talent I don't possess. Only now does it occur to me what a manipulative liar he was.

Man, I miss him.

"Focus," I tell myself, as if that will make any difference.

Hopefully Lilianne's doing better than me. There's been no sign that she made it to the other side of the river. Such worries evaporate the moment the door opens. I could start playing a tune in my mind, but I don't. Not today.

My interrogator comes in, and I'm jolted by recognition. It's the same young man who was there on my Testing Day. Joshua. Unless he, too, has a twin. He wears a mind auditor's uniform now. It shows off every curve of his muscled form, though judging by the stiffness in his walk and the way he keeps pulling at the collar, he's not used to it. His hair is longer now. Slicked back. It still shines gold.

"Caitlin Feral," he says. "We meet again."

It *is* him.

"Hello, Mind Auditor," I say. "Congratulations on the promotion."

His cheek twitches at that, as if the title pinches tighter than his outfit.

"Yes," he says. "There was a sudden vacancy."

I nod. "I'd heard that."

Joshua's brow crinkles in confusion.

He doesn't know about the video, I realize. *Not yet.*

"What video?" he asks, catching the thought. This is going to be brutal.

"Have a seat," I say, gesturing to the chair on the other side of the table, as if I'm the one about to interrogate him. "I have a lot to show you."

He sits, one golden brow arched, part curious, part concerned.

"You know that I'm here to find traitors who will then be put to death," he says. "Under article 20.2 of the Peace Treaty..."

"Let's not waste any time," I cut him off.

I reach across the table and grasp his hands. He tries to pull back and I tighten my grip.

"No need to be squeamish," I say. "You once told me the psychic connection is intensified through skin-to-skin contact, even for you."

He blushes, his cheeks turning rosy gold.

"That's correct," he says.

"Good," I say. "Let's begin."

I scroll back through my memories, and I can feel him pulling at one of me and Bradie in the hospital.

"We'll get to that," I say. "But it will all make more sense if we start at the beginning."

I focus on my trip to the library, on that long ago day when Normand slipped me that forbidden comic book. Joshua arches his brow, confused, surprised.

"That's the day you and I met," I say, even though it's unnecessary for me to speak out loud. "I'd just failed my final Testing Day."

I allow my story to unfold from there. I let Joshua feel what I feel. The more excruciating the emotion, the more hopeless or hopeful, the longer I linger on it. By the time we get back to Bradie lying in his hospital bed, I'm crying openly. Joshua's eyes grow moist. He doesn't try to break contact. He doesn't interrupt. He listens, he watches, and he feels. I get to the interrogator who was his predecessor raping my mind. The telepath flinches and for the first time tries to pull away. My grip tightens.

Is that what you want to become? I ask.

No, is his gentle reply.

He hears his predecessor's confession to the crimes against Supergenics like Lilianne, and I can see the rage on his face.

He didn't know, I realize. *How is that possible? He can read minds.*

"We have rules about where and how we use our powers," he explains. "And on whom."

"And they didn't prepare you for what you might find here?" I ask.

"They did not," he says. "My guess is they're testing me."

Sounds a lot like dealing with the agents. But it does give me a spark of hope. Joshua continues sifting through my brain, transfixed by my memories of Normand rescuing me from that other interrogator, dragging him down into some kind of psychic vortex.

It ends with me beating Trenton and sending Lilianne back to Jupitar City with the seeds to foment rebellion. Then, and only then do I let go of Joshua's hands. We've been at this for hours. He wipes away his tears and then gazes into my eyes.

They're going to execute you for this, he projects into my mind.

Only if you tell them the truth, is my reply.

"And what would you have me do?" he asks out loud. "Lie?"

"Yes," I say.

Joshua's Mind Audit of the Cube lasts over a week. He reads the minds of everyone on base to determine who is a "loyalist" and who is a "traitor." He's not the only interrogator, but he is the only telepath.

Fifty-two of the surviving protectors are found guilty of terrorist acts. I am not among them. Neither is Agent Samson. In fact, of the hundreds of us who were actually part of the revolt, none of our names are on the list.

Joshua singled out the loyalists instead. They are the ones to be executed, not the rebels like me.

He's taking our side, I realize, and he may be more powerful than even the Supergenics know. I start to suspect he's changing the memories of his subjects as he goes, and is mentally manipulating his fellow auditors to skew their results. There may be rules about using his telepathy on fellow Supergenics, but he seems to be ignoring them. By week's end, no one seems to remember me as "the girl from the video." She becomes some amorphous legend that no one can quite describe. The video itself has been wiped from the drives. What people do recall is a masked red-headed woman leading the rebellion. Her name: Shadowren.

On Joshua's last day at the Cube, I am among the entourage of protectors that escorts him back to his hovercraft. So is Liam. Sandie is in sick bay, recovering from a burn to her arm. As our boots thud on the tarmac, I hear Joshua's voice in my head.

The protectors who were found guilty are going to be put to death for doing their duty, he tells me. *That's on you.*

Yes, I reply. *I know.*

You really have changed from that girl on Testing Day, he says.

You wanted a legend, I reply.

Remind me to be more careful what I ask for, he says. *And you be careful not to change too much. You don't want to become what you're trying to fight.*

Our escort has stopped twenty measures from the hovercraft.

Are you aware that I will be subjected to a Mind Audit of my own when I get back? he asks me.

Why? I ask.

Now that I know the truth, they will need to be certain of where my loyalty lies.

Can you fool them? I ask.

I can try, he answers.

And if you fail? I demand.

Then I imagine we'll all be dead within a matter of days.

He crosses the final distance alone. I watch his shapely back, expecting him to turn around, to wink or wave. He doesn't. It was a childish thought anyway. I'm surprised when I hear him in my mind one last time. His voice is fainter, and I make a note of what his limit must be.

This rebellion of yours could destroy us all, he says.

So why are you helping me? I ask back.

I don't get a response. Maybe he didn't hear me. Maybe he's gone out of range. Or maybe he's not sure himself.

He climbs up a set of drop-down stairs onto the deck of the hovercraft, and then disappears into its hull. We watch as it floats a measure above the tarmac, and skims away across the river. Night is falling, the air is chill, and we are about to turn our backs toward the compound, but something across the river catches my eye. I squint at the beaming lights of Jupitar City.

"What's the matter?" Liam asks.

"That," I say, pointing at the skyline.

"I'm not sure..." and then he sees it too.

254

The lights in the tallest tower are winking out, floor by floor. And then the next building goes. And then the next.

"What the deuce?" Liam says. "Is one of ours doing this?"

My heart beats faster. Soon the whole island city will be dark. "Yes," I say. "She is."

An instant later, a projection fills the night sky, and the accompanying booming audio is easily carried across the river. It's of a lizard girl with hazel eyes flecked with gold. As usual, Lilianne is shining bright while Caitlin Feral fades to the background.

"Hello citizens of Jupitar City," her video projection says. "My name is Lilianne Whisper… And this is my story."

If you enjoyed this book, please take a moment to leave a positive review on Amazon.com and Goodreads.com. This helps the author a lot! Also consider buying an e-copy as a gift.

The author is hard at work on the sequel, tentatively titled *The Girl With Green Scales*. The more positive feedback he gets, the more he'll know that people are interested, and the quicker he'll get it done.

You can join his email list (used sparingly) at stevenbereznai.com to be the first to know of new releases. Keep an eye out for his next novel, *How A Loser Like Me Survived the Zombie Apocalypse* (release date TBD).

Pictures of fans reading the book, posted onto social media, are also very encouraging. Feel free to tag the author! He loves it.